Between Two Shores

Ruth Larrea

BETWEEN TWO SHORES

NEW YEAR'S EVE, ULLADULLA, NSW

Ellie tossed a log on the campfire. Sparks shot into the darkness, flames flared. She scanned the circle of faces lit by the glow, six friends she'd known for ever. Yes, it was good to be together again. Almost like old times. So why did this fury and restlessness linger?

She shivered, held out her hands to the heat. The night was chilly after the rain, so they all sat huddled in jumpers. The guys had caught a jewfish in the surf and they'd pan-fried it over the fire, baked potatoes and chunks of corn in the embers. You burnt and blackened your fingers that way, but it made you feel wild and free like pioneers, not a bunch of young professionals from the Sydney suburbs.

Around midnight they drank hot chocolate and toasted marshmallows. While the others joked about their plans for the year ahead – buy a batik business in Bali, back the winner in the Melbourne Cup, get a boob job – Ellie laughed with them, dodging the doubts. No, she'd made the right decision, leaving Brad. She was an independent woman now.

'What's your New Year's wish?' Cindy Chang asked her.

'A better job, worthy of my brilliance.'

The others laughed with her but Nic bridled.

'Lots of history graduates would kill to work in that museum.'

'It's like being buried alive. I want to be out in the real world, not stuck down in the archives.'

They all fell silent.

A greenish light glowed through the canvas when she woke and for the first time in ages happiness woke with her. She pulled on jeans and a sweatshirt, unzipped the flap and crawled out to the fresh morning air. The tents were pitched among the trees. A half-charred log lay like a twisted arm on last night's campfire. Towels and wetsuits hung on a fence by the bush, bikes and surfboards leaned against it.

Butch lay in a hammock strung between two trunks. He reached out a sleepy arm but it was only a game. The blokes knew how things stood.

'Hey, Ellie. Up early. How you going?'

'I'm good, off for a jog on the beach.'

'My head's spinning like a sledgehammer hit it. Think I had one beer too many.'

'That fish was wicked, though.'

In the clear morning light she made her way past the cabins and up a track through the bush. She kicked off her thongs, felt the sand cool under her feet, just like snow must be. Dad said it was soft and powdery when it first fell. Here, though, it never snowed. The undergrowth was vibrant, thick with ferns and coarse grasses. Pale patches scarred the tree trunks where the bark had peeled. Some were black from a recent fire.

Her foot pressed on something sharp and she bent to look. A tiny starfish. She cupped it in her palm, a sunburst with five golden rays, the underside a mass of fibres mottled cream and fawn, then slipped it into her pocket and moved on towards the distant boom of the surf. The sound lifted something inside her, restlessness, uncertainty, life's vastness and complexity. Freedom, exhilaration, the yearning to know more.

And Brad had the nerve to call her repressed.

'She's stubborn,' Mum always said but Dad defended her.

'No, she's not. Ellie finds her own way. She knows what's right for her and gets on with it, that's all.'

She smiled at the memory as she came over the ridge and saw the sky strewn with wisps of clouds that barely moved. The bay curved in a long, lazy sweep, edged with hills that faded into the distance. Way out from the horizon, waves rolled in, set after set, lifted, peaked and curled with a lace of foam that fizzed on the sand.

She stood, drank in the sheer vastness and isolation of this place. Nothing but the open ocean for thousands of miles halfway round the globe.

The sun came out from behind a cloud, the water brightened to a brilliant turquoise and she glimpsed a school of dolphins, their black backs cutting the surface. She watched until they disappeared then started to jog, the sand giving beneath her feet. When her mobile rang she checked it still running. A shaft of surprise made her stop. Mum never called when she was away.

'Hi, Mum. You okay?'

'Yes, I'm good but . . .' Her voice trailed off, hesitant, anxious.

'Is Karen all right? And baby Will?'

'Yes, they're here with me now. Listen, Ellie, there's no easy way to say this . . .'

'And Dad?' A chill trickled through her.

'It's not good news, honey.'

She gripped the phone so tight it hurt her fingers.

'He felt a bit odd before he went to bed, indigestion, he said, a discomfort in his chest. So he took some tablets and went to sleep and then . . .'

'What?'

'In the middle of the night he cried out and . . . '

She stared at the ocean. The relentless waves. A cormorant perched on a rock.

'He didn't feel anything, darling. He didn't suffer.'

'I'll come back,' she said. 'Right away.'

She swung round towards the camp and began to run, her voice bouncing with the impact of her body.

'If I leave now, I'll be with you by two, three at the latest.'

'Don't go too fast, sweetie. You know how dangerous the highway is. I'm okay, Karen will stay with me. Just take care. Love you.'

'You should have done something!' Ellie cried but Mum had already ended the call. Anger and impotence surged inside her, fought with the boom of the surf, the pounding of her feet, the thud of her heart.

Smoke rose from the campfire as she drew near. Carl was cooking breakfast. The others stood around chatting. Gabriella's belly bulged under her maternity smock.

Death, new life.

She stared at Nic perched on Steve's knee, his hand on her thigh. She wanted to scream, rip things apart.

First Brad, now Dad.

Cockatoos screeched. Cicadas drummed their deafening racket as the sun crept over the hill. She focused on the bush, the tangled vines, the ferns, the spindly paper-bark trees with fine pointed leaves.

'You're a koala,' Dad used to say. He was the only person in the world who had ever understood her. 'Koalas hide in gum trees and peep through the branches. Or you're a mollusc. They live in shells that snap shut when anyone threatens them.'

He can't die, not when I still need him.

The wind lifted and swayed the branches. She caught the scent of eucalyptus oil rising like incense as the leaves stirred. Someone passed her a mug of tea, strong and sweet. They made her eat bacon, pancakes with syrup. Her mouth was so sticky she could barely chew. Each attempt to swallow threatened to choke her. She forced the food down, not sure how long it would stay there, and scrambled to her feet.

Steve shifted Nic from his lap and put Ellie's bags in the boot of the Subaru.

'Sure you're all right? Want me to drive you?'

'I'll be okay.' She was strong, she had to be, this wasn't happening.

'Take care,' they all said, and hugged.

Cindy wanted to go with her. 'Ellie, you've had a shock. You shouldn't be alone.'

'No, I need to be. Honest.'

She started the engine and backed out the Subaru, fighting to find an answer. People couldn't die, not like that, without telling you first. No, that was insane. People died all the time, but not Dad. Maybe Mum had got it wrong, he was in a coma, if they tried hard enough they'd get his heart to beat. She stamped on the brake as a cloud of fury blurred her vision. Mum was a nurse, she should have known what to do. Why couldn't she have saved him?

No, it must be a mistake. If Dad had died, she'd feel pain not numbness. Life wouldn't go on as if nothing had happened, families outside their tents eating breakfast, campers coming back from the store, kids throwing balls. No, when she reached home, he'd be there the same as always.

He used to say anything was possible if you held onto it hard enough. The pot of gold at the end of the rainbow, the immigrant's dream.

'I made it, you see. I'm the living proof.'

Ulladulla. Mollymook. Falls Creek. The names of the places she passed had lost their meaning. The Princes Highway curved on and up, swept round and down, the drone of traffic incessant. Near the Nowra State Forest her throat tightened and she let out a shout of pain, a wail of disbelief.

Lake Illawarra passed in a blur and Kanahooka and Wollongong. She came to where planes lifted off from the airport, their bellies huge above the highway. On and on she went, north into the underpass where lights snaked through the darkness, out into daylight till the Harbour Bridge skimmed beneath her and the Spit Bridge lay ahead.

This road was so familiar she could have driven it blindfold. Almost too soon she turned into the driveway alongside the lagoon where Dad's car was parked. Only it wasn't his car anymore because he was dead, and the terrible, agonising truth was that she'd never really known him.

She switched off the engine, gripped the steering wheel and stared at the weatherboard bungalow he'd built with his own hands. She'd thought he would be here forever. All the questions she should have asked him, about his family, about England, his childhood, why he'd come here, and now it was too late. If only she'd spent more time with him, instead of distancing herself because of Brad.

'They're so cute,' Brad said when he first met her parents, 'living in their little time warp. It must be hard for you, Ellie, moving on to the twenty-first century.'

'What do you mean?'

'Please don't be angry. You see, my parents split when I was seven. What yours have, monogamy, commitment, it's so unusual these days. People are different now. Relationships have opened up, shifted, expanded, don't you think?'

'What are you getting at?'

His hand rested on hers. 'You know I'm crazy about you just as you are. I wouldn't change a thing.'

At the time, she'd felt pacified. She'd hooked a big fish, reeled him in, planned to keep him there. Older, been around a bit, knew what he wanted and meant to have it.

'The point is, Ellie, can you take me the way I am?'

Of course she should have asked what he meant by that, but back then she didn't want to know. Not while they played their little game of setting up home together, the perfect couple.

'Have you heard? Brad Steele? Looks like he's settling down,' his friends whispered, eyeing Ellie with awe.

She found out soon enough. Slowly, so that she barely noticed until it was too late.

With a rush of sick fury, she grabbed the keys from the ignition. The screen door opened with a squeak and Mum appeared, her face pale but determined. Karen followed with baby Will in her arms.

Ellie ran to them, they hugged, and the tears she'd been

fighting flowed until she sobbed and sobbed as if the pain would never stop.

When the funeral was over and Dad's belongings sorted and sent to the op shop, emptiness took hold. Nothing in the house had changed but everything was different. She woke in the morning to the strange familiarity of her old room with her childhood books on the shelf and her charcoal drawing of Dad on the wall. As she lay there, her mind turned over memories. They were all she had of him now, a few scraps, scattered like clues that might lead to an understanding of the father she'd loved but barely known.

At eleven o'clock she joined her mother on the veranda for morning tea. Shadows from the jasmine quivered over them. Mum cradled her mug and sighed.

'I should answer all those condolence cards.'

There were dozens of them, from friends, colleagues, neighbours. Ben Wright from the *Canberra,* the ship Dad had boarded for the long, slow journey from England.

'What a time we had of it, bands playing in every port, more food than we could eat. Blighty and post-war austerity seemed a distant nightmare.'

Michael from the migrants' hostel, Gerry Coombes who'd worked with Dad on a building site, Andy from the chess club, Phil who'd gone through accountancy training with him.

She'd had no idea that so many people knew him, or cared enough to write kind words about how he had touched their lives.

'I'll help with the replies if you like, Mum.'

'Will you have time? What about work?'

'I'm not due back for a week or so. How about you?'

Mum twisted a spray of blossom that had come loose from

the trellis. Her shoulders lifted and dropped.

'I could take more compassionate leave, but I'd rather get back on the ward and keep busy.'

Her face was set with the determination that Ellie knew so well.

'Why don't you go up to Uncle Charlie's?'

Mum's childhood home with its acres of sugar cane and mangoes. The hot earthy smell of the red dirt.

Mum lifted her chin.

'My life is here now, Ellie. I'll be fine, don't you worry. It's a shock but not a surprise. When you marry a much older man you have an inkling that one day you'll lose him.'

Ellie knew better than to argue. It was survival not hardness. Mum didn't come of pioneer stock for nothing.

If I could be as strong as her, I'd survive, too.

She gazed at the frangipane tree, its creamy petals tinged with yellow, and a realisation began to crystallise as if the network of branches, leaves and blossoms had given it shape.

'You know what? I'm sick of the museum. I want to do something with relevance to me, to us, to where we come from, our place in the world.'

'We all have to work, Ellie.'

'Poring over documents is so dry.'

'Didn't I say it was wrong for you? But of course you wouldn't listen.'

Give me patience, muttered Ellie and picked up the photos they'd found in Dad's desk, small monochrome snaps of the childhood he'd never talked about. His father, Ellie's grandfather, was an Anglican minister, but Dad claimed he'd had enough of religion to last him the rest of his life, so he'd never inflicted it on his children. Which was just as well, because from what she'd heard, most churches were riddled with intolerance. And all of Australia knew about the scandal of the British orphans who'd been sent to seminaries and treated like slaves.

In the photo, though, Grandad Jack and Grandma Lillian looked like sweet, gentle people. A little harassed, maybe, as they stood with their four children in descending order of age. First was big sister Dorothy, her back straight, her head held high. Next came Dad, in a suit with short trousers and thick knee socks. Beside him was a smaller boy with a scowl, his stomach pushed out. Then baby Frances, the little sister Dad had barely known. She was only a child when he left on the ten pound passage.

'Have you heard from Aunty Frances?' Ellie asked.

'I phoned Dorothy, and she promised to tell her. She did warn us her sister's hard to track down.'

'What was his brother called, the one who died?'

'Bobby.'

'So what happened?'

'Some sort of accident, I think. That's all Dad ever said.'

'How could he shut away the past like it never existed?'

'You know how your father was. He always said that things had been difficult and it was best to forget. Anyhow, by the time I met him he'd already been here for twenty years, so he thought of Australia as home.'

Mum gave Ellie one of her looks.

'It's no good being sentimental. Migrants have to leave the past behind or they can't move on. He did a bit of family research after his parents died, and that was enough for him.'

'But surely he could have gone for a visit? Or they could have come here.'

'It wasn't as easy back then, Ellie. The journey took a month by sea and cost a year's wages. Most people who emigrated never saw their families again.'

'Mother, I am a history graduate. I know all the facts. But it's why Dad never talked about them that puzzles me.'

'You could have asked him. He told you his story often enough.'

Ellie gasped. 'So that's it,' she said.

'What is?'

'The reason I'm bored in the museum. Whenever Dad told me about coming out here, he brought his story to life, made it exciting, funny, sad. That's what inspired me to study history, but all I do now is catalogue dead documents. Take them out of boxes, put them back again.'

'Well, there you go, Ellie. That's real life for you. Dreams don't always turn out the way we want.'

Mum picked up the empty mugs and turned towards the screen door that led to the kitchen.

'Dad's did, though, didn't it?' Ellie called after her. 'It brought him here to you, to Karen and me. That's what he always said. And don't forget I was only a kid at the time. What he told me was a fairy tale, a fable full of wonder. It never occurred to me to ask if he was upset about leaving his family behind. At least, I don't think it did . . .'

She stared at the lagoon as her mind travelled back over the years. In her memory, they're here on the verandah. How old is she? Four? Five? She's not sure. Dad's reading the newspaper and she pulls at his sleeve.

'Tell me your story, Daddy.'

'What, again?'

15

He folds up the paper and she climbs on his lap. Over his shoulder, the sky is white with cloud, the lagoon is silver, trembling. Feathery trees stir in the breeze, their roots in the shallow, sandy banks.

Karen isn't there. Maybe she's at school or out with her friends. Mum potters around, ties back the jasmine, prunes her roses. As long as she doesn't butt in, that's okay. This is Ellie's special time, just her and Dad.

'Go on, Daddy' she says and he opens his eyes wide as if what he's about to say is the most amazing truth in all the world.

'I was A Ten Pound Pom.'

He tells her about the war and how the planes came from Japan to bomb Australia. Everyone was terrified, he says, far away from the rest of the world, so the government hatched a plan to bring out more people to help defend the country if it was ever attacked again.

She's pretty sure they never talk about why he left his family. Maybe because she, Mum and Karen are his family now, and that's all that matters.

What she does remember is the way he turns all the facts into a game. Like when he tells her how every migrant had to meet three conditions. That's something she's never forgotten, because he counts them on her fingers.

'One, you had to be white, two, you had be healthy, three, you had to speak English.'

'Like you, Daddy.'

He pulls a funny face, says the trouble was it didn't work out as they expected. Lots of Aussies resented the Brits for pinching their jobs and as special buses took them to their hostels, locals shook their fists and yelled at them to go home. They even called them rude names. That's when she whispers the words, so that Mum can't hear.

'Pommy bastards.'

Dad chuckles, cuddles her closer and paints more pictures that she can see even now. How they slept eight to a room in old army huts left over from the war, and it was so hot they had to spray water on the tin roofs to cool them. Lots of men were homesick. They'd been conned into thinking Australia was a paradise, but instead there were flies, spiders and poisonous snakes. And it was so dry and dusty that they longed for green fields, sometimes even rain. But they couldn't go home, because it would mean paying the full fare themselves.

So Dad worked in the docks, saved money and bought a plot of land down by the lagoon in Narrabeen. She knows this bit by heart. How he went to evening classes, learned to be an accountant, made lots more money and built a little weatherboard bungalow the Australian way, on stilts with a tin roof and a dunny in the backyard. This always gives her a warm feeling, because that's her home, where she lives with him now. So when he says he used to be happy living alone, she asks why he married Mum, even though she knows the answer.

'Because a snake bit me.'

If Mum hears him, she laughs like it's a huge joke, but Dad says it's true – he was rushed to hospital and woke to see this lovely young nurse all dressed in white, with hair the colour of ripe corn and eyes like the sea, and he thought he'd died and gone to heaven.

'So I got down on my knees, asked her to marry me and took her home to my little wooden shack.'

'And then you had Karen and then you had me.'

'Double the trouble.'

'And twice as nice.'

When the story is all wrapped up, she rests her head on his chest while Mum has her say.

'You spoil that child, Jimmy. You're much too soft with her.'

'No, I don't, do I, Ellie Belly?' He buries his mouth on her tummy, blows hot and hard and loud until she laughs so much she has to beg him to stop.

That's all she remembers. The bits that matter. The rest of his life – England, his family, the people he left behind – is no more than a blur of names on birthday cards, strange stamps, ghosts from another world. Reality has always been here, in Narrabeen, the lagoon, the weatherboard house.

Until now.

Because now she can see that she knew only a part of him. The part he allowed her to see. Oh yes, she knew him, but not what shaped him, before he came here.

Maybe that was enough while he was with her, but now that he's gone she needs more than memories and a few old photos. She yearns to find what lay under the surface – his motivations, experiences, hopes and fears. Because, both as a daughter and a historian, she knows that what lies hidden is probably the most significant of all.

The following weekend, when Ellie went to search for a screwdriver to mend a broken rowlock on the dinghy, she came across a box of Dad's bits and pieces. It was under a pile of junk in the garage where he kept his tools and tackle, the only place they hadn't got round to clearing.

At the bottom of the box, under coils of wire, was a foolscap envelope with her name scrawled in pencil. She opened it and out slid a book, faded and spotted with age. The dust cover was grey, with a yellow lozenge behind the title.

Surprised by Joy – The Shape of My Early Life.

Apart from its historical value, the book meant nothing to Ellie, so why was her name on the envelope? Maybe Dad had recycled an old one. She flicked through the pages. The text seemed to be about atheism. Dad must have read it as a young man and brought it with him when he emigrated, because the date of publication was 1955, which was several years before he left.

The epigraph was a quotation from the Wordsworth poem that had given the book its title.

Tucked in the back of the book, she found a postcard and a photo. The card was a faded shot of The Three Sisters, the famous rock towers in the Blue Mountains, where they'd often spent family holidays. She could remember Dad telling her and Karen about the legend.

'The three sisters were turned into stone because they'd fallen in love with men from the wrong tribe. And they're still waiting, three huge rocks that tower up from the forest, for someone to come along and break the spell.'

'Ellie,' came Mum's voice from the kitchen. 'Your coffee's getting cold.'

'Won't be a minute.'

The other side of the postcard was blank. Maybe he'd just used it as a bookmark. She glanced at the photo. A child in an old-fashioned cozzie was squinting against the sun and licking an ice-cream. Her hair was gold and wavy like Karen's, but the style and muted colour of the swimsuit were from an earlier era.

'Who's this?' Ellie asked Mum when she joined her in the

kitchen.

Mum agreed it wasn't Karen. Maybe one of Dad's sisters, she said, probably Dorothy, because Frances looked darker in all the photos they'd seen.

Ellie didn't mention the book, but after coffee she took it to her room and opened it again. On a blank page just inside the cover was a handwritten dedication: *To my dear son, Jimmy, from Daddy, September 1958.* Jimmy, Ellie's Dad, would have been eighteen or nineteen at the time. But September wasn't the month of his birthday, and the date was a couple of years before he emigrated. So what was the reason for the gift?

As she mulled over the possibilities, it struck her that a book about atheism was a strange choice for a minister to give his non-believing son. She scanned down the resume inside the dust cover. It summarised the author's search for joy as a spiritual journey that saw him move from the Christianity of his childhood to atheism and then, through theism, to Christianity again.

So that was it. Grandad Jack must have hoped to persuade Dad that he was wrong, and win him back to the fold. Ellie couldn't help smiling. If that was his plan, then poor old Grandad had failed completely. But why had Dad brought the book to Australia? The only reason Ellie could think of, the only plausible explanation, was that he'd treasured it as a gift from the father he was leaving behind. The content wasn't what mattered to him, it was the inscription. That must be why he'd written Ellie's name on the envelope. Dad, too, had intended it as a gift, an heirloom for her, his much-loved child.

Then what was the significance of the photo? She checked it against snaps of Aunt Dorothy. Yes, she could see a resemblance, but this child's hair was curlier, her face thinner. The eyes were difficult to make out because they were screwed up against the sun. As for the style of the hair and the cozzie, Ellie's instinct as a historian nudged her towards a date in the fifties or sixties, which was too late for Dorothy and too early for Karen.

She looked again at the postcard, the only item that was familiar to her. Was it there by chance or had Dad intended it as some kind of clue? He'd written her name on the envelope. Was he trying to tell her something? She was well aware that he loved nothing more than a puzzle. Crosswords, treasure trails and secret codes were the games of her childhood. Had he left these items as some sort of cryptic gift?

The sun that shone into her bedroom faded, as if a shadow had passed over the fly screen. An unthinkable possibility gripped her. Did she and Karen have another sister, one born before Dad came out here?

She peered more closely at the photo. There was definitely a family likeness, not to Ellie because she was dark like Dad, but to Karen and Aunt Dorothy. The era seemed right, too, around the time that Dad had emigrated.

What was more, he'd put the photo inside a British book, with an Australian postcard, which also suggested a link.

But if he did have another child, and wanted Ellie to know about her, why not tell Karen, too? And why go about it in such an obscure way, leaving the envelope in the garage on the off-chance that she'd find it?

It took a surprisingly long time for the answer to click into place. The light from the window brightened and fell in a wedge of sunshine. Somewhere in the distance a voice called, and another replied.

Because he didn't know he was going to die yet, you idiot. And because you're a historian, and research is what you do.

'Karen builds,' Dad said when his elder daughter began to train as an architect. 'You dig, Ellie, and put pieces together.'

THE KENT COAST, JULY 1934

If he ever had a son, Jack mused as he lowered *Treasure Island* onto his lap, he would call him Jim. Not only for the plucky adventurer who outwitted pirates, uncovered dastardly plots and secured the treasure – though such feats were inspiring enough – but because Jim was his father's name, too. Jim Goodwin. That was a fine name for man or boy.

As the train steamed through the Kent countryside, Jack drummed his fingers on the window ledge, his excitement building. Fields and villages lay comatose under the sun and beyond them he glimpsed the silver sheen of the sea. He knew the dips and rises of this landscape as intimately as the contours of his own body, and even after years away it tugged and taunted him with memories. The closer they drew to Dover, the tighter his muscles tensed, as familiarity and estrangement tangled inside him.

He rested his head against the seat-back and let his mind rove over his childhood. He'd always loved books and was the first lad from the village to go to grammar school. But when Father returned from war, silent, his eyes staring, his hand trembling as he lifted his saucer of tea, Jack had to go out to work. He was just thirteen. By fifteen he'd grown tired of scrawling bills of lading at the docks in Dover and he fled to London. For a while he pushed a barrow round the Isle of Dogs, trying to make his way, until the call of the river, the hoot of the steamships and the smell of the ocean carried him East.

By the time he came back he was a boy no more.

He could recall only too clearly that last night on the salt-sprayed deck of the ship as they entered the Straits of Dover. He'd tossed a cigarette stub over the rail and watched its trail of sparks snap out in the wind. Through the mist a light flashed and a ghostly wall of chalk loomed and faded, once, twice. A sudden blast of the foghorn shot him back to his bedroom under the eaves, where that same mournful hoot had sounded again and again through his childhood dreams.

'South Foreland,' he'd called out as his heart soared and sank with the swell. Up there, nestling in the lee of the clifftop, behind the beam of the lighthouse, was his home.

Now, though, seen from the train, the air outside was clear. The sun blazed. The foghorn was silent. With a hiss of steam and a shriek of the whistle they sped into a tunnel. The carriage plunged into darkness. His eyes had barely adjusted to the glow from the bulbs when they came out into daylight and the train began to brake, slowing to a clanking crawl as it approached Priory Station. Dover's drab buildings lay all around, with the docks and the harbour ahead.

Jack reached for his battered suitcase from the rack above. What a poor receptacle for the proud certificate that he carried inside it. He chuckled to himself. You could start a sermon with an illustration like that, an everyday anecdote before the nitty-gritty of the spiritual lesson about this treasure we have in earthen vessels.

The train shuddered to a halt. He opened the carriage door and breathed in the sooty, salty tang of the air. How he'd looked forward to this break from London, where the misery of poverty grew ever deeper as the depression worsened. You could see it in the soup kitchens, packed with queues of destitute men and women, children too. He played his small part, helped when he could, snatched time to study. But all of them feared that the economic crisis and rumblings of conflict with Germany would have far more impact than well-meaning attempts at caring for the poor.

Clutching his suitcase he made his way through the crowds. Ah, there was Father with his slouch hat and cord trousers, a little more stooped but otherwise unchanged. He stood nattering to a farmer, and the two men glanced up as Jack drew near.

'Here's the lad now,' Father said, and they shook hands warmly. The farmer eyed him up and down like a bullock on market day.

'So what are we to call you now? University degree, your father tells me.'

'Plain Jack, the same as always, Mr Warren.'

'Not Reverend?'

'That comes later. After the summer holidays I'll start training for ordination.'

'We'll have to watch it then, eh, Jim?' Mr Warren said, and Father's face beamed.

In many ways the transition was as strange for Jack as it was for them. Who would have thought that a simple village lad would ever go to university, let alone end up as a vicar? But now, in his late twenties, five years after his dramatic turnaround in India, here was Jack Goodwin coming home with a degree in Theology from King's College, London.

Outside in the street, as if to underline this contrast, Bessie waited between the shafts of the cart with its faded inscription:

J. Goodwin and Son, Carriers, South Foreland.

'Remember me, old girl?'

Jack ran his hand over the horse's velvety muzzle. Her breath tickled his palm as he opened it to give her the lump of sugar he'd saved from his breakfast tea. He swung his suitcase onto the cart with the crates and boxes, then climbed up to the bench. Father took the reins, and Jack looked around him happily as Bessie clopped her way through the familiar streets. They were busy with shoppers, farmers in from the surrounding villages and children on their way home from school.

Once they'd left the town behind, the road grew steeper and the rhythm of Bessie's hooves slowed as she strained against the shafts.

Up above them loomed the castle, towering over the coast as it had done since medieval times, guarding the Straits between England and France. Once they reached higher ground a breeze rose from the Channel but the heat was still intense. The grass was pink with pollen, the air hummed with insects, the sun beat from a cloudless sky. Way below them the sea was a hazy blue, dotted with boats like specks of soot. Kittiwakes wheeled overhead and fold after fold of white cliffs faded to the east.

Sweat streamed from under Jack's hat and trickled down his back. Bessie's hooves sent up clouds of chalky dust that stuck to his skin and turned his shirt to a shroud. He mopped his brow with a handkerchief.

'What a scorcher!'

Father nodded and gave the reins a flick to urge Bessie upwards. She had travelled this way so many times that she knew exactly when to turn onto the lane that led to the village. They passed fields where Jack had played as a boy, now stripped bare from an early harvest, the stubble baked golden, scattered with sheaves of corn waiting to be taken to the barns.

Higher and higher they climbed towards a beech copse in the lee of the cliff where he'd snatched his first kiss. What was her name? Molly? Milly? Beautiful breasts, soft and yielding. She'd married and moved away long ago, but the memory reminded him that he was coming home to people who knew his strengths and weaknesses almost as well as he did, and would be curious to know how he'd changed.

What they didn't know were the struggles he'd been through and the transitions he'd made. All those experiences abroad that had shaped his character, until that awful night in Bombay when he'd found himself alone, robbed, beaten and penniless. It was one of those moments when a man cries out to the Almighty and makes all sorts of rash bargains.

He grimaced at the irony. As a boy he'd spent years kicking his heels in the choir stall of the village church while the vicar droned through the prayer book, and had never once stopped to ponder what those words meant. But stripped of everything in the far reaches of a foreign country, aware that his ship must long since have sailed without him, he'd been so frightened that he'd prayed in earnest for the first time in his life.

Perhaps that was why, when help came from the Consulate, he'd felt a rush of emotion that was more than relief. A strange conviction clutched him that an angel had been sent to save him, and a friendly angel at that. His rescuer was more like an uncle than a diplomat, and busied himself on Jack's behalf with a courtesy and concern that a young sailor in a scrape surely didn't merit. His parting words had branded Jack like a tattoo.

'Commit your way to the Lord, young man, and He will watch over you.'

Throughout the long voyage home Jack had felt strangely cocooned in a blanket of protection, yet with a rough prick of challenge, as if the one who watched over him might have something to ask of him, too. What that might be, he had as yet no idea. But it had left him alert and expectant, swaying between anticipation and blank terror.

Then had come a series of steps that had led Jack to make a commitment. While staying at the Toc H hostel he'd met its founder, Tubby Clayton, who'd been an inspirational army chaplain during the Great War. Clayton's friend, Dick Sheppard, the pacifist, housed down-and-outs in the crypt of St Martin's in the Fields. Jack did his bit to help, and while there he learned that these two inspirational leaders had set up the Knutsford Ordination Test School. Its purpose was to enable men like Jack, who'd left school early, to work towards the qualifications they'd need to study for a degree.

Thanks to them, too, he came into contact with that reassuringly masculine band of young men with a burning vision to build a better world out of the ruins of war. Reluctantly at first, but with growing excitement, he began to accept that someone as flawed and insignificant as Jack Goodwin could play a part.

'Whoa, Bessie!'

Father tugged at the reins as a wild apparition loomed from the brow of the hill and a bicycle headed towards them at an alarming speed. Two young women, one on the seat, one perched on the crossbar, shouted with laughter as they wobbled and swerved, propelled downhill by the pull of gravity. They whistled past in a whirl of dust and Jack caught a glimpse of sunburnt legs, dark hair with a plait flying loose, the flash of a smile.

'Bloody Londoners,' Father said, but the corners of his mouth twitched.

'Are they staying at the Guest House?'

'Been with us a fortnight. Convalescing, diphtheria, I believe. You'll have to ask Mother. She knows the ins and outs of it.'

So I'll see them at supper, Jack thought happily. He was used to a house full of visitors in the summer when Mother opened her tea garden and took in paying guests. He let out a long, slow breath as the strains of the city began to fade.

Way in the distance the open expanse of the Channel shimmered with heat. A stronger breeze reached him, bringing a tang of seaweed.

'Tide's out.'

Father glanced across and nodded, his eyes narrowed against the light.

The stumpy church tower came into view above a cluster of cottages. As always the village radiated an aura of peace, though many an invasion had threatened it over the centuries. They passed the flint and brick house where one of Jack's cousins used to live before he married a Dover girl and went to work at the docks. Then came the little shop, with boxes of cabbages and carrots and spuds stacked outside.

'Welcome home, luv,' a voice called. 'I'll be over later.'

It was Aunty Lulu. She waved from her doorway and Jack waved back.

They rounded a bend, and the sweet, sharp aroma of freshly baked apples drifted across the street. Mother made the best in the world, stuffed with raisins and honey and served with a dollop of cream. Jack's mouth watered. He'd eaten nothing apart from a meat pie at Victoria Station, but he knew that Mother would have a spread laid out for teatime.

The old house came into view and his chest expanded and tightened. The weatherboard facade was freshly painted a pale sea-green. Hollyhocks lined the path to the teahouse. All the sash windows were open, and from inside came voices and laughter.

A girl in a smock ran out from the garden gate.

'He's here,' she shrieked and two other children joined her, jumping up and down in excitement.

'That's never our Florrie.'

Last Christmas his sister's child was only a toddler, but now she was running around, chasing a hoop.

Father tied Bessie to a post and Jack lifted his case from the cart. Mother hurried towards him, wiping her hands on her apron. As she clasped him, the smells of childhood rose to meet him, milk and bread dough mixed with a tinge of sweat and a whiff of lavender. *It's good to be back, Mother,* he wanted to say, but the words stuck in his throat. He hugged her tighter and rested his cheek against hers.

'Welcome home, son.'

Her hair was greyer than last time and a dusting of flour smudged one cheek. She held him at arms' length to get a better look.

'Jack, my boy, we're more proud of you than words can tell.'

It was silly to feel like this because The Prodigy had arrived. But as Lillian and her sister came back from their bike ride, she was terribly hot and nervous. The sun beat full on their heads as they trudged uphill, taking it in turns to push the bicycle. Wisps of hair stuck to her face and her shirt was damp with sweat. Water was in short supply, so she had to make do with a quick splash under the garden pump.

Inside the house, in the kitchen, the butter had turned to oil on the dish with the blue willow pattern. As they all took their places at the supper table, Lillian was glad for the dimness now that the sunlight had faded. She kept telling herself there was no need to feel embarrassed. They'd known for ages that The Prodigy was due home soon. In the fortnight that she and Violet had been here, Mrs Goodwin had talked of little else.

My son this…Jack that…University…Ordination…Home soon.

These words had peppered the old lady's conversation as liberally as the thyme and rosemary that seasoned her stews.

So when the girls' bicycle had whistled past Mr Goodwin's cart, they'd guessed it was The Prodigy on the seat beside him. They already knew that he was due to arrive on the 3.43 from Victoria. Preparations were afoot to welcome him with a feast befitting his newly acquired status. But their bike had sped downhill at such a terrifying speed that Lillian could only grip the handlebars and shriek, while the dust flew into her eyes, blinding her to all but the image of a hot, red face, split into a grin.

That was what had surprised and unnerved her – the fact that he was laughing. It was so different from what she'd expected.

Until that afternoon, a picture of the soon-to-be-Reverend Goodwin had been forming in her mind's eye, painted with the brush of his mother's words. The Prodigy, as Lillian and her sister had christened him, would be a younger version of their parish priest in Streatham. Thin, sallow and a little bit too sincere. Like Father Leonard he would wear a black cassock buttoned to the neck and would squint over his books through horn-rimmed spectacles. His hand, if he shook theirs, would be bony and clammy.

'Creepy, like a beetle,' as Violet said.

Lillian was prepared for all that, plus lots of jokes at The Prodigy's expense once they were safely out of earshot. But she was quite unprepared for the young man who bounded downstairs two at a time, strolled into the kitchen with his shirt sleeves rolled up and tossed little Florrie to the ceiling.

She tried not to look at him as he took his seat opposite her, scraping the wooden chair against the bare stone floor. Thank goodness the only light came from one small window. The back door opened onto the garden, which was now steeped with shadows, so he couldn't see the heat rush to her cheeks. She half-closed her eyes, breathed in the fragrance of night-scented stocks that drifted into the kitchen, while the clock on the wall ticked its steady rhythm, soothing her nerves.

Violet sat beside her, but Lillian didn't dare look at her sister in case she made her laugh. Instead, she allowed her eyes to roam over the table, spread with a clean white cloth and laden with wholesome food. A ham glistened with honey, studded with cloves. She saw a loaf of white bread, a bowl of tomatoes and one of radishes. Plus a block of cheese, lettuce and cucumbers fresh from the garden, baked apples and a sponge cake still warm from the oven. Her mouth watered.

'Gosh, I'm ravenous,' she wanted to say, but felt too shy. She'd begun to relax with Mr and Mrs Goodwin, but now that the Prodigy was here, the words stuck in her throat.

A sharp jab from Violet's knee made Lillian stiffen. Whatever happened she mustn't giggle. She tried to blot out the words that her sister had whispered earlier.

'Did you see? He's hairy all over, except on his head.'

Now he sat bang opposite her, his collarless shirt open at the neck, wriggling his ears to amuse his nieces and nephews.

'Have a bit of ham, ducky.'

Mrs Goodwin took the carving fork from her husband and stabbed a fat juicy slice to pass across to Lillian.

'Now you see if that doesn't bring the colour to your cheeks. And one for you, dear?'

'Oh, rather.'

As Violet spoke, everyone's eyes moved towards her, but she smiled at them brightly and held out her plate. Lillian wished she had the confidence of her younger sister. Even now, well into her twenties, she felt almost more tongue-tied and awkward with strangers than she had as a child.

'Oh, rather,' echoed one of the little boys when his turn came. Mrs Goodwin gave him a look but tousled his head fondly.

Such an easy-going woman, thought Lillian with admiration. Much more relaxed than her own mother. Life here was less ordered than in Streatham, but the chores got done just the same. The wash might spill over the copper and hiss on the stove, but the linen came out beautifully clean. The lamps sometimes ran out of paraffin, but candles were much more fun. Chickens clucked and pecked their way into the kitchen, but they laid the most delicious eggs with the brownest shells and yellowest yolks. And still Mrs Goodwin found time to bake scones and cakes for her tea-shop, look after her grandchildren, organise her husband's business, and take in paying guests.

A bluebottle buzzed over the table and made for the cheese. Mr Goodwin rolled up a newspaper, waited for the fly to settle, and took a swipe that sent the milk jug toppling.

'Jim, you silly old fool!' Mrs Goodwin ran for a cloth to mop up the mess as a slosh of milk ran towards Lillian. The Prodigy leaped up, reached across to grab the tablecloth and trap the liquid in a pool, but Mrs Goodwin shrieked a warning.

'Whatever are you doing to Miss Cullen? Watch out! It's off to the other Miss Cullen now.'

'Miss Cullen? Miss Cullen? Don't these young ladies have names?'

He smiled across the table at them. His eyes caught Lillian's and the heat crept up her neck to her cheeks.

'Anyway, I answer to Jack,' he said.

Harebells, thought Lillian, that's the colour of his eyes. The delicate flowers grew up on the cliffs, scattered like snippets of summer sky. She snatched another look at him. The top of his head, almost as bald as his father's, glistened in the light from the window. His shirt, open at the neck, showed a fuzz of pale hair, and his forearms were soft and furry. Lillian stifled a smile, and a shiver ran through her.

'Well, I answer to Violet,' her sister said, her cheeks dimpling. 'When we came rattling down the hill on our bike we thought we might land in your lap.'

Lillian gasped. She could almost feel herself sitting there. She kicked her sister under the table, and struggled with a fluster of confusion. Violet already had a young man and should know better than to behave like a flirt.

Jack reached to shake hands, but Violet drew back.

'Oh, you mustn't touch. We've both had diphtheria.'

'That's why we're here,' said Lillian, amazed at her own boldness. But nobody noticed that she'd spoken. Tears stung her eyes while the babble of their voices swirled over her. Mrs Goodwin was telling Edward not to let the cat jump on the table. Violet was saying that diphtheria was a funny word, impossible to spell. Jack nodded.

'That's because it comes from the Greek.'

Mr Goodwin watched his son with a respectful smile. Everyone fell quiet, even the children, while The Prodigy answered their questions.

'Is Greek a hard language to learn?'

'Yes, it is rather, until you get the hang of it.'

'Do people still speak it?'

'Oh no, I'm learning ancient Greek, they speak something different now.'

'So what's the point of swotting at it then?"

'Is it to do with being a vicar?'

'Yes, the Bible was originally written in Greek, at least the New Testament was. The Old Testament was written in Hebrew.'

'Do you have to learn that, too?'

'Yes, I'm afraid so. They have different alphabets, so it's even more complicated,' he added with a smile.

Enjoying all the attention, thought Lillian, but she couldn't help smiling, too.

Little Florrie wanted to see his books.

'Tomorrow when I've unpacked them you can have a look. This evening I need some fresh air.'

He scraped back his chair and stood. His glance touched Lillian's.

'How about a walk down to the Bay? Anyone like to come?'

'Rather,' said Violet, and everyone laughed.

'And the other Miss Cullen?'

'Lillian,' she said, her cheeks flaming.

Now when he spoke his tone was more gentle.

'Will you come too, Lillian? It's a lovely walk on a summer evening.'

They all fell silent as they waited for her response. His smile drew her from across the table.

'I'd love to,' she said.

She could almost hear a collective sigh, while a grin, a ridiculous grin, spread across her face.

NARRABEEN, NSW MAY 2010

On the steps of the veranda, with the darkness soft around her and the laptop on her knees, Ellie opened Google Earth. In two weeks' time she would make the journey that her finger traced across the screen, the same journey Dad had made in reverse half a century ago. It had taken her a while to get up the nerve – communicating with her aunts, working out her notice at the museum, applying for a British passport so she'd have more freedom as to how long she could stay – but at last the ticket was booked, her luggage almost packed, and she was itching to go. A little nervous, maybe. But autumn was fading to winter, while in England it would soon be summer. Two summers in one year – that had to be good.

She zoomed in to the urban sprawl of London then east to Canterbury, tucked in a loop of the Kent coast. Beneath it was the port of Dover. A hop and a skip away along the cliffs was Grandad Jack's birthplace, no more than a dot above the English Channel. Way to the west was Aunt Dorothy's village, and further still, in the peninsula that narrowed towards the Atlantic, must be where Aunt Frances lived.

A sudden gust of wind reached her through the darkness and Ellie shivered. It was silly to feel nervous about leaving Sydney, but this was the only world she knew, the place where she felt secure. She peered across the surface of the lagoon, ruffled with reflected lights from the houses that fringed it. The tide was flowing fast and from the distance came a rumble of thunder. Spots of rain lashed the veranda. She grabbed the laptop and dashed inside.

Mum was baby-sitting for Karen and Tim, so the house was empty. She stood, and felt its silence settle. How strange that she'd lived here for most of her life but nothing much had changed. The screen door squeaked as it always had. The walls were the same pale green from decades ago. Patchwork cushions lay crumpled on the couch, and a picture of the farm where Mum was raised hung crooked by the window.

At least they'd replaced the lino and put a glass shower door where there used to be a plastic curtain. When Ellie was a kid, the rain bounced off the tin roof and they had to leave buckets to collect the drips, until Dad could afford to tile it.

His absence was the only difference.

With a sigh she went to the dresser and picked up her new biometric British passport, maroon with a gold crest. It struck her as unreal, like faking her identity. She was an Aussie through and through, but a thread of Dad's Britishness tugged at her now that he'd gone. She flicked over the pages with their delicate renderings of birds in muted blues, mauves and turquoise. The photo stared back at her like a stranger. Her smoky blue eyes had a startled look, her face was sunburnt and her hair, tangled from the beach, as wild as a gypsy's.

'Think they'll let you in?' Butch had joked when he'd seen it.

Dual nationality. What a strange concept. Like turning over that starfish and finding the other side was different.

Excitement sizzled inside her. In only fourteen days' time

she'd leave for England, for a new life, full of opportunities. A new Ellie, a new job, perhaps, new people for sure, maybe even someone special. Someone who would see through her stubbornness and love her the way she was.

As the countdown intensified, seven days, six, a yearning to visit old haunts gnawed at her. She wanted to say goodbye to places, as well as people. Now that she'd left the museum – a decision that Mum said she'd regret – kicking her heels at home made her nervy.

So the next day she drove down to Manly. A crazy idea. It was Monday, all her friends were at work, and an early winter gloom hung over North Steyne. She passed empty bars and cafes, then crossed to the Norfolk Pines that lined the promenade. The beach was almost deserted, so she turned north and began to jog towards the Lifesaving Club. Where the grass ended, she paused, took a bottle of water from her backpack, and without thinking, turned along the path to Queenscliff.

It led to the unit she'd shared with Brad in the days when they were an item, and she'd been that way a million times. But an unscheduled meeting with him now was the last thing she wanted, so she swung inland and over the cliff towards Freshwater.

When she neared the top of the rise, she stopped to draw breath. Back the way she'd come, she could see clear across Manly to the distant headland and behind it the skyscrapers of the City Business District rising in a hazy cluster. Somewhere among them, in a tiny side street, was the museum where she used to work. She'd never have to do that commute again, not now that she'd thrown it all in.

After another swig of water, she jogged on, past apartment blocks and down to Freshwater Cove, where a loop of sea licked its tongue between cliffs. Gulls cried, the waves rolled in and dashed in a fizz of foam on the shore. Several surfers were coming out of the water with a black dog running around them, barking. Surely they must have seen the signs warning that dogs weren't allowed here, but they didn't seem to care. Their wetsuits glistened and their boards streamed as they made their way slowly in her direction.

Their easy friendliness highlighted her aloneness, so she crossed to the scrub and sat with her back turned, trying to blot out their voices. Over the months since she'd split with Brad, she'd toughened up, put disillusionment behind her. But Dad's death was on another level. It had hit her hard, and time didn't seem to heal the pain. A boyfriend you could get over, one more crossed off the list, but a father could never be replaced. The roots of that relationship went far deeper.

Grief takes time, everyone told her, but what still gnawed at Ellie was the sense that she'd never really known him, not deep down, not the secrets he'd kept hidden, the person he really was.

Her only hope was to crack the puzzle he'd left her and see what it revealed about his past. But even while she'd been planning her trip to England, she still struggled with a deep well of emptiness. Maybe she should have gone for counselling after all. Mum had nagged on about it for weeks, and when Ellie had refused point blank, she'd lost her patience.

'You always have to do everything your own way. Too proud, too stubborn, too sure you're right.'

Or was it Brad who'd said that? He often resorted to gibes when she wouldn't do what he wanted. Opening up, he'd called it, being more inclusive. A sudden surge of sickness hit her and she tried to stifle a howl, but her body began to shudder, just as the surfers passed behind her, laughing and joking like they didn't have a care in the world.

She kept her back turned, but their dog, some ugly kind of bull mastiff, made for the scrub where she sat, shook a shower of drops from its coat, and began to sniff among the wiry plants. One of the guys called it back, and the others turned to look. The last thing Ellie wanted was a group of strangers gawking at her, so she gritted her teeth and focused on the cliff with what she hoped was a scholarly frown.

Sandstone, sedimentary rock, laid down aeons ago.

'Catch up with you later,' she heard one guy say, and sensed him coming towards her.

'You okay?'

She swung round and glared at him. What business was it of his? But his expression was so inoffensive and full of concern that it took her by surprise. She shrugged, sniffed, and to her horror, burst into tears.

'Hey,' he said, as he crouched down, but not too close, 'whatever it is, there has to be an answer.'

'Huh!' She wiped one hand across her nose which dangled with some disgusting sort of slime. He pulled a comical face, spreading his arms as if in apology.

'Too bad I don't have a hanky.'

She let out a reluctant laugh. His wetsuit clung to a muscular body, strongly boned, with a peep of tanned flesh at the edges.

'It's okay,' she said. 'I must have a Kleenex somewhere.'

She fumbled in her backpack, and while she blew her nose he called to the dog which had started to scratch up the sand.

'Gump!'

The dog slunk towards them, giving Ellie the evil eye. Its hide was black and hairless, a bit like its master's wetsuit. She glanced at him again. Why would a good-looking bloke choose such an ugly beast? Another of life's mysteries, she thought, and poked the snotty tissue in the sand. She jerked her chin at him.

'That dog shouldn't be here.'

'Yeah, I know. We left him in my mate's Ute but he jumped out. He'll be okay here on the scrub.'

She let her eyes touch his, but if he read her expression he didn't show it. It was time to get up and walk away, but she didn't have the energy or the inclination. Something held her there. Even without looking at this bloke she could feel his presence, and it was strangely soothing to sense him beside her as the beach emptied and fell silent except for the wash of the waves, while the dog, like a hideous chaperone, sniffed and staked out their territory.

Meanwhile its master stretched lengthways on the scrub in his wetsuit, as black and moulded as a whale, and leaned on one arm as if to settle in for a long chat. The dog flopped beside him, its chin on his thigh, and snorted contentedly. Two beady eyes watched Ellie as he spoke to her.

'So, what is it? Friends? Money?'

He sounded like some sort of shrink. But she was the one who sat stiff and upright while he reclined on his couch of weeds. Drops of seawater slipped from a strand of dark hair that hung over his forehead as he poked at the ground with a stick. The bits of skin she could see were tanned and caked with a silvery crust of salt.

Something reassuring about him disarmed her. It was almost like being with a brother, not that she'd ever had one. Or maybe not a brother, because when she looked at the breadth of those shoulders under the skin of the suit, sensations shot through her that she hadn't felt for quite a long time.

She shrugged and sniffed.

'It's just that my Dad died.'

The moment she spoke, it was like a cork popped from a bottle and the whole pitiful story came fizzing out, about how she'd never known him, had chucked in her job, wanted more from life, but now had cold feet about leaving for England.

The shrink listened, nodded and fiddled with the sand. Ellie sensed she was revealing parts of herself far too deep and intimate to share with a stranger, but the words flowed with a a delicious abandonment that purged her of pain. She even heard herself talk about Brad, how he'd tried to lead her into deeper and darker places where she didn't want to go.

While she rambled on, the shrink listened, with an occasional grunt as if to show that he understood. She took that as encouragement and carried on in the same vein, telling amusing little anecdotes about her and Brad's love life in more and more detail.

The dog fixed her with its eyes, but its owner's head stayed down as he watched the sand trickle through his fingers.

Ellie stopped. An unpleasant thought had hit her. By baring her soul she'd given this stranger a power over her that she couldn't reclaim. She darted him a look of suspicion, but he kept trickling the sand and gazed up at the sky which now scudded with clouds. Quickly she changed tack.

'So, what with one thing and another it's been a crap year, and I'm supposed to be flying to London next week, but now I don't know whether to go or stay put.'

This time the shrink did meet her eyes. His were dark, glowing, gentle.

'Hey, I know it's not me, but if it was me, I'd go. There must be a whole lot more to gain than to lose.'

His voice sounded friendly enough and Ellie nodded happily. Maybe he was just the quiet type. She could forgive him that. Not everyone came out all guns blazing like Brad. And, yes, he was right, a new country, new people, new experiences would be good for her. Now that she'd got things off her chest, the idea inspired her. The problem had shrunk.

Was that why people called them shrinks?

She took another peek at her confidant. One foot jigged, flapping his thong and sending a quick rhythmic throb up the muscles of his leg.

The sun slipped behind a cloud and plunged the beach into shade.

Ellie jumped to her feet.

'About time I headed back.'

He pushed off the dog and stood up beside her.

'My mates are in the car park if you need a ride.'

'Thanks, but I'm happy to jog back to Manly.'

'I'm Josh by the way,' he said, and held out his hand.

'Ellie. Hi.'

His handshake was firm, friendly, brief.

'Great to meet you, Ellie. Hope it comes good for you.'

He turned, walked away, and a cold breeze blew in from the ocean. She rummaged in her backpack for a jacket, while Josh and his dog headed towards a V-Dub. For a moment he paused, maybe to ask for her mobile number? Or say something about meeting again? But he climbed inside and the door slid shut.

She bit back her disappointment. This bloke had something. Special? Different? Whatever it was, the tiny taste she'd had of it set her all a-tingle. How cruel, so little and no more, only days before she was due to leave. Maybe she should have accepted that lift, not tried to play it independent. No, she'd sent out signals, and he hadn't responded. Could he be gay? A lot of the good looking blokes were.

The Ute had gone but she glanced again at the V-Dub, and as it turned up the hill, a flash of sunlight caught something on the bumper. A silver fish, twisted from a single line. She stared, blank for a moment, as a chill of recognition seeped into her. So, he was one of those religious types, was he? Northern Beaches Bible Belt, Christian Surfers, something like that?

Humiliation flared through her. Her feet stayed rooted to the sand. Who did he think he was, some sort of father confessor? And what did he take her for, a worthy cause? What a nerve, telling her what to do when he couldn't even control his own dog. Maybe she should call Warringah Council and report the Happy Clappies for breaking the law.

She hurried away, annoyed with herself for weeping and telling him things he had no right to know. Like her grief over Dad's death, for heaven's sake. How had she let him ferret that out? She'd even mentioned, without being specific, that Dad had set her a kind of challenge, and not even Karen or Mum knew that. She'd made a point of not telling them because she knew they'd only scoff and say it was all her imagination.

Then Brad. Sickness curdled inside her. Oh, she hadn't, had she? But yes, she had. All kinds of grubby details. Cold sweat broke out all over her skin and she tore off her jacket. Just stick your head in the sand and finish it all. But no, she hadn't sunk that low. At least she could see that to accept defeat would be to hand him the victory.

With new determination she strode uphill, glad of the silence and stillness. Where had he come from, like some apparition out of nowhere, precisely when she was at her lowest ebb? She'd never seen him around here before and with any luck would never see him again. Dad was right, those religious types always had an ulterior motive.

Next week couldn't come quickly enough now. She could see the advantage of flying to the other side of the world. An escape route that hadn't opened up a moment too soon. A new identity, a fresh start. If Dad could do it, then so could she.

We're so alike, she murmured, and the sun touched her cheek with a warm glow.

A couple of days later she drove into Manly to return a library book. She parked in a back street and was hurrying along the Corso, weaving in and out of the crowds, when she stopped with a jolt.

On the far side, perched on a low wall, sat Josh. He was leaning forward as he tapped on his mobile, so his head was down and he didn't see her. The ugly dog lay beside him, but its snout was pointed in the opposite direction. She snatched another glance at Josh, saw the curve of his back and how strong it was where it broadened to his shoulders.

He glanced up, and she darted into a doorway. She felt like a shelled shrimp. He knew all her darkest secrets. Quick, turn your back, she told herself, and pretended to take an interest in the real estate displayed in the window.

With a perfect north-easterly aspect this light and bright home appears to float above the world outside.

If only she could do the same. She sneaked a quick glance. He was still there.

A distractingly daggy and barely redeemable fibro shack.

That sounded more like her.

A stylish apartment in a boutique security complex.

No, she'd tried that one with Brad. She shifted her focus to where the plate glass window reflected the street behind. Josh hadn't spotted her, so it would be easy to slink away and keep her eyes straight ahead. Even if he did catch sight of her she'd pretend that she hadn't seen him. If he called out she'd ignore him.

A group of tourists passed, laughing and chattering, so Ellie used them as cover. Walk slowly, confidently, she told herself, and whatever you do, don't look back. She slipped into the first side street and headed for the library.

When she fumbled in her bag for the book, her hand was shaking.

It was unbelievable. In all the years she'd lived on the Northern Beaches their paths had never crossed, and now she'd seen him twice in one week.

She handed in the book, went out to the street, turned the corner and bumped straight into him.

'Hi, Ellie,' he said, and his face cracked into a smile.

'Hi.'

'Hey, I just need to hand Gump over to a mate, then I'm off to walk the Spit-Manly Trail. You want to come?'

In a more lucid moment she would have made an excuse, but like the first time on the beach when she'd blabbed everything, she heard herself agreeing to go. Why not? She had nothing better to

47

do for the rest of the day. Maybe she wanted to erase that earlier episode and pretend it had just been a blip. Prove that she was a normal person and could do normal things, like spending a day with a bloke she barely knew when she was about to leave for the other side of the world. Whatever it was, something tugged her forward, like a thread in an intricate pattern she was woven into but didn't understand.

They caught a bus to the Spit Bridge and walked down to Clontarf Beach to pick up the trail. Up near the cliff edge, he stopped to snap photos of Aboriginal rock etchings – fish and birds and animals and things – that she'd never really looked at before. But it was later on, when they'd reached the end of the trail and were sitting on the headland above Manly, that he explained his take on the Aboriginal dreamtime legend of The Three Sisters. She didn't tell him that the postcard Dad had left her was of those three rock towers. She'd blabbed enough about Dad the other day. But she kept her ears pricked in case Josh's theory threw any light on why he might have chosen it.

What Josh claimed was, that whether you believed the popular version – that the sisters were turned into stone because they fell in love with men from the wrong tribe – or his so-called authentic version – that it was a magic spell to protect them from the evil Bunyip – the whole point of the story was to show that the sisters were eternally trapped because of other people's actions.

'In a way we all are, but we don't have to be. If we're brave enough to face the truth, we can be set free.'

Ellie wasn't sure which version she preferred, or which linked better with Dad's challenge, but she couldn't help thinking that Josh would be an interesting person to get to know if he didn't have such rigid ideas about relationships. Somehow, he'd managed to drop in a couple of comments that made his values clear, but it was hard to credit that a bloke in twenty-first century Australia could be such a prude. There was something weird about it. Maybe he was in love with his dog. She chuckled to herself. No, that was gross. Or one of those hypocrites that Dad despised, who preached one thing and did another.

Of course she challenged Josh on the subject, a sort of return match of bare your secrets, and he said that if he ever fell in love, he and his girlfriend wouldn't have sex till they were married. He claimed that most of his friends thought the same way.

'It's kind of counter-cultural but for us it's no big deal.'

Ellie raised her eyebrows, both to show incredulity and to signal detachment. She was careful to speak with the impersonal manner of a researcher conducting an interview. The last thing she wanted was to give him the wrong idea. Especially when it was clear that he had more interest in a lump of rock than he had in her.

'What if – let's imagine the apparently impossible – you wanted to marry a non-Christian?'

'I wouldn't,' he said.

'Wouldn't want to, or wouldn't do it?'

He flicked a seed-pod onto the ground.

'I wouldn't do it.'

'So, a non-believer, if she was raggy enough to fall for you, wouldn't stand a chance.'

He grinned.

'We could be good mates. And there's always hope.'

Ah, she had him now.

'Hope that she'll become a Christian, you mean? So she has to change but you can't?'

'Look,' he said, 'I make these choices for my own life, I don't force anyone else to, so what's the problem?'

'It's discrimination – there should be a law against it.'

What else could she say while his eyes probed hers with their ironic light? But he let out a laugh as if she was the crazy one.

'We all make choices one way or another, Ellie. Vegetarians choose not to eat meat, environmentalists watch their carbon footprint, political activists boycott products and countries. What's the difference?'

'Quite a lot, I'd say.'

'Dead right,' he went on, getting onto his soapbox. 'There's harder things to live without than sex. Try going without food, for example, or shelter, like some people in the world have to. How would you fancy that?'

'So, wouldn't you even go out with a non-Christian?'

'Why should I? We'd only argue.'

They sat in a silent face-off. His eyes were dangerously dark and bright. She tried again.

'You should take people as they are. If you liked her and she liked you, what's wrong with that?'

'What's the point in having beliefs if you compromise them?'

'Have you ever?' Gone out with one, Ellie meant.

'A couple of times.'

'And so?'

'I grew up,' he said, and looked at her with something that was half grimace, half triumph.

AUGUST 1934

Where the bedroom was touched by the morning sun, the roses on the wallpaper were almost invisible. Lillian sat up in bed, her cheek warm, the pillow propped behind her, and listened to a robin sing. The open window let in the fresh morning air, with the smell of cut hay and a whiff of the sea.

Mansfield Park was on her lap but she'd stopped reading. The bars of the brass bedstead stuck into her back, and the mattress sagged towards the centre where Violet was sleeping beside her.

Behind the dressing table, painted cream, its mirror blotched with rusty spots, was a wall, and from behind the wall came a loud yawn. The room next to theirs was Jack's. The sound of him so close, with only a thin partition between them, made Lillian keep very still. If she could hear him, he could hear her. She held her breath to listen. His bedsprings squeaked and something fell on the floor with a thud. Water poured, china clinked. What a noise he made, splashing and snorting. She had the urge to laugh, but held it back, her body jerking.

Those were the sounds of a man, not a priest. Lillian had been reading about Edmund, Jane Austen's character with a vocation for the priesthood, and he was quite different. Jack – she blushed to use his name – was more physical. Last evening, for example, when they went down to the bay, he took the steep flight of steps three at a time. On the beach he picked up a piece of seaweed, frilly and slimy, dangled it in front of them and chased them with it. Lillian and Violet wept tears of laughter and had to beg him to stop.

As the sky faded, they sat on the rocks and watched the sun go down behind the western cliff. The sea was smooth with a pinkish sheen. Violet took off her plimsolls and dangled her toes in the water.

'The tide's coming in,' Jack said.

'How can you tell?' Lillian's voice was almost a whisper.

'At low tide the sea goes quiet. When it turns, the waves grow bigger and make more of a splash. It's the pull of the moon.'

She looked away from the touch of his eyes, and peered into the distance, where a tanker slid slowly along the horizon. Violet tried to skim pebbles, and Jack sent some in low leaps across the water while he talked about his childhood.

'The sound of the sea was my earliest memory, its smell what I most missed when I left home. The beach was our playground, but it was a place of work, too. We searched for shrimps in the rock pools, laver and mussels. When times were hard a family could keep alive with what they found there.'

Violet piped up and told him that Streatham used to be a village in the middle of fields when they were little.

'Our father kept a herd of dairy cattle on the common. Then he went away to war, and when he didn't come back, the cows had to be sold.'

Lillian clutched a shell in her palm. Even years later, those memories touched her with sadness. His love had been the fortress she'd lived behind, and as long as he was with her, she'd felt secure.

'We'll have to pull together now,' Mother had said when the news came. 'It'll be hard to make ends meet with your father gone.' She began to take in laundry and made Lillian help with the chores, when she'd rather have been doing her homework.

Mother scoffed, with a toss of her head.

'Book learning's a luxury.'

In the years that followed, Streatham had changed. Now, a maze of brick buildings spread over the pastures and tarmac had smothered the grass. Where Lillian and Violet and their brothers used to play, rows of shops had sprung up. The streets were noisy with passing trams. Half an hour's journey took them to work in the West End, and there were plans for extending the underground.

A cough from Jack's bedroom jolted Lillian to the present. She reached for her book, put it down again. It was hard to concentrate knowing he was so close. He began to hum, and she tried to make out the tune. Was it a hymn? No, far too light and jolly.

Heat pricked her skin as recognition struck. It was *Them There Eyes*. It talked about falling in love. The first time he looked into them.

An irritating itch crept up Lillian's thigh, and as she reached to scratch it, the bedsprings creaked. The humming stopped. She froze. Had he heard her? She knew that ears made good substitutes for eyes, and what they lacked, imagination would supply. Now, for example, she guessed he was pulling on his trousers, buttoning his shirt, tying his shoes. A coin fell to the floor and rattled around, a brush ran through his hair, not that he had much of it.

Then silence. Was he praying? Reading his Greek or his Hebrew? Presumably clergymen did things like that before they started their day.

Violet sat bolt upright. beside her.

'Quick! Where's the chamber pot?'

'Ssh!'

'But I'm bursting! She leaped out of bed, bent and grabbed the pot with a clatter. Lillian glowered in vexation.

'Ssh!' she whispered, but Violet lifted her nightdress to squat and out came a gush as loud as Niagara.

'Ah, that's better,' she laughed and slid the pot back under the bed.

Heavy boots passed their door and trod down the stairs to the kitchen. They heard Jack greet his mother and Mrs Goodwin reply. A moment later, her lighter step came towards them and she knocked and came in. Lillian snatched up her dressing gown. How embarrassed she would be if Jack caught a glimpse of her in her nightie.

'Hot water, ladies, if you're ready. Another beautiful day. You've certainly brought the sunshine.'

Mrs Goodwin left the pitcher of water and went back downstairs. Lillian went to the washstand and half-filled the bowl, soaped her face and neck, sponged under her arms and dried herself on the clean towel. It was soft and fluffy with a wonderful smell of fresh sea air.

'Your turn, Vi.'

While her sister washed, Lillian put on blouse and shorts, a bit like a man's, long and baggy. She was happy that all the fuss about women wearing them had passed. Much easier for climbing over stiles than skirts. A thrill rippled through her. Today they were going for a walk.

'Let me do your hair, Lil.'

Violet's was cut in a bob so it needed only a few strokes, but Lillian's had to be brushed and re-braided every morning. She sat at the dressing table while her sister drew a parting and wove each side into thick glossy plaits. Violet winked.

'We must make you beautiful for your beau.'

'Don't talk such foolishness.'

'But you know who I mean, don't you?'

She wound the plaits over Lillian's ears, took the hairpins from her mouth and fixed the coils in place. Her voice lowered to a whisper.

'He'd be just right for you, Lil. All that book learning. And gorgeous looking.'

'Rubbish. He's as hairy as an ape. Apart from his head.'

'He's sweet on you all right, though.'

'Don't speak so loud. He might hear you. Anyway, it's you he always talks to.'

'That's because you're so shy. I draw him out a bit. But you're the one he's trying to impress, what with his Latin and Greek and all the rest of it. You should see the way he looks at you. Can't take his eyes off you.'

'Well, he's got no right. I'm walking out with Albert Watson.'

'Some good a one-legged man will be for you, even if he did lose it being brave in the war.' She gave Lillian a nudge. 'He might be missing something else and all.'

'Have you finished?'

Lillian leaped to her feet, her face flaming. Her tummy turned over in excitement and terror, as if her predictable, ordered world had whirled off its orbit.

Since the Prodigy had arrived, they'd sat on the cliffs a dozen times, but today everything was different. It wasn't just the afternoon sun or the way the breeze ruffled her hair, or the turf smelled of wild thyme. No, it was the turmoil inside her, impossible to explain. How could she make anyone understand why she felt the way she did?

They sat side by side, Violet, then Lillian, then Jack, and looked out to where he pointed, beyond the boats as small as dots, towards a smudge on the horizon.

'That's France. It's clear today.'

'Blimey, who'd have thought it? Only a hop and a skip away.'

Lillian frowned at Violet to mind her language. The Prodigy might not be the paragon they'd thought he was, but even so. She snatched at a daisy and began to pull off its petals, while her sister rattled on.

'Oops, sorry, but I could say lots worse than that. When those travelling salesmen call at haberdashery, they make a girl blush, the things they come out with.'

Lillian picked off another petal. *He loves me, he loves me not.* Soon she, too, would have to go back to work, and memories of this summer would fade. At least bookkeeping was a step up from sales, and everyone said she was lucky to find a job like that after the disappointment of her School Certificate examinations.

Her tummy tightened at the memory. Nerves had set off a migraine, and what with travel sickness on the bus, she'd missed half of the paper. It was only because Mr Peterson, the maths teacher, had given her a special recommendation that John Lewis would even consider her for the counting house.

'You're a lucky young woman,' they told her when she went for interview.

'No, I'm not, I'm a bitterly disappointed one,' she could have said, but didn't. She'd hoped to matriculate for university.

'And who do you think you are, Miss-Give-Yourself-Airs-And-Graces?' her mother had said, scrubbing the sheets in the scullery. 'You'll go out to work and pay your way the same as your brothers. University's not for the likes of us.'

She'd straightened her back and peered over her glasses at Lillian.

'Even Lady Hilda didn't go to university.'

Lady Hilda was the daughter at the Big House where Mother had been in service before her marriage. But as far as Lillian could tell, all that Lady Hilda had ever wanted to do was ride her pony, dance at balls in beautiful dresses, and flirt with every man that came her way.

Lillian's tongue pressed between her lips as she pulled out the last few petals of the daisy. Yes, no, yes! Had she caught two together by mistake? The mutilated flower head slipped from her fingers. If only it were true. Then perhaps all her drudgery would end and a new life of possibilities begin.

Over the years her dreams of education had shrunk and faded. She kept them hidden, like the few mementoes that remained of her father, a button from his coat, a shoe horn, his tattered handkerchief. Instead of studying she'd had to make do with writing columns of figures in her immaculate copperplate script, totting them up in her head from the invoices on the desk-spike even before her pen could make the final strokes.

Two dozen pair silk stocking 12s 6d. Box gentlemen's collar studs, 5/-. Sixty yards knicker elastic, 1 shilling and tuppence halfpenny.

Up here on the cliffs, though, with a sea breeze cooling the summer heat, life in London was more distant than the coast of France. When she lay back on the grass and gazed at the sky, Lillian could see wisps of clouds that drifted like thistledown. Bees hummed and the honeyed scent of gorse mixed with a tang from the sea. The sun was warm on her face, and when she closed her eyes, dots of light danced behind them.

'So when do you go home?'

It was Jack's voice. She held her breath, not daring to look at him. Was his question for them both, or for her alone?

'Only two more days,' she heard Violet say.

'Worse luck.'

Was that actually her voice? It sounded fearfully loud and her heart started to leap uncontrollably. She could almost feel it lift the cloth of her dress.

Only two more days and everything would be clear. Did he like her or didn't he? Was he humouring her to pass the time, or had those invisible currents reached him, too?

When Lillian opened her left eye, she could see Violet with her knees tucked up and a pile of wild flowers in her lap, harebells and late thrift, pale pink and papery. She watched her pierce the stems, then thread through the flower heads to make a chain, chattering to Jack as her fingers moved.

When Lillian opened her right eye, she could see Jack stretched out with his shirt sleeves rolled up, leaning on one arm. But even with her eyes shut she could sense his closeness and hear how his chest rose and fell.

Something tickled her hand. It moved slowly up her arm. The ground beneath her head thumped with the blood pumping. As she turned to look, Jack laughed and darted away a piece of grass feathered with seeds. She laughed with him. His face had turned red from the sun and the top of his head was glistening.

Who'd have thought that she'd fall for a baldie? But over the fortnight he'd been here it had bothered her less and less. His expression was kind and his eyes had a clear light full of sensitivity and intelligence. Everybody here thought the world of him – his family, the neighbours, the friends he'd known as a lad.

Violet rested the flower chain on Lillian's head.

'There. Queen Lill of the Cliffs.'

In the distance, from the village, came the clop of horses' hooves and a two-tone whistle.

'That's Dad now with the post,' Jack said.

Violet jumped to her feet. 'Aren't you two coming?'

Lillian sat and brushed the dust from her clothes. She knew Violet was expecting a letter from her young man and would be eager to see if it had come. Her eyes slid towards Jack. Let him decide. Then she'd know.

'You go on,' he said to Violet. 'We'll see you back at Mother's.'

Once she'd gone, they both fell silent. Jack sat with his knees drawn up, his arms around them. The air was still, the downs parched, the white cliffs rose and dipped into the distance.

'What a lovely place to grow up in,' Lillian heard herself say.

'Yes, much better than London.'

His voice sounded different when he spoke to her alone. She wanted to tell him that the country was in her soul but that the city had suffocated it. Thoughts like those made her voice wobble, so she kept quiet.

'When I go back,' he said, and her heart jumped, 'perhaps we could meet again?'

'That would be nice.'

She lifted her eyes and dropped them again. Of course there was Albert, but nothing binding had ever been agreed between them.

'You'd like that?'

'Oh, yes.'

Her heart thumped so loud it was a wonder he didn't hear it in the silence of all that sky and sea. She could have stayed there forever, but as the sun sank lower the shadows lengthened. Jack got to his feet.

'We'd better be on our way. Mother will have tea ready soon.'

As he helped Lillian up, his hands lingered for a moment. She brushed the grass from her shorts and he reached to adjust her crown of flowers.

'You look beautiful,' he said and the heat crept up her neck.

They walked across the downs towards the village more slowly than usual, as if they both knew how precious these moments of solitude were. When they came to the stile in the thorn hedge, Jack climbed over first then reached to help her. He caught her round the waist as she jumped and she laughed as she floated towards him. Their faces drew nearer, till a sudden thought made her hesitate. What if someone walked by and saw them? But a hedge hid them, and his eyes, grey-blue like the sky, shone with a warm light.

When he kissed her it was like floating on a cloud. Albert sometimes kissed her goodnight, but it was never like this, just a quick peck on the cheek. Jack's kiss lingered and his arms were gentle but strong. She could swoon, be transported, drift with him into oblivion. So this is what they mean by bliss, she thought.

But Jack's lips eased hers open, and his tongue, which had

become a muscle with life and energy of its own, twisted on hers. Lillian tensed. No one, bar the dentist and Dr Gray when he'd looked at her tonsils, had ever invaded the privacy of her mouth, and that was with cold instruments. But this was no examination, this was a flame, a limb of fire to set her alight.

'No, Jack, please,' she said and wrestled from his grip.

He stepped back and took out a handkerchief to mop the sweat from his brow.

'Did I startle you? I'm sorry. You're so very lovely that I was carried away.'

Now she felt foolish. She reached to pick a burr from his shirt, he took one from hers, and they both laughed. Their clothes were covered in them. As they walked back through the field, Lillian slipped her hand into his so that he wouldn't think that she didn't care. Oh, life was so complicated and she was no good at negotiating all its trials.

Once they reached the house she moved quickly through the kitchen, glad of its dimness, and ran upstairs. She had dirt on her hands and her shorts, and her pulse was racing. In the mirror she saw that her hair was awry, wisps escaping from the braids round her ears, chin rubbed red and sore. An awful excitement stirred inside her and she had to take long, deep breaths to calm it.

Violet looked up from where she sat cross-legged on the eiderdown, a letter open in her lap.

'Well, well. Leave you two alone for a moment and see what happens.'

Lillian opened her mouth, but burst into tears.

'Whatever's wrong now?'

'Oh, Vi. What on earth am I going to tell Albert?'

Violet tutted, pity mixed with disbelief.

'It's not as if you're engaged or anything. He's lucky you've put up with him for as long as you have.'

Lillian sniffed, blew her nose. It was easy for Violet to speak, but she'd just crossed a divide into a world of terrifying possibilities. If only she could run away, open her wings like a bird and fly somewhere safe. But that was impossible. She must hang on to her little knot of courage and walk forward into the unknown.

Through the whole of that long sleepless night, under the eaves of their bedroom, the same wretched thought went round and round in Lillian's mind until the sheets were twisted and bathed in sweat.

Love and betrayal were bound together. One person's happiness meant another's pain.

ENGLAND 2010

Hour after hour the plane lumbered onwards while Ellie drifted in and out of sleep, fighting the pull of home and fears of what lay ahead. A sense of unreality nibbled at her, trapped in a capsule that sped her through the night towards an unknown future. She jolted awake to see the screen on the seat-back showing somewhere over Pakistan, still in darkness, while the arc of light to the west crept nearer. They'd been travelling forever but weren't even half way.

Later, her tummy churning from the breakfast they'd served in its plastic tray, she woke from another fitful sleep. Way below, framed in the porthole, was a sheet of silver that must be the Mediterranean, dotted with islands that conjured up tales of crusaders, invaders and brigands. Crete. Sicily. Corsica. Way more exotic for an Aussie than Fiji or Bali could ever be.

But as the plane bumped down through the cloud bank to Heathrow and scraps of fields gave way to a drab urban sprawl, a sense of hopelessness seeped into her. The terminal buildings were as sad and anonymous as others they'd taxied past, but the pale grey morning brought a sense of a different world, old and tired and weighted with history.

Solid ground swayed under her feet, her head swirled with tiredness and a slow fuse of anticipation. She cleared immigration and steered her way through customs towards the arrivals hall, her tummy tightening with tension.

Daylight hit her from the plate glass windows and she glimpsed a line of black taxis. The automatic doors opened and closed, letting in bursts of traffic fumes and the stale, polluted smells of the city. She scanned the semi-circle of waiting faces for two sweet old ladies, female versions of Dad, ready to surround her with support and solace. But she saw only businessmen, a woman in a sari, an African resplendent in robes, friends hugging, grandparents lifting babies, couples embracing. A buzz of excited voices rose around her, swamping her with sound.

'Eleanor!'

It took a moment for the name to register. No one called her that unless she was in trouble. A cool hand touched her arm and she swung round to see a lady with silvery hair tied back in a twist.

'You must be Eleanor. My goodness, you're so like your father.' Her eyes moved over Ellie's face and for a moment they were his. 'I'm Dorothy.'

Then the likeness vanished. Ellie hesitated. Should they kiss? Shake hands? Aunt Dorothy looked so serene, stately, a little aloof. And so much older than she'd imagined. A wave of jet lag sent the room swaying and she gripped the trolley.

A woman with hennaed hair ran towards them, her dark eyes dancing with excitement. A fringed scarf dangled from her head and hooped earrings flashed. Her mouth broke into a grin and two wizened arms shot out from under her kaftan.

'I'm Fran. Give your old aunty a hug.'

Untidy hair brushed Ellie's face with a blast of musky perfume.

'Mustn't miss you out, Aunt Dorothy,' she said, and ventured a kiss on the older lady's cheek. How soft and cool the skin was. 'And it's Ellie, please.'

She followed her aunts through the arrivals hall like a new lamb brought into the flock. Everything around her was familiar. The cafes, rows of baggage trolleys, signs and screens were universal, but something niggled all the same.

What had she expected to see? An older and wiser Australia? Dad reincarnated in his sisters? His young self waiting to welcome her home? Some trace of him, surely. This was his birthplace. These were his siblings. They spoke the same language, shared the same genes. Surely there should be a sense of kinship. Something should sit up in her and say, Ah, yes, now I understand.

But it didn't. All she felt was cold and tired, a misfit in an alien land.

A patter as faint as a whisper woke her. Where was she? Ah, yes, in Dot's cottage, in Somerset, on the other side of the world.

She threw back the covers and tiptoed across squeaky floorboards to the dormer window. Behind the curtains, tiny panes of glass were beaded with moisture from the finest of drizzles. She wrestled with the catch, leaned out to drink in the cool morning air, saw a cluster of honey-stone cottages nestled between folds of hills that merged into a misty sky.

This was a fairy-tale world, like the pictures in the storybooks Grandma Lillian had sent her as a child. Branches thick with foliage hung over a verdant lawn. Through the freshness she caught a whiff of damp soil and the strong, fermenting odour of manure. She knew that smell from Uncle Charlie's farm. But the smell of the rain was subtly different.

A bird began to sing and Ellie caught her breath. No Australian bird sounded like that. Its voice was full-throated and mellow as its song rose and trilled in an elegy of joy, loss and hope. Footsteps crunched on the gravel and the bird stopped. Aunt Dot appeared in a raincoat and wellies. Behind her trotted a spaniel, its fur dripping.

'G'day,' Ellie called down. 'Is it very late? I must have slept in.'

'Only ten o'clock. Come and have some breakfast when you're ready.'

A coffee would be good, but she wasn't sure she could manage food. Her tummy still churned from that breakfast she'd forced herself to swallow after the plane refuelled in Kuala Lumpur. Squashy oriental sausage, lukewarm omelette and strangely translucent Malaysian mushrooms. Then another breakfast, she couldn't remember where, two in a row as they travelled through the timelines, a bizarre start to a day that didn't quite happen.

Her suitcase lay open on the floor where she'd left it after they'd driven down from Heathrow. Exhausted, she'd gone straight to bed and slept through till now. She rummaged for clothes, surprised for a moment by the sight of the familiar garments in this unfamiliar room, with its low-beamed ceiling and sloping walls. Her vision blurred and she closed her eyes, sensing the huge distance from home to here, pushing against time through an endless night.

With an effort she dragged herself back to the here and now. She rummaged in her suitcase for shorts and a t-shirt, or maybe jeans, because although it was almost summer here, the air was chilly. Her body was uncertain, her mind muddled. She showered, dressed, and slid the photo of the little girl into one pocket. Nerves and impatience battled inside her. At the first opportunity she must pick her aunts' brains about Dad's puzzle. An educated woman like Dot, a former headmistress, who'd known Dad as a young man, would be the ideal person to help solve it.

Another rush of jet lag swayed her and she caught hold of the back of a chair. Her mind swirled with images of the journey – Mum fighting tears as they hugged goodbye, the white-sailed shell of the Opera House growing smaller as the city faded into a grid of charcoal along the snake of the Parramatta River.

She sank onto the chair, lowered her head to her hands. Even with her eyes closed she could still see the Blue Mountains like screwed-up tissue paper where their ridges caught the setting sun. Then darkness swallowed them, leaving nothing but the vast, empty bush and the thousands of miles from there to here.

The same sense of dislocation followed Ellie downstairs. Nerves fought with excitement, and despite her impatience to solve Dad's puzzle, all her certainty had vanished.

Dot was in the kitchen, loading the dishwasher. She'd taken off her raincoat and wellies and looked surprisingly chic in a white shirt and beige pants. Clio, the spaniel, sat cleaning herself in her basket. Fran leaned against the worktop in her purple kaftan, and flicked away a loose strand of hair as the toaster pinged.

After a few morning pleasantries, Ellie held out the photo.

'I was wondering if you'd know who this is? I found it in Dad's things.'

Dot put on a pair of spectacles that gave her face a startled, owlish look.

Fran stopped buttering the toast and peered over her shoulder.

'I don't recognise her. Do you, Dot?' she said.

'I would guess that it's one of our cousins.' She passed the photo to Fran. 'Do help yourself to cereal, Ellie, and fruit and eggs, too, if you'd like some.'

'Thanks, Aunty Dot, but I'll stick to coffee for now. I'm still a bit jet lagged.'

A frown rippled over Fran's forehead, as if chasing an elusive thought, and she tapped the photo.

'It's not Margaret or Vera. If anything it looks more like you, Dot. That determined scowl on your face as you devour the ice cream.'

Dot gave a bright little laugh.

'What imagination you've always had, my dear.'

'Better than having none.'

Ellie was used to sisterly spats, so she smiled at them fondly.

'Do you think she could be connected with Dad somehow?'

Both aunts looked at her in astonishment. Suddenly her theory about the little girl struck her as preposterous, a spectre of her own invention, and she couldn't bring herself to elaborate any further. So she slipped the photo back in her pocket, busied herself with the coffee and decided to play it vague until she was more sure of her ground.

'I just thought I might do a bit of family research while I'm over here.'

'I could tell you a few tales that would make your hair curl,' said Fran.

'The past is the past, Frances, but we have a visitor so let's try to focus on today. Now, Ellie dear, I must just finish my report for the Parish Council, then perhaps we could go for a drive and stop at a pub for lunch, if that suits you. I think the weather's going to clear.'

'Awesome, I'd love to have a look around. It's all so beautiful.'

Ellie sipped her coffee thoughtfully. She had the distinct impression that she'd been outmanoeuvred, but had no idea why.

All morning she waited for another opportunity to mention the photo, but none came. The longer she was with her aunts, the more she realised that shared genes weren't the same as shared experiences, and the less certain she was that her theories were right. It sounded crazy to suggest to these two sweet old ladies that Dad had fathered and abandoned a child who needed, like the sisters of the legend, to be set free from the wickedness of the past.

Maybe oral information was trickier to work with than she'd thought. How could you discern from casual conversation what was fact and what was evasion?

She reminded herself that the book where she'd found the photo was subtitled *The Shape of My Early Life*. That pointed to the author's childhood experiences, so maybe once she knew more about Dad's, she'd have a clearer idea of what he wanted her to know. With this in mind, she began to relax and enjoy the outing in Dot's car.

Every village they drove through, every twist and bend in the road, held wonders that oozed antiquity.

Wow! It's amazing!' Ellie gasped again and again as she saw cottages, churches and castles nestled in a miniature landscape of meadows, woods and hills, full of mystery and magic.

At lunchtime they went to a seventeenth century inn. Nothing in Sydney, not even Cadman's Cottage, was remotely as old as this. It was a little low building with a thatched roof and cob walls, and they had to duck their heads to go in through the doorway. As her eyes adjusted to the darkness, she saw rough-hewn beams and walls yellowed with age. Two gnarled old men sat by the bar, the burr of their accents like a foreign language as their eyes slid towards her and away again.

After lunch, Dot drove them down lanes that wound between banks until they came to a farm. It perched above a valley, all long grass and wild flowers and open sky, ragged with clouds.

Dot pulled onto a verge, switched off the engine, and beamed Ellie a smile.

'I thought you might like to see this very special place where your father and I spent our summers during the war.'

'Oh, wow, yes, I remember he told me about that.'

He'd once shown her a snapshot of him as a little boy in a singlet and shorts on the steps of a caravan, his face caught in a slice of sunshine.

'The happiest days of my life,' Dad had said, and she'd thought, How could you be happy in wartime?

'You were evacuated, weren't you?' she asked Dot as they sat in the car.

'Not exactly.'

Dot explained that Grandad Jack had been busy with parish duties, but Grandma Lillian had brought them here as often as she could, to get away from the bombing. She turned to Ellie with a smile.

'You know, I've often thought that we don't really appreciate peace until we've experienced discord.'

'What were those POWs called?' asked Fran. She'd been born after the war, but had heard some of the stories, and when Dot said their names were Mario and Lorenzo, she chuckled.

'Do share the joke,' said Dot, all bright and innocent.

'Two handsome Italians, and Mother a young woman on her own? I bet there were some goings-on.'

Dot tutted and started up the Audi.

'You've been watching too many American films, Frances. Not everybody behaved like that in the war.'

That evening, after supper back in the cottage, they all went into Dot's low-ceilinged sitting room. Ellie settled happily in one of the brocade armchairs. She felt more at ease with her aunts now that the initial strangeness had faded.

Clio flopped at her feet with a contented grunt and Ellie bent to tickle her head. This dog was way more attractive than the ugly beast that Josh trailed around with.

'Okay, Clio?'

She ran her fingers over the length of one silky ear, while the dog sighed happily.

Darkness had come early, and as the evening was cool Fran offered to light a fire. She placed paper and kindling in the grate, chatting to Ellie about her caravan on Exmoor.

'Open fires are the only thing I miss. But it's okay in other ways. You can come and visit if you like.'

'I'd love to. Did Dad ever go there?'

'God, no, by the time I moved there he'd long since buggered off. It's a sort of artists' colony. At least, it used to be. Now I'm the only one left.'

Dot winced at Fran's language, her mouth drawn tight, as her sister held a match to the paper. Ellie smiled to herself. How different they were, yet in both she glimpsed something of Dad.

Fran wiped a sooty hand across her face.

'There, that's drawing nicely.'

'Would you like to watch television, dear? How about a drink?'

Dot could offer sherry, Dubonnet or Bailey's. Ellie opted for sherry which turned out to be sweet and sticky, but she sipped at it happily. Maybe alcohol would loosen their tongues and help to reveal secrets, she thought, as Dot began her gentle questions.

'So sad about your father. How is your mother coping?'

'Oh, she's a tough cookie. Carries on just the same.'

'It must have been upsetting for you, too, Ellie. Were you very close to him?'

Ellie nodded and bit her lip, not trusting herself to speak, and stared at Dot's glasses that linked to a cord round her neck. Both aunts fell silent and tactfully sipped at their drinks. For some moments the only sound was the crackling of the fire. Fran reached for her knitting. Dot picked up *The Daily Telegraph* from the coffee table, put it down again, and sat with her fingers laced. Fran glanced across, her knitting needles clicking.

'Have you cracked the crossword yet?'

'Indeed I have.'

'Dad liked crosswords, too,' Ellie said.

'Did he?' Dot looked puzzled. 'You know, I don't remember.'

'Well, I do,' said Fran. 'He was always at them.'

'Perhaps later on when you've recovered from the journey we could take you to Bath, dear. There's more to interest young people there and it's not very far.'

'That would be great. And one thing I'd really like to do is go to Canterbury.'

'Canterbury?' Fran pulled a face.

'It's very historic, Frances. Don't forget that Ellie is a historian.'

'I can't stand the place. Oh, yes, it's very historic if you like the past. Personally, I prefer to forget.'

Firelight and shadows parried across the ceiling. Ellie watched her aunts, half in fascination, half in disbelief. Whatever she said seemed to cause tension between them.

Dot turned to Ellie brightly.

'From a literary point of view it's intriguing. Of course you'll be familiar with Chaucer's *Canterbury Tales*. Dickens lived there for a while, and Thomas a Becket was murdered there. T.S. Eliot wrote a play about that.'

Fran slid the knitting to the back of her needles, stuck them through the ball of wool, and tossed it aside.

'You know, people used to say to me, "Oh Canterbury, what a lovely place to grow up in," and I used to think, blimey, if only you knew.'

'It's different for Ellie, though. She's grown up in Australia. Naturally she wants to find out more about her father's origins.'

'Yes, that's why I've come here, really, to learn more about Dad. And to meet you two, of course.'

'You're not trying to find him, are you?'

'Of course she is, Frances, that's only natural.'

'Well, you won't. He's not here. He fucked off long ago.'

'Frances, please.'

A loud crackle came from the fireplace. The flames, scarlet gashed with yellow, shot light and shadows over the ceiling. Fran let out a sort of yelp, gulped down her Bailey's and brushed a sleeve across her face. Her eyes were those of a hurt child.

'I was nine when he went to Oxford. I worshipped the ground he walked on and he just disappeared out of my life.'

'Oxford?'

'He came back in the holidays, Frances. We both did.'

Ellie gaped at them in disbelief. Dad had never told her that he'd been to university, let alone to Oxford. He was a self-made man, he'd studied accountancy at night school in Sydney. His life-story was engraved on her memory with the indelible truth of countless tellings.

Now Dot was challenging that truth, saying she'd gone up a couple of years before him. So when he was accepted, too, their mother was over the moon.

'Huh! Then the next thing we knew he was off to Australia. I was twelve by then and he might as well have been going to Mars.'

'He was fond of you, Frances, you know he was.'

'Was he? Some way to show it.'

An awkward silence hovered over them. A log shifted on the fire and sent up a blaze of sparks. Ellie watched her aunts in wonder as they sat in steely opposition. They were like two members of a tribe tugging at an ancestor's bone, refusing to let go, but it was Dad's integrity that they were tearing apart.

'Didn't your father tell you any of this, Ellie?'

She shook her head.

'Why keep it secret? It's nothing to be ashamed of. On the contrary, to have studied at Oxford should be a source of great pride. At least, it was to me.'

'You didn't give up halfway through, though, did you, Dorothy dear?'

Ellie gasped in disbelief. Dad had the migrant's fighting spirit, he never gave up, she was about to protest, but a sudden possibility hit her. Could that have been when he'd got a girl pregnant? Maybe he'd been sent down in disgrace. Back then the authorities might well have considered it a serious enough offence for that sort of punishment. It might also explain why he'd never even mentioned Oxford. But she didn't want to set off more arguments by being too blunt. Better work round to it obliquely.

'Had he done something wrong? Did he fail his exams?'

'Oh, no, he did exceptionally well. An outstanding undergraduate, his tutor said.'

'So why did he leave?'

'He had to do his national service. But he could have gone back to his studies afterwards.'

'Oh, yes, if he hadn't emigrated. Sorry, Ellie, I loved him to bits, but – '

Fran clenched her mouth shut, unable to finish.

Dad was a very caring person, Ellie wanted to protest, but the words stuck in her throat. It was as if his sisters had pulled the shroud from his corpse to reveal someone she'd never known.

Dot leaned back in her chair with a sigh.

'We wrote to him, Ellie, over the years. He replied from time to time. When he married, when your sister and you were born, I sent presents, but we heard nothing. Did they go astray? I had no way of telling. It wasn't that I wanted thanks, only contact, to know that he was all right.'

Ellie cast her mind back, grasping at shreds of memories.

'I remember that Grandma Lillian sent me books, fairy tales with the most amazing illustrations.'

Had she written thank you notes? She couldn't be sure.

'It broke her heart.'

'That I didn't reply? I'm so sorry.'

'No, no, that your father left in the first place.'

'It's not your fault, Ellie,' said Fran. 'You were just a kid. But when he left, he was a grown man. He should have known better.'

'Young people leave home all the time,' Ellie said. She was hanging onto a cliff-edge, losing her grip.

'They do, they do,' Dot agreed, 'and of course the government made it so easy with the ten pound passage. Even so, we hoped he'd come back, eventually.'

'He was a good father.'

That was the least she could say to defend him. She'd come here to find answers, but not these answers.

'Well, that's something,' said Fran.

A look passed between them that Ellie couldn't decipher. You've run away, a voice told her as a sudden burst of rain lashed the window, straight into a trap. Dad isn't here, he never was. The person they remember is someone you never knew.

Upstairs in the low-ceilinged bedroom, sleep wouldn't come. Ellie lay on her back and stared up at the beams as niggles chased through her mind. It wasn't Dad's secrecy that bothered her, or even the row between Dot and Fran. Sisters were often like that. She and Karen used to argue all the time, about toys, clothes, what one was allowed to do and the other wasn't. But their fights flared in a moment and were as quickly forgotten. Now they were fine together, and when it came to what really mattered, they were always there for each other.

Dot and Fran were different Their ages, personalities and opinions were all at odds. But even that didn't explain the hostility that had simmered under the surface all day. A full-on fight would have been healthier, like her cousins – Wayne the hard-working, hard-drinking farmer, hostile to almost everything that his liberal, journalist brother believed. At family gatherings their arguments lasted well into the night, but the next day they'd go to the rugby match the best of buddies.

No, this was something else. Something Fran suspected and Dot knew but didn't want to say. A secret so deep that Dad had hidden it all his life. Even from her, his favourite.

She dreamed of Cousin Wayne's farm at shearing time. One ewe got away and she grabbed hold of its skinny, shorn body, stiff like a joint of meat. Bones stuck through its flesh and its eyes opened wide with terror. It kicked her, she let it go, and it turned and ran, bleating madly. The barn was empty. She was alone.

Dad was dead. The bare fact hit her as she jolted awake. He was dead and he would never come back. Blood pounded in her ears. He was dead, and his memory had been trampled into the dirt. Her pulse was painful, her skin hot and sticky.

When the bleating started again, it took her a moment to realise it came from her mobile. As she fumbled for it in the dark, the ring tone stopped. Who could it be at this time of night? She was about to check when she heard the beep of a text.

1 message: Josh.

Oh God no, the Shrink. Whatever did he want? She clicked on the screen.

Tried to call you. Are you ok?

Fine until you disturbed me, she felt like replying. She should never have given him her mobile number. He had a way of butting into her most intimate moments, that both enraged and excited her. She lay back on the pillow, her heartbeat racing. Hadn't he anything better to do than wake her in the middle of the night? Of course it would be morning in Sydney, but he must know the time difference. And why wasn't he at his desk, even if he did work from home?

That film he was making about Aboriginal rock art sounded interesting, though. A documentary, one in a series about artistic expressions of belief. Like those ghostly images on the boulders the day they walked the trail.

She cast her mind back to that unexpected meeting, so soon after the first one at Freshwater. She'd asked him if he'd ever go out with a non-Christian, and he was adamant.

'Why should I? We'd only argue.'

'Have you ever?' Gone out with one, was what she meant, and he said, yes, a couple of times.

Oh, no, she thought now in the quiet of Dot's cottage. Did he think she was asking him if he'd ever had sex? Maybe that was why he gave her such a strange look. But, no, it couldn't be that. He'd made it clear that sex before marriage was out of bounds.

How did these people manage? Were they allowed to hold hands? Could they kiss if they kept their lips closed?

This was no good. She'd never get to sleep if she kept laughing. But when you'd been dismissed as unclean, trodden underfoot like some disgusting kind of bug, revenge was sweet however you achieved it. Even if it did have a manic tinge and a sting of tears.

To marry or not to marry, that was the question. A few months ago it was no more than a discussion topic for tutorials. But now, as images of Lillian propelled Jack across the stile and into the grounds of Cheshunt College, it was an alarmingly personal possibility.

Rain splashed the mackintosh he held over his head as he sprinted up the drive. He made for the gabled building, its stone facade covered with ivy. To a stranger it might look foreboding under the late afternoon sky, but Jack could see lights from the common room gleaming behind the misted glass, warm with the promise of tea and conversation with his fellow trainees.

He dashed under the porch, shook his umbrella, left it to drip in the rack and hung up his waterproof. The small space was already cluttered with coats and shoes. He took off his wet boots and changed into leather brogues. His socks were damp, the turn-ups of his trousers splashed with mud, but he could live with that.

As he opened the door to the hallway, warm air met him, redolent with the aroma of steak and kidney pudding. His stomach rumbled. He paused for a moment by the oak-panelled wall, hung with photos of past students. He loved the solid, unpretentious comfort of this place, but the knowledge that he would soon be leaving it gave him a moment's unease. His future happiness depended on two things – a letter and Lillian.

At the end of the hall, the kitchen door opened. Marchant appeared with the afternoon post and began to lay it out on a mahogany side-table.

'Been for a walk, Sir?'

'Just across the meadow to the copse. Then the heavens opened.' He glanced at the letters. 'Any of those for me?'

The old man shuffled through the pile in his hands and his face creased into a knowing smile.

'I do believe there is. Let's hope it's good news, Sir.'

Jack reached for the envelope with a quick intake of breath. It was addressed to J.K. Goodwin, Esq., A.K.C., and postmarked from the south London parish where he had applied for a curacy. He slit it open with the paper knife, and let out a cheer.

'They've accepted me! What a relief!'

Marchant turned, on his way to the kitchen.

'Congratulations, Sir. And it couldn't happen to no one better, if you'll pardon me saying so.'

'Go on with you,' laughed Jack, touched by the old man's fondness. For some time now he'd been aware of a hint of special treatment, like an extra biscuit with his morning tea, or his cassock brushed and laid out neatly before chapel.

'There's some that has their heads in the sky,' Marchant had said soon after Jack started. 'Strikes me you're the sort of man who'd understand a man, if you know what I mean, Sir.'

Jack did know, only too well. His fellow students were mainly ex-public school, Oxbridge men, far more learned than he was, with an ease for ritual and etiquette that he'd had to pick up along the way. They all got on well enough, but sometimes he had to remind himself that their differences were not as important as the values they shared – a spirit of fellowship born of a common faith, and the belief that their service to others could somehow contribute to a better world.

Clutching the letter he leaped upstairs two at a time, in a hurry to get out of his damp clothes. At the landing under the stained glass window he changed his mind. This news was far too good to keep to himself.

He dashed back to the common room with its comfortable masculine ambience that he so enjoyed. It was filled with the rumble of men's voices and the smell of pipe tobacco, damp tweed, leather and beeswax. Lambert stood by the coal fire with one elbow on the mantelpiece, polishing his spectacles, while he chatted to Barker, who balanced a cup and saucer in one hand, stroking his reddish moustache with the other. Jack smiled to himself. The tash was a relic of Barker's army days, and a source of much banter among the men.

Near the windows was a table scattered with newspapers and writing materials. Jack spotted the tea things, slipped his letter under one arm, poured himself a cup, and took a digestive biscuit from the plate. He joined a group of men who sat in armchairs by the fire. They appeared to be in the middle of some sort of noisy contest.

'Here's Goodwin,' said Barnes. 'Maybe he can help you out.' He turned to Jack. 'They were doing pretty well but they've fallen at the last fence.'

Hugh Gregson made room for Jack beside him. His rugged face radiated camaraderie.

'The thirty-nine articles of faith of the Church of England. We've been discussing whether we need to commit them to memory before our ordination service.'

'I jolly well hope not. We just read them out, don't we?'

'Barnes reckons he has them by heart. So he bet us all a pint that we couldn't recite them, and blow me, we've got as far as thirty-four but now we're stumped.'

Barnes leaned back in his chair, his eyebrows drawn together with a quizzical expression.

Phillips held up three bony fingers.

'We've had the marriage of priests, ex-communication and traditions of the church. But then what? Come on, you fellows, we can't let Barnes fleece us like this.'

Jack put down the envelope and stirred his tea thoughtfully.

'Homilies isn't it?'

A circle of faces turned to him as Gregson let out a whoop.

'Homilies! Goodwin has it. That's right, isn't it, Barnes?'

A nod from Barnes confirmed it. Gregson gave Jack a friendly slap.

'Well done, Goodwin. Now come on, you fellows, only four to go.'

Jack's inspiration had dried up, and in any case, his mind was on other matters. He glanced at his friend. Gregson's curly hair had threads of grey but there was still something of the rugby blue in his muscular frame. His strong-boned jaw and steely expression sometimes made him look stern, but he was a man of empathy and good sense. His face brightened as he caught sight of the envelope on Jack's lap.

'They've accepted you?'

Jack nodded.

'I knew they would. Congratulations, old chap. And well deserved.'

He seized Jack's hand, gave it a hearty shake, then raised his arm to silence the others, who were still arguing over article thirty-six.

'Goodwin's got his curacy,' he announced to cheers and cries of congratulation.

Jack fielded their questions about the parish. The rector was getting on in age, but was open to new ideas. It was in a fairly prosperous area on the edge of the stockbroker belt. Yes, it had a good-sized congregation, mainly of older families, plus some retired people. New housing had been built, which had caused some controversy. And yes, to help bring about reconciliation between these disparate groups was one of the reasons it appealed to him.

He didn't mention the niggle of doubt that it didn't quite fit his original calling of ministering to the poor. After all, those who were better off could be just as spiritually needy, if not more so. Nor did he say that it was within easy reach of Streatham.

Conversation drifted back to article thirty-six and the chances of depriving Barnes of his beer. Jack caught Gregson's eye.

'Do you feel like a stroll later on? When you've got a moment, I'd appreciate a quiet word.'

Gregson nodded and glanced at the window.

'No time like the present. I've been stuck in here all afternoon and fresh air will do me good. This lot can fight it out without us.' He got to his feet.

'Goodwin and I are going to leave you fellows to it, I'm afraid.'

Jeers and laughter broke out.

'Cowards!'

'Some men have no stomach for the long haul.'

'We'll see you later in The Red Lion. First pint's on Barnes!'

Outside, the sky was still heavy, but it had stopped raining and the air was fresh with the scent of wet earth. A thrush started to sing in the chestnut tree, and the purity and poignancy of its voice brought hope more eloquent than any words.

They walked in silence and turned into the parkland behind the house. A ray of sun came from behind a cloud. Jack drew in his breath and glanced at Gregson. He sensed that the moment was right.

'I've made up my mind, Hugh. When I see Lillian at the weekend I shall ask her to marry me. I'm jolly nervous though, in case she turns me down.'

Gregson looked pleased but unsurprised.

'It's the right decision, I'm sure. Of course she'll accept you, you old rogue. You're a lucky man.'

'Yes, I know.'

He could almost sense Lillian beside him, the softness of her body unbearable when it was forbidden for him to caress.

They kept up a steady pace past the cedars towards the sports field. Jack took time to choose his words, glad that Gregson was the sort of chap one could speak to frankly.

'Celibacy's not for me,' he said with sudden determination. 'I know it suits some men, and for a while I did think about it. After my conversion it seemed that the spirit had overcome the flesh, so to speak, and I managed to curb my feelings rather successfully.' He gave a wry laugh and fiddled with the loose change in his pocket. 'But when I'm with Lillian, I realise they're as strong as ever.'

They sat on a bench by the cricket field, and Gregson took out his pouch of tobacco.

'Yes, I believe the Anglican Church has it right on this issue. Why impose unnecessary burdens on priests? The job can be difficult enough, and we're none of us superhuman.'

Jack murmured his agreement.

'Have you discussed it with your spiritual advisor?'

'In general terms, yes. Benson quoted the text from Genesis about it not being good for man to be alone, so he had made a helpmeet for him. He said that God's original plan was for man to have a mate, and he claims Paul's epistles endorse that, though some scholars argue otherwise.'

Gregson puffed at his pipe and nodded.

'There'll always be some who disagree, but I think Benson's interpretation is correct.'

'One rather wonders why he doesn't put it into practice himself.'

'I don't suppose Benson has been near a woman in his life.'

'Or that a woman's been near him, more like.'

'A man perhaps? The old public school tradition, so to speak?'

'Somehow I can't see that either.'

'No, Benson's married to his books. There's something about him which is, how can I put it, asexual.'

Jack watched the wind lift the branches of the trees. Life would be easier without the struggle against one's natural urges. Even the memory of Lillian's breath on his cheek was enough to stir them. The wind blew chillier and he buttoned his coat.

'We'd better be getting back,' Gregson said.

'There's just one more thing I wanted to ask you. Would you consider being best man, Hugh? It would mean a lot to me if you would.'

'My dear fellow, I'd be delighted. Honoured that you'd ask me.'

'That is, assuming Lillian will have me. I'm rather running ahead. Of course it won't be anything fancy. Not like the sort of dos you're invited to.'

'You know full well that I wouldn't care if I never went to another society wedding in my life. I'm sure that yours will be a refreshing change.'

Gregson's handsome face beamed. He tapped out his pipe and the two men began to retrace their steps towards the building.

'Well, well, the curacy, marriage. It looks as if everything is falling into place for you.'

'Without a curacy I couldn't ask Lillian to marry me. As you know I don't have a penny of my own. But with a house and a stipend, I should be able to support a wife.'

If Lillian would accept him, Jack thought as they drew nearer to the house, his happiness would be complete. What more could he ask? For the first time in his life he was deeply in love. Lillian was unlike any other woman he had known, not only beautiful, but intelligent and sweet-natured, too. Her quiet but firm reluctance to let him overstep the mark was agony, but he admired it as a sign of her modesty and virtue. Thank goodness he'd never compromised himself with any of the village girls. Not one of them would have made a vicar's wife.

He thrust his hands into his pockets as his excitement mingled with relief. Life as a parish priest would have its challenges, but with Lillian at his side, the blessings of domestic comfort would help him to face them. Together they would live secure in a relationship based on mutual love, admiration and trust.

'Your husband will guide you. There may be blood.'

As Lillian posed for photographs, one hand on Jack's arm, her mother's words shivered through her.

'Come on, Lil, give us a smile!'

'Say cheese!'

She snapped out of her thoughts and beamed at the box camera Hugh Gregson was holding.

There was every reason to smile. It was a glorious afternoon, the leaves turning colour on the trees, the garden bright with late flowers. Everybody Lillian cared about was here – her family and Jack's, their friends and neighbours. She had just married the dearest and kindest man in the world. Now at long last she could leave her mother's miserable regime for a home of her own.

'All right, Mrs Goodwin?' said Jack with a grin.

'I've never been so happy. It's like a dream.'

A gust of wind stirred the leaves of the apple tree. Shadows fluttered over the lawn.

'Now let's have one of Mrs Cullen with Mr and Mrs Goodwin senior.'

Jack's parents, a little tipsy, lined up beside the bride, while Lillian's mother, stiff and erect in her best dress, stood next to her new son-in-law. Lillian gripped Jack's arm, her fingers pale against his sleeve. If only Father had lived, how proud he would have been to see her now.

Beside her, Jack's mother gave off a whiff of sweat and lavender, her cheery face split into a smile.

'Who'd have thought it, dearie, when you and your sister came to my guest house, that it would have ended like this?' She tugged at her husband's sleeve. 'Come on, Jim, you silly old fool, we're all waiting for you.'

With a docile grin, Jim Goodwin turned towards the camera. His cheeks were red and shiny. Lillian's mother didn't approve of alcohol, but they'd persuaded her to have a flagon of cider and one of ale to drink with their lunch. And even she had sipped a glass of Auntie Lulu's rose hip wine to toast the bride and groom.

Once the photo session was over, Lillian helped clear the trestle table that they'd covered with a cloth outside the scullery door. All that was left of Auntie Winnie's ham, cooked in Somerset cider, were the bone and a few tattered slices of pink flesh. The slab of cheese was now a misshapen lump, the freshly-churned butter a greasy mess in the dish. Crumbs and flour from the crusty loaves dusted the tablecloth as well as the ground beneath it.

A sharp pain stabbed her tummy and she looked suspiciously at the dish of pickled onions. They always gave her the cramps. She should have avoided them, but it was too late now and she was determined not to let them spoil her day. Perhaps the turmoil inside her was only excitement and nerves.

Her mother looked up from where she and Violet were stacking the dirty plates..

'We'll do this. You two had better be on your way.'

'Come on, Lil, I'll help you get ready.'

Violet slipped her arm through her sister's and they went across to where Jack was laughing and joking with Uncle Barney. He looked up happily as she drew near to speak to him.

'I'll just pop upstairs, and then we can leave.'

Jack's hand touched hers and she felt like dancing. I could almost dissolve with love for him, she thought.

The sisters turned back to the house and went up to the bedroom they'd shared for more than twenty years. How rough the floorboards are, thought Lillian as if seeing them for the first time. The rug was threadbare, the wallpaper faded.

On the eiderdown that covered the bed lay her new suitcase, brown and shiny with metal tabs on the corners. She'd packed nightclothes, sponge bag and towels, brush and comb, a couple of dresses, several jumpers and a coat in case the weather turned chilly. Each evening after work she had stitched every garment herself by the light of the gas lamps.

Her brothers had already taken down the trunk with her trousseau of bed and table linen, books and other belongings, ready for Jack and his friend to strap to the motor car. How good it was of Hugh to drive them to the honeymoon cottage. Once he'd dropped them there, he would take her trunk to their new home in the parish where Jack had started as curate. Hugh's well-to-do speech and manners had unsettled Lillian at first, but he was a kind and generous man, and she was proud to see how easily Jack moved between two such different worlds.

So now she was a clergyman's wife. She closed the suitcase with trembling hands. This new role both excited and terrified her. People had already started to look at her differently, and even her family treated her with new respect.

She lifted her felt hat from the dressing table where she'd left it when they came back from church, and put it on her head. It was hard to secure the hatpins, her fingers were shaking so. Her face, reflected in the glass, was ashen, and her limbs had gone cold. Her palms were sweating. Violet reached for the pins.

'Here, let me. You look a picture, Lil. And that trimming I got for you goes just right.'

Their faces, side by side, smiled back at them from the mirror. Lillian's hat with its low crown and gently flared brim, dipped over one eye. A ribbon ran round it, tied in a neat but saucy bow. She'd trimmed the hat herself, and cut the dress from mauve and lavender crepe de chine. It hung beautifully. For modesty she'd tucked a gauze scarf in the v-neckline, edged it with a fluted frill, and finished it off with a fabric gardenia.

Violet squeezed Lillian's arm.

'What's the matter? You're shaking like anything.'

'Oh, Vi, I'm scared stiff…about you know what.'

'You silly goose, whatever for? Just do what comes natural.' She lowered her voice. 'I wish it was me and George.'

Jack called from downstairs.

'Are you ladies ready? Hugh's cranking the car, so if you're decent I'll bring your suitcase down.'

'Just a moment.' Lillian's heart fluttered like a fledgling. 'Wish me luck, Vi.'

'Go on with you, it'll be fine. Write to me as soon as you can and tell me what it's like,' said Violet, giving her a playful nudge.

Lillian followed her onto the landing, marvelling at the lightness in her sister's step. Every muscle in her own body clenched tight as a twinge in her belly made her gasp. She clutched the banister and took each stair carefully, as if one wrong step would pitch her into the chasm below.

It was a tiny brick cottage that backed onto woods in the heart of the Surrey countryside.

'You should be peaceful here,' Hugh said to Jack.

'Thank you for everything. You know how much it means to me.'

'Don't mention it. My pleasure.'

They unstrapped Lillian's trunk from the back of the Morris Minor, took it indoors, then went back to the car. Hugh had polished the bodywork until the paint gleamed. The spokes of the wheels glinted under the mudguards, and as the engine ticked over with an occasional shudder, it sent the white ribbon on the bonnet into a shiver.

Hugh stood with one foot on the running board and buttoned his jacket, his face ruddy in the setting sun. He climbed into the driver's seat and wound down the window.

'Enjoy yourselves. Forget about parish business. This time is for the two of you.'

As Jack watched the car disappear down the lane, a sense of solitude settled over him, spiked with anticipation. The days were shortening but the nights were star-studded and full of promise.

He closed the garden gate and glanced up at the dormer window. Behind it was their bedroom. The small panes of glass reflected the last rays of sun. Some sort of climbing plant spread up the wall of the cottage with dry, twisted stems, but Jack had no idea what it was. His mother would know, he thought with a smile.

His parents had enjoyed themselves famously. In fact everything had gone off well, the ceremony, the celebrations, the journey here. Now a whole week of uninterrupted bliss lay ahead, with all its promise of new delights. No wonder his heart whirled in a turmoil of joy.

Through the open door of the cottage he could see Lillian take bottles and jars from the hamper that Hugh had left them. His heart surged. How beautiful she looked in the half-light, her body stroked with shadows.

'Look,' she said as he came in. She held up a bottle of champagne, her eyes bright with excitement. She'd taken off her hat, and a strand of dark hair had come loose and stuck to her face. He lifted it from her cheek and slid his arms round her waist. Only the softest of fabrics lay between them.

'I've never had champagne before, have you?'

'Just once, at King's, when the results came through. Mandeville's family sent a bottle.'

Her eyes opened wide, full of love and admiration. He lifted her up and spun her round for the sheer fun of it and she laughed like a child. When they came to a stop he drew her close, but she planted a kiss on his cheek and wriggled free.

'I must get this food unpacked, and our clothes, too.'

She shuddered, rubbed her hands up and down the thin sleeves that covered her arms.

'Are you cold? I could light a fire.'

He had noticed a coal scuttle next to the Rayburn and a crate of sticks with newspapers on top. On the table were a paraffin lamp, a bundle of candles and a box of matches. The stove would take the chill off the cottage, make it cosier and help them to relax.

He rolled up his sleeves and set to work, trying to contain his excitement. He tore the newspaper into strips which he twisted and placed in the grate, layered with twigs and pieces of coal. Once the fire began to blaze he closed the iron door and opened the vents. They would need plenty of hot water for tea as well as for washing. And to fill a stone bottle to take the chill off the sheets.

'Are you hungry?' Lillian asked him. 'There's a tin of salmon here, plus fresh bread and oranges. What a treat.'

'Don't worry about food. You must be tired.'

He longed to scoop her in his arms and carry her upstairs. But something in the way that she fell quiet warned him she would need more time, and he was afraid of startling her.

'As soon as I've lit the fire in the sitting room,' he forced himself to say, 'we'll have a bit of supper.'

'That would be lovely.'

She took out plates and cutlery. When he came back from lighting the fire, she'd arranged the food like an artist, the shapes and colours placed just so. This wonderful creature he had married was a new universe that he had the rest of his life to discover. There was no need to hurry.

By now it was dark outside. Jack drew the curtains and lit the paraffin lamp, and they sat side by side on the settee with their plates on their laps. The flames of the fire flickered and the candles glowed with a golden halo. Lillian chattered happily.

'What fun this is! Mother would be shocked if she knew we weren't eating at the table. And didn't we have a lovely day. Did you see Aunt Florrie's hat? She looked a scream.'

'Yes, it was a bit like a bird's nest, I thought.'

'Mother's looked as if she'd sat on it. She hadn't worn it since Father's funeral.'

Her voice wobbled, but Jack came quickly to the rescue.

'Hugh's mother-in-law joke was a bit near the knuckle.'

'Oh my word, did you see her face? I thought she'd choke on

her own tongue. She wouldn't have taken it from anyone else, but she's in awe of Hugh because he went to Public School.'

'Talking of Hugh…'

Jack reached for the champagne and untwisted the wire. The cork hit the ceiling and the liquid fizzed into their tumblers. They were the only glasses he'd been able to find. Lillian took a sip and screwed up her nose.

'It's awfully sour, isn't it? I'd rather have Auntie Lulu's rose-hip cordial. Though it was kind of Hugh to give us it, of course.'

'I suppose it's an acquired taste. Let's have some more and see if that's true.'

He refilled their glasses. Lillian kicked off her shoes and drew her feet under her.

'Isn't it lovely and cosy here?'

The firelight flickered over her face. Jack slipped his arm round her and she snuggled against him, stifling a yawn.

'Tired?' His heart started to thud with a strong, rapid beat.

She nodded and rested her head on his shoulder. Hot currents raged through him as he breathed in the heady scent of her flesh. Her fingers twisted as she played with the wedding ring.

'Just think, I shall wear this every day for the rest of my life.'

They sat in silent contemplation. Then she yawned, and the gold band glinted as she covered her mouth.

'Shall I take you up some hot water?'

He could see that she was nervous, and he wanted to reassure her, but he felt as jittery as a novice.

'Yes, in a minute thank you, that's very kind.'

She shivered. He reached for her coat which lay draped over the back of the settee, and helped her to draw it round her shoulders. She gazed at the fire.

'The flames are so pretty. They dance as if they're alive. I'd like to paint them, or write a poem, or both.'

She closed her eyes. Jack went to the kitchen and heated the kettle. It took an age. He paced around and sucked on a cigarette to calm his agitation. If he had to wait much longer he'd boil over like the water that spluttered onto the hot stove. He poured some into the stone bottle, the rest into a jug, and took both upstairs. When he came back to the sitting room, her eyes were still closed.

'It's ready,' he said.

She gathered her coat around her and went up the stairs, step by step. He waited in front of the fire, fiddling with the loose change in his pocket. The bedroom door squeaked and the floorboards creaked overhead. He heard a chink of china and the splash of water. Better to stay here while she went through her preparations.

His body was ridiculously tense. He reached for the champagne bottle and poured himself another glass. His hand was unsteady, his blood pumping fast, but the alcohol did nothing to soothe him. He tried to master his thoughts and pray, but the knot of desire made it difficult to concentrate. Gradually, though, an unsteady peace seeped into him.

But the relief was only temporary. He paced up and down, his teeth clenched, his blood burning. At last he could contain himself no longer. He raked out the embers in the grate, secured it with a fireguard, put out the paraffin lamp, snuffed the candles and went upstairs in the dark. He had to stoop so as not to bang his head on the ceiling. His heart hammered with a loud, uneven beat as he opened the bedroom door.

She stood in her nightgown, white cotton trimmed with lace. The candle on the washstand behind her lit up the curves of her body. Dark hair rippled over her shoulders. As she lifted one arm to flick back a loose strand, her breasts rose under the fine fabric.

He reached for her hands, surprised at their coldness.

'They're lumps of ice,' he said, rubbing them between his.

When he drew her to him, she laid her head on his chest like a child. The soft mounds of her breasts trembled against him. He stroked his hands down her back to calm her, holding her close.

'I'm scared, Jack.'

'I'll be gentle.'

But his voice sounded hoarse and rough. He cleared his throat, and was about to lead her to the bed when she let out a cry and clutched at her tummy.

'Whatever is it, Lil?'

She steadied herself, her fingers sharp on his arm. Then, with a sudden swift movement, she bent double, contorted with pain.

'Quick, I need a towel!'

He stared, uncomprehending.

Her eyes, wide open with horror, met his.

'The curse has started.'

She snatched at her nightgown, and in a shaft of moonlight from the window, he saw it was streaked with the crimson of blood.

SOUTH SOMERSET, 2010

People change when they marry. The little intimacies, jokes and secrets that Ellie and Karen had shared as kids didn't flow any more. Like bad Skype connections, their chats jerked in and out of interruptions or distractions, till Ellie felt that her sister was there but not there. Her affections had moved away and nested elsewhere.

She mused about this as she walked through the wood behind Dot's cottage, mobile to one ear, Clio's lead in her free hand, and let out an exasperated sigh.

'Come on, Karen, it's not that late.'

The dog stopped to sniff at the wet undergrowth. It gave off a strong, musty smell. The path was narrow and muddy, overgrown with nettles and brambles where it twisted between densely-leaved trees.

'Yes?'

Her sister's voice shrilled in her ear. Ellie could picture the scene, Karen and Tim, the exclusive twosome. Annoying little sister breaking in like a burglar to their domestic intimacy. Their secret world put on hold.

'I'm feeding Will,' Karen said.

'How is he? Is he walking yet?'

'Duh. How old is he? He's teething, tetchy, hungry all the time.'

'Does he miss me?'

'Oh yes, he asks about you every day.'

Bite your tongue, Ellie told herself, and took a deep breath.

'Look, there's something I wanted to run past you.'

As usual Karen ignored her and started firing questions.

'How's it going? When are you coming back? What are the aged aunts like?'

'Nice, but slightly cracked. At least one of them is. The other's more like Dad, kind of secretive.'

She told Karen what they'd said last night about Dad leaving university. Ellie hadn't mentioned her theory about the child in the photo before, fearing scorn and ridicule, but now, instead of treading carefully, she blundered straight in.

'So what do you reckon? Could we have another sister? And if there was a scandal, maybe that was why Dad emigrated. What d'you think? Would you mind?'

'That he had a kid? Hang on, I need to change boobs.'

Ellie picked up a stick and whipped it through some nettles until Karen's voice reached her again.

'So what if Dad did put it around a bit? He was a young man when he came out here. Presumably he had a life before Mum. It doesn't mean he abandoned a kid.'

While Karen chattered on, Ellie followed Clio out of the wood into fields. They started to climb a steep hill towards the open sky. The clouds had cleared, and where the sun brightened on the slope, it lit up horizontal ridges. Maybe some sort of archaeological remains lay beneath the surface.

'So you wouldn't mind?' Ellie asked.

'If he'd got a girl pregnant? Why should I? At least it would prove he was human.' The line crackled. 'Are you there? Look, Ells, you're not still moping about him are you? You need to get over it, you know. People die. He was an old man. He had a good life.'

Ellie let out an exasperated huff. From the mobile came a gurgle, a fart, then her sister's voice again.

'Hey, have you met any decent blokes yet?'

'What here? You must be joking. Everyone I've set eyes on is over seventy.'

She sat down at the top of the hill, gazed out towards the horizon, hazy in the distance, and poked with a stick in the dust while Karen began a lecture.

'Single life doesn't suit you, Ells. We always agreed you'd be the one to marry and have kids, and now look at us.'

'Well, yeah, maybe.'

'Maybe what?' Karen's voice rose with excitement. 'You have met someone, haven't you?'

'It's not that simple, Karen. There's always something wrong.'

'Yay! I knew you had. What's his name?'

Ellie stopped moving the stick. No, she couldn't believe it. She'd started to doodle in the dust, two letters, J, O…

'John,' she said. 'His name's John.'

'So what's wrong with this one?'

'He's got religion.'

'Oh, shit, that's the last thing you want. What is it with you, Ells, you don't half pick'em. A sex maniac, and now the God Squad. Just a mo, I need to burp him.'

From down the line came a loud belch. Clio had given up whining and flopped at Ellie's feet.

'So?' Karen said. 'Tell me more.'

'Don't get excited, he's just a good mate. He'd be okay if he wasn't always trying to sort me out. Too convinced that he's right and everyone else is wrong.'

'Whew, that's a relief. For a moment I thought you were a goner. Look, as soon as you come home, we'll fix you up with someone. Hang on, Tim's trying to say something.'

Ellie could hear her brother-in-law's voice in the background, then her sister laughed.

'He says he's got a whole rugby team lined up for you when you get back.'

It was typical of Karen to treat her theories as if they were worthless, Ellie grumbled to herself as she made her way home. Just like big sister used to do with little sister's treasures. Her cicada chrysalis, the snail shell, the lump of turquoise sea glass that Bossy-Boots had chucked into the bin. Well, this time she would show her. As soon as she got back to Dot's she would confront her aunt about the photo, hunt down this mystery child of Dad's, and see what Karen made of that when she came face to face with the facts.

But a dark blue Rover was parked in the driveway next to Dot's Audi and Fran's old van, and from behind the closed door of the dining room she could hear a man's voice underscoring her aunt's soft, modulated tones. Clio sniffed at the crack under the door and wagged the stump of her tail.

Should she go in and disturb them? The stairs behind her creaked and she swung round.

It was Fran, dressed to go out in a poncho and jeans, a tasselled bag slung over her shoulder, one hand massaging her jaw.

She caught sight of Ellie and her face brightened.

'Apologies for the hoo-hah last night. The thing is, Dot's very sweet and kind and generous and all that, but she drives me up the proverbial wall. What she really needs,' Fran gave a theatrical wink, 'is a jolly good you-know-what.'

Ellie's mouth dropped in stunned amusement.

'Can you imagine living all your life without it? That's what makes her such a tight-laced old crab.'

Ellie glanced at the closed door. From behind it came the steady murmur of voices.

'Wasn't she ever married?'

'No, far too busy clocking up qualifications and being the perfect career woman. Any normal, healthy man would have run a mile.'

Fran pulled Ellie away from the door and began to fill her in on the details. Dot was funny with men, she said. That old boy in there clearly had the hots for her, but every time he asked her out she made an excuse. Fran mouthed the words.

'I think she's terrified of sex.'

The dining room door opened and Dot appeared, glasses perched on her nose, a streak of blue ink across one cheek.

'Oh, it's you, dears,' she said, shooing Clio out of the room. 'I wondered what was going on. Why don't you both go out somewhere today? I'm busy with the parish council, or I'd come with you.'

Fran jabbed one finger at her chin.

'Have you forgotten? Dentist? Emergency appointment?'

She gave a cheery wave and went out to her van.

Dot sighed, and passed Ellie a bag bulging with papers.

'Just some old bits and pieces that might interest you. Do make yourself a coffee, if you'd like one.'

With a mug in one hand and the carrier bag in the other, Ellie sped upstairs. She propped a couple of pillows on the bed, made herself comfortable and took a bundle of documents from the bag. This was more familiar territory, where her expertise would come into play.

The first bundle turned out to be Dad's old school reports. *Shows great promise. Must concentrate more in class. Will go far.* The irony of that last comment made her smile, but fascinating as these little treasures were, they didn't offer the kind of details that she had hoped to find.

Next came some of his primary school exercise books, filled with childish handwriting and crayon drawings. She flicked over the pages. These, too, were charming but irrelevant to her present task, so she left them on the bedside table to look at later.

The only other items in the bag were rolls of parchment, tied with crimson ribbons. As soon as she unfurled them it was clear that they had nothing to do with Dad. Even so, Ellie handled them with awe, aware of their beauty and historical value. The text was written in elaborate calligraphy, and they were stamped with seals of red wax and signed by past Archbishops. She had worked with all sorts of documents in the museum, but never seen anything quite like these. They appeared to be licences for every step of Grandad Jack's ecclesiastical career, peppered with solemn declarations to live a 'pious and virtuous life'.

She retied the ribbons and put the scrolls back in the bag. Men who made promises like that must have their reasons, but they were a mystery to her.

A snuffle came from the door and Clio nudged her way inside.

'You should be back downstairs,' Ellie told her, but the dog settled on the rug with a contented whimper and she didn't have the heart to move her.

'You're a lucky girl, you know. Uncle Charlie's dogs aren't even allowed in the house.'

They slept in a barn and called to you if they caught your scent. Up there the night skies were so vast and clear that you could see every constellation, dominated by the Southern Cross. The very sight of it conjured up the national flag, with its six stars scattered across in a wild and ragged freedom that squeezed the Union Jack into one corner.

A sudden insight struck her.

The Australian flag had something to do with the origin and development of identity. The old homeland had seeded itself in a new continent that had, in time, outgrown it.

A shiver of rebellious pride shot through her. Josh wasn't the only one who could have deep thoughts. And she was an Aussie, too, even if she was half English. What was he, three-quarters Italian?

Besides, he'd never even been to Europe, so he wouldn't understand how coming here to this world of dark corners had opened a crack in her sense of self. It was like when the crust of baked dirt breaks open at the thrust of a tender shoot.

How strange it must have been for Dad, when he'd made that journey the other way round. How untamed and incoherent the Lucky Country must have seemed at the end of his ten pound passage. No wonder he'd spent hours shut in his office, with his books and papers.

She was beginning to understand him better now – a sensitive man who'd fled from some secret unhappiness, affectionate as a father but a little distant. Gentle, courteous to a fault, but reticent. No one ever mistook him for an Aussie.

But thoughts of home were making her restless. She leaped to her feet and began to pace back and forth across the room. She could almost smell the salt-spray of the ocean, hear the bush crackle with heat, and not for the first time she longed to be back there.

With a sigh she reached for her laptop. *Facebook* was a poor alternative but it was an easy link to home.

Gabriela and Cindy had both messaged her. She keyed in replies then skimmed through her newsfeed. Nic had dumped a bloke she'd met in Bali and was back with Steve. Butch and Megan were 'in a relationship'. She hesitated before clicking *like*. It was a mad kind of musical chairs with Ellie the one left standing.

Her heart flipped when she saw the next message. She clicked on the name of the sender. Josh Bellini. His profile picture, nose to nose with his dog, stirred the same old mix of intrigue and uneasiness. The animal was grotesque, with folds of flesh under its eyes, but Josh in profile was impressive, his nose strong-boned yet touchingly kinked as though it had been broken. His hair was cropped, cut clean round neck and ears where it dipped to the hint of a sideburn. It flicked up at the front, combed through like a fine field of grasses. Black grasses, if such a thing existed.

Another shot showed him doing a headstand in his wetsuit, dark hair in the sand and a lunatic lop-sided grin on his face.

She couldn't help chuckling. This guy was seriously wacky and way more likeable than he had a right to be.

He'd uploaded a video clip from his series on Aboriginal representations of natural phenomena, visual images interwoven with words. His voice, with its perceptive, slightly ironic tone, was uncannily familiar. Yes, he had talent, and originality, too. What he said made you take another look. His choice of images, juxtaposed with comments, formed a counterpoint, a pattern of sound and meaning with a rhythm almost like music. His artistry impressed her more than she cared to admit.

She went back to the message.

Hey Ellie, how you doing? No regrets? Hope the research is coming good.

He didn't mention why he'd called her last night, just said that he was off to film some interviews with Aboriginal artists living in the Northern Territories.

She keyed in a reply.

I'm ok. It's interesting but complicated.

That would keep him guessing. It would take more than a film-maker to tell her how to separate historical fact from fiction.

She clicked *send* with a flourish, and her own mission leaped into new focus. Once she'd cracked the mystery of the little girl in Dad's photo, she would put all her information about his life into some sort of memoir.

Her mind buzzed with new energy. The finished work would focus on Dad's mysterious child, framed with details of his early years in England and his adult life in Australia, interspersed with her own memories and research. It would be a lasting tribute to him, and the creative approach would look awesome on her CV.

At the very least it would be an heirloom for baby Will, who was too young to remember his lovely grandfather.

Feeling more positive, she shooed Clio out of the bedroom and went downstairs. Sounds of movement came from the dining room but the door was still closed. She flopped on the sofa, and waited. It seemed like an age before her aunt appeared, followed by a man with a lick of grey hair, bushy eyebrows and the nose of an eagle. He shifted a pile of document wallets from one arm to the other.

'Ellie, I'd like you to meet Raymond. He and I are treasurer and secretary of the PCC.'

'Partners in Corporate Crime,' Raymond said and winked.

He wore the sort of tie covered in little crests that veterans sported on Anzac Day. Could she see these two together? Ellie wasn't sure.

'But more to the point, he knew your father.'

'Oh, you're kidding.'

She sprang to her feet and Raymond clasped her hand, scanning her features.

'Isn't she the image of him?' said Dot.

'As a matter of fact, she reminds me of a young lady I used to be sweet on.'

Mischief flickered across his face, but Dot drew herself straight and spoke with a bright, professional voice.

'Do sit down, the pair of you. I don't know why we're all standing.'

'I can't stay, Dorothy, much as I'd like to. My goodness, who would have thought I'd see a daughter of Jimmy Goodwin's after all this time.'

He explained that they were at school together.

'Then Jimmy went to university and I joined the navy. Clever chap, your old man. Fine cricketer, too. I used to think of him every time you Aussies made off with the Ashes.'

Ellie laughed politely. It was probably better not to mention Dad's divided loyalties. But Raymond's mind had moved to other matters.

'Dorothy, do you remember when Jimmy was hauled before the Headmaster?'

'How could I forget? Mother was furious.'

'I suppose we were sixteen, seventeen at the time, Ellie, and some busybody reported seeing him in town with – God forbid it – a woman. A blonde, no less. Horror of horrors! He'd broken a cardinal rule. Of course we boys were all agog. Good old Jimbo!'

Dad was with a blonde woman? Every tendon in Ellie's body tightened as she made a quick calculation of dates and possibilities. She glimpsed the two old people communicate some secret understanding, but before she could interpret it, Raymond glanced at his watch and turned towards the door.

'It's later than I thought. I must dash.'

Dot went to see him out, and came back looking a little flustered.

'Raymond talks a lot of nonsense but he has a good heart. His wife was a friend of mine.'

Fired by visions of Dad and the blonde woman, Ellie seized the initiative.

'Dot, you know that photo I showed you of the little girl. Do you have any idea who her father was?'

'Her father? How should I know that?'

'It's just that I've been thinking about Dad dropping out of university, and I wondered if there was some sort of . . . scandal that caused him to emigrate.'

Dot's smile was the kind that a headmistress might give to a wayward and stubborn pupil. With a low, calm voice, she suggested that Fran had put these ideas into Ellie's head, and that Ellie shouldn't credit them.

'You see, Fran has been damaged by a difficult life, not only as a fourth child that our parents could have done without, but also as an adult in her three disastrous marriages.'

'Three? I never knew that.'

'Oh, the first boy was nice enough, intelligent, educated and so on, but they were both very young. It's not for me to comment, perhaps, but Frances wanted to go to art school, and while she was there she met this awful musician. At least that's what he claimed to be, but as far as the rest of us could see he was a complete waste of time. Anyhow, Frances left her first husband for him, and that's when Janis was born.'

'Janis?'

'Your cousin.'

'So I have an English cousin?'

This was becoming a recurring motif – facts that James Goodwin never told his children. Perhaps she should include a section on that in the memoir, too.

'So of course, that relationship ended in disaster as we all predicted it would.'

Later, Dot said, Frances had met quite a nice fellow, but sadly he suffered from depression, and one day she came home to find that he'd taken an overdose.

Ellie listened dumbstruck to the deepening tragedy. Could this be true? She began to see Aunt Frances in a new light. No wonder she carried so much hurt and anger.

'Yes, they did what they could for him but it was too late, the damage had been done. He died in hospital.'

Dot shook her head as if to say it was a hopeless case.

'So she's not had a very happy life. It's such a shame, she was a lovely, gifted child. Oh, I don't deny that by the time she was born there were problems, but she understood very little of what happened. I was twelve years older, and that makes quite a difference in the context of family life.'

'But what did happen? That's what I don't understand. Please tell me, Dot, I really need to know.'

Ellie's voice tangled and she had to stop.

Her aunt faced her with a steady smile that mixed sensitivity and stubbornness. Ellie knew that expression, but in a strange context it took a moment to place. Of course – it was Dad, gentle, benign, but impenetrable.

They knew but wouldn't tell. Sister and brother. Guardians of a secret.

Painful as it was, she forced herself to speak.

'There was a child, wasn't there, Dot? That's why Dad went away.'

'Oh my dear, there were many reasons. Life is so horribly complicated, and what we choose to tell others is always selective. Can anyone claim they have nothing to hide?'

A van screeched to a halt in the yard and out jumped Fran. Dot spoke in a low rapid voice.

'Should we not respect a person's wish for privacy? I believe that we should.'

Fran dashed inside, her face flushed with excitement, her hair awry, and beamed them a look of triumph.

'You'll never guess what I've just found out. I phoned Jan, she's in LA with her father, I woke her up but never mind, and told her about the photo. Oh don't glare at me like that, Dot. Jan remembered something Mother told her ages ago when she was a little girl.'

Dot raised her eyebrows. *There you are. Do you see what I mean?* her expression said.

But for once Fran didn't rise to the bait. She surveyed them both, her lips enigmatically pursed, then announced that her visit to the dentist had been a success. Even better, she said, a friend who ran a gallery had texted to say that one of her paintings had sold. So she'd bought a bottle of fizzy to celebrate.

She whipped it from her bag with a flourish, and danced around with her poncho flying. When Ellie asked about the photo, she laughed, skipped towards the stairs, and said that they'd have to wait.

'All will be revealed. Not now. Tonight.'

When at last evening came, the cottage was filled with light and laughter. They sat at a small table by the open window with the rapidly emptying bottle of Cava and a homemade pizza margarita that was surprisingly yummy. A breeze from the garden brought the fragrance of night scented stocks, full and heady with sweetness.

As the sun dipped over the rooftops of the village it painted them red. Her aunts' faces were flushed. Ellie's felt fiery and full of promise. Tonight would be the night of revelations. The truth was only a glass or two away. Once she had revealed her theory and Fran had confirmed it, the facts about Dad would be out in the open.

Dot was already a little tiddly. She sniffed the air.

'Night stented socks. Mother's favourites.'

'Bring out the family album, sister,' said Fran.

While Dot went to fetch it, Ellie uncorked a bottle of Australian Shiraz, her contribution to the night's festivities, and filled their glasses. Fran sat munching her third slice of pizza, a rose from the garden behind her ear. Dot bustled in.

'Here we are. And more sterviettes for sicky fingers.'

She placed the album on the table and brushed dust from the cover. The leather binding was pitted with indentations, the corners were worn. Ellie imagined Dad as a little boy on his mother's knee, turning the pages and pointing to people he recognised. Her excitement soared. He'd drawn her into his family and now they would guide her to the moment when she'd uncover his momentous secret.

Dot opened the album. The clematis round the window trembled in the breeze as their heads drew together. Light and shadows danced across a sepia studio portrait of a little girl with ringlets and bows. The caption read, *Lillian Cullen, aged 4, 1910.*

'Here she is, our mother, your grandmother.'

'Oh, she's so cute. Look at the frills on that dress.'

The grandmother Ellie had never known sat on a button-back chair with one foot tucked under her. The other foot, in its white sock and shoe, barely reached the edge of the seat. Her chin was down, but her eyes peeped up at them.

A shiver shot through Ellie. She might have been looking at herself.

That first day at school, all those kids staring. The horror that gripped her in a room of strange people.

'She was shy, wasn't she?'

It was easy to say that about someone else, but when they'd said it to her she'd crumpled. In Grandma Lillian's day it was different. Kids were supposed to be seen but not heard. Now, though, shyness was a weakness, worse, a mental illness. The syndrome even had a name. Social Anxiety Disorder. If you weren't confident and assertive, something was wrong with you. Ellie had learned to fight against it, but it hadn't been easy.

So that's where it had come from, the dreaded gene, handed down through the generations like a curse. Thank you, Grandma Lillian. But Fran was pointing to a snapshot of a young woman on a bike, with baggy shorts rather like a man's.

'Mother looks pretty wild in this one. And to think she had the cheek to criticise my mini-skirts.'

'Frances grew up in the Singing Swixties,' said Dot, and took another sip of her wine.

'Rock'n' roll, make love not war. And look, in this one she's even more brazen.'

In the photo she pointed at, Lillian sported a swimsuit and perched on the edge of an upturned boat. Dot nodded.

'Yes, South Foreland, 1934. That's where she met our father.'

'Wow, she has lovely legs.'

'And showing them must have been quite daring back then. But Mother did have her unconventional side.'

Ellie began to warm to Grandma Lillian. The timid little girl had blossomed into someone who looked like a lot of fun. What a pity she'd married a vicar. He must have knocked all the budding freedom out of her with his rules and regulations.

But on the next page Lillian smiled happily at her husband from under a soft-brimmed hat. A long-sleeved dress slipped over her slender body and flared down to a scalloped hem. In one hand she held a bunch of violets, while the other rested on Grandad Jack's arm. His chin lifted awkwardly above a clerical collar, but his mouth was spread in a broad grin. He looked surprisingly normal, and except for his baldness he was painfully like Dad.

'They look happy,' Ellie said and Fran agreed.

'He's the cat that got the cream all right.'

Next came the children, Dot as a little girl with golden curls, then one of Dad in a short-trousered suit, his hair brushed back from his face, receiving a book at a school prize-giving. How could anybody doubt the sweetness of his character? Whatever they said, she would always defend him.

On the next page was a photo of toddler Fran, clutching a knitted rabbit, the little girl's sweetness hard to reconcile with the wild-eyed woman she'd become. Beside her stood a boy, a cricket bat under his arm. Dot brushed one finger across the snapshot. This was Bobby, she said, who had died in a tragic drug-related incident, only weeks after Ellie's father left for Australia.

'Of course Jimmy couldn't come back. The ten pound passage was one-way. He would have had to pay a fortune for a return ticket.'

Ellie gazed at the child's happy face, his mouth spread with laughter, innocent and unsuspecting of what the future held. She thought of Dad, stranded between two continents, burying the loss of his brother deep inside. It was almost a relief when Fran turned the page to the staid black and white of Grandad Jack's clerical robes. Here was the image of a nice boring minister with answers to everything, and not a whiff of drugs, sex or rock'n'roll anywhere. His eyes squinted against the sun, his smile was gentle and unassuming, as if he felt uncomfortable in such formal attire. Behind him was an arched doorway set in an elaborately carved medieval porch.

'Canterbury Cathedral,' said Dot. 'The photo was taken when he was made an honorary canon.'

'A canon? Isn't that something quite important?'

'It's not as grand as it sounds, but it was an achievement nevertheless, especially for a man who came from a very ordinary family and left school at thirteen.'

'Really? I didn't know that.'

Dad's secrecy about every aspect of his family made her feel more and more uncomfortable. It was one thing to be reserved, but this was ridiculous. She sat tight-lipped and pensive while her aunts flicked through the rest of the photos, but by the time the album was closed, Ellie Goodwin was ready for action.

She poured the remains of the Shiraz between their glasses, leaned back in her chair and faced the two old ladies.

'Fran, I'm dying to know what Janis told you.'

Dot's face twitched, but an enigmatic smile spread over Fran's. A petal fell from the rose she'd put behind her ear and settled on the table. She flicked it aside with one finger and spread her hand in a dramatic flourish.

'As I said earlier, I phoned Janis, and while we were chatting I happened to mention the photo of the little girl that none of us recognised.'

Dot's mouth clamped shut. She folded her napkin, corner to corner, square to triangle.

'And guess what? Jan wasn't a bit surprised. She said, "Oh, didn't you know? Grandma told me ages ago that Grandad had another little girl, and he kept a photo of her in his wallet."'

'Grandad?'

Dot nearly choked. 'She said what?'

Fran repeated the words with a touch of triumph. Ellie stared at her in confusion.

'But why would Grandma say that?'

She felt like Alice falling down the rabbit hole into a world of inexplicable madness. Surely Janis must have got it wrong. She grabbed her glass, sending the wine swirling.

Dot regained her composure and injected a note of sanity.

'I'm afraid Mother could sometimes be rather indiscreet. However, that in itself proves nothing. It was probably a misunderstanding, or even paranoia.'

Fran clutched Ellie's arm.

'So you see, the girl in the photo is my sister.'

'No, she can't be your sister. She's your niece. It's okay, I more or less guessed that Dad got someone pregnant before he went to Australia.'

At last she'd let out the crucial revelation. She sank back in her chair with relief. The room was dark, but the truth was clear for all to behold.

But Fran clicked her tongue.

'No, Ellie, don't you see? It wasn't your father's. It was *our* father's. Your grandfather – Canon Jack Goodwin – the great man himself.'

'Grandad Jack? No, no, you've got it all wrong.'

'Look, this whole business started when I was a kid. He was having an affair and it made our mother bitterly unhappy. That's what all the rows were about.'

Dot drew in breath, smoothed her skirt, brushed off a crumb. Fran shot her a look of challenge and continued.

'Of course, if you want to believe the gospel according to Dorothy, there was no little girl. Well, Janis says there was. Mother told her quite clearly.'

'Mother was a lovely person, Frances, but rather insecure, and I'm afraid she, too, had an over-vivid imagination.'

'What about that row over the anonymous letter? That wasn't imagination. I was there. I heard it. And saw it.'

Ellie watched with astonishment as her aunts glared at each other. Dot lifted her chin.

'People can be beastly, Frances, and the best thing by far is to ignore them. Unfortunately, once a seed of suspicion is sown, it takes on a life of its own.'

'No smoke without fire, though.'

Dot rose from the table and began to gather the pizza plates, scraping crumbs from one to another. A strand of her hair had come loose, and she looked tired and distant as she let out a sigh.

'That's what Mother said the day those women came.' Her hand froze. She snatched at the plates and began to stack them in a pile.

Fran frowned, her eyes narrowed.

'What women?'

'Oh, it was nothing, just some parish dispute probably. You know how people can bicker.' A weary expression had settled on Dot's face. 'Now, this is all becoming rather silly. Ellie will think that our family has nothing but problems and disputes.'

Ellie screwed up her paper serviette and held it tight. The nerve ends throughout her body were ragged. All her reasons for coming here – Dad's quest, her theories about its meaning, the plans to honour his memory – depended on her version of events being correct. She let go of the serviette and held onto the seat of the chair to stop her shoulders trembling.

'Dot, those two women, who were they? Why did they come?'

'Goodness, now you're asking. It was a very long time ago, soon after I'd started at Oxford.'

'Yes, but who did they come to see? Dad or Grandad Jack?'

For one moment Dot hesitated. Then she sighed and faced her niece with a look of resignation, as if in that split second she'd made up her mind.

'I think that the younger woman was an employee at the theological college where my father worked. She came to consult him because she was expecting a baby.'

Now they were getting somewhere. The moment of truth was upon them.

'In those days a pregnant woman wouldn't have been allowed to carry on working, and if she was single it would have been a disgrace. Obviously, as my father had some influence and was a caring person, he would have done what he could to help, I'm sure.'

Fran snorted. 'Especially if the child was his.'

Dot walked to the window, drew the curtains, and switched on the standard lamp. A gentle glow suffused the room.

'We can never know the precise facts, Frances. It is my understanding that we have in this country a presumption of innocence until guilt is proven. There are all sorts of possibilities. Anyone could have been the father.'

'Anyone?' Ellie's mind was numb. It was like waiting to see on whose neck the executioner's axe would fall.

'Yes, in theory. She might simply have come to ask for help or advice.'

'Or to blackmail him,' said Fran.

'How old was the woman?'

She calculated that Dad would have been sixteen at the time, as Raymond had said when he'd talked about the blonde woman. Yes, and the child in the photo was blonde, too.

'Oh, much the same as age as I was, I imagine. Early twenties, perhaps?'

'The dirty old sod,' said Fran. 'Having it off with a girl young enough to be his daughter.'

Or was it a young man of sixteen, having his first sexual encounter with a more experienced woman? Confusion whirled through Ellie's brain. Father or son, which had it been? She turned back to Dot.

'Do you remember her name?'

Dot's expression, as she spoke, was not unkind.

'You know, my dear, when I was a headmistress, I used to say that once someone had been found out, very often the shame of it was punishment enough.' She shivered and drew her cardigan closer. 'Just think, whoever she is, she'll be a very old woman by now, perhaps even older than I am. What good does it do to dig up the past? People think they'll find buried treasure, but more often than not it's just a rotting carcass or a pile of bones.'

Fran let out a hiss of exasperation, knocked back her wine and went stomping upstairs.

As soon as the bedroom door slammed, Dot turned to Ellie.

'The surname was Latimer. Unforgettable, really, the name of an Archbishop, a famous school. Such a sad irony, I thought. I'm afraid I don't remember her Christian name.'

She glanced up to where Fran's footsteps creaked overhead.

'Investigate by all means, Ellie, if you must, but please don't let my sister turn this into a scandal.'

Ellie didn't get into bed, or even bother to undress. All thought of sleep had gone. When a pale dawn broke she went to the window and looked out at the grass, heavy with dew. Tiny beads of moisture sparkled as the first light caught them. She watched a blackbird peck at the lawn, pull out a worm and fly away.

Despite last night's breakthrough she was flooded with doubts and confusion. Miss Latimer might have been her father's lover or her grandfather's. If Fran was right and the culprit was Grandad Jack, it would mean that Dad wasn't the one who had caused the unhappiness at home, and that would be some consolation. It might also explain why he'd wanted to escape family conflicts and build a new life of his own. So would any young man in that situation.

But the problem with Fran's version was that it left her own theory in tatters. Why would Dad challenge her to find this child if it wasn't his? Until tonight, her quest had seemed straightforward, but now she had to reconsider its whole purpose.

She cast her mind back to Fran's comments about Grandad Jack. Ellie had never met him, so why should it matter to her if he'd had an illegitimate child? Everyone knew that ministers weren't all they appeared to be. So what if he'd had a child out of wedlock? Lots of people did, even in those days. A man was a man even if he had taken a solemn oath to live a pious and virtuous life. Not everyone was superhuman like Josh Bellini.

The truth was that these people tied themselves up in ridiculous rules that they couldn't keep. Just wait until she told Josh about Grandad Jack's double standards. He'd probably think she was making it up, which was all the more reason to find solid evidence. But that might be tricky. If someone in her grandfather's position had got a girl pregnant, he wouldn't have blazoned the news around. Any hint of a scandal and he'd have been defrocked, or excommunicated, or whatever they called it in the Anglican Church. No, he must have hushed up the whole affair.

From the little that Ellie knew of clergymen, they only mixed with worthy women who went to church. That at least was the impression Aunty Phyll had given her. So maybe this woman wasn't an employee at the college where Grandad was bursar. Dot might have muddled up the details. He'd also run a small parish, so she could have been someone who played the organ, arranged flowers or taught Sunday school. That would have given them ample opportunity for secret liaisons.

She imagined their hands touching over hymn books, groping in the vestry. Or maybe he'd met her while making pastoral visits, a young woman who'd been bereaved or abandoned, who was lonely and upset, and he'd tried to comfort her. When one person was emotional and the other was trying to help, concern might turn to solace, and solace to something else.

Like that day on the beach at Freshwater. The day she'd felt all choked up, and a group of surfers had appeared out of the water, and one of them had come over to ask if she was okay. Yes, she could see it clearly now. Because Josh had been kind and concerned, she'd been drawn to him. He could have acted all macho, but he came across as a decent human being, and that very decency made him attractive. Irresistibly and infuriatingly attractive because, after all, there was nothing on offer. Except for unwanted advice.

She sat back on the bed, grabbed a pillow and sank her teeth into it. The last thing she needed was for her aunts to hear her weep. Was there anything more miserable in life than to want a bloke who didn't want you? Either that, or they tried to manipulate you, to mould you to their own appetites. She should have learned from her experience with Brad and kept her resolve to steer clear of the lot of them.

Instead she'd fallen headlong into this impossible situation with Josh. Someone she found herself liking, let's be honest, liking a lot, though he clearly wasn't right for her, was too hung up on his own ideas even to consider her, had rejected her outright because of her beliefs, or lack of them.

It was prejudice, pure and simple.

On the bedside table was a box of tissues with a fancy cover, probably crocheted by Dot. Ellie grabbed a handful, blew her nose and peered in the mirror. Her face was blotched, swollen, hideous.

She undressed in the en suite bathroom and stood under the flow of the water until it began to soothe her. When she spread soap over her body she could almost imagine that the hands that touched her were his. No, his were strong, sensitive, olive-skinned. They had never touched her and they never would. She might as well have copied Grandma Lillian and fallen for a minister. And look what had happened to that relationship.

Allegedly.

SOUTH LONDON 1935

Lillian smiled to herself as she pegged the unfamiliar garment with its buttoned fly to the line that Jack had strung up from the apple tree. He'd made her a clothes prop out of an old branch, and these little attentions filled her with a disproportionate joy.

In return she laboured over the wash with a devotion that would have astounded her mother had she been there to see it. The scullery filled with steam as the suds heated in the copper, while Lillian danced and sang *By the light of the silvery moon*. It talked of spooning and crooning and singing about love.

Sunshine slanted over the garden and the washing flapped in the breeze. She lifted Jack's undershirt from the basket and span round in a twirl. The sleeve caught in the branches and sent down a shower of leaves, but she broke off a sprig and tucked it behind her ear.

The buttons on the front of his shirt were open as she'd opened them last night at his prompting, slipping her palm inside to where his heart quivered like a tiny bird under his chest. He took hold of her hand, moved it down to that part of him which still startled and fascinated her, as if a third party lay between them with a life and a power of its own.

'It's the measure of my love for you,' he said. 'You shouldn't be so irresistible.'

After the disaster of their first night and the pain while her period raged, Lillian had begun to relax to his touch. Dear Jack had been so patient, so attentive. He brought her hot drinks and aspirins, massaged her back and temples. By the time the curse left her, she'd grown used to his closeness, the comforting warmth of his body bent to the curve of her back. Once the agony passed, she wanted nothing more than to make him happy. If that meant allowing herself to be led down paths she'd never dreamed existed, she could only marvel at her good fortune in having such a guide.

Afterwards she felt moist and tender and surprisingly empty. It was as if Jack had claimed a new part of her, discovered a hitherto unknown inlet which would be forever stamped with his identity. Her fear that the experience might remind her of that awful day when her brother had trapped her on the back staircase and rubbed his fingers between her legs, was exorcised. Or that other time, when she'd opened the door to the privy where he sat with glazed eyes, pumping his hand on what looked like a skinned rabbit, huge and purple. That memory had lost its power, too.

A rustle in the hedge made her freeze. A dog with hair like wire wool appeared, and a woman's voice called after it, ringing clear with the rounded vowels of the aspiring well-to-do. Lillian flushed. How embarrassing to be caught in such intimate musings by her blue-rinsed neighbour, whose husband left each morning with his bowler and brolly for the train to London Bridge and his desk at the Prudential.

She pegged up her knickers, and as she took the empty basket back to the scullery, the front door bell rang. It couldn't be Jack. He had his own key. Besides, he'd gone to a meeting with the vicar to plan next month's services and wasn't due home until lunchtime.

Could it be a parishioner? Her courage dipped at the thought of some well-meaning wife, so different from herself, making a social visit. One or two had brought scones or cakes, and Lillian had no choice but to invite them in and offer a cup of tea. They sat making small talk, sizing up the few possessions that she and Jack had added to the sparsely furnished house.

'You'll soon fit in,' they assured her.

It made Lillian feel as if she came from an alien tribe.

Impossible to explain to these confident, worldly women that everything was strange for her. Not only marriage, but giving up work and moving somewhere new and – worst of all – trying to adapt to the role of curate's wife. Even Jack didn't understand why she found it so difficult. He'd had months of training to help him prepare, whereas everyone assumed that she would know instinctively what to do.

The doorbell rang again. Lillian smoothed her apron and hurried down the hall, tidying back a loose wisp of hair. Behind the glass panel she could see a portly figure with a bulging bosom. Could it be the vicar's wife? She opened the door and there stood the fearsome neighbour in a tweed skirt and twin set with a string of pearls.

Two sharp little eyes skimmed down Lillian's work clothes and up to the twig in her hair.

'May I speak to the lady of the house?'

It took Lillian a moment to grasp the implication. The wretched woman thought she was a housemaid. What? On a curate's stipend? she was about to retort, but bit her tongue for Jack's sake and managed a polite reply. Her neighbour smirked.

'Ah, Mrs Goodwin. Yes, I realise that you are new here, so no doubt you are unfamiliar with our ways. That is why I wanted to give you some discreet advice.'

'Advice?'

'I saw you in the garden, hanging out your…garments. My dear, it just isn't done. Not where anyone might see. We have standards to maintain.'

A tide of anger surged through Lillian. Standards? Of cleanliness or godliness? she could have said, but the gate squeaked open and Jack appeared, all smiles.

'Good morning, ladies. What a beautiful morning.'

'You're back early.'

'The vicar was called out unexpectedly, so we'll have to finish our meeting some other time. No peace for the wicked, eh, Mrs Jenkins?'

At the sight of his clerical collar she simpered.

'Oh, Father…delightful morning, isn't it? But I must be getting on. It's Ladies' Day at the Golf Club.' She glanced at them doubtfully. 'Do either of you play?'

'Only the piano, I'm afraid,' said Jack and steered Lillian indoors.

'What a dreadful woman,' Lillian said once the door was closed. She told Jack about the underwear on the washing line.

'What does she expect me to do, drape it all over the house?'

'Take no notice. Her bark's probably worse than her bite. Wait till you meet Mr Jenkins. He's churchwarden at the Smells and Bells place. Used to ruling the roost, God bless him.'

'I don't know how you put up with these people. Will you have a word with her sometime? She'll listen to you.'

'Of course I will, darling. And by the way, I didn't want to say this in front of the dragon, but old Simmons has had another turn. That's why the vicar had to dash off. Looks as if it might be the end, I'm afraid.'

'Oh, no. Such a lovely man.'

He had been kind to Lillian in the short time she'd been here. It was all very well for Jack to joke that dragons and death were part of the challenge of ministry, but it made her feel that her new life was going to be harder than she'd thought.

'Anyhow, it meant I could get away early and home to my lovely wife.'

'Have you had elevenses?'

As Lillian lit the gas under the kettle she smiled to herself.

One of the perks of her new role was having an adorable man who came home for coffee and a cuddle in the middle of the day. Even if he did wear a dog collar.

Mrs Denham was in the vicarage garden, her knees in the flower bed, a pail of weeds beside her. Wisps of grey hair had escaped from under her floppy hat. She stabbed at the earth with a trowel and looked up as Lillian approached.

'Well, thank the Lord you've come. Now we can have a cup of tea. This ground is more unyielding than the souls of some of our parishioners.'

She struggled to her feet, brushed the dirt from her skirt, and Lillian followed her into a spacious hall with chequered tiles and a majestic staircase. A ginger cat sat cleaning its paws on a strip of threadbare carpet. The hallstand was almost buried under coats, hats and umbrellas.

They went into the back kitchen. The table was littered with pamphlets, a vase of dead flowers and a pile of laundry. Mrs Denham pushed aside some books and moved the dirty plates.

'Do excuse the muddle. I should have done the dishes earlier, but the garden is so much more rewarding, don't you think?'

While she washed her hands at the sink and put on the kettle, Lillian sat at the table and scanned the titles of the books. She'd never seen so many scholarly looking volumes in anyone's home before. She was about to open one when Mrs Denham turned.

'Yes, do have a look if they interest you. They're from the lending library. I'm looking into the history of women's education. We've made some progress but there's still a long way to go. Would you believe it, when I was your age I was allowed to go to university but not to receive a degree?'

'You went to university?' gasped Lillian and Mrs Denham gave her a sympathetic smile.

'Yes, my dear. I am one of the fortunate few.'

'I'd have given anything to go. My teachers encouraged me to think I might, only I missed my school certificate examination. And anyway,' she added morosely, 'we couldn't afford it.'

Mrs Denham nodded as if she understood. Something soft touched Lillian's leg, and she looked down to see the cat rubbing himself against her, his tail in the air.

'Ah, Macavity has taken a liking to you. That's a good sign. Charles calls him my baby and it's true I spoil him terribly. It's what comes of not having children, I suppose, but perhaps that's a blessing or I wouldn't have time for my research.'

She poured the tea and passed a cup across.

'Have some sugar. I take two as I need plenty of energy. Now, my dear, I have a proposal. We need to act speedily because I am sure that a healthy young couple like you and Mr Goodwin will soon become parents, and then your chance will be gone.'

Lillian's mouth dropped.

'Parents? Oh, not yet.'

'Are you taking precautions?'

'Precautions? No…at least, I don't think so.'

'Well, none of my business, of course. Charles says I'm too outspoken, but to my mind we women have to take the initiative in these matters. It's our health that stands to suffer.'

Lillian froze, like a non-swimmer on the edge of dangerous waters.

'The point is, once you have children, your chance of education will be gone. What with the demands of a parish, a vicar's wife never has time for much else.'

'I think the church has a cheek to get two people for the price of one.'

'Indeed it has. One day perhaps they will allow women to minister in their own right. Until then, we have the choice of opting out of our role, or turning it into an opportunity.'

'It's not that I don't want to help Jack. But it's his work, not mine. I had a perfectly good job before I met him, but they wouldn't let me stay on after I married. If I'm not good enough for one thing, why am I all right for another?'

Mrs Denham waved a wasp away from the sugar bowl. She took off her glasses and polished them on her sleeve.

'Well, now, that makes it rather awkward. You see, I asked you here for a purpose, apart from the pleasure of seeing you, of course. I hoped that I might persuade you to take over the Young Wives. They need new blood. They're tired of an old battle axe like me.'

'Oh no, I couldn't – I mean, I wouldn't know how.'

She pictured all those confident women sitting in a circle, waiting for her to speak. Married to men who'd made a bit of money, they turned up at church with their smart clothes and affected voices, chattering about coffee mornings and having their hair waved.

The vicar's wife gave her a shrewd look.

'You underestimate yourself, my dear.'

She reached to touch Lillian's hand. Her skin was rough with calluses, but Lillian felt she would burst into tears, unused as she was to such kindness.

As if to rescue her, Macavity sprang onto her lap, and clawed at her skirt.

'Turn him off if he's a nuisance.'

'It's all right. I like animals.'

She stroked his fur while he lifted his head, closed his eyes and purred.

'And animals seem to like you. People, too. Yes, I see it, even if you don't. You've a lot to offer and I hate to see an intelligent young woman held back by lack of confidence.'

Lillian swallowed. The failures of her life loomed up to taunt her.

'Now, listen to me. Why do you think you are here? Because you fell in love with a charming young man who happens to be a priest, or because someone up there has an interest in you? No, you don't need to answer, but it would be a jolly good thing if you'd think it through. There may be a purpose here for you, too.'

A gust of wind blew the door open and several hens came in, clucking and pecking around. Mrs Denham flapped a tea towel at them as she continued.

'I'm not going to pressurise you. Give it some thought and let me know. In the meantime, if you're free tomorrow, I'll take you down to the library and we'll see about evening classes. The WEA is a wonderful organisation. Archbishop Temple is their president, so no one can object if the curate's wife enrols on a course, can they?'

'That would be wonderful. Thank you so much.'

But if she accepted help, how could she refuse to give it to others?

On fine evenings they sat on the lawn under the trees. Jack had found two fold-up chairs in the shed and Lillian had cleaned the cobwebs from their canvas seats. When he took off his dog collar and rolled up his shirt sleeves, she felt as happy as when they were courting up on the cliffs at South Foreland. It was hard to believe that little more than a year had passed since then, such a lot had happened in that short time.

The garden faced west, and they could see across rooftops to where the sun sank, colouring the sky with streaks of flame. Jack read the newspaper and Lillian darned socks or worked on the tablecloth she was embroidering. She found it comforting to hear him turn the pages that fluttered in the breeze as dusk fell.

While she stitched, he told her the latest news. Hitler had become Chancellor. Oswald Moseley was stirring up trouble. But even the nationalists' rallies in London seemed too far away to touch their peaceful world.

A train hooted. From their neighbour's open window came the murmur of Mr Jenkins' wireless. He had put up a high wooden fence, presumably so that his good lady would not see the offending underwear. Jack still hadn't found time to talk to her and Lillian didn't want to nag.

'The old dear will have to put up with the sight of my knickers once in a while,' she joked.

The air was cooler now. Lillian shivered and drew her cardigan over her shoulders. Mother was due to visit on Saturday. Strange how one thought led to another. That would mean the house had to be cleaned, the washing dried, ironed and put away neatly. Heaven forbid that her highness should find anything out of order. At lunchtime there'd be the challenge of producing a meal which was both frugal and nourishing.

Lillian's marital status made no difference to her mother's interference. Quite the opposite. It was only when Jack was present that she slipped into an awestruck silence. Lillian chuckled to herself. There were some advantages in being married to a vicar.

Jack folded the newspaper.

'It's getting a little chilly. Shall we go inside?'

'I'll make a cup of cocoa.'

It was their bedtime ritual. Once they'd finished and she had rinsed the cups, he would check the doors and windows, take her hand and lead her upstairs. Often he liked to undress her, opening one button at a time and stroking her skin. He was now skilled at unclasping her brassiere, and if she wore stockings he would release the suspenders and roll the silky softness down her legs, tracing its path with his fingers. His attentions had redefined her body from a mechanism that fulfilled its functions to a landscape of endless sensations.

Only her corset baffled him.

'Why women want to squeeze themselves into these things, I'll never know,' he said, and let her unhook it herself.

'What do you know about women?' she laughed and he gave her a quick look.

'I have sisters, don't I?'

Tonight, though, she wasn't wearing a corset. Since she'd spent all day at home there was no need. She sat on the bed while he unfastened the back of her dress.

'By the way, Mother and Violet are coming on Saturday.'

'Oh, blow. There's a wedding.'

'Do you need to be there? Won't the vicar do it?'

'He wants me to learn the ropes.' Jack slipped the flowered georgette over her head. 'I'll try and get out of it, or at least get away early.'

Spread out on the mattress, Lillian lay still and tried to relax. She was growing used to it now, and he was so gentle that it no longer hurt her. But she still found it puzzling that men had such urgent needs, when more often than not she'd have been content with a kiss and a cuddle. What a shame that babies couldn't be born that way, she sometimes thought. One more issue that she'd have to take up with the Almighty when her time came.

'Well, my girl,' Mrs Cullen said at lunch on Saturday when Lillian reached for the spring onions she'd left on the side of her plate. 'You certainly seem to have taken a fancy to them.'

'They'll make your breath smell,' said Violet.

Lillian lifted one to her mouth, crunched the white part and savoured its succulent juices.

'They taste different here. It must be the soil.'

'Humph.' Mrs Cullen eyed her shrewdly. 'Stuff and nonsense.'

All three of them turned as a key sounded in the lock. The

132

front door opened, followed by Jack's familiar 'Coo-eee.' He'd come straight from the wedding, so still wore his cassock, and the sight of the priestly garments silenced Mrs Cullen.

'Hello, Mum,' he said, then bent to kiss Lillian. He smiled at Violet. 'My word, Vi, your George will have to watch out. You look prettier every time I see you.'

Mrs Cullen pursed her lips and raised her tea cup, being careful to crook her little finger.

'Shall I show him, Lil?' Violet whispered.

Lillian nodded in excitement and her sister lifted one hand to display the ring with its single amethyst.

'They're engaged, Jack, and want you to marry them.'

'Gosh, I'd be honoured. Congratulations to the pair of you. It's a good job I've been having a bit of tuition. So George finally popped the question, eh?'

Violet laughed. 'Yes, I was beginning to think I'd have to wait for a leap year.'

While Jack ran upstairs to change his clothes, Lillian went to make a fresh pot of tea. She'd just begun to pour on the boiling water when her mother appeared in the doorway.

'So you'll have both daughters married now, Mum.'

Mrs Cullen sniffed and straightened her shoulders.

'Not before time, I might say. All that gallivanting around, I was fast losing patience with the pair of them.' She ran one finger along the edge of a shelf as if to check it for dust. 'I don't know what young people are coming to. They'd even begun to talk about going away together for a cycling holiday. Whatever next?'

'I thought you liked George.'

'He's a polite young man, I'll give him that. And he holds down a responsible position at John Lewis. But a man is a man and if you give him an inch he'll take what he has no right to.'

'You seem to know a lot about it,' Lillian wanted to say but didn't have the nerve. She turned away to hide her amusement. When she picked up the tea pot and moved towards the door, her mother barred the way. Her eyes slid down over Lillian's dress. Was there a button missing? Or a stain she hadn't noticed?

'As for you, young lady, you'd better get yourself to the doctor's. Don't leave it too long. There are some things a woman should go easy on when she's in that condition.'

Lillian's mouth opened and shut again. Her face flamed, her hand trembled and tea sloshed all over the floor.

'What do you mean?'

'Spring onions, indeed. With me it was radishes. Except when I was expecting Violet and then it was apples.'

She lowered her voice, and glanced at the door.

'The time for pleasure is over, my girl. Your responsibilities are just beginning.'

She decided to forget him. It was the logical and responsible thing to do. A bloke you'd met once on a beach, then outside a library in Manly, wasn't worth the grief. No matter that you'd walked the trail with him, talked and bared your soul, tried to dig into his. That had been a mistake. Or maybe what Mum would call a blessing in disguise. It had revealed what a totally impossible person he was.

If she'd forgotten Brad, whose DNA was written all over her, how much easier it should be to forget Josh, who'd never so much as touched her. Apart from that handshake. The memory shot a flash of fever up her arm. She would douse it out with a cold dose of reason. It was no more than a formality, what you'd expect after a session with a shrink.

She whiled away the evening reassessing her plans. The empty cottage groaned and creaked. Outside, the sky scudded with clouds that chased the light from the dormer window. Fran had left for her caravan in Devon, Dot had gone to a meeting about the village fete. Clio was whining down in the kitchen.

The suspense and confusion about Dad's past, the hopelessness of her situation with Josh, plus creeping fears of joblessness, had sapped Ellie dry. Her quest had come to nothing. The whole idea now taunted her as a misguided fantasy, a desperate attempt to turn misery into happiness. All the same, a fascination lingered. Even if the child wasn't Dad's, he must have left Ellie the photo for a reason. Did he know about the tensions between his sisters and want to help them? After all, Dot and Fran were far more bound by the past than she or Karen were.

She began to warm to this new scenario. The prospect of trouble-shooting other people's woes gave her an unfamiliar buzz. She would come out of it as a heroine, a contemporary saviour. How impressed His Holiness would be.

Light and shadows played across the wall, the breeze whispered in the curtains. No, it was a mistake to do good for ulterior motives, like celebrities who posed with famine-stricken orphans. Besides, Josh would see right through her.

Something, though, she had to do. She stared at the beams that crossed the ceiling like bars on a cage. If she stayed here any longer she would go stir crazy.

Why not visit Canterbury? The thought hit her like a revelation. She sprang up, went to her laptop and clicked onto the internet to check out the trains. It was time for action. Dad had lived in that city for years before he emigrated. If she could ferret around and unearth a nugget of information about the mysterious and pregnant Miss Latimer, what a scoop that would be.

Only one little niggle still lingered. Did Mum know more about the girl in the photo than she'd let on? Maybe she hadn't wanted to talk about it while Dad's death was still so raw. Ellie glanced at the clock. She couldn't call her now. It was still night time in Sydney.

She paced around the cottage until Dot came in, had a nightcap with her, went back to her room and waited till she knew it would be morning down under.

A car went by and in the distance she heard a train hoot, but otherwise it was silent. Not even a whisper of wind or tides like she was used to at home. How ironic that on a tiny island she hadn't yet seen the ocean. Or that she could be surrounded by people but feel so alone.

At the stroke of midnight she called the number on her mobile. Mum answered right away. In the background a TV was blaring, and the blunt Aussie voice caught Ellie with a tug of nostalgia.

'Hi, Mum.'

'Just a moment, I'll go out in the yard. Charlie's watching the farming news.'

'You're in Queensland? I'd forgotten you said you might go.'

They went through the usual chit-chat. Charlie was the same as ever, Phyll was good most days but her back played her up if she didn't rest. Adam and Wayne and their wives had been over with the kids. Mum's voice took on a more tentative tone.

'Karen said you called the other day.'

Ellie bristled. What had Karen told her? To stamp on her irritation she leaped straight in with a question.

'Did Dad ever say anything about another sister?'

'Another sister? What, apart from Dorothy and Frances? I don't think so.'

Mum listened with little huffs of surprise while Ellie filled her in on the details of Grandad Jack's love child.

'Well,' Mum said, 'I never had the impression there was anything like that.'

'So you don't think it's true?'

'Dad did say the old man could be a bit of a flirt, but it was more his mother's reaction that upset him.'

'How do you mean?'

The signal was breaking up and Ellie moved closer to the window. Outside, the breeze stirred the leaves of the trees. Mum's voice tightened, and Ellie could sense her struggling to keep control.

'Sweetie, Dad wouldn't want me to talk about this, but I guess it can't hurt him now. He said his mother was touchy about anything to do with sex, and was always jealous and suspicious of other women.'

'That's what I'm trying to tell you. She had reason to be. Grandad was having an affair.'

'No, no, it was all paranoia. She was one of those people who are so insecure that they spend their whole life imagining things.'

What was Mum insinuating? Ellie clenched the phone so hard, her nails dug into her palm.

'So it's not true about Grandad Jack?'

'Look, honey, what really bothered your dad was the way his mother clamped down on him. And on Dot. I'm not sure about the others. They were quite young when he left.'

'Yes, I know – Fran was only twelve, and she was bloody upset about him going.'

'Well, don't get cranky with me. Why didn't they come out here and see him, if they cared about him so much?'

This would get her nowhere. Ellie almost slammed down the phone, but there was one more fact she needed to clarify.

'So,' she said in a nonchalant way, 'Dad must have had lots of girlfriends before he emigrated. Maybe the kid was his.'

'Listen, Ellie, his mother put the fear of God into him. He was terrified of going anywhere near girls and it took him years to get over it.' A pause. 'You're not getting carried away again, are you? It's about time you came home, got a job and straightened yourself out.'

'Oh, give me a break,' Ellie muttered. She tried to moisten her mouth with saliva. The vision of Jimmy the lad, dating blondes and having flings with older women, had faded to a picture that made her mouth go dry. Dad was sexually inadequate. No, he was gay, her parents had never had sex, maybe he wasn't her father at all.

She lowered herself onto a chair, her heart thrusting in her chest.

'But he married you. Did you . . . am I?'

'For heaven's sake, Ellie, he got it together eventually. He was very shy and took a bit of coaxing, that's all. Do I have to go into details?'

Ellie bit her lip. She tried to speak, but her throat had knotted. Maybe Mum realised, because her voice softened.

'Sweetie, we were very happy. Let's just say he was a late developer.'

Ellie found herself laughing, for relief, for joy, she wasn't quite sure.

She took the bone-shaker from Victoria, calling at all stations to Canterbury East. The slower the better. Mum's jibes about sorting out her life had worked their poison. What did she expect her to do? Beg for her job back at the museum? Live at home in Narrabeen where every nook and cranny reminded her that Dad wasn't there? Go on with the purposeless life she'd tried to escape?

No, she told herself as the train rattled through the drab conurbations of the Medway towns, she'd had enough of people's taunts and demands. From now on she'd do exactly what she wanted and ignore them all.

The rough upholstery of the seat rubbed against her bare legs. She should have worn jeans instead of a skimpy little sundress. The day was barely warm, and a smell of sludge and seaweed seeped through the open window. Way across the Thames she could see what might be the Tilbury Docks where Dad had boarded the boat to Australia. He'd worn an overcoat, carried a battered suitcase, and had left behind at least two broken hearts, his mother's and Fran's.

Did he feel guilty? Or apprehensive? Maybe he didn't care. He was young, setting out on a great adventure.

When you emigrate you can reinvent yourself. You cross a border and nobody knows who you were, where you grew up or what happened there. Dad would have shed his identity along with his thick clothing as the ship moved south. Gone were the overcoat, the tweed jacket, the woollen jumper. Take off your tie, roll up your shirt-sleeves, strip off altogether, sit in your singlet and turn your face to the sun.

He was no longer the private school boy, Canon Goodwin's son James, who'd once gone to Oxford. Somewhere, between one hemisphere and another, he changed into Jimmy the regular bloke, who roomed in a hostel and worked on a building site, called people mate, slapped them on the shoulder and had a beer with them in the evening.

If he really had escaped a dark scandal, no one would have a clue. So what if your father had got another woman pregnant? No one would care. A few lewd jokes and it would be forgotten. You wouldn't have to creep about a cathedral city, listening to snide remarks, rumours or gossip, watching people nudge and whisper when they saw the man of the cloth walk down the street. Of course Ellie was speculating, but every historian had to have a theory. That was what engaged your imagination. True, but only researching the facts would show if you were right.

So, Ellie Goodwin, the scent of the chase is drawing you. The grit to hang on like a terrier and solve a puzzle is still strong.

That quality had come to her from Dad, too, as well as the dark colouring and quietness. The hours they used to spend together playing chess, or putting piece after piece in a jigsaw. They'd started a new one each Christmas – the map of Australia, animals of the bush, the Great Barrier Reef.

Fancy Dot not knowing that Dad liked crosswords. He'd cracked one every day for as long as she could remember, persisting till the last detail was complete. She shook her head in bemusement and took out one of his old school exercise books that she'd shoved in her backpack. Its faded cover was held together with rusted staples, the name pencilled on in a childish script: *James Goodwin, Class 3, Local Studies, 1947- 48.*

After Fran's revelations, Ellie had felt like chucking all these books in the bin. She was sick of the whole saga of Dad and his family, what had or hadn't happened, so much misery that tossed her from one person's theory to another.

Alone on the train, though, this was calmer territory where no one could intrude. She turned the pages of his schoolwork with new gusto. Here was a doorway into a little boy's world in an age of innocence, the child who had become her father. Now at last, she had him to herself.

In September, in East Kent and West Kent, people go hop picking. Hops are dried in the oast house then they go to the brewery to be made into beer. Hops give beer its bitter flavour, which people like.

He'd left out the 'o' in 'people' and the teacher had added it in red ink. This was what she'd come here to find, Dad as a sweet little boy inviting her into his life.

One side of her face was warm. The sky had cleared, the sun had brightened, and the train gathered speed as it moved into open country. Dad had mentioned oast houses, and right on cue Ellie caught sight of two of them, their wind vanes like fins on the conical cowls. Around them spread orchards in a regular chequerboard of trees, steeped in long grass.

She pulled open the window and peered out. The foliage was dotted with fruit, like spots of colour in an Impressionist painting. So different from the fiery reds and yellows she was used to down under. There was beauty in both and she was no longer sure which she preferred.

As the train approached Canterbury, it began to slow. In the distance, rising from the plain like silver fingers pointing up through a hazy sky, she could see what must be the towers of the cathedral. The city spread around it in a collage of low-lying houses, trees and fields.

So this was Dad's home town. Her palms were damp with excitement as she turned from the window and picked up her backpack. Her fellow passengers began to stir. A nun reached for her suitcase. A soldier shouldered his knapsack, a businessman folded his newspaper, a workman in overalls passed down the corridor with a bag of tools. In the seat opposite, a woman took out a mirror and daubed on some lipstick.

They were like Chaucer's motley band of pilgrims, drawn by varied motives to a common destination.

She glanced again at the grimy glass where her reflection stared back at her. Did coming here make her a pilgrim, too? The

142

idea had an uncomfortable whiff of self-discovery. Find yourself, medieval style. No, her reasons were purely historical. She would visit beautiful buildings and learn more about Dad's roots.

A gust of wind surprised her with the smell of the ocean. She'd seen on the map that Canterbury nestled between estuary and channel. But for a second, the salty sea-weedy tang swept her back to the beach at Freshwater with the surf rolling in, gulls crying overhead, and a black dog scampering across the sand.

It was a moment only, then the carriage filled with a metallic heat as they drew into the station. The train jolted to a halt. She grabbed her belongings and tore herself from the memory. It had gripped her with an urge to be there, not only to relive the encounter with Josh, but to re-write it.

But as she shuffled forward with the other passengers, she resolved to focus on the picture she was building of Dad's early years. The urge to make sense of his life, to create beauty and coherence from brokenness, hadn't lost its power.

It was a bit like the time she'd worked with the fragments of an amphora, once graceful but now smashed into pieces. Whether she failed or succeeded in piecing them into a coherent whole, what mattered was to try.

The cathedral dominated everything. As Ellie walked from the station, its towers loomed over the narrow medieval streets like a giant watching Lilliputians scurry at its feet. Was it oppressive or protective? She couldn't decide. But it had a different effect from the skyscrapers of the City Business District, sleek, confident, stylish, that clamoured for attention in the Sydney skyline.

She'd made an online reservation at a B&B run by a retired

couple in a lane near the Westgate Gardens. Dot had suggested it.

'It's always nice to stay somewhere homely.'

The house was small and unpretentious, built of brick and flint, so different from the stone cottages in Somerset. A man in a sleeveless jumper answered the door. A pair of bright, shrewd eyes met hers.

'Welcome to Canterbury.' He introduced himself as Bert, 'proprietor, chief cook and bottle-washer' and insisted on carrying Ellie's backpack. His wife came out from the kitchen and shook hands.

'I'm Doreen. If there's anything you need, just ask. Breakfast is from half past seven to nine.'

She handed Ellie a list – sausages, kippers, scrambled eggs, bacon, veggie option available – and told her to tick what she wanted then leave it on the sideboard. Bert shouldered Ellie's backpack and chatted as he showed her upstairs to her room.

'So you're from Australia? There's quite a few Goodwins in these parts. Finding your roots, are you?'

'Yes, my father grew up here.'

'Canterbury family, were they?'

He paused at a turn in the staircase. From the window she could see the River Stour, green and sluggish where it wound between weeping willows.

'Well, kind of.'

She had no idea if Granddad Jack's private life was already public knowledge, or how far she dared probe without digging up a termites' nest of scandal. She followed Bert up the remaining stairs and decided to take a risk.

'My grandfather, Canon Goodwin, used to work at the theological college.'

Bert turned, his eyebrows raised.

'Canon Goodwin? Not Canon Jack Goodwin?'

'Did you know him?'

'Oh yes. Everybody knew Canon Goodwin.'

His expression showed the hint of a smile, whether benign or mocking she couldn't tell. But Bert was enthusiastic in his praise.

'He was a lovely man. We all thought the world of Canon Goodwin. I worked as a groundsman at the college, so I remember him well. Always had a kind word for everyone. No matter who they were, high or low, he was always the same.'

'Really?' She could have hugged him with relief. Maybe Fran's claims had no foundation. If Bert's point of view was anything to go by, public opinion had shone kindly on Grandad Jack. She guessed that the goings-on of the clergy would spawn no end of gossip in a city like this, so either Granddad Jack was innocent or his secret had never been discovered.

While Bert stopped to unlock a door, Ellie spoke as nonchalantly as she could.

'Did you know a Miss Latimer?'

He turned, pursing his lips. 'Latimer? Doesn't ring any bells.'

'She worked at the college, too, at one time, I think.'

'When would that have been, then?'

'Oh, in the fifties, maybe, or early sixties?'

'That was before my time. I started in the late sixties, just a couple of years before Canon Goodwin retired. Relation of yours, too, is she?'

'No, just the friend of a friend.'

That was as close to the facts as she dared to go.

Her room was small but comfortable with a rose-coloured bedspread and patterned carpet. From the window she could see the flower beds of the Westgate Gardens, and a path with benches alongside the river.

She unpacked her clothes, wondering where to go first. Of course she wanted to see the college and all the other places connected with her family, as well as the major historical sites. But first it would be good to soak up the atmosphere of this amazing place where Dad had spent his childhood, and see it through his eyes.

Rather than use a guidebook, she would let his school work be her guide. She flicked over the pages and read what he had written.

Archbishop Alphege was imprisoned in the Northgate by the Danes. The tower no longer exists but there is a stone in the pavement to show where it used to be.

He'd marked the site on a map, along with other vanished buildings like Whitefriars, Blackfriars and Burgate. His sketches of the city wall and the Westgate were childish, but they showed the love of detail that she recognised so well.

She put mobile, purse and a bottle of water in her backpack, and a few minutes later Dad's words led her under the archway of the Westgate, between two towers that once formed part of the City Wall.

Through this gate came many famous people in history. William the Conqueror, Richard Coeur de Lion, the Black Prince, Chaucer, Henrys VII and VIII, Queens Mary and Elizabeth, Oliver Cromwell and many others. In fact most of England's history has passed through Westgate.

'And now it's Ellie Goodwin,' Dad would have said if he'd been here.

She turned the page and glimpsed him as a little boy with a fascination for the gruesome and bizarre:

The head of Bluebeard the Hermit was stuck on top of the tower. Then it became a prison complete with instruments of torture. In 1852 a circus owner tried to have it demolished to allow a procession of elephants to pass through.

She chuckled to herself, wondering how had Dad grown into such a quiet and serious man.

By the time she reached the cathedral a service had begun. She dodged into a row of chairs at the back of the nave as choir and clergy passed in a long procession. A white-robed minister held the cross aloft, its surface gleaming as it caught the light. The organ resounded with crashing peals that were almost enough to put the fear of God into even a cynic like her.

She sat on a hard wooden seat and focused on the stone pillars that rose gracefully to fluted arches. She had come here to admire the architecture, not to have a religious experience.

The organ fell silent. Then the choristers' voices rang out with a purity that resonated through the lofty space. She watched the clergy take their seats and wondered if Grandad Jack had played a part in rituals like these.

She pictured him here with his colleagues, carrying a secret that not even those closest to him suspected. Did he tremble at the awful contrast, or hide behind his role as priest, just as the robes that he wore masked his body? These people believed that God saw everything, didn't they? So why hadn't the Almighty struck him down if what he'd done was so sinful? Or, if it was so easy to get away with, what did that prove? That God didn't exist?

That he knew but didn't care? That you paid for it later? That, as a certain person said, he was infinitely merciful?

The most likely explanation, she reasoned, was that all this talk of sin was nonsense. In any other job, if Grandad Jack had had an affair no one would have raised an eyebrow. He was in love with a woman who wasn't his wife, and that was that. If people were hurt, that was their problem.

Like the way she'd been hurt when Brad cheated on her.

'It wouldn't be cheating if you were more open, Ellie.' Throwing the blame back on her because she didn't want to swing with some friends he'd lined up.

'So it's my fault, is it?'

Well, she could throw things, too. His hand-engraved glass platter, an award for innovative publicity, shattered against the wall. His Smartphone whizzed into the pool.

'You bloody bitch,' he yelled at her. 'You're too used to getting your own way.'

'I'm not turned on by all that group stuff, Brad. I like it with you, just the two of us. I've never been good in crowds. I'm sensitive. You don't understand.'

'Up-tight, more likely. Possessive. Clinging on like a clam.'

That made her laugh. It reminded her of what Dad used to call her.

'I'm a mollusc, didn't you know?'

Brad's cool exterior shattered.

'Shit,' he said. 'I've been shagging a loony.'

That did it. She packed her bags and left.

Yes, it was tough when you didn't fit in, but you had to get over it. Move on and live your own life, set your own priorities. Tell yourself that a man like that wasn't worth beating yourself up about, and you could live quite happily without a single one of them.

She closed her eyes until the memories faded. The choristers' voices lifted her to another plane, peaceful, ethereal, triumphant. This was the achievement of great art. It helped you to see beyond all the daily dirt and disappointment.

When she opened her eyes, she could see how the light filtered through richly coloured figures in the stained glass windows. Gothic art was didactic, her tutor had explained, inseparable from its symbolism. The idea was that simple people could learn about faith from what they saw, because the message appealed to the heart, not the head.

So was that why places like this had an aura of otherworldliness? It was a bit like the vibe you felt when you went to Ayres Rock, or Uluru, as Josh insisted on calling it. Uluru was a natural phenomenon, not man-made, but both places attracted people who claimed to see beyond the material, and both had a power that was hard to explain by rational means.

The day they walked the Spit-Manly Trail, Josh pointed out shapes of fish and birds etched in the rocks along the path. Ellie had passed them before, but seeing them through his eyes brought them alive. He talked about the cave paintings at Uluru, of boomerangs and human forms, waterholes and abstract symbols, and how those so-called primitive peoples had used art to make sense of the world around and beyond them.

Ellie agreed with him on that. But when he said that everyone longed for meaning beyond the material, even now, despite this materialistic age, she disagreed.

'We're rational beings. People don't have the same certainties anymore.'

'Don't they? Depends who you speak to. Maybe some people can't see them.'

'Oh, so I'm blind, am I? Well, thanks a lot. Maybe I just don't need a crutch.'

He laughed and went on taking photos, and it bugged her that he wasn't more offended.

'I've got to convince a backer,' he said, 'so I'm putting together some stills for a pitch. Let's have one of you beside the boulder. For a sense of proportion. And because it's a cool photo.'

'Okay. Then I'll take one of you.'

She'd saved the shot on her mobile, his handsome mug grinning at her like an ape.

Ellie slipped from her seat, out into the brightness of the precincts, and wove her way through the tourists queuing to go inside once the service had finished. She took out her mobile and flipped to the photos.

There he was. Dark hair, dark eyes with a look of sympathetic mischief that saw everything, as if he knew her better than she knew herself.

She clicked *delete*. There, I've zapped you.

If only it was as easy as the touch of a button.

When she let herself in at the B&B, a lamp glowed in the hallway. On the sideboard was a note asking her to come into the lounge as they had some information for her. Behind the *Private* sign she could hear canned music and peals of laughter from the TV.

She knocked, and Bert opened the door.

'Come in. No, no you're not disturbing us. It's only some silly quiz programme. Doreen, it's Miss Goodwin.'

'Do have a seat, dear.' Doreen flipped the TV to silent. 'We've thought of someone who knew your grandfather. He's an old man now, but he and his wife joined the college staff in the fifties. I still see her occasionally at the WI. So I took the liberty of giving her a ring and she said, oh yes, they remembered Canon Goodwin very well. If you'd like to have a chat with them, they'll be in all day tomorrow.'

Bert handed Ellie a piece of paper with their name and address.

'It's just off the Old Dover Road. I could drive you there if you like.'

'Thanks, that's really kind but I could do with a walk.'

She didn't want Bert getting wind of her mission.

Up in her room Ellie drew the curtains, switched on the bedside lamp and looked again at the name on the paper. Rev and Mrs Arnold Whitaker. She groaned. You probably couldn't move in a place like Canterbury without meeting ministers. But the prospect of entering that world gave her the creeps.

She lay back on the bed with her arms folded under her head. It would be a lot easier to forget all about Grandad Jack and what he had or hadn't done. Who was she to go raking up his past mistakes? Besides, even if these people did remember him, that didn't mean they knew all the intimate details of his affair with Miss Latimer. Anyhow, the whole story might be a pack of lies.

But what if Miss Latimer really had had his child? Fran clearly thought so and even Dot hadn't denied it outright. Dad's photo and postcard could well point to that possibility. Even the book, with its link to Grandad Jack, began to make more sense in this context, too.

Then what were Dad's motives in setting her the puzzle? Had

something happened to the little girl that made him feel concerned or guilty? No, once Dad had left for Australia he'd more or less cut off contact. If her birth had been kept secret, how could he have known what happened to her later? Not even Dot or Fran knew that.

She glanced up at the ceiling, swept by the lights of a passing car. If Dad had wanted to find the little girl, he could have looked for her himself, or at least told Ellie what he wanted to find out and why. But no, it had never been his way to make revelations. A secretive man, his true feelings were always hard to guess.

'Still waters run deep,' Mum used to say. Even she didn't know much about his past. He'd left it behind, built a new life far away, and buried whatever it was that had caused him to leave. Yet something must have gone on gnawing at him, deep inside.

Ellie would probably never know what his true feelings had been. But at least she could try to uncover the facts. If he did have another sister, she could track her down, put her in contact with Dot and Fran, though there was no telling what the result would be.

Explosive, probably, knowing Fran. That was what Dot had implied with her warnings.

But if Dot was so opposed to uncovering past secrets, why had she recommended a B&B owned by someone who knew Grandad Jack? It was hard to believe she wasn't aware of the connection. Dot was such a savvy old so and so.

Unless it was simply that Canterbury was such a small place that, as Bert said, everyone knew Canon Goodwin.

She stood up and went to the window. Outside it was dark except for pools of light under the lampposts. The street was silent.

Another explanation struck her. In Dot, just as in Dad, deeper currents ran beneath the surface. Maybe she, too, was using indirect means to point Ellie to the truth.

SOUTH LONDON, 1936-37

Jack was so absorbed in writing his sermon that the cries didn't register at first. The text about the sins of the fathers being visited on their children was a beastly one to preach from, and he was pretty sure that was why old Denham had passed it his way.

He struck through what he had written and ground his teeth in frustration. How to put across that our actions have consequences, while reassuring the congregation that we can trust in a loving and forgiving God? If he over-emphasised the fearful implications of sin he risked frightening the vulnerable. But unless he highlighted the need for repentance, those who saw church attendance as a payment on an insurance policy, would go away with their consciences unruffled.

Through the study window, open to let in the fresh spring air, came a horrifying scream. His first thought was of the abattoir – he was used to the squeals of animals when slaughtering took place. But that was on Tuesdays and Wednesdays. Sermon-writing day was Saturday.

Another cry sped him back to reality. It came not from outside, but from above his head.

Lillian! He leaped up, his senses alert.

Silence. Only the curtain sighed as it swelled and sucked flat again. From way in the distance a train hooted as its rhythmic rattling passed through the valley. He listened, still clutching his pen. The floorboards above him creaked, voices murmured and a low moan grew to a fearful shriek.

Jack tossed down the pen and began to pace. He must insist on seeing Lillian, even if mother-in-law Cullen and the midwife had forbidden it. How could they expect him to keep away while his wife screamed with pain? Women could die in childbirth, couldn't they? He ran his fingers across his forehead, wiped them on one sleeve and saw too late that they'd left an inky stain. He stared at it dumbly, while his mind reeled with the midwife's command late last evening.

'You've done your bit. This is women's work. If we need more water or towels we'll give you a shout. Otherwise please keep out of our way.'

As if it hadn't been bad enough to endure the months of pregnancy, his adorable wife wracked with nausea and swollen with hypertension. The bigger her belly had grown, the more miserably their pleasures had dwindled. Gone were the nights of passion, the tender caresses of early morning. Once Mrs Cullen had arrived, all remnants of domestic peace were upturned in an earthquake of activity. She had banished Jack to the guest room, installed herself on a camp bed beside Lillian, and taken over the running of the house. Meals were served promptly and eaten in silence.

Last night she'd allowed him to take a bowl of thin gruel to where Lillian lay in bed as the labour pains began. He bent to kiss her, breathing the warm, citrusy smell of her skin.

'Not long now,' she said. Pregnancy had made her more beautiful than ever, filled out her cheeks and given them a rosy bloom.

'Thank goodness.'

He slipped his hand under the sheet and rested it on her belly. Between them they'd produced a new life. It was both wonderful and terrifying. When the midwife appeared, brandishing a thermometer, Jack snatched out his hand, took down Lilian's empty bowl and sought refuge in his study.

That night, much to his surprise, he'd slept surprisingly well and woken to the sound of women's voices. Business-like. Efficient. Enough to send a man packing.

As he'd crept downstairs, hoping to slip into the kitchen for breakfast and a quiet read of the newspaper, his mother-in-law had appeared, the sleeves of her blouse rolled to the elbow.

'Her waters broke during the night. We thought it best not to disturb you. If you are needed, we will call you.'

For hours since then he'd been shut in his study, wrestling with his sermon, just as Lillian wrestled with the interminable labour overhead. No, that was an ignoble thought. There could be no comparison.

Another shriek shrilled from the bedroom. He dashed into the hall and bounded upstairs. The bedroom door was ajar but Mrs Cullen's back blocked his view. As she stepped aside he saw the midwife thrusting apart Lillian's thighs. To his horror, the sheet was gory with blood. Dear Lord, let it not be true. She was bleeding to death.

He drew nearer. Lillian's skin was shiny and wet with perspiration. Her hands gripped the bars of the bedstead, her face was contorted with pain.

'Push,' the midwife said.

'I'm pushing! I'm bloody pushing!'

The sound of the blasphemy on his wife's lips made him

gasp, whether with shock or admiration he was not sure. But Mrs Cullen turned, saw him and thrust up her hand imperiously.

'Out!'

He hesitated. Blood smeared the midwife's forearms. Between her hands was something dark and slimy. She barked at Jack.

'Bring more hot water. Quick.'

He rushed down to the kitchen, convinced that he would never see his wife alive again. God was punishing him for his sins. A trickle of shame and self-pity chilled him. Of course, he had repented and mended his ways, but if someone had to die, it should be he, not Lillian. The thought that he would sacrifice his very life for her gave him new courage.

The kettle took an age to heat. He lit a cigarette and paced up and down, trying to make sense of the sounds above his head. More cries from Lillian. The midwife firing commands.

'Chin to chest and push! Bite on this!'

A grunt, a wail, a loud shriek. Then Mrs Cullen:

'Do as you're told, girl. You're not the first woman in the world to give birth.'

Silence. An awful silence that lasted an eternity.

Jack could bear it no longer. The water had only just begun to sing but he stubbed out his cigarette, seized the kettle and ran upstairs, slopping water over the threadbare carpet. As he reached the landing, he heard a yelp. It sounded like a fox cub, or a puppy if you trod on its foot. He raced into the bedroom, expecting to see Lillian gasping her last breaths.

'Hello,' she said with a smile.

It was a weak smile, her hair was damp and tangled, but she sat propped up on pillows. In her arms was a bundle, a white bundle with a small, sticky head.

'You have a daughter,' the midwife said. 'A fine little girl, seven pounds two ounces. Congratulations.'

Mrs Cullen raised her eyebrows as if to say, *A fat lot a man has done that deserves congratulation.* Her lips were drawn tight but her chest swelled with pride.

Jack pulled up a chair and sat beside Lillian.

'Are you all right? I was terribly worried.'

'Here.' She raised the bundle towards him, laughing at his awkwardness. 'Hold her. Go on.' A spasm of pain passed over her face and she clutched at her stomach.

'What's wrong?'

If this creature had hurt her, he would happily crush it.

'It's nothing. Go on, cradle her. She's yours, ours, our first. Isn't she gorgeous?'

Our first? Was she mad? Could she even think of putting them through this again?

He stared at the tiny face. It looked for all the world like a plum that had fallen from the tree and been left to shrivel. Tufts of damp hair sprouted from its head. Its eyes were a milky blue, and its little mouth opened in a circle. The fingers of its hands were as slender as skinned shrimps, the nails as tiny as the petals that fell from hawthorn blossom. He reached out his thumb and the little fingers curled around it. She was warm. She was soft. She was the most beautiful thing that he had ever seen.

'That's enough for now,' the midwife said. 'We need to get her to suckle and then let Mrs Goodwin rest. She's had a long labour and lost a lot of blood.'

Jack passed the baby back to Lillian and kissed the top of her head with a sheepish smile.

'I had no idea it would be so difficult.'

Mrs Cullen snorted.

'There's a man for you. They have all the pleasure and we have all the pain.'

'And while we're on the subject of pleasure,' said the midwife, 'you'll abstain from intercourse until I give you the go-ahead. Is that clear?'

Jack's eyes met Lillian's. She went on cooing at the baby and gave him a shrug. He surveyed the feminine forces rallied against him, their expressions victorious, unyielding. So he had served his purpose, had he, like a bull that is kept for stud? He'd produced what was necessary and was no longer needed. The tyranny of women had reduced his passion to a function.

He slunk out of the room, aware that his tail, metaphorically speaking, was between his legs. Humiliated and defeated, he returned to his study. It looked as if he would even have to make his own coffee.

By the end of May the weather was warmer, and on sunny days Lillian put the pram out in the garden. She could see it from the kitchen window while she washed the dishes. Shadows from the apple tree danced over the hood, and every now and then a butterfly landed on the quilt. If she heard a bee buzz she rushed outside with a tea towel and flapped it until all was safe and peaceful again.

Dorothy slept in the pram with her little fist curled tight. Sometimes she woke and gurgled, kicked her legs and wriggled so much that the covers fell off or tangled with her toes. When she was hungry the gurgle rose to a whimper, and when it grew more persistent, Lillian washed her hands and lifted her from the pram. It came quite naturally now to take one breast from her brassiere and hold the nipple for the baby to suck.

Her breasts were swollen, and the moment when Dorothy's lips fastened on them sent a sharp but exquisite pain into her flesh. As the milk started to flow and the sucking slipped to a soothing rhythm, an almost sensual pleasure flooded her. In the early days of their marriage, Jack's mouth on her breasts had thrilled her, too, but she no longer remembered whether that had the fullness and completeness, the sense of nurturing and being nurtured, that she experienced now. This too was love, she thought, only purer and simpler, and drawn from unfathomable depths.

The rhythm slowed, stopped, started fiercely again for a moment then loosened and fell slack as Dorothy slipped into sleep.

When the doorbell rang, she opened her eyes, sighed and closed them again, as if the world inside her head was more beautiful by far. Lillian stood up and adjusted her clothing. She held the tiny body against her own, rubbing one hand up and down the baby's back to release any bubbles of air.

'Aunty Violet's come to see you,' she said, slipping her palm over the silky head as she went to open the door. It squeaked on its hinges so she made a mental note to find the oil can. She'd asked Jack several times, but really it was easier to do things herself. You learned that when you grew up without a father.

Violet wore a soft, flowing dress with a narrow belt round the waist. She took off one glove and stroked the baby's cheek. Her amethyst engagement ring had been joined by a gold band.

'Oh, she's so soft. And she smells of vanilla. Can I hold her?'

Lillian passed little Dorothy to her aunt. 'I've just fed her, Vi. She might bring it up. Be careful of your nice new frock.'

'Do you like it? It's rayon crepe, quite the rage for daytime wear. George got it at a discount, and now that he's fashion buyer I get first pick.'

'Lucky you. Come on, let's have a cuppa, the kettle's just boiled.'

As they went into the kitchen, yellow liquid trickled from the baby's mouth onto Violet's shoulder.

'Oh, Vi, I'm so sorry. Here, dab it with this.'

Lillian handed her a cloth. After a few pats Dorothy let out a large burp and they both laughed. Violet sighed.

'Motherhood suits you, Lil. You're a natural.'

'You will be, too, Vi. Just you see. Give it time, you've only been married a few months.'

'It's not for want of trying.' Violet glanced over her shoulder and lowered her voice. 'Is Jack here?'

'He's gone to take the Young Wives' group. I gave it up while I was pregnant.'

'What a shame, they liked you so much, didn't they? I knew they would. See, all that worrying for nothing.'

'Yes, but they like him better.'

She measured a couple of scoops of tea leaves and poured boiling water into the pot.

'The Prodigy. Do you remember all those things we used to imagine about him?'

'How could I forget?'

'Well, that's what they think he is, some sort of hero who can do no wrong. You wouldn't believe the way people idolise him. Sometimes I think women go to church to worship the vicar, or the curate, in this case.'

'You're not jealous, are you?'

'Oh Jack doesn't even notice. He's friendly and charming to everyone, so wherever he goes, people take to him. Anyway, Mrs Denham says it's just human nature. Congregations are notoriously fickle. There's a saying that in the first year a vicar can do no wrong, and in the second he can do no right. But they always love a curate.'

Lillian carried the tea tray out to the garden. She wouldn't breathe a word to Violet, who was still in the throes of married bliss, but once you'd been together a while, your relationship mellowed from that first fiery passion to something more slow and tender. It was like moving into a new season, where you felt at ease with one another, contented to curl tummy to back in mutual comfort, needing neither words nor actions to know that you were no longer two, but one. Secretly, she preferred it that way.

On Dorothy's first birthday, Lillian baked a cake. It was a Victoria sponge made with eggs from Mrs Denham's hens, and she used cochineal to colour it pink. It sank in the middle but she filled the dent with butter icing. Jack always said the gooey bit was what he liked best.

Dorothy sat in her high chair and clapped her hands as they lit the candle and sang Happy Birthday. Jack showed her how to blow it out and she made a circle of her mouth, but there was more spluttering than air. He blew with her till the flame vanished. She insisted on eating her slice unaided, but most of it stuck to her fingers and smeared over her cheeks.

The little girl's hair had turned the colour of sand and her eyes were now grey like her father's. She had the rounded cheeks of the Goodwins, and Lillian could see glimpses of Jack's sisters when she laughed. How strange that the child had so many of his features but none of hers, as if she were no more than a mechanism to perpetuate his genes. However much she searched, she could find not a hint of the Cullen's dark wildness. Even Dorothy's placidity, like a gently gurgling stream, came from Jack's side of the family.

He adored her and she adored him. While he worked in his study, she sat happily in her playpen, stacked bricks or chewed on the ear of her teddy. But as soon as his door opened she pulled herself up and called to him. *Dada* was her first word, and soon it rang through her chatter again and again.

When she started to walk, she toddled towards him and hung onto his knee till he scooped her into his lap. Soon she learned to take out the stud at the back of his dog collar. To her delight he let her lift it off and put the white circle on his head like a crown. She loved nothing more than to be cuddled by him, and often fell asleep while he stroked her curls or whispered sweet nothings.

At bedtime Lillian bathed her in a tub by the fire. Most nights, when she'd tucked her into the cot, she read her a story or sang a nursery rhyme. Then she switched off the light and tip-toed downstairs to the sitting room, where Jack sat reading the newspaper.

Sometimes they listened to the wireless, but the news was ever more depressing. Unemployment had reached a record high, and the new King was carrying on with that dreadful American divorcee.

Occasionally in the evenings, or even for an hour or two in the afternoon while Dorothy had her nap, Lillian read a book. She felt guilty for missing flower arranging or the committee for the village fete. But if Jack could read novels when he should have been doing his report on the leaky roof for the Archdeacon, why shouldn't she put her own interests first?

She'd realised what he was up to when he snapped shut a book as she took in his coffee. Later, when she was dusting, she saw it under a pile of papers. *The Thirty Nine Steps*. The following week it was Kipling's *Kim*.

To enrol for classes was no longer an option for Lillian. Several evenings each week Jack had parish clubs or meetings and she couldn't leave the baby alone. If the meetings were held in their house she had to make tea and serve sandwiches or biscuits.

Even Mrs Denham believed that a woman's first duty was to her husband and children. Deep down, Lillian knew that she no longer had the energy or motivation to study. Even so, one thing was clear in her mind. Her own opportunities for education might have slipped away, but she would make sure that her daughter didn't suffer the same fate.

Towards the end of his second year as curate, a letter came for Jack from Leonard Barnes. For a moment the name stumped him. The handwriting was vaguely familiar, but it was the mention of Cheshunt College that took him back to the common room on that summer afternoon and the bet on the thirty-nine articles. It was the very day he'd heard that they'd accepted him for his curacy, which was an uncanny coincidence, because the purpose of Barnes' letter was to offer him a job.

Offer was perhaps too strong a word. He re-read the paragraph where Barnes explained his reason for writing.

I seem to remember that prior to training for the ministry you were in the navy, which, if my memory is correct, would make you an ideal candidate for a post which is soon to become vacant.

Jack glanced up from the notepaper with its spidery, slanting scrawl. The thin winter sun barely touched the windows of his study and the only heat came from an electric fire. As his eye caught its glow, an image of a port in the Indian Ocean came vividly to mind.

Bombay was it? Singapore? The intensity of light, the sizzling heat, the smells of oil and tar and coconut and spices, the clanking of chains and cranes, the bustle of traffic, cries, shouts and laughter, hit him so clearly that it was like a revelation. Until this moment he had never once thought of returning to that life, or regretted leaving it. But as Barnes' letter transported him there he realised how deeply he missed it.

Of course it was impossible. His brain ran through the objections even as his fingers, numbed by the cold, struggled to re-fold the letter.

He was a married man with a child who was the joy of his life. It was unthinkable that he should leave his family. Whatever would they do? True, his curacy was shortly to end, and the time had come for him to find a new post, but they'd always assumed it would be in a parish of his own.

Uneasiness niggled him. This would mean a move to a strange place and people, with the added difficulty that the vicar's wife would be expected to play a part in church life. Lillian seemed to think she was unsuited to that role. But at least they'd be provided with a home, which was more than the navy would offer. Unless there were married quarters.

He placed the letter to one side and began to pace. The carpet had worn thin between his desk and the window. Their current house, sparsely furnished as it was, came with the curacy.

But a vicarage they would have to kit out themselves. Most were rambling old buildings, Victorian mainly, and Jack's stipend would never run to all the furniture needed to fill them. True, Violet and George could buy at a discount from John Lewis, and Lillian had suggested that they might try an auction house. If they were lucky, some of the wealthier parishioners might even pass on the odd piece or two.

His eyes slid back to the letter. He unfolded it again and scanned Barnes' words in one crucial paragraph.

You will be aware that the remuneration for a naval chaplain is considerably more generous than that of a parish priest, as it goes some way to compensate for what many would consider to be the inconvenience and deprivation of a life at sea.

Jack walked across to the window and peered at the tiny yard between their house and the street. The paving slabs were uneven. He'd promised Lillian that he'd replace them, but never seemed to find time. She worried that Dorothy would trip and hurt herself, but he could see no real danger. Just dry soil and the stubby stems of rose bushes, bare except for thorns and the remains of a late bloom.

What exactly was the pay of a naval chaplain, he wondered? If it brought in enough for Lillian to rent a small flat and cover her daily needs, it might even leave them enough to save. His expenses would be negligible, as on board ship everything would be provided.

No, the very thought gave him a chill. Now that he'd tasted the delights of marriage, how could he leave the comforts of home? To sleep alone in a narrow bunk would be worse than those years of celibacy. True, he would no longer be a common sailor, confined to cramped quarters amongst the snores and farts of other men. A chaplain would have his own cabin and the comradeship of dinner and port with the officers. There would be the usual masculine conversation and banter, the jokes and the leg-pulling, the fresh salty tang of the ocean, the excitement of unfamiliar shores emerging from the horizon and taking the form of strange cities with new colours, sounds, smells and tongues.

Naturally a chaplain could not partake in the pleasures that ports in faraway places offered to sailors. That was out of the question. Still, one could visit sites of antiquity and culture. He could picture himself on a camel bound for the pyramids, or hunting for bargains in some souk, choosing an embroidered shawl for his lovely wife, trinkets for his daughter.

He looked again at the letter. Was the appointment for a fixed length of time? Five or six years would be far too long. One or two, though, might be feasible. Barnes didn't say exactly, only that it was likely to be on a temporary basis, as deployment of all vessels was being reassessed in the light of political developments in Europe, not least the incessant demands for rearmament by Germany.

War did not bear thinking of and in Jack's opinion those who claimed it was inevitable were scaremongers. He would never consider a naval chaplaincy if there were the slightest risk of war. Hitler was a nasty piece of work and Oswald Moseley wasn't much better, but plenty of people opposed them. Besides, the Anglo-German Naval Agreement had fixed the size of German fleet. It was inconceivable that Britain would engage in a second conflict after all the slaughter of the first.

From the kitchen he heard Lillian tell Dorothy to get down from the chair or she would fall and bang her head. Smells of Irish stew and boiled potatoes drifted his way.

He glanced at the clock. Twenty to one. He'd have just enough time to write a quick note before lunch. Nothing definite, of course. Simply to ask for more details, how long, how much, that sort of thing.

His mind moved back to the possible paths ahead. Until he knew the facts it would be better to say nothing to Lillian that might upset her. But if the salary were generous, and the time short enough, there would be a persuasive argument for accepting Barnes' offer.

If, and only if those conditions were met, he told himself. And, of course, if it was God's will.

CANTERBURY, 2010

At a quarter to eleven Ellie turned into the street where the Whitakers lived. She paused under the shade of a sycamore tree and scanned the houses on the opposite side. They were tall, built of red brick, Victorian, she guessed. Their bay windows reflected the ripples of passing cars, while they faced her like a watchful barrier, both forbidding and daring her to cross.

She took out the slip of paper and checked the house number. A shiver chilled her. She felt like a spy on the edge of enemy territory. These people lived in an alien sphere among cloisters and precincts, Archbishops in mitres, clergy in robes, rites and rituals from centuries past. It was one thing to come to Canterbury as a tourist and admire the beauty of church buildings, but quite another to penetrate its inner workings.

You're a researcher, she told herself. There's no reason it should touch you. Yes, but the family connection took her deeper, as if that seductive but oppressive belief system had woven itself into her genes.

She looked again at the row of silent houses. Sneak away and never know fact from fiction? Or steel herself to take a risk?

A motorbike stuttered past and she darted across in its wake towards the wrought iron gate in a low brick wall. Her hand touched the latch. If it opened easily, she would go in. If it was stiff, she'd pretend she'd made a mistake and belt round the corner.

The gate swung smoothly on well-oiled hinges. The gravel crunched under her sneakers like thunder claps.

A brass knocker in the shape of a fish gleamed on the door. She lifted it, let it go. Footsteps sounded from inside. She had no idea what to expect – did ministers wear robes when they were at home?

The door opened to reveal an elderly man with silver hair, a newspaper tucked under his arm. He wore an open-necked shirt, a cardigan, corduroy trousers. A pencil stuck out from behind one ear.

'Aha, you must be Miss Goodwin.'

'Reverend Whitaker?'

'Come in, my dear, delighted to see you.'

His bony hand shook hers vigorously. He closed the front door and led her down a dark hallway.

'My wife is in the conservatory. I hope it won't be too hot for you, but you must be used to the heat down under.'

Mrs Whitaker was watering plants that grew like a miniature jungle under a hexagonal glass roof. She dried her hands on her apron and greeted Ellie, as bright and chirpy as a little bird. Her hair was as white as her husband's, but she barely came up to his shoulder.

'Well, well, what a lovely surprise. Canon Goodwin's granddaughter. Now, it's Arnold who knew him better, so I'll go and make us a nice cup of coffee and leave you two to chat.'

She bustled off to the kitchen. Ellie sat opposite her host, in a wicker armchair, and politely answered his questions. Yes, Australia could be very hot, and yes, there were sometimes bush

170

fires, and sharks, too, and crocodiles, though people were only occasionally eaten by them.

Mrs Whitaker reappeared with milky coffee and digestive biscuits on a plate with a doily, then hurried out again. Ellie sipped her coffee and listened with an unexpected glow of pride as Rev Whitaker praised Grandad Jack. He had brought the college through its early struggles with funding shortages and inadequate facilities, to establish it as an institution that was respected throughout the Anglican world.

'Everyone admired his dedication and efficiency, and above all his integrity.'

Her antennae were alert for irony but she couldn't detect any.

'What's more, he was such a lovely person. No one had a bad word to say about him.'

As the praises continued, Ellie's head bobbed in polite appreciation. It was flattering to hear such good reports of Grandad Jack, but the longer the list grew, the more she dreaded shattering this old man's illusions. Her jaw ached with smiling. The air was warm and oppressive. Her eyes began to glaze. A bluebottle hit the glass with an angry buzz.

She placed her empty cup and saucer on a glass-topped table beside a faded photo of three children, one black, one white, one Asian. Silence gathered around them. Even the fly stopped its rasping and settled on a curtain. It was time to ask the crucial question or leave. Nerves and the coffee swirled inside her as she moistened her mouth to speak.

'Rev Whitaker, there's something I wanted to ask you. It's a bit delicate and I hope it won't sound too shocking, but . . .'

Her voice startled the bluebottle into a new fit of fury, and the old man tilted his head.

'My good ear,' he said.

Relieved that no one else could hear her, Ellie raised the volume and told him that while researching her father's early life, she'd stumbled across rumours of unhappiness in the family.

'As far as I can tell, it was during the time that my grandfather worked at the college, and had something to do with another employee – a Miss Latimer. So I wondered if you knew what happened. There was talk of a relationship, and I'd like to establish the truth. You see, I think there was a child. And if there was, then I'd like to find her.'

Rev Whitaker laced his fingers. The light in his eyes was shrewd but gentle.

'With a view to what exactly?'

His question took Ellie by surprise. She snatched at the first response that sprang to mind.

'So, my aunts are both getting on in age and I think it might bring them . . . closure,' she said, wincing at the cliché, 'to know the truth about their father. And if it is true, to try and right the wrongs of the past.'

Rev Whitaker rubbed his chin thoughtfully. The bluebottle buzzed, then fell silent.

'Let me ask my wife. She worked at the college, too, for a while. In fact that was where we met. She was on the administrative staff and may well have known Miss Latimer. The faculty was full of stuffy old men like me, I'm afraid, and the name rings no bells.'

Ellie sank back against the cushions while her host shuffled out to the kitchen. Her heartbeat was racing and it took several deep breaths to calm it. All this personal stuff was scary and made her want to run back to the safety of the archives. But something held her, like the time when Dad had taught her to swim, and she'd come up spluttering, trying to cling to him, but he'd stepped back so that she had to thrash forward in order to reach him. How exhilarated she'd felt in the brief moment when she'd stayed afloat on her own.

So that was it. That was why Dad had set her a challenge and not explained what to do. It was his way of coaxing her to the place where he knew that she needed to be. And here she was now, just as he had intended, exploring the past through the memories of living people.

'Goodness, it's hot in here.' Mrs Whitaker bustled in and opened the French windows. The bluebottle whizzed out and fresher air drifted in.

'Now my dear, how can I help you?'

'Your husband mentioned that you worked at the college, too, and I wondered if you knew a Miss Latimer?'

'Oh yes, Maureen. She left soon after I started, so I didn't know her well. She was Canon Goodwin's secretary, I believe.'

Mrs Whitaker's expression had the same calm impartiality as her husband's. Its implication seemed to be that any worthy woman who worked for the church was above suspicion.

Maybe, thought Ellie, but not above a fall from grace. Her finger traced the rough edge of a nail as she deliberated her next step. If there had been a scandal, these people would almost certainly have closed ranks to keep it secret. Somehow she had to break through that barrier of loyalty and discretion to get to the truth.

A sudden boldness gripped her.

'Do you remember why she left? You see, my aunt told me that she was pregnant.'

It was pure inspiration, but the direct approach cracked Mrs Whitaker's composure. She flinched, then let out a sigh as her shoulders relaxed.

'I did hear noise on the jungle drums that she'd left under a cloud. Though it might have been no more than office gossip.'

'In those days, I suppose, a pregnancy in a single woman would have caused quite a scandal?'

'Yes, indeed.'

'Do you have any idea what happened to her after she left?'

'Goodness, it was a very long time ago. Let me see, yes, there was one thing. A couple of years later, we had a query from the Church Pensions' Office in London about one of our staff who had retired. To my surprise, it was Maureen who made the call. Apparently she'd moved up there to work.'

'Really? The church took her back, even after she'd "left under a cloud?"'

Mrs Whitaker's eyes met Ellie's.

'I honestly don't know what their policy would have been, but if we practice what we preach, then forgiveness and a second chance are what Christianity is all about. And who knows, she might have had help, good references, a recommendation. Everyone agreed that she was a very efficient secretary. But of course this is pure speculation.'

Rev Whitaker appeared in the doorway.

'Any luck?'

'Yes, thanks. You've both been amazingly helpful.'

Ellie beamed them a smile. The interview had gone so much better than she'd dared to hope. She now knew Miss Latimer's first name and Mrs Whitaker had confirmed, or at least not denied, her suspicions. Now all that she needed was the date.

'Just one more question, if that's okay, then I won't take up any more of your time. Do you remember exactly when Maureen left?'

'Oh, yes, it would have been nineteen fifty-five. I'm sure about that, because I started in the autumn of fifty-four, and it could only have been a few months later.'

Nineteen fifty-five. Just as Dot had suggested. Only five or six years before Dad had left for Australia. The age, more or less, of the little girl in the photo.

'That's awesome. Thank you both so much.'

She felt like giving these dear old people a hug. It looked as if she'd hit gold. A rough scenario was sketching itself in her mind. Around nineteen-sixty Dad must have heard about his father's love-child, and instead of returning to Oxford, shock and disgust had propelled him to emigrate.

'I'm sorry I couldn't be of more help to you,' Mrs Whitaker said as she showed Ellie out.

'Oh, but you have been. Far more than you could imagine.'

It took less than twenty minutes to find the information she needed. Her phone was out of credit, and besides, she fancied a stronger coffee, so she went to a cyber cafe in one of the narrow streets near the cathedral. It was in a half-timbered building with an overhanging first floor supported by carved struts. Inside was a seating area with leather couches and a row of computers along one wall.

She ordered a cappuccino at the counter then logged onto the internet. All her doubts and hesitations had evaporated in the heat of excitement. This was like an archaeological dig magnified a hundred times, and now the search was not for distant relics, but for real people, flesh and blood relatives, Dad's half-sister, her aunt.

When she googled *birth certificates* it took her straight to the government webpage. A glance through the relevant information showed that it was even easier than she'd thought. The law allowed any member of the public to access records of births, marriages or deaths. Copies of certificates could be ordered for a small charge.

A click led her to the relevant link. She knew that illegitimate births were usually registered under the mother's surname. The father had to give consent for his name to be used, and with Grandad's position in the church, that was unlikely.

Luckily Latimer was not a common name. Good thing it wasn't Smith or Jones.

She entered *Maureen Latimer* and left the father's name blank, selected Kent as the county, and approximate dates between January and December 1955. Almost immediately a result showed on the screen. *Amanda M. Latimer, born in November 1955, in Dartford, Kent*. The mother's name was Maureen but, as expected, the father's name wasn't given.

It seemed almost too easy. She leaned back in the chair and considered her options. To be absolutely sure, she should widen the search. Maybe Maureen had been taken further away to have her baby. She extended the place option countrywide, and half a dozen or so births appeared for babies with parents named Latimer. But in every case the surname was the father's, except for a boy called Norman, who was born in Scunthorpe.

She felt uncannily certain that Amanda M was the one. The next step would be to request a copy of the birth certificate, but for that there was a fee. Should she order it now and pay with her credit card, or discuss it with Dot and Fran first?

Why delay any longer? Her aunts had spent most of their lives denying the truth. If she went ahead now, the proof would be with them within a few days.

Her stomach rumbled and she realised that it was hours since breakfast. In the chiller they had a selection of salads and quiches, and above it a board listed today's specials. Pasta with pine nuts, spinach, sun-dried tomatoes and parmesan shavings sounded good.

'And I'll have one of those Sicilian Lemonades.'

As soon as she'd finished eating she went back to the screen, completed the request for a certificate and clicked *submit*. Mission accomplished. By the time she reached Dot's, the evidence would be on its way and her aunts could decide for themselves if they wanted to take the search any further.

Or she could go it alone. Why not? After all, Amanda was Dad's sister, too, a living person, out there in the real world. What a scoop it would be if she came up with a current address. Then, maybe, while she was still in England, they could all get together.

The online telephone directories showed a number of Latimers but none of them tallied. Of course, Amanda would be in her fifties by now and might well have changed her surname on marriage. That would complicate the search, which was a pain because other people were waiting for the computers. Anyhow, after all this sitting around, Ellie needed fresh air and exercise.

She logged off, paid the bill, and went outside on more of a high than she'd felt for months. A tour bus from Hungary was unloading passengers by the cathedral gates. The street glowed in the afternoon sun and the buildings were ablaze with flower tubs and hanging baskets. Groups of tourists lounged at cafe tables, a busker whipped up a violin concerto and a clown juggled skittles.

This place looked like fun and she might have been tempted to stay, but now that she was hot on the trail, wild horses wouldn't hold her.

It was later, back at the B&B, that it struck her. A tiny but significant fact. She'd got through the whole day without once thinking of Josh.

The rush hour was over by the time Ellie crossed London. When she reached Somerset the sky had faded through crimson to a lemony glow. The spell of good weather had turned the fields golden, and where the corn had been cut they bristled with stubble, scattered with rolls of black plastic.

She didn't want to bother Dot, so blew twenty pounds on a taxi from the station. Her money was disappearing fast, but what mattered more was success in her search and the opportunities it might bring.

The Audi stood in the drive, but the cottage windows were dark. Had Dot gone out in someone else's car?

As Ellie let herself in, Clio came to greet her, and she crouched down to stroke her.

'Hey, Clio, how you going? Have you missed me? Strange smells, hey?'

On the table Dot had left a note telling her to help herself to food from the fridge.

She found some lasagne, span it in the microwave, tossed a few salad leaves with dressing and opened a beer. In the sitting room, she stretched out on the sofa with the plate on her lap and her bare feet on a cushion. This place felt like home now, cosy and welcoming. A few days away had made all the difference.

178

She opened a window and the night air brought a waft of newly mown hay from the fields. The sky was dark, pricked by a few stars. A car passed and the lights of another swept into the drive. It was the blue Rover. Ellie chuckled to herself. So Raymond and Dot had been on a date. But as the key turned in the lock, the car reversed and drove away, and Dot came in alone, her cheeks flushed.

Had she drunk a bit too much wine? Or was it being with Raymond that had affected her? In her navy silk dress and pearls, her hair swept up into an elegant twist, she looked surprisingly attractive for a woman in her seventies. She put down her handbag

'How was Canterbury? Did you have an enjoyable time?'

'Awesome. How about you?'

'Yes, very pleasant. We went for dinner in a pub up in the Mendips. It was really rather good.' She seemed a little flustered. 'Excuse me while I check the answer phone.'

Oh my, thought Ellie as she carried her empty plate and glass to the kitchen, Dot's as frisky as a kitten. A moment later her aunt appeared, patted her hair and reached absent-mindedly for the kettle.

'Would you like a hot drink before bed? I'm going to have a tisane.'

'Okay. Shall I make it?'

They took their mugs into the sitting room. Dot sank into an armchair, kicked off her shoes and rested her stockinged feet on the stool, rubbing the toes of one foot against the other.

'Frances left a message while I was out. She has decided to stay in Devon for the time being and says you're welcome to visit whenever you want. I should warn you she sounds a bit fraught. Now tell me about Canterbury.'

'Wow, it's an amazing place. And guess what? I've made a discovery.'

A flicker of alertness passed over Dot's face.

'It seems that Miss Latimer – her first name is Maureen – did have an illegitimate child.'

Dot put down her tisane and nodded slowly.

'Well, I can't say I'm surprised.'

Ellie took the computer printout from her bag and passed it across, watching Dot's reaction.

'Of course the father isn't named, and I guess only DNA tests could prove conclusively who he was.'

The light from the lamp touched Dot's cheek. She lifted her eyes to Ellie's. 'There's no need for that. The child was almost certainly my father's.'

Ellie gasped. Was it the evening out with Raymond that had brought about this change, or simply the fact that Fran wasn't here? She listened, spellbound, as Dot continued.

'Of course I have no proof, only instinct.'

Dot began to explain that she'd always had suspicions, but never known for sure. Then later, after both her parents had died, she'd found the photo of the little girl while clearing their possessions. She'd sent it to Jimmy in Australia. Neither of them knew how their father had come by it, or if the child was his. But it had brought back vividly that awful evening when the two women had turned up at their house in Canterbury.

'You might find it hard to credit,' Dot said, 'but although I was almost twenty at the time, I was unbelievably innocent. And yet, when I opened the door to them, mother and daughter demanding to see my father, I had a dreadful foreboding of why they'd come.'

She said that the younger woman wasn't visibly pregnant, but her embarrassment, and the mother's distress, made Dot suspect the awful possibility. When sounds of argument came from her father's study, she put on her coat and ran from the house.

'My mother was out and I dreaded her coming back while those women were there. But I couldn't find her. I must have wandered around the streets for hours. So I gave up and went home. All the windows were dark, apart from a light in Jimmy's bedroom, where he was swotting for his exams.'

'So Dad was there when the women arrived?'

'No, he was out at choir practice. But he heard our mother screeching hysterically as he came up the street. He tried to creep in unseen but she burst out of our father's study, her face red, streaming with tears, and screamed at him:

"Did you answer the door to those women? They've accused Daddy of fathering a child!"'

Dot paused to gather breath.

'Then she ran off sobbing, and our father came out and told him to get on with his prep. "Don't bother Mummy," he said. "She's in a bit of a state."'

'So Grandad didn't admit or deny it?'

'No, he went back to his study and Jimmy went up his room. None of us ever talked about it again.'

Ellie sat, dumbfounded. The emotions Dot had described – shock, anger, outrage – burned in her, too, but for different reasons. Dad had set her a challenge, even though he'd known every detail right from the start!

She pointed to the computer printout, barely able to keep her voice steady. 'I can't believe that you both knew about this, but never breathed a word to anyone.'

Dot leaned her head back on the armchair and closed her eyes. She looked old, frail, weary. Her chest lifted and dropped, the navy silk dress as crumpled as used wrapping paper. In a low, tired voice she began to explain how she'd convinced herself that the whole episode had never happened.

'I was in denial, I think they call it now. It was the shame, probably.' Her hands worked in her lap as she forced out the words. She simply hadn't wanted to believe that her father could have done such a thing, and besides, she was worried for his reputation.

'You see,' she said and her eyes opened to meet Ellie's across the shadowy room, 'I loved him. I told myself that anyone can make a mistake and that when they do, we should forgive them.'

A hot wave of anger surged up through Ellie. Wasn't that more or less what Josh had said when she'd told him about Brad? 'Forgiveness clears the way for reconciliation.' It was the sort of glib comment that he excelled in. Forget all the shit as if it had never happened. She seized the empty mugs and turned towards the kitchen.

'I'm not surprised that Dad emigrated. Or that he didn't want anything to do with churches and all their religious hypocrisy.'

She strode out. Wearily Dot followed her and when she spoke, it was with effort.

'Ellie, I daresay your father wanted to forget the whole sordid episode just as I did. But his way of dealing with it was different from mine.'

He was younger, she said, more impressionable, a sensitive and pious sixteen-year old, a proud and adoring son. In a single moment his illusions were shattered, his confidence in the values he'd been brought up with, shaken.

'But speaking for myself, I can only say that although it made me very unhappy, I never once blamed what had happened on the church.'

'Well, Dad did. He wouldn't let us have religious education or go anywhere near a church. He said that too many parents brainwash their children.'

Dot raised her eyebrows.

'Isn't that brainwashing in reverse?'

'No – it's having the courage of your convictions.'

She was too churned up to say more. Clio was whining to go out and her own irritation was about to explode.

But Dot put on her headmistressy face and gave her a smile, half in sympathy, half in challenge.

'When a clergyman does something wrong, people stop going to church. But when Dr Shipman killed all those patients, we didn't stop going to the doctor.'

'That's different!'

Exasperation smouldered. Clio scratched at the door, but they both ignored her. Ellie sighed.

'Look, Dot, the point is that Grandad Jack had an illegitimate child. Fran thinks so, Dad must have thought so, and now even you've admitted it. That child is a real person. She's your sister. So the question is, do you want to find her, or don't you? It's as simple as that. The ball's in your court, I've done all I can.'

Clio started to yelp and Dot opened the door to let her out. Ellie offered to go with her, but Dot said she'd be all right on her own for a minute or two. She began to tell Ellie that for years she'd barely given a thought to the fact that a half-sibling, their own flesh and blood, might be alive somewhere. If their paths had crossed they wouldn't even have known.

'But as I've got older, my feelings have changed. When you've had your three score years and ten, you begin to review your life. You want to set matters straight while you still have the chance. Partly out of curiosity, I suppose, to know the truth before you die.'

She forced a smile. 'But more and more I want to find her because I realise that she must have suffered, too. Through no fault of her own. I'd like to do something to put that right.'

'What about Fran?'

'Fran?'

'She's suffered just as much, hasn't she? Doesn't she need help?'

'I've tried, Ellie, I swear I've tried. But Fran is, well you've seen her . . . so defensive, so prickly. Whatever I say, she takes the wrong way.'

'I think she's lonely. And unhappy.'

'Yes, I daresay. She's had husbands, boyfriends galore, but as far as I could see they were all a waste of time. And Janis is a lovely girl – well, she's a grown woman now – but she's got her own life and is rarely there for her mother.'

The clock in the hall struck twelve long chimes, way past Dot's bedtime, but she appeared not to notice.

'She has no one, I have no one.'

'There's Raymond.'

Dot laughed softly.

'Ah, Raymond. That's another story.' She gathered her book, glasses and water to take upstairs. 'I think we've had enough revelations for one day.'

Outside in the garden Clio was growling and snuffling at the hedge. The night air carried a strong, rank odour that might be fox. The sky was starless, thick with cloud, but with a tinge of a sulphur glow from street lights in the village.

Back home in Sydney they'd be starting a new day. The urge to be there still pulled at Ellie, but less than before. Despite the irritations, something kept her here.

'What you start, you finish,' Dad used to say. 'Giving up is a euphemism for failure.'

She followed Clio around the shadowy lawn. Dad's secrecy exasperated her, but it couldn't outweigh the good things about him that she loved. He was the one who'd always understood her, seen how she struggled and tried to strengthen her.

Whenever she'd wavered in her studies or was unsure of her career path, he'd always encouraged her with maxims like that one. But neither of them could have predicted its significance to her here. She had come to England to dig up the past and, boy, had she found secrets, but they weren't inanimate objects covered with dirt. They were the lives and emotions of two old ladies, and now that she'd exposed them she owed it to them to continue. The dead were dead, but the living still needed make sense of life.

An owl hooted. The trees were motionless, the flowerbeds sunk in darkness. It was airless, humid, suffocating. Clio gave up her scratching and trotted towards the house. Ellie was about to follow when her mobile bleeped.

1 message: Josh. In UK at wkend. Give u a buzz?

She stared at the glow of the screen as the blood pounded in her ears. Just when she'd forgotten him, he'd barged back into her life. Suddenly the past seemed very safe territory compared with the present.

She wiped the palms of her hands on her jeans, and keyed in a reply.

OK.

No, that was too abrupt. She added: *Wd be great to see you.*

Deleted it.

OK was too little but she couldn't think what else to put without giving away the ridiculous swirl of hope and excitement that scattered all reason. Anyhow, her fingers were trembling too much.

Long after she'd clicked *send* her pulse went on racing as questions and objections whirled in her head.

People didn't come all this way for a weekend, did they? But Josh wasn't people. Josh was Josh. But why was he coming? Where was he staying? For how long?

It did and it didn't matter. It meant everything and nothing. It kept her awake half the night.

SOUTHERN ENGLAND, 1938-40

'I don't understand it,' said Mrs Cullen for the third time that morning. They were sitting on Hay Tor in the clear autumn sunshine that Lillian so loved. The moor, purple with heather, buzzed with a few late bees.

'If she goes on like this, I'll go completely barmy,' Lillian muttered to herself. She drew little Dorothy closer and straightened her dress, which had got caught under her coat. Thank goodness the old lady's visit was nearly over and she'd soon go back to Streatham.

'What don't you understand, Mum?'

'Oh, nothing.'

Mrs Cullen stared into the distance. Her hat, a bit like Lillian's cakes that sank in the middle, perched on her head. A gust of wind might have scooped it off had it not been for the ferocious pins.

'Go on. There must be something. You keep saying it. What have I done now?'

'You? Did I say you? The world doesn't revolve around you.'

Dear Lord, give me patience, thought Lillian as she watched Dorothy sit on the ground in a patch of mud. Let her get her dress dirty. What did she care?

'So what is it then? What don't you understand?'

Mrs Cullen held her back straight and lifted her chin as if making a stoic attempt to be tolerant.

'It strikes me it's a strange husband who leaves his wife with a baby and goes off to sea.'

'Dorothy's not a baby. She's two and a half.'

So that was it, the old crow. Getting at Jack again.

'But who am I to judge? He's knows what's right and wrong, I suppose. A minister of the church, not a mere mortal like me.'

Lillian picked a piece of heather and stroked Dorothy's cheek with it.

'Tickles,' the little girl said and prised it from her hand.

'Dad left you when he went in the army and you had five children.'

'That was different. He had to defend his country, and anyway he went to Flanders, not gallivanting half way across the world.' A flicker of distaste passed over her mouth. 'Goodness only knows what terrible diseases they might give him out there.'

What diseases? Who might? What was she trying to insinuate? A rush of heat sent Lillian's neck flaming. She scrambled to her feet and led Dorothy towards some Dartmoor ponies that had gathered to graze, their tails flicking off flies.

'Look at the horses, darling.'

'Want stroke them.'

'All right, then, if they'll let us. We'll have to be quiet, though, so we don't frighten them.'

Anything to get away from the old witch. If this went on much longer, she would commit a murder. The worst thing was that she missed Jack terribly, but would never admit it to her mother. She bit her lip, fighting the tears.

'Why you crying, Mummy?'

'I'm not crying, it's all right, my love.' She brushed a hand over her eyes. 'Look, the horses are watching you.'

The ponies' heads turned, their jaws still munching, ears alert.

'Why, Mummy, why?'

'They've heard us, that's all. We mustn't go too close, or we'll scare them. They're wild ponies. They live on the moor.'

'Why?'

'They like it here. They can go where they want for miles and miles.'

That's what I would like to do, Lillian thought, live wild and free with no one to bother me, not cooped up in a tiny flat with Mother watching every move. Nag, nag, nag, all day long. 'How some people find time to read while there's work to be done, is a mystery to me.' The washing was never clean enough. 'Scrub, girl. A bit of elbow grease won't hurt anyone. The dirt won't move itself.'

Whenever a postcard came from Jack with a scene of some colourful far-off place, Mrs Cullen huffed through her nose.

'Well, at least he finds time to write to you.'

Or when morning sickness struck, and she caught Lillian leaning over the sink, retching and sweating:

'Men have it easy, I'd say. Give them a dose of what they put us through and see how they like it.'

One of the ponies whinnied and stamped its hoof. The others swung round, tossed their heads, and they all bolted, tails and manes streaming in the wind.

'Why horses go, Mummy?'

'Why? Because they want to, that's why.'

Lillian pointed clear across the moor towards Plymouth, the sea hazy beyond it.

'Look. That's where Daddy's ship is. Out on the bright blue sea.'

'Daddy ship? Why?'

'Because…because…oh, I don't know. Look, there's Grandma waving to you.'

When they went back, the old dear seemed more cheerful.

'Did I tell you about the new cabinet in the kitchen?' she asked Lillian. 'George put it in.'

'Did he?'

'He's very handy like that.'

'Good for him. Lucky old Violet.'

Her mother darted her a look.

'Yes, he's a good boy. Like a son to me. Nothing's too much for him.'

'Please spare me,' mumbled Lillian, stifling a groan as her mother continued the eulogy. She was fond of her brother-in-law, but if anything was calculated to turn her against him, it was hearing the old lady sing his praises.

She sprang to her feet.

'We'd better be going, Mum. We don't want to miss the last bus home and have to walk, do we?'

In the evening, when she'd put Dorothy to bed, Lillian sat by the window to read. The sash had frayed and the wood had swollen, so it only opened half way, but it let in the cooling air and sounds of the dockyard in Devonport. They had been busier lately with long convoys carrying freight or naval recruits on training.

'We'll be at war before the year's out, you mark my words,' Mrs Cullen said from the armchair where she sat knitting. Click,

click, click went her needles as the maroon wool flicked between them.

'Oh, don't say that.'

Lillian lowered her book. War meant darkness and misery. A father who never came back.

'Mr Chamberlain said it'll be all right now.'

'Humph,' said her mother. 'Mr Chamberlain.'

Plymouth had always been a busy place, Lillian told herself. What with the Admiralty, the dockyard and the transatlantic seaport, it always bustled with activity. Her mother simply wasn't used to it. Besides, the old dear relished in spreading gloom and doom. In a minute she'd have sunk Jack and his vessel to the bottom of the ocean.

Right on cue Mrs Cullen ended her row of knitting, changed needles and released another barb.

'Hardly the time to be on a battleship.'

'They're not at war, Mother, they're only on routine exercises. In any case it won't be for much longer. Jack'll be home soon.

'I should think so, too, with you in your condition. You'll have your work cut out then, with two of them to contend with.'

What, two husbands? Lillian could have joked, but a glance at her mother told her it was unwise. She took up her book and pretended to read. The uncertainty of the future was a subject to avoid. Thoughts of a return to parish life were as daunting as the months of loneliness still to endure without Jack.

Which was worse, she asked herself, to push Dorothy's pram through the streets of a strange town and come back to an empty house, or to cope with the demands of being Mrs Vicar? At least the locals here in Plymouth were friendly, but that wasn't the same as a husband to go out for a stroll with, or to welcome her home.

Not that the old battle-axe would understand. You made your bed. Now you'll have to lie in it, was her philosophy.

In her bleakest moments, Lillian thought fondly of the South London parish where everyone had eventually accepted her. Such laughs they'd had at the Young Wives' Group, once all the holy stuff, as they called it, was finished and they could have tea and a chat. Dear Mrs Denham had helped her tirelessly, given advice and encouragement, boosted her confidence. But a month ago the vicar's wife had died suddenly of a stroke. Now Lillian couldn't even look forward to her letters.

When Jack took on a new parish, the challenge would begin all over again. Lillian would no longer be the curate's wife, able to slip into the background and plead inexperience. She'd be elevated to a position where more was expected of her. Many of the congregation would keep a respectful distance. She'd have to fight with her shyness, her nerves, the feeling of inferiority, all of which they would misunderstand as aloofness. It was easy for Jack to say that she worried too much. He had an ease that charmed people. They looked up to him and he loved his work.

'I chose you, not your job,' Lillian tried to tell him, but he didn't understand.

Dear Jack. She loved him as much as ever and missed him terribly. Whenever she woke, her first thought was of where he might be. Somewhere in the Mediterranean was all he could tell her. *It's perishing hot,* he had written. *The top of my head got sunburned.* The silly goose, he knew he should wear a hat. Even walks along the Hoe with Dorothy had left her quite tanned. Mrs Cullen had scolded her for looking like a gypsy.

'A lady keeps her skin lily white,' she had said.

'Well, I'm not a lady. I'm me.'

That was the trouble, Lillian thought as she put away her book and got ready for bed. I'm not like other people. Wherever she went, the sense that she didn't belong set her apart. It was only when Jack was with her that she felt secure, cocooned in his love.

There were days, though, when she loved this place, its air of bustle and busyness, the hooting of ships and the fresh salty tang of the sea. It was a joy to walk with Dorothy onto the cliffs where you could see the long loop of coast that unravelled into a distant haze, or watch the sun go down behind Rame Head.

'Sing Daddy's song, Mummy,' Dorothy would say every time.

With a glance to make sure that no one could hear, Lillian softly sang the sea-shanty that Jack had taught them the last time he was home on leave.

'Sea-shanties are songs that sailors sing,' he'd told Dorothy. 'This one talks about the landmarks we spot when we're coming home from far away.'

He'd held Dorothy's hand and they'd danced a jig while he sang:

The first land we sighted was call-ed the Dodman,
Next Rame Head off Plymouth,
Start, Portland and Wight;
We sail-ed by Beachy, by Fairlight and Dover,
And then we bore up for the South Foreland light.

'Look – the bit that sticks out there is Rame Head. Further along is South Foreland, where Daddy was born.'

'Where? Can't see.'

'No, it's a long way off, near where Grandma Goodwin lives. Next time I come home we'll take you there.'

At first it had been hard for Lillian, a mother alone with a young child in a strange town, but she soon found that she wasn't the only one. Naval wives were used to spending long months by themselves while their husbands were at sea. Children saw their fathers come and go. Nobody looked at you strangely, the way they would have done in Streatham. It was taken for granted that men had to go away while women held the home together. Fishermen, too, were often out for days, with all the dangers of storms to contend with. Their wives were a hardy breed, who rolled up their sleeves and slapped another fillet of fish onto Lillian's meagre purchase.

'Hubby back soon?' they'd ask, with a glance at her belly, and she'd nod.

'By Christmas, all being well.'

'All right, me lover?' they'd say to Dorothy, and Dorothy would repeat the words as she played with her dolls, the broad Devonshire accent creeping into her speech.

At Christmas Jack was home, his term of service completed. The day that Lillian waited on the dock with all the other families and watched a tiny speck on the horizon draw nearer until it was a huge ship nudged by dozens of tugs, then a leviathan that loomed above them, was one of the happiest in her life.

The excitement of the waiting crowds, the hoots and manoeuvres of the vessel, the bands playing, the naval ratings lined up on board to give the salute, the shouts and whistles of greeting, brought a lump to her throat, mixed with a surge of joy. All around her people called out and ran to greet their loved ones. Her heart skittered as she scanned the crowd.

'Daddy!'

Dorothy spotted him first. Lillian swung round and saw him run towards them, his arms outstretched. He scooped up the little girl, hugging Lillian, too, and all three of them laughed with happiness.

'Give me hat, Daddy.'

Dorothy pulled off his cap and he put it on her head.

'I won't need that anymore. Daddy's home to stay now.'

'Thank goodness,' said Lillian, and she slipped her arm in his as he led them through the crowd.

He looked different, sunburned of course, his face more lined, his body a little more portly. The chaplain's uniform made him even more handsome than she remembered. Lillian sighed. Somehow they would have to buy a new suit so that he could be interviewed for a parish of his own. Money had been easier during his time in the Navy, but soon they would have the struggle of living on a stipend again. And until he found a position, they would have only their savings.

'Don't you worry, Lil,' he said to her that night after supper when Dorothy was in bed. 'It looks as if there's a parish all ready and waiting for us.'

'So soon? What a relief.'

She nestled against him on the settee, her head on his shoulder. He'd changed into grey serge trousers and a jersey that smelled of moth balls from where she'd stored it while he'd been abroad.

'Don't you want to know where?'

She did and she didn't. A new place always brought the sense of coming to a precipice and struggling to fly. Parish life again, strange people, a rambling old house to furnish and keep clean.

'Go on, tell me then.'

'Somewhere that's special to both of us.'

Her mind ran through the places where they'd been. Plymouth, Streatham, his village.

'Not South Foreland?'

'Nearly, you're very close.'

Where else could it be? She could think of nowhere.

'Do you give up?'

She nodded.

'Dover.'

'Dover?'

Dover wasn't special to her, not really. She'd always thought it was an ugly place, noisy and run down. The castle was impressive, though, and there was a busy port, not unlike the one she'd grown to love here. But Jack had been at grammar school in Dover. He'd started his first job there. He still had a lot of friends in the town. The vicar had known him since he was a lad, and considered him a protégé. Now, Jack said, the old man had retired and put in a good word for him.

Wherever Jack went, people liked and remembered him. To Lillian that was both a relief and a source of pride.

He rested his hand on her belly as the baby gave a sudden kick.

'Just think, our son will be born there. He'll be a man of Kent like me.'

'It might be a girl.'

'Then she'll be a maid of Kent.'

'Not a Kentish maid?'

'No, no, Dover's east of the Medway. And anyway, I have a feeling that this one will be a boy.'

He was right. Early in February, on a grey morning, the sky slaked with sleet, James Peter Goodwin was born. He gave his first cry, opened his eyes and looked around the little, low-ceilinged room as if to say, Where on earth am I now?

The cottage belonged to Jack's cousin. It was just round the corner from his mother's guest house in the village where he and Lillian had met. As she sweated and writhed through the hours of labour, a gale howled against the window, while the moan of the foghorn on the Goodwin Sands wove in and out of her cries.

The birth was easier this time. Lillian sat up in bed, freshly washed, her hair brushed, the new baby in her arms, to receive a procession of visitors. Jack's parents came, his sisters and brothers, his cousins, aunts and uncles. Half of the village was related to him and everyone wanted a glimpse of the new arrival.

It was like being part of a tribe, Lillian thought, and while the sense of community sometimes soothed her, at other times it was suffocating. Your life was never your own. Everyone had an opinion on it, what you should and shouldn't do, how you brought up your child, what you chose to feed your husband.

Jack, who to her mind looked well-fed enough, ducked under the bedroom doorway to show in each new visitor. He wore what he called his civvies, a collarless shirt open at the neck, sleeves rolled to the elbow, his trousers held up with braces. Until he was licensed for his new incumbency, he could dress like any other man, go out for a walk on the cliffs, help his father with deliveries, or call round for a cup of tea with one of his old chums.

In the morning he stoked the kitchen boiler, and in the afternoon he laid a fire in the sitting room. It was almost like being on honeymoon again, bar the intimacy. Pregnancy, childbirth and breastfeeding had mellowed all that. Lillian was secretly relieved to have an excuse to lie quietly at night and regain her energy.

The first person allowed to her bedside after the birth was Dorothy, bursting with pride at the sight of her new little brother. She wanted to touch him and hold him, to climb under the eiderdown and cuddle her Mummy. Lillian had to explain that since there was a new baby, Dorothy would have to be a good, sensible girl and a kind big sister.

During Lillian's lying-in, Dorothy had stayed with her grandmother at the guest house, and the older Mrs Goodwin had won over the little girl. She fed her freshly baked scones and home-made jam, and let her collect eggs from the hens. Now, though, she held Dorothy's hand and pulled her away from the bed.

'Don't poke your fingers in his eyes, Dotty. He's a real little boy, not a doll, dearie. My word, Lillian, this one's turned after your family, I'd say. I've never seen a Goodwin as dark as him.'

Lillian stroked her hand over the baby's head. The black hair was soft and thick, his little face crumpled and creased, but with all its tiny features so perfectly formed that she couldn't resist planting a kiss on his warm, soft skin.

'He's beautiful. Aren't you, Jim, my boy?'

'Jim, eh?' Mrs Goodwin nodded in approval. 'Father will be pleased.'

Lillian smiled. It was an obvious choice, her own father having been christened James, too. What a comfort to think that her son carried the name of the father she had so loved. Her lips pressed against the baby's cheek and a surge of pure joy filled her.

She had loved Dorothy, too, from the moment she was born, but this little boy, with his strong legs kicking against her, his lips sucking lustily at her breast, had stolen away her heart.

Jimmy was three months old, solid and sturdy, when they moved to the vicarage in Dover. Lillian, still breastfeeding, exhausted from broken nights and busy days, scrubbed and swept and did what she could to organise their few possessions in the dank Victorian house that fronted a busy street in the centre of town.

Jack and his father went back and forth with the cart, helped by a band of relations, and soon the rooms began to look more habitable. Everyone chipped in with gifts of sheets and blankets, an old kitchen chair, a settee that the springs poked through but that would see out the summer. The bare floorboards rang hollow as Lillian walked from room to room to hang curtains so that people in the street couldn't see their every move.

Directly outside was a bus stop, and one morning when she opened the front door to bring in the milk, a man toppled into the hall.

'Beg pardon, ma'am,' he said and doffed his cap.

Several other passengers huddled beside him to shelter from the rain. From then on, Lillian gave a thump on the door before she opened it.

Just before Easter, about the time of Dorothy's third birthday, Jack was instituted as vicar. His study was in the vicarage, but he went back and forth to the church, or to visit parishioners, and these concerns were woven in and out of their family life.

Because of all the slum clearances, the parish had shrunk over the past few years. Unemployment had risen, and although some men found work at the docks, the town had an air of neglect and desperation. Jack laboured away, took services, visited the sick and elderly, tried to encourage youth activities, but Lillian could see that his efforts bore little fruit. For her own part she was relieved that nothing much was expected of her. Even better, there were no meddling middle-class women to tell her what she should and shouldn't do. The few regulars at church were working people. But much as Lillian tried to be friendly, they looked up to her as a lady, which she'd never felt herself to be.

As the weather improved she walked out more often with Jimmy in the pram and Dot linked by a strap to the handle. They watched ships load and unload their cargo in the docks. Sometimes, when Jack had a day off, they all went up to South Foreland and picnicked on the cliffs, or went for tea at his mother's.

With his family nearby, life was less lonely for Lillian. Even so, it was Jack whom everyone loved and admired. She sensed that they still saw her as an outsider. To the close-knit village community any Londoner was thought to be hoity-toity. But now that the children were the centre of attention, it was easier for Lillian to fit in, and over time her in-laws began to see that her quietness was shyness, and to appreciate her gentle ways.

Summer came, the grass turned dry and yellow, the petals of the poppies dropped from their swollen seed-pods, and Lillian began to feel more settled in her new home. From time to time news reached them of Hitler's rants and his increasingly tyrannical power, his hatred of Jews, his lunatic and grandiose ambitions. But disturbing as this was, most people were optimistic that Mr Chamberlain would keep Britain from being drawn into hostilities.

Then, in September, war was declared.

'Don't worry, it'll all be over in a couple of months,' Jack said, as sanguine as ever.

Lillian was numb with dread. Memories of the First World War, from which her father had never returned, crept back to haunt her. And if this war did develop, there was hardly a worse place to live than Dover. Only twenty-two miles from the French coast, it would be in the front line of any invasion.

Throughout the long months of winter the war remained no more than a distant rumble. Of course troops were embarking, and neighbours had sons who'd enlisted for service. Calls came for everyone to dig up their flower beds and plant vegetables, or hand in aluminium saucepans for the war effort. But in other ways life went on as usual. Lillian began to relax and hope that Jack was right.

In the evenings they switched on the wireless and heard reports of battles in places with strange names that sounded mercifully distant. But as Poland fell, and winter turned to spring, Hitler's relentless progress across Western Europe brought his troops nearer and nearer to the English Channel.

One night, towards the end of May, when the German invasion had swept through Holland, Belgium and into France, there came a chilling announcement. Dover was to be declared an evacuation area, and school children would be moved to safety.

'But Dotty hasn't started school yet,' said Jack, 'so she won't have to go.'

Yes, that was true. Dot had only just had her fourth birthday and Jimmy was barely a toddler. But would it be any better to stay in Dover? Lillian listened to the news with growing horror. British troops were stranded on the beaches at Dunkirk, and that very evening the Admiralty began to evacuate them. Soon there would be nothing between their little family and Hitler but the Straits of Dover.

Six days later, when the evacuation of troops was at its height, the first train pulled out of Priory Station, carrying over seven hundred children to safety in South Wales. It was a Sunday morning and Lillian, on her way to church, passed mothers walking home, tear-stained but stoic. One woman she knew came out of the crowd and sobbed on her shoulder.

'I know the littl'uns had to go,' she said, 'but it's breaking my heart.'

Lillian did her best to comfort her, but her own heart was heavy.

'Where have they gone, Mummy? Why?' Dorothy asked.

Lillian tried to explain, but it was hard for a child to understand why her playmates and neighbours had suddenly disappeared. By the end of the day, nearly three thousand children and over two hundred teachers had left Dover. The next morning, when Lillian took the children for a walk, the town seemed empty and hollow.

As fear of invasion grew, even Jack began to worry. He wanted Lillian to take the children away, if only to Streatham.

'I'll have to stay here, but it would be some relief to know that you are all safe.'

'I'd rather die with you here than live with Mother. What sort of family life would that be, if we're apart?'

She had coped with separation while Jack was in the Navy, so she would manage again if she had to. But another fear was so chilling that neither of them dared speak of it. Hitler had twisted religious doctrine to justify his slaughter of Jews, but at the same time he was persecuting dissident church ministers. This was less publicised than his treatment of Jews, gypsies and homosexuals, but it was happening all the same. Any churchmen like Dietrich Bonhoeffer, who spoke out against the Nazi regime, were rounded up and sent to concentration camps.

'What if I go away and never see you again?'

'Other women and children are going,' Jack said.

The town was almost empty of everyone but the men.

'Couldn't we stay up at South Foreland?'

'Lill, if I can walk there in half an hour, how long do you think it'll take the Germans to get there with their tanks and guns? Anyway, if they start to shell us from the French coast, we'll be as much in the front line there as we are here.'

A couple of days later, while Lillian was hanging out the washing, Jack came to her with a suggestion. A friend of his from Cheshunt College knew a family in Somerset who were willing to have evacuees on their farm.

'There's no time to dilly-dally. It's only a caravan but if you don't take it, someone else will. So I told him yes.'

'Oh, Jack, no, please…'

He reached into his pocket and drew out four railway tickets.

'I've arranged with the churchwardens that I'll take you there next week and help you to settle in. I'll have to be back by Sunday, but I'll come down as often I can.'

Lillian stared at the destination printed on the tickets. *Chard*. It was the name of a cabbage, wasn't it? So that was to be her new home, yet another place to get used to, and again without Jack.

We are aliens and exiles on this earth, she thought, not knowing where the words had come from. Ever since they'd been married, it was her destiny to shunt from one location to another, always a stranger, and horribly out of her depth.

LYME BAY, 2010

The road unwound beneath the wheels of the hire car that had cost Ellie a hundred pounds plus seven hundred excess. All this for a bloke who thought contact with her would contaminate him. But the railway had long since closed, and the bus journey to Lyme Regis, changing at places like Chard and Axminster, would eat an unbearable hole into the few short hours they'd have together.

She fixed her eyes on the road that unwound between banks thick with grasses, and flowers whose names she didn't know, pale frothy lace starred with pink and mauve. As the car laboured uphill she had to change down the gears. It was a wonder she knew how, after years of driving an automatic.

The road passed through woods heavy with summer foliage. It snaked round bends that opened to views of the downs in a sweep of green and gold, the sky pale with drifts of clouds as soft as cotton.

Way in the distance was a haze as indistinct as the sky. Could that be the ocean? It looked too tame, too insignificant. The road dipped and the view disappeared, but on the next rise there it was again, wider, clearer, a cleft of blue between steep slopes. So it was the ocean. It must be. An ancient fingerpost that might have been there in Hardy's time showed only five miles to Lyme Regis. She was Bathsheba Everdene riding to meet Sergeant Troy. Stop it, stop it. You're Ellie. He's Josh. He's far too serious for that sort of swordplay. Gabriel Oak then. No, Bathsheba's insides would never dissolve to cola for him.

When she drew into the car park, there he was, sitting on the wall with one knee drawn up, talking on his mobile. His t-shirt hung loose over sun-faded shorts and his legs were as brown as the outback. She honked the horn and he spun round and waved. His hair looked as if he'd used fingers instead of a comb.

As she cruised round for a park, she saw him slip the phone in his pocket. He came towards her, looking ridiculously happy. Or maybe it was her own joy that made her see him that way.

She checked in the mirror and saw that the open windows had blown her hair to a snarl. Her cheeks were flushed, her eyes had an unfamiliar brightness, and the sleeveless silk top she'd chosen reflected their smoky blue. Her black linen cut-offs were crumpled from the drive, but there wasn't much she could do about that. Silver earrings shaped like lemon leaves. A silver chain, rings and bracelets. A cord over one shoulder with a velvet hip purse in the form of a diamond.

When she got out, he was standing there.

'Well, g'day.'

She zapped shut the lock, trying to pull back her idiotic smile.

'Hey.'

His face was sunburned and his eyes were darker than she remembered, and more luminous.

'Good to see you, Ellie.'

'You, too, and great to hear an Aussie greeting.'

He lifted one hand to give her five, and as she thumped it, his other hand touched her shoulder. He smelled of apples and wood smoke. They stepped apart and stood laughing.

'You're looking good, Ellie.'

'And you.'

'Are you hungry? Shall we grab a coffee? Or you want to go walkabout?'

'A coffee would be good. Then maybe we could check out Lyme Regis. Jane Austen, John Fowles, how cool is that?'

'Did you see the movies?'

'The books are even better. But I forgot you don't read novels.'

He darted her a grin.

'What me? All that emotional gulch? Technical manuals are more my line.'

'So you're not into words.'

'Words are fine but the visual image wins out every time for a filmmaker. You have to set the scene before you add the dialogue.'

'Let me guess – Hitchcock?'

'Spot on.'

If he hadn't reminded her, she'd have forgotten to put a ticket on the car. He insisted on paying because she'd had to drive here, and he got it for the whole day, because he hoped she'd be able to stay that long.

Just as long as you want, she could have said, but managed to get a grip and focus on what he was telling her about a wedding and camping in someone's orchard.

'Tomorrow I'm going to London to meet with some friends for a few days, then heading back home.'

'You came all this way for a wedding?'

'A mate of mine just married this English girl. They met in Sydney but all her family live here. They own this really quaint old cider farm. I promised them I'd do the filming. Catch up with one or two people along the way.'

'Today's Sunday,' she said. 'I thought you'd be in church.'

'I was in church yesterday. Today I'm with you.'

She darted her head aside so he wouldn't see her ridiculous grin, and they strolled down the narrow street towards town. As they turned a corner he stopped, touched her arm and pointed beyond a jumble of houses towards the harbour and the open sea. He drew his thumbs and forefingers together to frame a rectangle.

'See what I mean? One shot says it all.'

'Depends what you want to say.'

'You'd know if you saw it.'

When they reached the harbour he had her sit on a low wall above the pebble beach.

'Just look out there, whatever catches your eye. Don't look at me.'

She gazed beyond the cottages of grey, pink and cream to where the cliff slanted to the ocean. The sun was in her eyes so she had to lift one hand to shade them. The bay was a soft blue under the sky, with no more than a ripple where the water touched the beach. But the smell of salt and seaweed brought back all those other beaches, Ulladulla, the cove at Freshwater, the pounding of the surf, till the yearning for all she knew and never could know was so strong that she swung round with a gasp to face him.

'Okay. That's good.'

He showed her what he'd filmed. She looked different somehow, her knees drawn up, a bare arm raised to shade her eyes. There was a grace in her movements she didn't know she had. And when she swept round at the end, her face gave away more than she'd intended. She wondered if he saw it, too.

'What d'you reckon?'

She nodded. The right words were hard to find. The Ellie Goodwin he'd shown her was someone she didn't know. The simple sequence had a directness that made you sit up and take notice, and again she sensed a sneaking feeling that Josh Bellini had a spark of brilliance.

'It's good. Impressive.'

He laughed the compliment aside.

'Nah, it's nothing. Gift of a shot, that's all.'

The smell of freshly ground coffee led them to a sea-front cafe, cluttered with buckets and spades, shrimp nets and a stand of postcards. They sat side by side on high stools at the window looking out to where boats bobbed in the harbour. The sun fell across them in a diagonal line. It caught the hairs on his arm where it rested on the counter, and as he tapped with his toe on the frame of the stool, his thigh almost touched hers.

A girl with an accent straight out of Hardy brought them cappuccinos in tall glasses. Ellie scooped up the froth with a spoon. The bittersweet foam dissolved on her tongue.

They looked at each other and laughed.

'Sad about the coffee over here.'

'The beer's better, though.'

His eyes, when he spoke, danced dangerously close. They were deep pools that she could dive into and drown.

'How's the research going?'

She put down her spoon and began to fill him in on what she'd learned about her father, and how his unhappiness was linked to a dark family secret. She explained her idea of writing the story in some sort of memoir.

Josh nodded as she spoke, his arms on the counter, his

fingers beating a rhythm.

Then she told him about her grandfather and their discovery of his illegitimate child. It gave her a sly satisfaction to reveal the religious hypocrisy and wait for his response.

'That was the minister, right?'

'Yes.'

'Too bad. Another own goal. What with paedophile priests and telly-evangelists who hire hookers, the church has done itself a good demolition job.'

'I'd say it's rotten to the core. It's no wonder people want nothing to do with it.'

The points were clocking up fairly evenly, so she was surprised by the gentleness of his next question.

'Tough when it's your own grandpa, though?'

'Yes, crazy, isn't it, when I don't even believe in all that. As you know.'

He drained his cappuccino, pushed back the glass and turned to her.

'Did I ever tell you about my grandpa? The Italian one?'

She shook her head. Being with Josh was like standing on the shore of a new continent.

'Grandpa Bellini was in prison. He was a Communist, couldn't stand Mussolini. He wanted to emigrate with my dad, but the Aussies wouldn't have him because of his criminal record. Ironic, really, when you think how we all started out.'

When he laughed, the corners of his eyes crinkled.

'Anyhow, Grandpa's brother was a fascist sympathiser. Politics and religion split the family. That's why my dad left Italy. He hated both state and church with equal loathing. One propped up the other and both were corrupt.'

'So weren't you brought up as a Catholic?'

'No way. Dad had left all that behind, and Mum's family had long since assimilated. Australia's always been a place where people can escape from the past.'

'Same as my dad, then. Ditch your problems and move on.'

'Or be ditched, like the convicts. Or those poor kids that the Poms sent over back in the sixties.'

'The orphans?'

'Yeah, though it turned out that half of them weren't orphans at all. Must have seemed like a good idea to some government bureaucrat to send a crowd of kids to the other side of the world. And I thought I had it bad when my oldies split up.'

Something else she didn't know about him. His head was down as he fiddled with the coffee spoon.

'I was fifteen when my dad moved to Brisbane with some woman he'd met. I don't know what I thought I'd do – kill him? Plead with him? But I took Mum's car and got as far as Gosport. Then a wombat ran out and I swerved and flipped off the road. The car was a write-off. I was lucky to get out alive.'

'A wombat?' Ellie had to laugh. 'But you couldn't drive at fifteen.'

'I thought I could. I was wrong.'

'Well, well, Mr Bellini. So you have a past, too.'

'Don't we all?'

She shrugged. She'd told him enough already. He tossed up a sugar lump and caught it in his mouth.

'So what happened?' she said.

He crunched, swallowed, and passed her the bowl.

'You want one of these?'

'No, I want to hear the rest of your story.'

'So, the cops came. They did what they had to do. It could have been a hell of a lot worse, but I was a kid, no one else was hurt, and there was all the stuff about my dad. So they read me the riot act and that was that.'

His eyes touched hers.

'You know, it's kind of humbling to be let off when you deserve a lot worse.'

Her fingers closed on the empty glass.

'Anyhow, it was one of the things that helped turn my life around. You know all about that.'

'One of those dramatic conversions, was it? What do they call them? A road to Damascus experience? Or in this case, the road to Gosport.'

'Yeah, a bit slower than that, but it stopped me in my tracks all right.'

'It blinded him, didn't it, that Damascus bloke?'

Josh chuckled, and signalled for the bill.

'My shout,' said Ellie, 'you paid the park.'

As they walked out to the street, she turned to him.

'So,' she said with just a hint of irony, 'do you still have problems with seeing things clearly?'

He threw back his head and laughed.

'You're on good form, Ellie. Yes, maybe it does dazzle you a bit at first, but you know what? It turns out to be more like cataracts. Once they've gone, you see better than ever.'

They walked through the town, past shops, pubs and cafes hung with baskets of brightly coloured flowers. The traffic was backed up where a truck couldn't make it round a narrow corner, and the pavements were crowded with holiday makers, so they dropped down to the beach. The tide was out, leaving wet pebbles and rock pools slimy with weed. Above them towered the cliffs, with thin ridges of limestone in the clay.

'When the rocks crumble,' Josh said, 'they expose fossils from millions of years ago.'

They sat on a boulder, warm from the sun. The balmy sea air brought a drowsiness, and she felt at ease with Josh, as if they, too, had been together for a very long time. She watched him pick up stones, turn them over and toss them aside.

'This place is like Uluru,' he said.

'Uluru? It couldn't be more different. That's red, a huge island in the desert.'

'What I mean is, they both tell us about the past. Who we are and where we come from. Aboriginal dreamtime and ancestor creators. Or geological ages. Triassic, Jurassic, Cretaceous.'

He held out a pebble. One side was grey but the other was coiled and ridged like a snail shell.

'An ammonite?'

'Revealed from the layers of time. Like the secrets that you've uncovered, Ellie.'

He passed the fossil to her and she cupped it in the palm of her hand.

'This is beautiful, though. What I've churned up is more painful.'

He listened while she told him about her dad, his sisters and the brother who'd died, and how their parents' problems had scarred them all in one way or another. When she'd finished, his eyes met hers with a gentleness that almost melted her.

'I guess that's why it matters.'

'What matters?'

'What we do or don't do. Because every action has consequences. Because the things that we do affect others. For better or worse.'

She knew what he was getting at, but refused to be drawn. When she passed back the ammonite he shook his head.

'No keep it. A memento. There's millions of them.'

It rested for a moment in her palm. Then her stomach rumbled and they both laughed.

'It's the smell of the ocean,' she said. 'It always makes me ravenous.'

'Me and you both. I could murder some fish and chips.' He nodded towards the town. 'Race you back?'

She sprang to her feet and leaped over the rocks, her espadrilles sliding on the pebbles. Something wet and slimy caught her shoulder and she swung round to see him dangling a piece of seaweed. She laughed, grabbed the free end and tugged.

The slippery ribbon grew taut. He drew her closer.

'Come here.'

She stood with his arms around her, her head on his shoulder. His body was as warm and solid as the rock they'd sat on. They both smelled of seaweed, sweat and salt, and their chests pumped from the run. He lifted one hand and moved a loose wisp of her hair.

'Look at you.'

His lips touched her forehead. It was a moment, an eternity. It was not the way she meant it to be.

They stepped apart and walked in silence, side by side. She couldn't think of a single word to say. That touch had set her head whirling.

The rest of the day passed in a haze of sounds and images that faded into insignificance compared with the one emotion that ran through them all like a silk thread on which beads are strung.

Later that night, as she drove back along the dark lanes, the day's images replayed in her mind. The fish and chips they'd eaten from newspaper as they sat on the wall of the harbour. A Punch and Judy show they laughed at with a crowd of kids, while Josh rested one arm on her shoulder and played with a strand of her hair. The musty interior of the church where his friends had been married, still filled with roses and gypsophila, cream and pink and mauve. A footpath that climbed up to cliffs where the view stretched in all directions, south across Lyme Bay, east and west to places whose names resonated with history and the endless possibilities of imagination.

Lulworth Cove, Golden Cap, Durdle Door.

They lay on the turf and watched the sun sink lower and the shadows grow longer. Josh made shapes with his hands – rabbits, a roo, a pelican in flight. The fronts of the cottages flushed pink as they strolled back to town. In the garden of a pub they sat on a wooden bench, and the beer that Josh carried from the bar was strong, malty, but way too warm.

'Just one,' he said because she had to drive home and he didn't want her to crash. Because he wanted to see her again. Because she was special.

She'd have forgiven him anything then, everything, but he spoiled it.

'Like that ammonite. Millions of us, but each one is unique.'

On the way home, with the car window open, and the heavy scent of honeysuckle that drifted in from the hedgerows in the darkness, his words still rang clear in her ears.

'When you hit Sydney, you call me.' He pressed one finger to her lips. 'Promise?'

'I promise.'

He was a nice bloke, that was all. It meant nothing. Because he was Josh. And Josh wasn't like other blokes, who acted first and talked later and thought last. He was different, and that difference was something she had to wrestle with and make up her mind about one way or the other. That was all.

SOUTHERN ENGLAND, 1944

In her dream the siren sounded its high-pitched wail. Ten minutes to get the children down to the shelter. She groped for the baby mask for Bobby – *Yours first, then his*, she'd been told again and again, but could never bring herself to obey. He was so small, so vulnerable, so nervy, the poor little mite. In his short life he'd known nothing but warfare. Thank goodness Dot and Jimmy knew the routine and could manage alone.

But where was Jack? He should be on his feet by now, dragging on his ARP uniform. In the blackout she could see nothing, but his side of the bed was cold and empty. As her eyes adjusted to the darkness, it formed into cupboard, doorway, window, and relief flooded her. She was in the caravan, in Somerset, on the farm.

If she kept very still, she could make out the rush of water in the stream, which heavy rain over the last few days had filled to a muddy swell. She reached across and lifted one corner of the blanket that covered the window. Even here, in the depths of the country, you couldn't be too careful. Enemy planes sometimes passed on their way to Bristol, and a stray light might tempt a pilot to release a bomb for the devilry of it.

She pushed open the window and leaned out to the mild

summer night. The air barely stirred. A full moon appeared from behind a cloud, and the dark shapes of barns and machinery took on a ghostly glow. Across the valley an owl hooted. Then all was silent.

For some time she sat there, her arms on the sill, too restless to sleep. In the hours before dawn her fears were always more acute. She worried about Jack, braving the onslaught in Dover. True, the worst of the Blitz was past, though occasional doodlebugs whistled in to cause damage. Shelling continued, too, but less strongly. The Allies were bearing down on Hitler's troops, closer and closer to their gun positions at Calais.

But what if – and she barely dared think this even to herself – if while she was away, Jack met someone else? The war had forced many husbands and wives apart, and illicit relationships had sprouted up all over the place like the weeds on the bomb sites.

From Dover to Somerset and back again, her life had become a nightmarish merry-go-round. Summer in the caravan, and the rest of the year at the Vicarage. The people of 'hellfire corner' as Dover had come to be known, prided themselves on their stoicism. Blow the shelling, everyone said. If we die, we die.

Even she almost preferred to endure danger with Jack than safety without him. Never mind that her nerves were in tatters, that day or night they might have to grab the children and rush to the damp burrow of the Anderson shelter. At least they'd all die together.

Relaxation and pleasure had become as alien to her as the far-off places to which the war had now spread. Her emotions were inflamed and exhausted with the struggle to survive. Whenever Jack felt amorous, which was less and less often these days, she lay under him and listened through the squeak of the bedsprings for the warning wail of the siren. What with the bark of anti-aircraft guns, the drone of the planes and the thud as shells exploded, sleep was near impossible.

Her ears followed every sound like the words of a new language. That awful whine as the bombs fell, mixed with the knowledge that if you could still hear it, they hadn't yet hit you, while you prayed they'd explode somewhere else. The relief once the all-clear sounded. But you could never relax, not really, when at any moment the horror might begin all over again.

My shattered nerves are an inner reflection of the devastation outside, she often told herself. During the last few years, endless buildings in Dover had been destroyed and hundreds of people killed or injured. Strangers, neighbours, shop-keepers, members of the congregation – no one was immune. Coffin-makers and undertakers flourished, and poor Jack was worn out with conducting funerals. Half the population was numb, the other half verged on insanity.

Some have even taken shelter in caves deep in the cliffs,' Jack had written. *It's as if civilisation itself is crumbling. In the mornings, the air is full of the acrid smell of burning. I can pinpoint where the bombs have fallen by the smoke that rises in this street or that, from the port or a factory or the railway station. Sometimes I pass the front of a house, still intact like a stage set with roof and facade untouched, curtains at the windows, only to find nothing behind it but a pile of rubble.*

Yes, only here in Somerset, in the summer, could she experience something like peace. Yet while the children slept, she often wept through the long, quiet nights, releasing the fear and exhaustion of this endless ordeal.

In the morning, the face of an old woman stared at her from the mirror, as pale as a ghost, eyes puffed, skin shrunken and lined.

'Mummy! Mummy! Look what I've found!'

Jimmy ran towards the caravan, where Lillian sat on the step in the cool of the evening with Bobby on her lap, thumb in mouth. His free hand clutched a fistful of her dress as his brother drew near.

The older boy's hair was red with dust, his face flushed with excitement. Grass seeds covered his clothes and his knees were scratched. He opened one hand and a shower of berries fell like drops of blood into Lillian's palm.

'How lovely! They're wild strawberries.'

'Me, me, me,' said Bobby and she popped one into his mouth.

'There's lots and lots of them, Mummy, down by the stream. Dot's guarding them case anyone comes.'

Lillian stood Bobby on the ground, went inside the caravan and came out with a piece of paper, rolled into a cone.

'Take this to put them in and when you get back I'll have a treat for you. No, don't ask, it's a surprise.'

She watched Jimmy run off, then walked across to a can that stood in the shade under a stone slab. The milk came fresh each morning from Mr Winter's cows, and a thick yellow cream always settled on the top. Carefully she scooped several spoonfuls into a jug. When Jimmy and Dot reappeared, Mario was with them, holding the paper cone full of strawberries. He passed it to Lillian with a flourish.

'For the beautiful Signora.'

She went inside for a bowl, poured cream over the berries, and handed round teaspoons so that they could all have a taste.

'It remember me my home,' Mario said. He'd taken off the brown POW jacket with its yellow flashes, and sat in a vest that revealed his muscular arms.

'Where's your friend?' she asked him.

'You don't hear? He make music on pipe.'

The soft sound of a flute drew nearer and Lorenzo appeared. In the evenings when their work was finished, the two Italians often sat with Lillian in the dusk on upturned crates by the caravan. While Lorenzo serenaded them, Mario showed the children how to carve instruments from pieces of wood.

In the broken English he'd picked up from the Tommies, he talked about his work as a stone mason in a village high in the Apennines. He was only eighteen when the war started. In the battle for Tobruk he'd been taken prisoner, and from there they'd sent him to Britain.

The two POWs slept in the barn. They helped Mr Winter feed the animals, plant crops, cut the hay and bring in the harvest. For this they were given food and a ration of one packet of cigarettes a week, plus a couple of shillings if they worked especially hard.

'Better here than in prison,' Mario said as he spooned up his strawberries. 'But some Italian soldiers angry. They say Mussolini shoot us when war finish.'

Lorenzo flicked his fingers in a gesture of disgust.

'Mussolini run like rat now the Americanos in my country. When the Partisanos will catch him, they will finish him quick.'

He drew one hand like a blade across his throat.

'Already Americanos in Firenze,' Mario told Lillian. 'And today take Parigi, also.'

'Paris? Are you sure?'

'Mr Winter say yes.'

She hardly dared believe it, but it looked as if Jack was right after all. At long last the Allies were gaining ground. Perhaps before long this dreadful war would finally end.

'When war finish you come to my country, meet my Mama and Papa.'

'I'd love to, Mario, I'd love to.'

If only it were possible. The two Italians had told her so much about the mountains and the vines, the music and food, a world full of sunshine and laughter. They flirted with her outrageously, brought gifts of wild flowers and taught her to dance, but Lillian knew it meant nothing. Not only was she married, but she was nearing forty, her hair was well on the way to grey, and childbirth had slackened and spread her body.

Whenever Jack came to visit, they kept a respectful distance. They couldn't quite believe that he was a priest. What a strange religion in this country, where the priest had a pretty wife and three children. But Jack's easy-going ways soon won them round, and once they knew him better they slapped him on the back, cadged cigarettes and taught him their songs. While he was there they were more distant and formal with Lillian, but the moment he went they relaxed into their chivalrous ways.

Sometimes, as Lillian drew the curtains at night, she caught sight of them slipping away towards a neighbouring farm where there were land girls. Once, when she'd woken early she'd seen them return, yawning but happy in the pale light of dawn, their uniforms crumpled and red with dust.

Contact between the two groups was strictly forbidden, but the war had brought a wildness and freedom that Lillian had never known, and which she both feared and envied.

Towards the end of October Jack went to Canterbury. It was a clear autumn day, the berries bright in the hedgerows, the leaves gleaming gold in the morning sun. He sat on the bus for the fifteen-mile journey with a sense of excitement he'd not known for a very long time. It felt almost like those Sunday School outings when he was a boy.

As they laboured uphill towards the downs he glanced over his shoulder at the pale spread of sea, as peaceful now as if hostilities were already a distant memory. Here, on his own, away from work and responsibility, he could rest his head, close his eyes, and relive the extraordinary events of the last month.

When Canadian troops had captured the gun emplacements at Sangatte, which had been shelling Dover for the past four years, the town had erupted with huge celebrations. The King and Queen had come to pay tribute to its people's fortitude, and he, Jack Goodwin, local boy turned vicar of one of the parishes, had been privileged to line up with the mayor, town clerk and other dignitaries in a welcome party to greet their majesties. The channel port might have been battered and broken, its people depleted and scattered, but it had survived, and the white cliffs that towered serenely above it really did seem to be a symbol, not only of endurance, but of peace.

Fired by these memories, Jack unfolded his newspaper to catch up on the latest developments. All over Europe, he read, as the Allies advanced, the enemy was surrendering. Nobody wanted to tempt fate, but it really did look as if victory could be only a matter of time. Hitler's power base was crumbling, though sadly too late for many. As the death throes of his regime resounded, so the shocking extent of its terrors had begun to emerge. Soviet forces, advancing through Poland, had found gas chambers at Majdanek, Belzec, Sobibor and Treblinska. No one could say how many thousands of Jews had been put to death, but it was clear that very few survivors remained. The Allied troops, already worn down and depleted, were pressing doggedly forward with the hope of liberating others before it was too late.

When Jack re-folded the newspaper, his hand was trembling with horror and relief. His war had been painless by comparison with what others had suffered, but even so he was exhausted. By night he'd helped to patrol the streets, enforce the blackout and tend the injured. By day he'd done his best to comfort the bereaved, find support for the homeless and impoverished, and answer the unanswerable questions of those who railed against God for permitting such carnage, while bolstering the faith of those who found in it their only source of strength, comfort and hope.

He was a young man no longer. It was hard to believe, but next year he would be forty. Middle-aged, past his prime, however you looked at it, it was a depressing thought.

But as the bus rattled its way through farms and villages, the autumn sunshine fell on his cheek and shoulder with a soothing warmth. The bus jolted; he opened his eyes; he must have fallen asleep. Where were they? Ah yes, the village of Bridge, its brick and flint cottages as bright and cheerful as if they'd seen too many ups and downs over the centuries to worry about one more. The only signs of the war were occasional craters where a stray bomb had fallen, and gardens full of 'dig for victory' vegetables instead of flowers.

The surrounding farms were busy harvesting corn. In the

orchards he glimpsed apple pickers on ladders that reminded him of Somerset. If only Lillian had agreed to stay there all year, it would have spared him a lot of worry. He could have managed on his own with a cup of tea and a sandwich, or meals with his family up at South Foreland. Of course it was a comfort to feel her close to him at night, but what with the air raids and the three little ones, they were both too exhausted to do more than lie like corpses on a medieval tomb.

Everyone's nerves were frayed by the war, but Lillian suffered physically, too. One week it was a migraine, the next a tummy upset. She worried over the children, and complained if he didn't. Dot's uniform was shabby. Jimmy had picked up bad language at school. Bobby was so nervy and irritable. Jack was their father, so why didn't he do something? As if there was anything that anyone could do.

She was afraid of everything, not only bombs and the shelling, but the risk of infection, meeting strange people, or going out on her own. It was a mystery to Jack why habits that were so straightforward to him caused her such distress. The lavatory seat left open, shirt sleeves at the table, tea drunk from a saucer, were all signs of ill-breeding. If they went to South Foreland she complained that his mother was too lenient with the children, his father too passive, his sisters too interfering. Parish life was anathema to her, not that there was much of that now, with half the congregation dead or scattered.

Jack, too, was disillusioned. A church service didn't take itself. A lot of thought and preparation went into each one, and when only a handful of old crones turned up, it was hard to find the motivation. If he took a funeral, the pews might be full or half empty, but each time he had to find something to say that would be tailor-made for the deceased, while giving comfort and reassurance to those who remained.

He even caught himself wondering why God had called him to the ministry if there was so little visible reward. All very well to be told that we don't do it for our own reward, but in thy service, Oh Lord. That was easier said than done.

No, it couldn't go on like this. He had decided to take matters into his own hands. Parish life was wearing him out, and Lillian had never taken to it. The theological college at Canterbury was about to reopen its doors and had a vacancy for an administrator. It might be the opportunity that they both needed. Didn't Lillian always say how much she loved learning? An academic environment would be ideal for her. Didn't she revel in history and culture and beauty? Where better, then, than Canterbury?

He had thought about consulting her first but decided against it. No point in raising her hopes when he might not even be offered the job. And what if she found fault with the idea before he'd even tried? Far better to present her with a *fait accompli*. No, that was too callous. A surprise, then. By taking the initiative he would spare her unnecessary anxiety.

The bus groaned and strained up the last hill. The one thing he had always wanted, more than anything he could ask for himself, was to make Lillian happy. How sweet she was when they first met, so unassuming, with no idea of how her eyes and her smile affected him. He'd had precious little to offer her, but she had fallen in so compliantly with all his plans. If only she would realise how much people liked her and not worry so much. She was like the princess in a fairy tale, blessed with umpteen qualities but cursed with the one that threatened them all.

Of course money was scarce, of course the war had blighted

everything, and of course three children took the youthful spring out of a marriage. But for some inexplicable reason, she had taken to jealousy. If he so much as spoke to another woman she accused him of flirting, when nothing could be further from the truth. It was his job to be pleasant to people, and if they warmed to him, it was hardly his fault.

The bus jolted, hiccupped, and wove into the traffic. He lit a cigarette and drew on it deeply. So had he stopped loving her? No, no, a thousand times no. Was he still in love with her? That was a different question. He gazed ahead as the towers of Canterbury Cathedral came into view above the rooftops of the city. In amongst the buildings were gaps where bombs had exploded. But whether by chance, divine protection, or Hitler's plan to keep its grandeur for himself, the cathedral had survived.

Jack rubbed his chin, which he'd shaved that morning with his last decent blade. In some ways his love for Lillian was like his love for God, he mused. It wasn't so much that it lessened with time, rather that it grew more complex. Early on, in the euphoria of innocence you thought all your problems had vanished, but each new struggle or disappointment took some of the air out of your naivety. Yet these trials made you more resilient and shaped you in a way you could never have foreseen.

So could you do without this love? No. Perish the thought. Why not? Because it had become part of you, like the air you breathed. Without it you would shrivel and dry.

He brushed a fleck of cigarette ash from his jacket. No, wedded love had to do with commitment. When you married, just as when you offered your life to God, the commitment you made was voluntary. Yes, at first you might kick and struggle against it, but in the end you succumbed. You made the decision of your own free will, as much as it could be free when something as powerful as love had ensnared it.

The sound of bleating reached him and he glanced out of the window. A farmer was driving a flock of sheep towards an enclosure. It must be market day. The animals' eyes were wide with terror, and their frightened cries rose above the noise of the engine.

So, wondered Jack, when you made this commitment, were you like those sheep, led blindly to the slaughter? No, you were a willing collaborator who chose to be branded with the red-hot iron. In marriage, the ring was the symbol of that voluntary bondage. In ordination, it was the ridiculous plastic circle that people jokingly called a dog-collar.

Yes, it was rather like being led on a lead, albeit by a master to whom you were devoted.

There must be a sermon in this somewhere, he pondered, as the bus reached the terminus. He gathered together his briefcase and raincoat, turned the threadbare sleeve face-down, and walked through the busy medieval streets. Ancient buildings closed around him and the towers of the cathedral gateway appeared ahead. Kings and archbishops had passed through them, as well as countless ordinary mortals like Jack Goodwin, one-time sailor and barrow-boy, husband of Lillian, father of Dorothy, Jim and Bobby, now on his way to an interview that might change all their lives.

With a spring in his step he set out through the precincts towards St Augustine's Abbey. At the far end, he spotted an empty bench in a garden just inside the city wall. Blow me if even these flower-beds weren't filled with cabbages and carrots.

He glanced at his watch. The appointment wasn't for another forty minutes and it could be only a short walk from here. He sat on a bench, reached into his jacket pocket for notebook and pencil, and began to write.

SOUTHERN ENGLAND, 2010

A week or so later, like a rabbit tearing itself from a trap, Ellie bolted to Devon. More expense, more blind panic. She made the excuse of wanting to see Fran, which was true, but the real reason was that a hole gaped, where loneliness lurked, fear of unemployment. The only way to dodge it was to keep moving.

Thoughts of Josh lured her, too, but she had to resist them or before she knew it she'd tumble into the hope that maybe, just maybe, he'd get in touch before he flew home.

No, she would fix her mind on the reason she'd come here, and focus on her own survival.

The route to Fran's caravan was complicated. She headed west through a downpour, the wipers squeaking back and forth. After Taunton the road led into open country, and up ahead she could see hills. As the lane narrowed and climbed higher, she glimpsed a stretch of blue way below. That must be the Bristol Channel. The rain stopped, the sky began to clear. She pulled off the road. In the distance the coast of South Wales was just visible, with a haze of mountains beyond it. Sunlight came and went as clouds scudded across the sky, and the sea below shimmered.

Why, every time that she glimpsed the ocean, did thoughts of Josh creep in unasked?

You're special.

She wanted so much for those words to mean more, but the barrier of beliefs that he refused to cross was impenetrable. Instead, he swung back and forth, playful one minute, lecturing the next.

She reached for her bottle and took a swig of water. It dribbled down her chin but she barely noticed. Her mind had drifted back to an earlier incident, on another coast, thousands of miles from here.

It was the second time that she'd seen him, the day they'd walked the trail. All the way past Balmoral Beach and onto the headland they talked about university, where their paths might have crossed, people they'd both known. He told her about his majors in indigenous Australian studies, art history and film, and she talked about hers in historical research and archaeology.

When they stopped to look at the rock etchings, he said something about their spiritual significance, and it struck her that he had a nerve to steer round to religious topics so soon.

'Why are you so interested in the Aborigines?' she said. 'All that the missionaries ever did was try to Europeanise and brainwash them.'

'Yeah, they got a lot of things badly wrong.'

That wasn't the response she'd expected but it riled her all the same.

'So why are you? Because you think you've got something to offer?'

'I'm interested in the way they see things,' he said in a voice that was much more level than hers. 'Don't you think we can learn a lot by looking at other cultures?'

'What, like how to change them, you mean?'

He was clicking away on his camera so he didn't answer at first. Then he put it down slowly and surveyed her with an irritating little smile.

'Why are you so hostile, Ellie? Whatever I say, you turn it around. Did I say that?'

'And whenever I ask a question, you answer it with another. It sends me crazy!'

He moved towards the cliff, and once she could breathe more calmly she joined him. They sat for a while looking out at the ocean, which was a ridiculously bright blue. It made you feel that all the little irritations and anxieties were a waste of time.

'Tell me about your project,' he said.

She told him. That led them on to their families and where they'd come from, and he said he'd like to go to Italy sometime to find out more about his. As long as he kept to topics like that he was nice enough to be with and she began to soften to him.

'When history gets personal it's exciting, but scary, too,' she said.

'Does that put you off?'

'No, but if we don't like what we uncover it could be tough.'

'Don't you think that if we search deep enough we're all bound to find stuff we don't like?'

What, even you? she wanted to say but didn't.

'When you think about it,' he went on, turning a stone over in his hand, 'we've all come from somewhere or something that we might not like.'

He talked about invaders and immigrants, lost empires, trade, secret liaisons, and said that if they dug deep enough they'd all find plenty to be ashamed of. She pointed out that no one was responsible for what their ancestors did.

'No, but it affects us all the same. Look at the angst we're going through as Australians. We stole land from the Aborigines, wiped out their culture and gave them diseases and alcohol instead. And what were we? A bunch of convict exiles, most of us, when we came here. Or poor immigrants who grabbed what we could, because where we came from we had nothing.'

'At least Rudd's apologised to them. That's something, isn't it? Or are you one of those people who think we can't say sorry for what we didn't do ourselves?'

Josh thought for a bit then said he wasn't sure.

'But I think it makes a difference to say sorry if people got hurt, so, yes, in that sense it is important.'

That was when he talked about how forgiveness and understanding could open the way to reconciliation. He claimed there were links now with indigenous churches, and more respect for their spiritual traditions.

'Did you know, percentage-wise, more Aboriginals than white Australians identify themselves as Christians? They say that Jesus set foot on this continent long before the whitefellas came.'

She raised her eyebrows but said nothing.

'So, you're right, I agree, we did get a lot wrong. But what matters now is that we face up to those mistakes, both in our collective past, and in our personal lives.'

He stopped, his eyes met hers, and for a moment she thought he was going to open up about something personal. Then his knee jigged, he looked down at his hands, and his brow creased into a frown that was difficult to read. She decided to help him along.

'Yes, I agree it's important to be honest about our own mistakes, too.'

He nodded, but side-stepped her meaning. 'Part of the

problem is that we all start with misconceptions about one group of people being this or that, when in reality there's often good and bad on both sides.'

'Possibly.' She suspected an underlying snipe, but couldn't quite pinpoint it.

'If we see flaws and imperfections in others, we should also see our own,' he went on, 'and seeing our own should help us not to be so hard on those who are different. Nobody's perfect.'

'Not even you?' She was goading him but of course he wasn't fazed.

'The difference is, Ellie, that I know it.'

'You mean I'm not perfect?'

He laughed, the way he always did, eyes crinkling and a grin that shot creases down his face.

'You're within a cooee of it, I agree.'

'Say that again. That was really cool. Can I have it in writing?'

He took out a scrap of paper. She passed him a pen.

Ellie G's within a cooee of perfect.

'But? There's always a but.'

'You have these unrealistic expectations. You're drifting around, snatching at fads, trying to be someone you're not. Find out about yourself, who you are, where you came from, what you really believe. Then maybe you can move on.'

A muddy track pitted with potholes led up to Fran's caravan. As it grew steeper, the view opened over woods and fields, scattered with farms. A pointed hill loomed in the distance, moody purple against the sky. That must be Dunkery Beacon. She recognised it from a painting Dot had in her cottage.

Ellie pulled up beside a shed. A goat ran out, followed by Fran in overalls and wellies. She grabbed it by the collar and tied it to a post.

'Blessed thing's giving me the run-around. Come and have a look at the estate.'

She led the way past a barn used as a studio, cluttered with easels, a potter's wheel and kiln, shelves stacked with tins and boxes. Beyond it, ragged clouds ran across the sky and the wind rippled the grasses. The hill sloped down to a copse of trees.

'What an amazing place. I can see why you like it.'

It was half a globe away from Narrabeen, but its isolation and slightly zany independence reminded her of Dad, and how he'd built his shack on the lagoon long before it was suburbanised. What had drawn him and his sisters to such lonely locations? Even Dot didn't exactly live in the heart of civilisation. Maybe Dad's family were just weird, and a little bit of that weirdness had come down to Ellie, too.

Fran had lunch ready in the caravan – radishes and spring onions from her garden, and home-made goat's cheese. Shells on cords hung from the windows where they tinkled in the breeze. Indian bedspreads covered the seats, and the small space was bright with paintings and varnished pots. Up on a shelf a cross-legged Buddha gazed serenely beyond them, as if floating above the squalor of the world. A dish with a sea-blue glaze and a design of fishes glinted where the sun reached it.

While they were eating, Ellie told Fran what she'd learned about Maureen Latimer. She rummaged in her bag for the birth certificate and read it aloud. '*Amanda Margaret, born November 1955, mother Maureen Latimer, father not named.* Look – the words *Adopted – Superintendent Registrar* are handwritten in the margin.'

234

'What a strange way of recording an adoption. Is that what it means?'

'We weren't sure. Dot phoned the registry but they wouldn't tell her. Apparently siblings have no legal right to that information.'

Fran let go of her fork.

'*Dot* phoned?'

'She's come round to the idea of finding her.'

'That bloody woman. She's doing it to spite me.'

'To spite you?'

'Yes. She knows that I wanted to find her and she can't bear to be upstaged. So what better way to get one up on me than to make the discovery herself?'

She leaped to her feet and started to clear the table. Her eyes had a hurt, angry look.

'I think Dot's just lonely, Fran. It would mean a lot to her to have another sister.'

'She's got me, for God's sake. Not that she's ever cared about me. Oh no, I'm just a problem, or an embarrassment, or both.'

She flung a fork in the sink and stormed outside.

Ellie wriggled from her seat, cleared the table and washed the dishes under a trickle of lukewarm water. How long had she been here? Half an hour? And her aunt was on a rant already. Poor old Fran, her emotions were never far from the surface. It couldn't be easy for her growing old, all alone in the ruins of her chaotic life.

She made a pot of tea and took two mugs out to the yard. Fran was stabbing a spade into her vegetable patch, rows of leeks and lettuces, canes with beans and sweet peas.

She wiped one hand across her face.

'Sorry, Ellie. I don't know what it is about that woman but she always gets to me.'

'No worries. Come and have a cup of tea.'

They sat side by side on a wooden bench. Fran warmed her hands on the mug and seemed calmer now.

'So, what else did you find out?'

'Nothing much, I'm afraid. We tried court adoption records, but the ones for that period have been lost.'

'Lost? Is that some sort of cover up? What's the betting the church is involved. You know how they close ranks if there's any hint of a scandal.'

'Yes, I wondered that, too. The adoption took place around the time when social workers and journalists were beginning to investigate rumours of maltreatment. In many cases the authorities tried to cover their tracks.'

From across the valley came the hum of a tractor. A dog barked and another answered.

'So what next?'

'We've registered with a couple of agencies that help to reunite blood relatives who've been separated by adoption. You have to give them as much information as possible,. then, if her name is on their books, they'll check the connection and eventually put us in touch. But only if both sides are willing.'

She lifted her mug, took another swig of tea.

'The problem is that Amanda's name might have changed on adoption, not just her surname, but her first name too. I've already checked registers of marriages and deaths, and there's no one who matches her date of birth. So either her name really was changed or she's disappeared off the face of the earth.'

'Shit.' Fran tossed the dregs of her tea onto the dirt.

'There's an Amanda Latimer on *192.com,* but she turned out to be a twenty-year old student.'

'So we're scuppered.'

'Looks like it.'

A bee buzzed round the sweet peas and they watched it nudge open the soft hinge of petals.

'What about Maureen? The scarlet woman – my father's lover.'

'Oh, I've found her. She's in an old people's home in Herne Bay.'

Fran's eyes widened.

'You mean you've been to see her?'

'No, I just found her address. It's got to be her. Everything else tallies.'

Fran nibbled at her nail but said nothing. For a while they both watched the goat browse on some brambles, stretching its neck to the juiciest berries which grew almost out of reach.

Her aunt swung round to face her.

'Listen, if I can get someone to look after Nanny-Nancy here, we could go and visit her. Maureen Latimer, I mean. Take her a bunch of flowers and tell her who we are. Say we're not leaving till she's told us the whole story.'

'Fran, she's an old woman in her eighties. She's probably kept this secret all her life. What would we gain by outing her?'

'Well, I'm an old woman, too, and I'd like to know the truth before I snuff it.'

Ellie nursed the empty mug. Part of her, the selfish part, wanted to forget all about this saga, head home to Sydney and get on with her life. No, it was nothing to do with Josh, just that her bank balance was shrinking rapidly. Zooming across England in hire cars wasn't going lead to a job, however much she liked to think it would. And by the look of it, Fran's van was a wreck.

It was time to be sensible and face up to reality. That was what Mum would say. Besides, in a few weeks she'd achieved far more than anyone could have predicted. She had plenty of material for a memoir – the details of Dad's unhappy childhood and his motives for emigrating. Her aunts were now real people, not just names on birthday cards. She knew all about her grandparents and the affair with Maureen Latimer.

But that relationship had produced a child. That child was Dad's half-sister. Somewhere out there was a person, a real person that they were all related to, and if she could track her down, maybe three old ladies could lay the whole trauma to rest.

From across the valley a voice barked commands as a dog raced around driving sheep into a pen. Shadows of clouds chased over the hillside and leached it to monochrome. The sun reappeared, the colours flowed back, green and bronze and purple.

What we choose to do matters.

She scuffed her toe in the dust. He'd preached at her so much that she was beginning to think like him.

Our choices and decisions affect others.

She could see him on the cliffs at Lyme, his brow creased as he listened while she spoke. Intimate secrets about struggles she should have kept to herself. When she finished he turned, and his eyes had a penetration that seemed to understand rather than judge.

What we want isn't always the best way.

He'd learned by experience, he said, had become stronger as a result. One day she would see for herself. He wouldn't pressurise or persuade.

Damn him. Ellie broke off a stem of grass and ran her nail along it until the seeds sprayed in a shower to the ground. Damn,

damn, damn.

'Okay,' she said to Fran. 'How soon can you leave?'

They drove south-east towards Dorchester. Another tank of petrol, thirty-five pounds. The day was much like that other day, bright, the countryside green after rain, and the road was like that other road, rising and dipping over the downs with glimpses of the sea.

She ignored the signs to Lyme Regis, gripped the steering wheel and kept her foot steady. No, Ellie, he won't be there. He's on his way home to Sydney.

From time to time she glimpsed a silver sheen beyond the hills. Surely that was Lyme Bay. The sun was in her eyes and the shadows of trees came and went in black strips that dazzled and confused.

They stopped for coffee in Wimborne with its Abbey and timbered cottages, rusticity giving way to bourgeois chic, Thomas Hardy and the Tolpuddle Martyrs reborn as tea shops and tourist attractions.

In heavy traffic they skirted the urban sprawl of Southampton and Portsmouth, and by lunchtime neared the Sussex coast with its blight of bungalows and post-war semis, the beaches broken by dark lines of breakwaters. Fran knew a place on the downs towards Lewes where they could picnic. She'd brought homemade bread, cheese and elderflower cordial, home-grown salad and raspberries. They spread a blanket on the grass and Ellie listened as she reminisced about childhood holidays, when they'd stopped here on the way to Devon.

'Our mother used to bring a steak and kidney pie, baked the

day before. The meat was amazingly tender, set in its jellied gravy inside the pastry crust.'

'So there were happy times, too?'

Ellie wanted to think so, for all their sakes.

'Holidays were happy. We were a real family then, and all the problems seemed to slip away the further we went from Canterbury. Mother was in her element. Father wore an open-necked shirt and rolled up his trousers to paddle in the sea. Jimmy gave me piggy-back rides over the pebbles.'

Ellie remembered him charging along the beach at Narrabeen, splashing through the waves with her on his back. He was like a child himself sometimes. 'Faster!' she'd say, kicking him with her heels.

She bit into her sandwich. It was still a struggle to accept that he wasn't here, but not as much as before. Now she knew that Fran, too, had struggled with losing him, and she guessed he'd want her to speak.

'Fran, I'm sorry he hurt you so much when he emigrated.'

To her surprise, Fran laughed.

'What really upset me was that he wouldn't take me with him. I'd have gone like a flash if they'd let me.'

By early evening it had started to rain. As they approached Canterbury, the towers of the cathedral hovered grey and murky in the darkening sky.

Bert opened the door of the B&B. 'Welcome back.' He shook hands with Fran and said he could see a family likeness. 'Another of Canon Goodwin's lovely offspring. I had no idea he had so many.'

This time he gave them a room at the front of the house, overlooking rooftops towards the old town. Twin beds with flowered doonas, pink and white towels folded at the corners, sweet Williams in a vase on a table by the window. Fran flopped onto one of the beds.

'Crikey, it's weird to be back in Canterbury. That old bloke Bert's like something out of Dickens, isn't he?'

'Yes, he's quite a character. But he picks up on a lot, so be careful what you say in front of him.'

This time when they walked into town, Ellie saw it through Fran's eyes. It was decades since she'd been here, but slowly the landmarks began to slot into place.

'All these streets and gardens by the River Stour were my playground. Look – the Lepers' Hospital. I remember that. The river runs underneath it, and sometimes we used to hire a boat and row all the way through a tunnel. It was dark and scary, but wonderful fun.'

In an alleyway near St Augustine's Abbey she'd had her first serious snog.

'A Hungarian boy who'd come here to escape the occupation. My God, he was hot. I thought he'd swallow me whole.'

Ellie remembered hers with a guitar-strumming dreamer who tasted of salt and coca cola. She'd been crazy about him for all of two weeks.

In a back street they passed what used to be a jazz club, where Fran and her friends stomped to four old men playing Acker Bilk's *Stranger on the Shore*. 'Every time the door opened, our hopes were dashed at the sight of yet another spotty youth. But we cadged cigarettes and puffed them in a huddle, vowing to escape one day to somewhere more exciting.'

Ellie smiled with a tinge of sympathy. A caravan on Exmoor probably wasn't what she'd had in mind.

The sat nav showed the nursing home in a residential street on a hill above Herne Bay. But first they wanted to buy flowers, so Ellie drove to the sea front with its ice cream parlours and fish and chip shops, where she parked by a line of beach huts that stretched along the shingle.

In a bizarre sort of way it reminded her of Bondi without the sand or the surf. The tide was out and she could see rock pools where children crouched with nets and jam jars.

'They're probably looking for cockles,' said Fran.

They found a flower shop and settled on carnations and chrysanthemums in yellow and white. Enough for a gesture but not too showy. Part disguise, part peace offering. As if delaying the moment of truth, they strolled along the promenade, past Victorian villas and public gardens gaudy with municipal planting. The sky was bright and the air smelled of seaweed, hot dogs and petrol fumes. Fran pointed towards a low cliff with twin towers that overlooked the bay.

'Reculver. It's a Roman fort. I worked on a dig there once.'

'I didn't know you were into archaeology.'

'I wasn't really. But I fancied this guy who was.'

For a moment longer they gazed out to sea, then turned uphill, walking slowly, in silence. The Hollies was a double-fronted brick building with bay windows and half-timbered gables. Several cars were parked in the drive. Nerves tightening, they paused to read the sign.

A residential nursing home offering 24-hour quality care.

The front door was open but an inner door, with intercom and security codes, was closed. 'Let's go for it,' said Ellie. She rang the bell. They waited, but nobody came. She was about to ring again when footsteps sounded from inside and the door clicked open.

'Goo-afternoon. Can I hell you?'

The young woman who stood there wore a pale blue uniform. She looked like Cindy Chang, and had a sing-song accent that clipped the consonants.

'Good afternoon,' said Fran in a brisk manner that took Ellie by surprise. 'We've come to visit Miss Maureen Latimer.'

'Jussaminute, please. I ass Manager.'

She hurried away and came back with a middle-aged woman, who peered at them over her glasses.

'Are you family?'

'In a manner of speaking,' said Fran. 'We're related to a very close friend of Miss Latimer's, and since we were in the area we felt sure he'd have wanted us to pay our respects. He had such a high opinion of her.'

Ellie clenched her jaw tight. Nerves, and the way her aunt spoke, made her want to giggle like a schoolgirl.

The manager's eyes fell on the bunch of flowers.

'Come inside for a minute. I'll go and see if Miss Latimer is in her room.'

While the click of her heels receded down the corridor, Ellie avoided eye contact with Fran and looked around her at the reception area. The walls were cream, the carpet an institutional brown. Framed certificates for fire inspections and health and safety checks hung behind the desk. From a corridor came the hum of a vacuum.

A door opened and an elderly man shuffled towards them, leaning on a Zimmer frame. He cocked his head and put one hand to his ear.

'Is that a siren I hear?'

'I think they're vacuuming,' said Ellie.

'I'd better get down to the shelter, quick.'

A care assistant hurried towards him. 'Now, now, Mr Jones, you know you shouldn't be out here.'

'They're after me again, they know where I am, I told you not to tell them.'

'Come along, dearie. No one's going to hurt you.'

She led him back to his room, and a moment later the manager reappeared.

'Would you come this way? Miss Latimer is in the lounge.'

They followed her down the corridor with its whiff of boiled potatoes and furniture polish, past a room where elderly folk sat in armchairs, their heads drooping. At least Dad didn't have to go through all that, Ellie thought. Sudden death was a shock, but senility and slow deterioration must have their own horrors.

The lounge was in a sunny annexe at the back of the house, overlooking a garden. Several elderly men clustered around the television watching a cricket match. Two women were playing cards at a small table. Another sat knitting in an armchair by the window. She wore a pair of silver-framed glasses and her grey hair was neatly waved. She glanced up as they drew near, but continued to slip the wool between the needles with a rapid click.

'Maureen, your visitors. I'll leave you to chat. Would you all like a cup of tea?'

'That would be lovely,' said Fran. 'Milk but no sugar. We're sweet enough.'

'These are for you, Miss Latimer,' said Ellie as she laid the flowers on the table. Miss Latimer nodded her thanks, but kept up the rhythm of her knitting until she reached the end of the row.

'A jumper for my great-niece. She'll be fifteen next month. How time flies.'

She slipped the knitting into a cloth bag and folded her hands in her lap. The skin was loose, the bones visible, and she wore no ring. Her face was wrinkled and dry, but when she spoke, there was a liveliness in her features that might once have been attractive.

'So please tell me. Should I remember you? My memory is a little vague.'

Before Ellie could explain why they'd come, Fran jumped in with alarming boldness.

'We know someone you know. Your former boss.'

Miss Latimer took off her glasses, polished them on a cloth, and smiled calmly.

'Now which one would that be? I had so many, you see. I worked for nearly fifty years altogether, mostly for the church, though I did have a stint in a solicitor's office in the West End. Of course, I've been retired for nearly twenty. Not a bad innings.'

A care assistant came with the tea tray and they waited while she passed round the cups. As soon as she'd left, Fran spoke again.

'This was in Canterbury. Canon Goodwin.'

'Oh, Canon Goodwin. Yes, I worked for him for several years. A lovely man.'

Ellie didn't dare look at Fran. She stared into her cup, where a few tea leaves swirled on the surface. What had she expected? A burst of anger? Tears, embarrassment, denial?

'That's the one,' said Fran. 'You both worked at the theological college in the nineteen fifties.'

'My word, that was a long time ago. It was my first job, you know. Well, well, there's been a lot of water under the bridge since then.'

Fran's foot reached Ellie's and nudged her into action.

'So, do you remember a Mrs Whitaker? Molly? She came to work at the college not long before you left.'

A flash of something crossed the old lady's face. Had the name stirred a suspicion? Or was she puzzled by the Australian accent?

'Yes, I do vaguely, but we weren't particularly close.'

'It's just that I happened to meet her a week or so ago and she said she remembered you very well.'

A burst of excitement came from the cricket-watchers by the TV.

'Test match, I believe,' said Miss Latimer. 'I always thought cricket was the most dreadfully boring game.'

She rubbed the back of one hand with the fingers of the other, then lifted her tea cup.

Fran and Ellie glanced at each other, wondering how to work round to what they wanted to say. But before either of them could speak, Miss Latimer put down her cup with a polite smile.

'Well, it's been lovely to see you. Thank you so much for the flowers.'

It was now or never. Pink blotches had appeared on Fran's cheeks and Ellie could tell that she was about to pounce. So she leaned forward quickly, speaking softly so that the other residents wouldn't overhear.

'Miss Latimer, I think we should be honest about our reason for coming to see you. My aunt here is Canon Goodwin's daughter.'

The old lady went rigid. She flashed Fran a look, opened her mouth, closed it.

'Please believe me when I say that we wish you no harm. But my aunt is very keen to find her half-sister, Amanda.'

'Amanda Margaret,' said Fran.

Miss Latimer began to tremble. She reached for her tea but her body was shaking so violently that the cup rattled on the saucer.

'No, no, please, I can't, don't . . .'

Ellie took the cup gently but firmly from her hand.

'So do you know what happened to her? Was she adopted?'

Miss Latimer's eyes closed, her jaw clamped tight, her whole frame shuddered. Ellie turned to Fran.

'Should we leave? We're obviously upsetting her.'

'No way,' Fran mouthed.

For the first time, the implication of what they were doing to this old lady struck Ellie in all its cruelty. They were like conjurers taking her grubby secrets out of a hat, playing with her life. How would she feel if someone did that to her? It had been bad enough when she'd poured out her woes to Josh, but he hadn't asked to hear about all her mistakes, and at least he'd had the decency not to pass judgement.

On the table was a box of tissues. Ellie passed it across but Miss Latimer waved it away, slid a handkerchief from her sleeve and worked it between her fingers, her face contorted in the effort to control her emotion. The card players had stopped their game and were watching. One of them stood up and left the room, while the other glared in their direction.

'Please, Miss Latimer,' said Fran, 'we just need to know if Amanda was adopted and then we'll leave you in peace. Was it through an agency? The Children's Society, maybe?'

The old lady shook her head, clenched her eyes tight. Her voice was more like a croak than a whisper.

'It was Hugh – Hugh Gregson.'

They both stared at her blankly.

'Who was? The father?'

'No, Hugh . . . he . . . arranged it.'

Ellie looked at Fran, but she shrugged as if to say she didn't have a clue.

'So did Hugh work for the adoption agency?'

Miss Latimer waved one hand in despair.

'He was a friend . . . of . . . of . . .'

'Who? My father?' Fran looked like a tiger about to spring.

'You mean it was a private adoption?'

Miss Latimer's fingers tore at her handkerchief. She caught her breath and gasped out the words.

'Hugh knew a . . . a clergy family . . . in Cornwall, I think . . . who couldn't have . . . children of their own. Henderson, they were called.'

Her eyes opened wide and stared full at them.

'I wasn't supposed to know. I was supposed to put it all behind me. But how can you forget something like that?'

She sank her face in her hands, her body quaking. Ellie reached to comfort her but she shook her away.

'Don't. Please. I can't . . .'

The manager came towards them, followed by a portly middle-aged man, who was glaring at them.

'What is it, Aunty? Have these people upset you?'

'I think you'd better leave,' the manager said, and ushered them towards the door.

Ellie glanced back at Miss Latimer. She sat with her shoulders drawn straight and was composing herself with amazing stoicism.

'Really, Colin,' she said, 'it's nothing. Nothing at all.'

'But, aunty –'

'Please. I don't want to talk about it. Just some sad memories, best forgotten.'

The door closed behind them, and like two naughty schoolgirls, they followed the manager down the hall.

CANTERBURY, 1949

Really and truly, it was not because she was pretty that Jack offered her the job. She came with excellent testimonials from the secretarial college, having been placed top out of thirty-five trainees in the final exams. Her speeds were startlingly good, her reliability and respect for confidentiality outstanding. Composure, deportment and personal presentation, though lesser qualities, were equally highly praised.

The other candidates weren't a patch on her. For goodness sake, would anyone expect him to appoint a woman whose skills were mediocre, just because she was plain?

Naturally Jack hadn't mentioned this rationale to Lillian. She simply knew that in his new job he needed a secretary. Besides, they'd moved to a village near Canterbury where he was helping with a parish in addition to his college work, so the paths of wife and secretary would never cross. Home and work life could remain separate. Calm and good order would prevail.

From the start, Miss Latimer made her presence known in the nicest possible way. On her first day, when he arrived late and a little harassed because baby Frances, still in nappies, had kept them up half the night, she made him a calming cup of tea, with extra sugar, despite the rationing.

'For energy, Reverend Goodwin. Vital for a busy man like you.'

Vaguely, in the background to his work, Jack was aware of her opening and shutting the drawers of the filing cabinet. It was an unfamiliar pleasure to have someone sort out his muddle of papers, and make quiet, unobtrusive and well-informed decisions as to which he should keep. His mind was engrossed in the perilous state of last year's college accounts, and how to balance them with the limited income expected in the year ahead.

Just as he began to feel the need for a cup of coffee, it appeared in front of him with two chocolate digestives on a plate beside it.

'Ah, my favourites, how did you know?'

Miss Latimer was on her way to the door but she paused and turned.

'All men like chocolate digestives, don't they, Reverend Goodwin? They were my father's favourites, too.'

This reference to her father comforted Jack. It helped him to relax, as if Mr Latimer were a chaperone quietly maintaining decorum. Some weeks later he learned by chance from a colleague who'd ministered in a neighbouring parish, that Fred Latimer had died years before at the age of forty-five, which was uncomfortably close to Jack's own age. He had left a widow and one daughter, now a blooming young lady in her early twenties.

One Monday morning his coffee came not with a biscuit but a slice of Victoria sponge.

'Mother and I had a baking day,' Miss Latimer said. 'We thought you might enjoy a taste. Don't worry, it's very light, you won't put on weight,' she added, just a little playfully.

This witticism, with its delicate touch, lightened the tension between them, while introducing the sense of a watchful maternal eye. Father had gone, but his good lady was there to monitor proceedings. Jack might even have mentioned these treats to Lillian, but Fran was teething at the time and her nerves were on edge. That night she went to bed early with a headache.

From then on these little exchanges between Jack and his secretary became the norm.

'Give my compliments to your mother. This shortbread is quite delicious.'

When he'd enjoyed a hint of sloe gin in the chocolate cake, Miss Latimer took off her coat the following morning and said,

'Mother was pleased you approved of her new recipe.'

Years later, when it was far too late, he discovered that Mother had known nothing at all about these delicacies.

He, in turn, began to talk about his children.

'Little Frances spoke her first word yesterday.'

'Oh, how lovely! What was it?'

'*No!*' he said. '*No, no, no.*'

They both laughed, hers a rippling little tinkle like the water of a stream.

'Really, Reverend Goodwin, you're such a tease.'

'Dorothy came top in both her English and French exams,' he said proudly on another occasion. 'She will receive two books this year at the grammar school prize-giving.'

Miss Latimer nodded, pen poised for dictation. Her knees, held modestly together where they emerged from the hem of her skirt, led via a pair of very trim legs to a flattering but practical pair of court shoes.

'I would have expected nothing less. A child with such a clever father is bound to be clever, too. Now, where were we?

have, *Dear Sirs, With reference to your communication of the 10th instant . . .'*

Naturally Jack made no mention of Lillian. A man does not talk to another woman about his wife.

Was it the angora jumper or the perfume, Jack wondered later, that first gave him the frisson of danger, a stir of attraction that he should have stamped on like a lit match on a tinder-dry floor? Or perhaps it was something more mundane, like the time when Miss Latimer phoned to apologise that she could not come to work because she was 'under the weather'.

When pressed (because he was truly concerned) she admitted that she had a tummy ache.

Jack put down the phone, his neck hot under the clerical collar. How clumsy of him. Of course it was her period but she was far too delicate to say.

No man is a lover of that time of the month when women become particularly crabby, with a tendency to burst into tears over nothing. But this incident would have brought home even to a blind man the terrifying and wonderful fact that Miss Latimer was not only a secretary, but a woman, too. More, she was a young woman, with those soft jerseys that moulded to her breasts, and the skin of her face and arms so velvety smooth. No, no, no, he must not even think of such temptations, but he couldn't help it. She was a woman, and, God forgive him, despite being a priest, he was a man. Yes, he was a man with needs that didn't seem to diminish with age, equipped with an alarmingly visible barometer of his animal responses.

If he could have relieved his desires in the normal way, he might not have succumbed. But Lillian had just begun the upheaval of that time known ominously as 'the change of life'. Her emotions soared and crashed at the least provocation. At night she flung off the bedclothes, lathered in sweat. She couldn't bear Jack to touch her. Frances, born as they both entered their forties, had come as an unwelcome surprise. They could barely afford to feed and clothe three children, let alone four. It was one mistake too many and Lillian wouldn't risk another, nor go through the agonies of pregnancy, childbirth and broken nights again.

'It's all right for men. You don't know what women suffer.'

More and more she reminded him of Mrs Cullen. 'All women grow into their mothers eventually,' someone had once said to him. Youth and beauty were the pollen that drew you, but once you'd tasted it, you were trapped.

If Jack came home a little late, if his face was flushed, or Lillian's acute sense of smell picked up something floral when he pecked her on the cheek, she flew into a rage.

'I suppose that bit of skirt can afford perfume even if your wife can't.'

'Why are you so late, Daddy?' one of the children might ask in all innocence, but before he could answer, Lillian would slam down a plate.

'He's been with his bit of fluff, that's why.'

Hearing the ice in her voice, the children froze, afraid to speak, and they all ate their supper in silence.

'Are you all right, darling?' she would say to Frances who hadn't touched her food. 'You'll be a clever girl when you grow up, won't you, not a silly secretary.'

Frances, with her thumb in her mouth, would climb on her lap and bury her face.

'What's a secretary?' Bobby might ask, always the bold one.

'A typist, dear. Nothing but a typist. Click, click, click, writing letters all day long. When I was at John Lewis I had twenty typists under me.'

Later, when Jack went up to bed, his pyjamas and dressing gown had disappeared.

'They're in the spare room. Go and play with yourself there. Then perhaps I can get a decent night's sleep.'

It was uncanny how well he and Miss Latimer understood each other. They both knew implicitly what they could and couldn't do. There was no need to speak, to warn or discuss. It was almost as if they worked by telepathy, so that a glance conveyed everything.

The office was sacrosanct. However tempting it might be to reach out and draw her to him when they passed in a narrow corridor, he did not. Nor could they risk an embrace in the store cupboard, when at any moment footsteps might pass, or the door spring open to reveal them. At work they remained in the roles cast for them, secretary and boss, respectful, courteous, distant.

At the end of the day, they always left separately.

'Good night, Miss Latimer.'

'Good night, Reverend Goodwin. Have a pleasant evening.'

'Thank you, and the same to you. See you tomorrow.'

At lunchtime he ate his sandwiches in the office. She went to a cafe in town with some of the other staff, or on her own, with a book.

'What was on the menu today?' he might ask.

'Shepherd's pie,' she would answer, or, 'toad in the hole. But not as good as Mother's.'

She didn't ask him about his sandwiches. He wondered if she'd got wind of the fact that they were always cheddar cheese, although Lillian sometimes added chutney. If they'd had a row the day before and she'd turned Jack out of the bedroom, he'd eat them as if in penance, feeling sorry for himself. But actually he liked crusty white bread, and cheese was his favourite filling.

'How was the Daphne Du Maurier?' he asked Miss Latimer one day, as she put down her book after lunch.

'Gripping. Mrs Danvers is a truly evil woman. But love and goodness will win through in the end, I am sure.'

It did not happen quickly. Months passed, a year or more even, but like a pot of water on a slow, steady flame, sooner or later it had to boil.

The clergy conference was the unlikely location. A fusty old building stuffed with black-robed vicars from every corner of the Anglican Communion. Meetings of this committee and that, where minutes had to be taken and capable secretaries were essential. The training of staff worldwide was on the agenda, and since the college was a prominent centre of such learning, and funding at the heart of the discussions, Miss Latimer was essential to proceedings.

Nobody blinked an eyelid at her presence. She took to the role superbly, dressed in a sensible tweed skirt and twin set with a sturdy pair of Irish brogues, and some alarmingly efficient-looking glasses perched on her nose. Jack could not remember her wearing them before.

They travelled up with Canon Cooper, the college principal. Naturally the men sat in the front, and Miss Latimer, her hands folded in her lap, in the back with the files and folders. She spoke only when spoken to, brightly, in an intelligent voice.

'Yes, I'm perfectly comfortable, thank you. Indeed, the roads have improved greatly since the war. And, yes, I do begin to feel rather hungry. A jolly good lunch will be most welcome.'

On the second day, when everyone had settled into the routine of matins, meetings and meals, and her presence was no more noticed than that of the coffee ladies, it seemed perfectly natural that Miss Latimer should breeze into her boss's room with a portfolio under her arm and a notepad and pen in one hand.

'I'll leave the door open for a breath of air,' she said, and sat on the hard wooden chair to take dictation. While floorboards in the corridor squeaked to passing parsons, her pen dashed over her pad without a falter.

On the third day she came in the evening, after supper, walking briskly, carrying a pile of portfolios. Jack looked up from the desk where he'd been going over the accounts. The corridor outside was silent. Everyone was down in the Common Room for after-dinner tea and coffee, but Miss Latimer spoke in a bold voice as if to invisible ears.

'Oh dear, Reverend Goodwin must have gone for a walk. Never mind, I'll come back later.'

She stepped inside, closed the door, turned the key and smiled at him with a look full of meaning. He stood and faced her. His erection was instant and painful and he knew it must show through his trousers. She walked swiftly towards him, tossed aside the portfolios, undid his clerical collar and threw it on the desk. He fell upon her, clasping her breasts, soft and yielding through the powder blue jersey, but had to let go as she loosened the jacket from his arms.

As she began to unbutton his flies, that untameable part of him sprang through the thin fabric of his pants. She stepped back, lifted her jersey over her head and unclipped her brassiere to reveal two beautifully formed breasts.

He clutched them, he took them in his mouth, he devoured them even as he fumbled with her skirt. She kicked off her shoes, stepped out of her knickers, and stood naked before him.

In vain he tried to control himself, but as her hand encircled him he knew he must have stained the rug. She drew him to the bed and covered his body with her own, gently writhing until he had regained enough strength to enter her. He found release inside her, and again during the night, gorging himself on her as if dying of starvation.

Her hunger matched his. By the time they were sated, night had long since fallen. Vaguely he was aware of footsteps in the corridor, doors opening and closing, deep voices saying goodnight. Languidly he moved his hand over her satin smooth skin. It was creamy pale in the moonlight, soft with down as golden as her hair that now lay tousled and tangled on his chest. Her body curved from shoulder to waist, hip to thigh with the graceful fluidity of youth.

She lifted her head, smiled at him, drew her lips over his cheek.

'Jack.'

'Maureen.'

They whispered their names back and forth, caressing each other until they drifted into sleep.

He didn't hear her leave. He woke suddenly, aware that he was cold. The window was open, the room empty, but with a strange smell that he couldn't identify. It turned out to be Vim from the bathroom, which she had used to eliminate dangerous odours. The rug was free of stains, albeit a little damp.

She was not a virgin. No tell-tale drops of blood coloured his sheets. Later she told him about a sweetheart who'd had to leave to fight in Normandy. He had pleaded with her to give herself to him, and although she wasn't in love with him, she had agreed. A few weeks later, he was killed. She was sad, but for him not for herself, and glad that she'd given him a taste of heaven before he went into that hell.

During devotions the following morning, Jack's Bible fell open at the book of Proverbs, where Wisdom exhorts her son to flee from enticement and rejoice in the wife of his youth, to be satisfied with her, and not be captivated by an adulteress who will lead him down to death.

Throughout the journey home, while Canon Cooper rambled on about drawing ordinands from other countries to the college, Jack wrestled with his conscience. He tried not to look at the driving mirror, where Maureen's – Miss Latimer's – face was clearly visible to remind him of the enormity of what he had done. His body was alive with the memory of its delights, but his mind was in torment.

They dropped Miss Latimer – he must remember to call her that – at her mother's home in Faversham, a semi-detached council house in one of the pleasanter estates. Canon Cooper was out of earshot as Jack opened the boot for her suitcase, so he spoke rapidly in a low voice.

'This must never happen again.'

She visibly started.

He closed the boot and shook her hand with deliberate formality.

'Thank you so much for all your hard work, Miss Latimer.'

For a moment their hands remained clasped. She slid hers away and reached for the suitcase.

'A pleasure, Reverend Goodwin.' And with a smart step, her golden head held high, she glided down the path to her door.

For the last few miles to Canterbury, Jack drove in silence. A horrible tingle of tension crept through his body, despite his attempts that morning to purge it of all traces of infidelity in a lukewarm bath.

His mind whirled with the awfulness of what he had done. Once he had delivered Canon Cooper to the college, he would have to face Lillian. All his skill would be needed to keep her from spotting the signs of betrayal. The uncomfortable business of subterfuge would begin. Now that he had deceived her, he could never again face her in the assurance of innocence.

He had slipped, he had fallen, he had satisfied a deep craving and could not truly say that he was sorry. The pleasure had been intense, the release tremendous. But a man in his position could not continue on such a dangerous path. He had broken not only his marriage vows, but those made at ordination.

Yet he served a God who was in the business of forgiving sinners. Even King David had committed adultery, and although God had rebuked and punished him, he had restored him to the kingship. He'd even allowed him to take the adulteress as his wife. Jack drew strength from that knowledge. Men were fallible beings, but God was merciful. Of course, he must exercise his free will and play his part. He had slipped once, but once only. From now on he would be strong.

Perhaps, even then, Jack knew that he was deceiving himself. That night, as he lay by Lillian's side, his guilt tangling with tenderness for the wife he still loved despite all the trials they had weathered together, he had the sneaking conviction that feeding an appetite does not kill it, but makes it grow.

LILLIAN

When had the snake of suspicion first slunk into her? Lillian could not be sure. Was it before that girl came to work in his office, or after? For a long time now, Jack's easy friendliness with women had made her hot with fury. Almost worse was how they reacted to him. They simpered, smirked and wriggled like worms in a blackbird's mouth, as if to be gobbled up by him would be a pleasure.

Now this. A cold accusation from an unknown hand, with the spelling and punctuation of an oaf.

Madam!! watch out for yor husband you aint the only lady frend hes got and him a vicar!!!

Tears stung her eyes as she held Frances by the waist and jumped her down from the bus. The bell pinged, it drew away, and silence settled. All around them the trees were green with the freshness of spring, and shoots pierced the rotted undergrowth.

She sighed. In another month summer would begin, after which Frances would start school. All of her children were bright and healthy, and she should have been full of joy. Dot was expected to achieve top grades in eight subjects at 'O' level. The girls' grammar school had an excellent reputation for Oxbridge entrance, and if all went well, Dot would add to that privileged number. The boys' school was going through difficulties, with poor discipline reflected in disastrous results. But to Lillian's relief, Jimmy, the delight of her life, had started as a day boy at the local public school, aided by a bursary for sons of poor clergy. Bobby, equally clever, but a bit of a pickle, would go there, too, in due course.

Yes, she should have been bursting with joy, but her stomach heaved, her mind swirled, her throat was tight with pain.

'Where are we going, Mummy?'

Frances clung to her mother's hand, as nervy as always. Since birth the poor child had known nothing but rows and upsets. They'd started as occasional skirmishes, built to a full scale war, and driven the little girl deep into herself.

'To find the pretty flowers.'

Blow the dirty bathroom and the pile of washing. If Jack could enjoy himself, why shouldn't she? Year after year she'd slaved for him, put up with hardships and deprivations, and now he had betrayed her.

She led Frances down a lane until they came to the path that led into the woods. The primroses had faded, but bluebells swam in a blue haze under the beech trees, filling the air with their scent.

'Here they are, Mummy!'

'Yes, they're lovely, darling, but we're looking for white bells, not blue. We'll have to walk down to the stream. They grow at the bottom of the hill. That's why they're called lilies of the valley.'

As they went on their way, the quiet of the wood settled over them. Frances let go of her mother's hand and ran around happily. The grass was starred with celandines and anemones, so they picked some as they went, making them into a posy. Here, in the dappled light that fell through the branches, the awful pain seemed far away. The path wound deeper down through the trees. A chaffinch sang *chip-chip-chooee-chooee-chee-oo*, while butterflies danced in spots of sunlight. Slowly, as these sounds and sights soothed Lillian, her mind tip-toed back towards the events of that morning.

The cruellest blow of all was that the day had started so well. Jack had brought her up a cup of tea, smiling as he passed her a letter that had come with the early post. He was in shirt sleeves from where he'd been stoking the boiler. It was their only source of hot water, and the mornings were still cool.

'It's going to be a lovely spring day.'

He kissed the top of her head and a wave of happiness calmed her, like it used to when they first met. Whenever Jack was affectionate, all the suspicions and rows, the screaming and shouting of the past weeks and months, faded like last year's leaves.

Lillian smiled at him. Perhaps he was right. All her fears were imaginary. She mustn't be jealous, it was only because she was so insecure. They had both been through so many hardships that it was hardly surprising her nerves were on edge. He had never loved anyone else and never would. Of course he didn't mind that her hair was grey and her waist had thickened. What would he want with a silly young girl when he had a lovely wife, the mother of his children, a woman who was worth more than twenty others?

She had wanted so much to believe him, even if it meant closing her eyes to the fact that, deep down in some secret place at the centre of her being, she knew that his need for physical love was and had always been greater than hers. It was an unspoken secret they skirted around, like unstable ground that might collapse under their feet.

Over the years she had grown used to that part of their lives. But at first, when they were courting, the heat and fierceness of

Jack's embraces had startled her. Each time they were alone his mouth pressed harder, his hands strayed further, until she had to wrench herself free. Her face and neck were raw and red, his clothes covered in fluff from her mohair jumper.

All this was normal, Lillian supposed. Her mother had drummed into her that most men found it hard to control themselves before marriage. Once he was wed, so Mrs Cullen claimed, the urgency of a man's passion subsided. Before marriage it was a woman's duty to restrain him. After, it was her duty to submit.

But Jack's passion hadn't subsided. From those first nights once her period was over, when Lillian lay taut with nerves as the man she loved thrust into her, right up to the present, Jack's desires were as strong as ever. That brief interlude when she had blossomed under his embraces was a distant memory. Now when he'd finished, all she felt was tired, sore and dirty.

A rustle in the undergrowth startled her. Out of the tangle of branches a fox cub appeared. She snatched Frances by the hand.

'Ssh!'

The tiny red snout twitched as the cub looked this way and that. They were upwind, so it couldn't catch their scent. It trotted out, and a second later another followed. They sat on their haunches and boxed with their paws, tumbled on the ground and rolled together, play-fighting. It was hard to believe that these sweet, cuddly creatures would soon grow into fierce killers who tore their prey to pieces.

'Are they cats, Mummy?' Frances whispered.

The cubs' sharp ears picked up the sound. They froze, looked round, and disappeared swiftly the way they had come.

'They're foxes. They're probably afraid that we'll hurt them.'

The world is a cruel place, she thought, and it must be a cruel God who made it that way. With each new blow that came to her, Lillian's faith shrank a little more, like a withered balloon.

Frances said nothing, just clutched her mother's hand. The poor child, she'd probably been woken by their awful row this morning. Her bedroom was across the landing and the walls were thin. She must have heard Lillian shouting, because when that letter had arrived, with its chilling accusation, she had lost control. The humiliation, the deception, the shame, overwhelmed her. She flung the scrap of paper at Jack and shrieked at him.

'Read this! See what people are saying about you! It's not just me, you see, others have noticed, too!'

As he read it, his face flushed, then went pale.

'People gossip about all sorts of things. It doesn't mean they're true.'

Something sly in his look fuelled her anger.

'How could you, and with that tart, that typist, that common little slut!'

She wanted to hurl more insults at him but the words tangled in her throat. He was guilty, she knew he was, but he wouldn't admit it.

The thought of the two of them together made her want to vomit. A priest, who was supposed to set an example, fornicating with a girl young enough to be his daughter. She wanted to smash things, hurl the cup at the wall, but Jack stood meekly and smiled and shrugged while she was the one who was shattered and broken. How could she go on like this, day in day out, putting up with him and his damned weakness for women?

'I can't *stand* it anymore!' she sobbed. She sank her head onto her knees and tugged at her hair like a wild creature. Her eyes felt sore and puffy. She wanted to hurt him, make him feel pain, see him suffer as she suffered. Her rage flared, and a new, wild sense of power gripped her. Yes, he had betrayed her, but she could destroy him. If the truth came out, he would be finished. Knowledge was the key and she, Lillian, weak and abused as she was, held it.

The words burst from her in hiccups.

'I'll tell the – bloody Arch – bishop!'

Slimy stuff dropped from her nose onto the sheet. Jack stepped towards her and she screamed. At that moment Frances appeared in the doorway, clutching her knitted rabbit and sobbing.

'No, Daddy. Don't hurt Mummy.'

He turned, gaped, and fled from the room.

It was all very well to threaten him, Lillian thought, as they walked downhill to the stream, but what could she do that wouldn't hurt her and the children even more? Yes, if the church found out, Jack's career would be finished. He would lose his job. But with his job went their house. She and the children would be homeless, too.

How would she manage? As a young woman, she had enjoyed her work and taken pride in it, but now, nearly twenty years later, worn out and middle aged, who would want to employ her? Bookkeeping had moved on and adopted new methods. She was out of date, out of touch. Besides, who would look after the children? Where would they live? Lillian would wear herself out going to work and trying to run a home and family, while Jack would be free to do as he pleased. That girl would get her clutches on him and she, Lillian, would be left to cope alone.

'Mummy, look! The flowers.'

Lillian turned to where Frances pointed. All along the banks of the stream, in pale swathes like a bridal veil, grew lilies of the valley. Their leaves covered the moist ground, and from the centre of each sheath arched a stem hung with creamy-white bells.

Tears sprang to Lillian's eyes. The flowers were so pure, so perfect, with a fragrance at once sweet and delicate. Here, in the depths of the wood, with no one to disturb them, they declared themselves quite simply to be what they were – gentle, innocent and beautiful.

When they reached home after their walk, a huge florist's bouquet wrapped in cellophane lay on the kitchen table. Roses, carnations and chrysanthemums were skilfully arranged so that red, bronze and yellow harmonised against a background of foliage. Tucked inside was a card with a handwritten inscription.

To my darling wife, Lillian, from your ever-loving husband, Jack.

She ripped the card in two and flung it in the bin. This was what men did when they felt guilty, wasn't it? They bought their wives flowers.

All the peace and happiness that had soothed her in the woods now vanished. Unbelievable! Men committed adultery and thought they could buy forgiveness with an extravagant gift. Oh yes, it must have cost him a packet, far more than they could afford. Better to have spent the money on a new pair of shoes for Bobby.

She seized the bouquet and strode out to the garden. In the far corner was a rubbish tip where Jack put the grass clippings when he cut the lawn. She hurled the flowers onto it, turned back to the house and slammed the door behind her.

A week later it was still there, decaying inside its cellophane, the corpse of their love.

CANTERBURY, 2010

They walked from the nursing home in silence, all the excitement of discovering Maureen Latimer strangled by the pain they'd caused. Ellie slid the key into the ignition. Fran sat beside her, fists clenched on her lap.

'Bugger,' she said. 'Bugger, bugger, bugger.'

Traffic whizzed past in both directions. Across the road was a dingy looking cafe.

'Would you like a coffee?'

'What, in that crappy place? Sorry, it's just that, oh God, I'm sick of everything.' Fran thrust her head into her hands.

A truck whistled past and sent their car swaying in its wake. Ellie slumped against the steering wheel, numb, sick, exhausted. Beside her, Fran's body heaved with emotion, and she remembered that day at Freshwater when the struggle had been hers. Somehow Josh had found the right words, but now she couldn't think of a single one.

Spots of rain hit the screen. The wind had got up and the sky was heavy with cloud.

Fran blew her nose and let out a strangled laugh.

'Crazy, isn't it? That it still hurts so much after all these years. Oh let's get back to Canterbury, go out and get plastered.'

'Drown our sorrows?'

Why not, she reasoned, now they were wrecked on the rocks of everyone's misery. She pulled out into the traffic, her hands sticky on the wheel.

'D'you know what I'd really like to do?' Fran said. 'Pick up a gorgeous guy and take him home, just for one night. Long enough for him to screw me senseless and bring me breakfast in bed the next morning. Then he could eff-off.'

She tilted the mirror, took out a comb and tidied her hair.

'God, what a hag. Who'd look at that. Anyway, all men are a waste of space in the end. Rotten bastards, the lot of them.'

'Most of them, anyway.'

'Let me know when you find one who isn't. Look at my father. A vicar, who should have known better, having it off with his secretary.'

'I don't suppose vicars are any better than anyone else.'

'Well, they should be. Or if they're not, then they shouldn't be vicars. At least other men don't pretend.'

Maybe not, mused Ellie, but honesty could hurt, too. She dragged her mind out of that pit and tried to focus on the hazards ahead. Before long they reached Canterbury where the streets were narrow and tourists overflowed from the pavements, gaping up at the buildings. Two priests in black cassocks darted across.

'Look at them. I hate the lot of them. Hypocrites.'

'That's what Dad used to say.'

'Jimmy? Did he? Well, he was right. We all knew, you see, what the old man was up to. He had what people used to call a roving eye, for what Mother, bless her, called a bit of skirt. He couldn't resist a pretty woman.'

'Why didn't she leave him?'

'How could she? She'd have been penniless and homeless with four kids to support. Not to mention the scandal. The disgrace, as they used to say. Anyway, they sort of patched it up. People did in those days.'

'Did she know about Maureen and the baby?'

'Of course she did. We all knew, deep down. We just never talked about it, brushed it under the carpet and pretended it had never happened. In the end you began to believe it. Now I can see that my whole childhood was one bloody big lie.'

When they reached the B&B. Fran swung round to face her.

'You know what really hurts, Ellie? To find it wasn't just a rumour. She shagged my father and had his baby and made my mother miserable. And the rest of us, too.'

'She probably loved him.'

'Love!' spat Fran. 'Who believes in love anymore?'

Bert was in the hall, watering a maidenhair fern with a long-spouted can. He glanced up as they came in, and smiled.

'Did you have a pleasant trip down memory lane?'

'Oh, roses all the way,' said Fran.

'Nothing that a nice cup of tea won't put right, I'm sure. You'll find kettle and teabags in your room. Give us a shout if there's anything else you need.'

'Thanks.' Ellie followed Fran upstairs. Another Englishman who thought that tea would cure everything.

The River Stour at Fordwich was slow and sluggish. Brown water pulled at the weeds, unfurling their strands in its current. Willows overhung the banks, and through the threads of their branches Ellie could see fields where cows grazed in the long grass.

She lay on her tummy, chin on hands and gazed at the sky. Dad would have been seven or eight when the family moved here, the year that Fran was born. But he wasn't the one whose life she tried to picture now. It was Fran, her fragile identity slashed by discord. Ellie listened, letting her talk. She watched a bee slide into the spotted throat of a foxglove. Seedpods had formed lower down the stalk, while new blossoms opened towards the tip.

'My earliest memories were of rows,' Fran said. 'The two of them shouting and screaming. Like the day that anonymous letter came. I didn't know what anonymous meant at the time. But even as a child you sense when something's creepy.'

'How long did the affair with Maureen last?'

'No idea. Mother often made snipes about women, but it might just have been paranoia. I never knew if he really was having affairs or not.'

'It's a miracle the news didn't get out.'

'Yes, I spent my whole childhood in constant fear that, if it was true, he'd be disgraced. It was like hiding in an eggshell that might get trampled on at any moment.'

'Did Dot know what was going on?'

'Of course she knew. She just pretended she didn't. Jimmy was the only one who cared enough to spend time with me, but even he didn't talk about it. And then he went away. All the men I've ever loved have left me in the end.'

'I'm sure he loved you, too, Fran. He just wasn't the sort of man to talk about his feelings.'

Fran snorted. 'Do you know a man who does?'

Ellie rolled onto her side and gripped her eyes tight. The grass felt damp, the river murmured and chuckled.

After a while they brushed the dirt from their clothes and

wandered back to the village past houses of brick and flint. Some had weatherboard facades painted white or sea-green.

They stopped by the sixteenth century Guildhall. An information panel explained that in the Middle Ages, when the river was navigable, Fordwich was one of the Cinque Ports. Here, on this dock, stone was unloaded for the building of Canterbury Cathedral. Weeds choked the river now.

At any other time Ellie would have gone inside the little museum, but Fran wanted to find a path that led to a field where violets used to cover the banks.

'Mother knew the names of all the wild flowers. Once she took me to Littlebourne, down to a stream where lilies of the valley grew wild.'

The path to the violets was impossible to find. Cul-de-sacs of executive semis had wiped out the landmarks, and only some name plates hinted at what used to be there. *Marlowe Meadows. The Drove.* Fran took out a map and rummaged in her bag for glasses.

'Spring Lane, I remember that. It was like a dark tunnel under the trees. Blimey, these names ring bells. Stodmarsh Road. Wickhambreux. Bekesbourne.'

'Place names tell stories, too, don't they.'

She thought of Manly Cove, Broken Hill, Freshwater. A tug of nostalgia pulled her, but she took the map from Fran and scoured the dense network of fields, lanes and villages marked on it.

'These Kentish places must be steeped in history. Saxon, Latin, Norman probably.'

The names were the relics of countless invasions, shifts of population, the mixing of genes and languages. Dad was one small individual who'd come and gone, insignificant in the scheme of things. Yet what he and his siblings had experienced here, had shaped their lives.

'Does anyone find life easy?' she wondered aloud. 'It's as if we're all cast in a role – fornicator, prude, long-suffering wife, mistress, damaged child, rejected lover – and try as we might we can't escape it.'

'Huh,' said Fran. 'Take control of your life and you'll succeed – isn't that what they say? Load of rubbish.'

Ellie's thoughts went back to Maureen Latimer living out her last days in the residential home. What sort of happiness had she found, sharing brief moments of love with a married man, bearing his child and giving it away? Love must be a wretched thing if it was paid for in so much hurt to others and oneself.

Yes, a wretched and a powerful thing that, however much you struggled, sometimes would not let you go.

Back in Canterbury, Fran was hungry, Ellie starving, so she parked the car near the centre of town. The cyber cafe was just round the corner.

'Why don't we grab a sandwich and do an online search at the same time? Miss Latimer's gifted us two new facts – the surname Henderson and the location Cornwall.'

'Okay. I guess it won't hurt to have a quick look.'

'But are you sure you want to do this, Fran? She's Maureen Latimer's daughter. If we find her, it might open more wounds.'

'It's not her fault she was born, is it? And, anyway, if we don't hunt her down, Dot will.'

Yes, thought Ellie, what a coup to go back to Somerset armed with all the details. And to Sydney. Quest completed. Sisters reunited and reconciled.

When Ellie logged on, they found several Amanda Hendersons in the marriage register, but none that matched her date of birth. She switched to the register of deaths but the outcome was the same.

'Shit,' said Fran. 'Where is she?'

'Let's keep positive. The results confirm two things. Amanda hasn't married and she's still alive.' Her hand froze on the mouse. 'That is, unless she's not called Amanda anymore. Adoptive parents often choose their own name for a child.'

'Then we could spend a lifetime and never guess it. Bridget? Samantha? Lily Rose?'

'Maybe we should search for Reverend Henderson instead. Where did Miss Latimer say he lived? Cornwall? There must be parish records, that sort of thing.'

An hour later the cafe had filled, emptied and filled again, and still they'd found nothing. The ecclesiastical sites either refused unauthorised access, or stated that documents were available only from local offices. But Ellie was able to verify one small fact.

'The mysterious Hugh Gregson, who brokered the adoption, died decades ago.'

'So we'll need a medium to contact him.'

She logged off the computer, leaned back in her chair and rubbed her eyes.

'Let's get out of here and have some fresh air.'

Afternoon had faded towards evening and the narrow streets were deep in shadow. The half-timbered buildings jutted forward, closing off the sky. Lights had come on behind some of the windows and the pebbled glass gave a sense of secrecy.

'I guess in medieval times people must have felt safe here,' Ellie said, 'clustered inside the city walls, with the gates barred against intruders.'

'I think I'd feel trapped, shut off from the world.'

'Yes, I guess I would, too.'

You were wrong, Dad, she thought, I'm not a koala or a mollusc. I need open spaces. If I stay here too long, this city will stifle me.

They walked a bit further, and as they turned into Burgate, an elderly lady came out of a cake shop. With her white hair and tiny stature, Ellie recognised her straight away.

'Mrs Whitaker, remember me? Ellie Goodwin.'

'Ah, I thought your face was familiar. And yours, too,' she said when Ellie introduced Fran. 'You look just like your mother. I always thought Mrs Goodwin was such a lovely lady. So what brings you back to Canterbury?'

'We've been to see Maureen Latimer. She's in a residential home in Herne Bay.'

'How is she, poor dear?'

They stepped aside to let a group of French teenagers pass with their teacher, while Ellie explained.

'I'm afraid we upset her, raking up the past.'

'Poor Maureen. What she must have gone through. How very sad.'

'But now we've hit a brick wall. We can't find a trace of this Rev Henderson anywhere.'

Mrs Whitaker tapped her chin.

'Henderson. Let me see. No, I can't say it rings any bells. Cornwall did you say? My husband might know. The clergy all meet up at conferences, you see, always hobnobbing together like a lot of old crows. I'll ask him when I get home.'

'Fantastic. I'll give you my mobile number.'

The old lady was discretion itself, but she didn't want her to phone the B&B and let Bert get wind of anything.

They said goodbye, and went on their way. Ellie linked her arm through Fran's. She felt more optimistic now. Just when she'd least expected it, another lead had opened up, shining a slender ray of hope.

They'd barely been back at the B&B for half an hour, when Ellie's mobile rang. She gestured to Fran who lay on the bed resting her feet on a pillow, her toes pink and swollen.

'Mrs Whitaker,' Ellie mouthed. She could hear Bert coming upstairs.

'Rat-a-tat-tat. Are you ladies decent?'

She asked Mrs Whitaker to hold, and went to open the door.

'Sorry to disturb you, but we was wondering if you'd be going out this evening. Only me and the missus have got our whist night, so if it's all right with you we'll take your breakfast order now.'

Ellie chose the full English, passed the list to Fran, and escaped to the bathroom. At least Bert couldn't follow her there. The fan came on with the light. It made a bit of a racket but she could just about hear Mrs Whitaker say they were in luck.

'Once I mentioned the name Henderson, my husband remembered right away. It's Reverend John Henderson. Only it wasn't Cornwall where he lived. It was Devon.'

She paused, and when she spoke again there was an ominous catch in her voice.

'There's a bit of a fly in the ointment, I'm afraid.'

Ellie braced herself. A whole string of illegitimate children? Child abuse? Suicide?

'There's no easy way to say this, my dear.'

Ellie lowered herself onto the side of the bath and took deep breaths. Who was the idiot who'd said it was better to know the truth?

'My husband is absolutely adamant – I told him that we couldn't possibly mention it if there was any doubt, but he insists that he's remembered correctly. You see, there was a car crash.'

'A car crash?'

'Yes, my dear. It must have been the late fifties, early sixties, he's not too sure about the date. The whole diocese was in shock when the news came. He can't believe that I've forgotten it, but as you know my memory's a bit wonky these days.' Her voice wavered. 'Apparently they'd only had it a couple of weeks.'

'The car?'

'Yes, they drove out of the village onto the main road and a lorry ran into them.'

'What happened? Were they okay?'

'That's the terribly tragic thing, my dear. It's so cruel to have to tell you this after you've come so far, but no, they didn't have a chance. Their little Morris was crushed by a huge great juggernaut. Of course it would have been mercifully quick and they wouldn't have known a thing, but a dreadful tragedy all the same.'

Ellie clutched the phone, too stunned to speak.

The extractor fan whirled. A spider hung by a slender thread from the curtain rail, swaying in the draft.

'I'm so very sorry, my dear. I wish it was better news.'

'And Amanda was killed with them?'

'Arnold thinks so. He's as certain as it's possible to be after all this time. To tell the truth, his memory isn't what it once was, though he won't admit it.'

'But they definitely did have a daughter?'

'A little girl, yes. He can't remember her name. He sometimes forgets his own grandchildren's names, come to that. Yes, he thinks they adopted her. Of course that would have stuck in his mind. It was a sensitive subject for us as we were trying to adopt, too, at the time.'

Ellie remembered the photo in their conservatory, the three children of different races. She searched for something appropriate to say, but her mind was numb.

'He thinks the parish was called Midford or Mudford, or something like that, but place names are bit of a blur for him, too.'

'Okay, no worries. Thank you both so much. If it hadn't been for you, we'd still be looking for someone who doesn't exist.'

They said goodbye, but Ellie didn't move. The bathroom fan droned on with its manic whirring as she pictured the scene. A car crash. The huge truck bearing down and thundering into them. Flesh, blood and bones smashed to oblivion. Three lives crushed in one horrendous moment of impact.

So Amanda was dead. She had been dead for fifty years and Dad had never known. The distress he'd felt at her birth, his concern later on, had been in vain. This quest was pointless. She was dead. Nothing could alter that.

Slowly Ellie got to her feet. She felt chastened, foolish. All her efforts had been no more than a stupid game. Her hopes and illusions were mere self-deception, spawned from the emptiness of her life.

The photo and the postcard were mere mementoes, dry documents long since redundant. Dad did not have three sisters. There could be no reconciliation. The trail had reached its end.

THE EAST END, 1955

Hugh Gregson's church was easy enough to find. A dingy Victorian monstrosity, not far from where Jack had lodged when he'd worked as a barrow boy a quarter of a century ago. How ironic that Gregson, the Oxbridge rugby blue, had ended up here, while Jack, from a simple village family, lived among the pomp and splendour of Canterbury.

Or as Lillian called it, 'The City of the two Esses.'

'The two Esses?' said the mystified Bishop's wife, who'd enquired how Lillian enjoyed living there.

'I don't,' she said. 'It's full of Slums and Snobs.'

Really, Lillian was impossible, Jack thought as he turned the corner towards the church, but he couldn't help admiring her grit. She saw through people's pretensions and wasn't afraid to say so. The trouble was, she offended them and embarrassed him. He'd moved from one post to another, hoping to please her, but if the truth be told, she simply wasn't suited to being a vicar's wife.

He looked around him at the grimy street. If they'd come somewhere like this, would she have been happier? He doubted it. Snobs might be scarce in the East End, but slums there were a-plenty, bombed buildings in disrepair, whole families crammed into single rooms.

As he walked up the weed-infested tarmac to the church door, his pulse quickened and he sent up a silent prayer. Of course he had no right to ask anything of the Almighty, serial sinner that he was. Time and time again he'd fallen to his knees, begged for forgiveness and sworn to mend his ways. Sometimes he'd succeeded for months on end. But once a chink of opportunity came, temptation tightened its coils and he succumbed. Wretched from months of enforced abstinence while Lillian turned him from their bedroom and slammed the door in his face, Jack convinced himself that he was justified. Gorged with desire and the memory of its sweet consumption, he fed himself on the ever-willing Maureen's tender flesh, until sated at last, he could take no more.

How innocent they had been, how foolish. And now this, the inevitable result. No, for himself he could ask nothing, but for Maureen, who had risked so much, for Lillian whom he had hurt too often already, and for his children – all of his children – he must.

He braced himself for the ordeal ahead. The south door of the church was open, and from the crypt came whoops and shouts as if a game were in progress. As Jack headed in that direction a familiar figure appeared. He wore a clerical collar and his shirt sleeves were rolled to the elbow.

It was Hugh, an older Hugh, but unmistakable all the same. His hair was a steely grey and his face showed signs of ageing, but he had the same strong-boned jaw and wiry frame that Jack remembered from their days at Cheshunt College.

'Jack, old boy. How terrific to see you.'

They shook hands warmly, searching each other's faces for signs of the young men they'd once been.

'Thank you for making the time, Hugh. I realise how busy you must be.'

'Come into the office. The lads are having a ping-pong tournament, so they'll be fine for a while, and we've got an excellent youth leader to sort out any squabbles.'

Jack followed him into a ramshackle room which doubled as a vestry. Cassocks and coats hung from pegs, and dog-eared prayer books toppled in an untidy pile on top of a cupboard. A moth-eaten rug half covered the floor. Hugh's desk was an old kitchen table littered with books and papers. He could see no sign of the pipe or an ashtray, and was glad he'd just had a quick cigarette to calm his nerves.

'How's Lillian?'

'She's in Devon with the children.'

He had expected this question, so had prepared an answer that was truthful enough.

'We rent a chalet down in Branscombe, well, it's more of a beach hut really, but the children love it. They'll all stay there for the rest of the summer, but of course I can only manage a couple of weeks.'

'Remind me, how many is it now, three?'

'No, four – two boys and two girls. Our youngest is seven.'

He could have added that the eldest, Dorothy, had just completed her first year at Oxford, but proud as he was of her, he knew this wasn't the moment to boast.

Hugh drew out a chair for him and brushed some crumbs from the cushion.

'Have a seat. My word, you must have stamina. Remember what old Benson used to say, that marriage is for the strong hearted?'

They laughed at the memory, Jack with a twist of discomfort.

'Nature, nurture or personal choice, wasn't that what he said about celibacy?'

'Yes, in a nutshell. Some are born that way, some are made that way by experience, and some renounce marriage for the kingdom. But whichever path you choose has challenges.'

'So you've never tied the knot, Hugh, or the noose, as some might say?'

'No, though in my case it was probably a combination of all three factors.'

He laughed, throwing back his head in the way that Jack remembered so well. Had he, too, struggled with certain inclinations, Jack wondered? But Hugh had never confided in him and now was not the time to probe.

The stained glass window above them brightened, and a wedge of ruby light fell over the papers on the desk where Hugh sat waiting for him to speak. This was the awful moment when he would have to reveal the reason for his visit. He cleared his throat.

'Thank you for agreeing to see me at such short notice.'

'It's always a pleasure to see an old friend. How can I help?'

'I don't want to take up your time, so I'll come straight to the point.' His mouth was dry and he had to moisten it with saliva before he could continue. 'It's a rather delicate matter, Hugh, and whatever your decision, I know I can depend on you to let it go no further than these four walls.'

'Of course, dear boy. I give you my word.'

The rugged face, lined with age, showed only gentle concentration.

'You see, there's someone who works at the college who's in a bit of trouble.'

He swallowed hard, bracing himself for the revelation of gender that he'd have to make. Already he sensed a new alertness in the glance his friend gave him.

'She's an excellent employee, hard-working, efficient, came with top-class references, but she's very young and, unfortunately it seems that…she's single, you see…and, well, there's no easy way of saying it…she's expecting a child.'

'I see. And the father?'

'Oh, her father died some years ago, and her brother is in the army, stationed abroad, so she has no one but her widowed mother, who's taken it very hard.'

'I meant the father of the child,' Hugh said gently. 'Is he able to marry her?'

The sun danced over the desk, the air swirled with dust motes. Jack could feel sweat form on the palms of his hands. His throat knotted under the clerical collar.

'No. The father is already married.'

His blood flared then ran cold. He did not want to lie, but neither did he want to reveal more of the truth than necessary. The less that anyone knew, including and especially Hugh if he were willing to help, the better. His heart hammered as he waited for his friend to respond. Hugh sat like a chess player contemplating a move, the fingers of one hand tapping the knuckles of the other.

'Forgive me if I ask a few more questions, simply for the purpose of clarification.'

He waited, while Jack nodded.

'Firstly, when is the child expected, and secondly, does the young lady in question wish to keep it once it is born?'

With growing relief at Hugh's discretion and lack of censure, Jack provided the answers. The child was due in mid to late

November, and no, the young lady did not feel that she was in a position to keep it. As a single working woman with limited means, that would be impossible.

'And one assumes that the father,' said Hugh with the greatest delicacy, 'is not in a position to support them?'

'No, that is correct.'

'And her mother can't be persuaded to help?'

Jack shook his head, and shuddered at the memory of the dreadful day when Mrs Latimer and a tearful Maureen had appeared in his study at home. This was no Mother-in-law Cullen, confining herself to icy barbs. This was a fierce and furious Amazon who threatened to see Jack and his family out on the streets begging for a crust if she didn't 'get satisfaction' as she put it.

'No, I'm afraid that her mother could make things very difficult indeed.'

There was no need to say more. Hugh knew as well as he did what that might mean, not only for the guilty father, but for the reputation of the church.

'They are Baptists,' Jack added, and at once regretted it. He'd meant to imply that Maureen, despite her condition, was a devout Christian, but perhaps it sounded like a slur on other denominations, which had not been his intention.

He shifted uncomfortably on the lumpy cushion while Hugh weighed up the situation. What Jack dreaded more than anything was sympathy but no offer of help. In that case he would be in despair. On the one flank he faced Mrs Latimer and her threats, on the other the rumbling volcano of Lillian's wrath. He'd tried to deny the accusation, claimed that anyone could be the father. There was no proof it was his. But a pregnancy was not like an anonymous letter that one could brush aside as malicious hearsay. Its awful evidence was visible in Maureen's swollen belly.

Ever since the news had broken, he'd wrestled with the stark choice that confronted him – leave his wife and children, or abandon his mistress and baby. Whichever he chose, someone would be unhappy, and Jack would be branded as villain. God might forgive, but people did not.

At times he felt that the Almighty was unjust not to allow a better solution. Look at Solomon with his hundreds of wives and concubines. Solomon, the offspring of David the adulterer and murderer of Bathsheba's husband. Why, David had even been allowed to marry his mistress, and have her bear his children!

Oh no, God did not strike down those men. On the contrary, he blessed them with untold riches and wisdom. And look at Abraham – he'd sired a child not only with his wife but with his slave girl, and both offspring went on to be patriarchs of great nations. Why, in some parts of the world, even today, men were allowed two or more wives.

Not that Jack wished for that solution. One wife to contend with, day in, day out, was hard enough. All that he wanted was help for Maureen and peace with Lillian. And also that he, if possible, might be rid of his confounded weakness.

A knock on the door jolted him from his thoughts. A tousle-haired boy put his head round, glancing from Hugh to Jack and back again.

'You comin' down yet? Only Forbesie's worried there's going to be a bit of bovver if them lot win.'

'Ten minutes, Sam, and I'll be with you.'

The boy left, closing the door behind him.

'Sorry I've caught you at a difficult time,' Jack said.

'Not at all. These minor scraps are routine.'

Hugh took out a pen and reached for some paper. The ray of sunlight had moved onto his desk, and he shifted his chair.

'Now, let's consider solutions. I'd say there are three steps we need to take. Tell me if you agree. Firstly, find a place for the young lady to be cared for while she waits for her confinement. Secondly, locate a suitable family to adopt the baby, once born. Thirdly, when the young lady has recovered, help her to find employment in a new location where she can make a fresh start.'

Relief swamped Jack and he nodded vigorously, trying not to grin like a fool. The mask of pretence meant he had to moderate his joy.

'What sort of work does she do?'

'She's a secretary.' A very good one, he would have liked to add, but didn't dare.

'And she'll have no trouble obtaining references from your end?'

'None at all.'

Hugh made a note and nodded as he did so.

'That point should be fairly easy to resolve, as long as she's prepared to move. In fact I would say that a fresh start is essential. How about London? I can think of a number of church offices there where a good secretary with the right recommendations would have no trouble in finding employment. The Church Commissioners, Church Pensions, Lambeth Palace, and so on. What do you think?'

'I'm sure she'd take any opportunity that's open to her.'

'Good, good. Now, a number of places in discreet surroundings specialise in helping young women in these situations. In a parish like this, as you can imagine, such problems aren't uncommon. So the question of confinement is also straightforward, assuming that she is willing to move from her home.'

'That's definitely not a problem. In fact her mother refuses to let her stay.'

'So,' said Hugh, putting down his pen, 'the only other step we need to take is to arrange an adoption.'

Jack swallowed. To help Maureen find solutions was easy compared with the challenge of disposing of a child – their child – who must never know the truth about its birth.

Strange though it now seemed, they had never taken action to prevent a pregnancy. Opportunities for love-making were rare and often unexpected, and the fact that they both struggled with guilt and swore never to fall again, had somehow immunised them from reality.

'Will she agree to an adoption?' he heard Hugh say.

'Yes, yes, she feels that she has no choice.'

To his relief, Maureen had made no demands of him, but had kept up a stoic independence. 'I could never ask a man to desert his children,' she had said.

Jack had taken her words at face value. He knew it wasn't a baby she wanted. It was him. But he could not, would not, abandon Lillian. Secretly, though he'd never have admitted it, he felt too old and worn out to start a new family with a young wife.

Hugh was speaking again, so Jack tried to concentrate as he mentioned a clergy couple who might be persuaded to adopt a baby. For some time they had been trying for one of their own, but without success.

'I'll have a discreet word with them and let you know. Their name is Henderson. They're caring, reliable people, who'd give child a secure and loving home. He was a colleague of mine some years back, but didn't take to life here in the East End, so they moved to a small rural parish in Devon.'

'Devon?' Jack thought of Branscombe and the possibility of their paths crossing, but Hugh's mind was on other issues.

'Yes, it's a long way, I know, but that's probably better for all concerned.'

'No, no, it would be ideal.'

Hugh glanced once more at his watch.

'Look, Jack, leave this with me and I'll be in touch as soon as I can. I appreciate that time is of the essence in cases like this.'

'Thank you, you're a true friend.'

'I'll need a few details, the young lady's name, address, age, qualifications and so on.'

He passed across pen and paper. When Jack had finished writing, Hugh glanced through the information without comment, stood up and moved towards the door. As Jack followed, Hugh turned.

'One last thing.' He lowered his voice.

'Please tell Miss Latimer to expect me to contact her within the next week or so. I'll keep you informed of proceedings, but I think it's better for all concerned if you take no further part.'

'Quite, quite,' Jack heard himself say.

'And finally, both she and the father must agree to give up all claims on the child. That means no contact with it, either now or in the future. Or with each other.'

Hugh rested one hand on Jack's shoulder. Every muscle in his body tautened.

'Do you understand?'

He nodded.

'And agree?'

'Yes, yes, of course.'

He drew deep into himself for strength to speak the words that he'd promised Maureen he would say.

'Only, when the baby is born, might…they…be allowed to have a few minutes together with it?'

For the first time, a trace of annoyance passed over Hugh's face.

'I'll see what's possible. Mind you, I can't promise.'

Jack followed him out of the office and down the nave towards the south door. All noise from the crypt had subsided and the church was perfectly quiet, with only a dull hum of traffic from outside.

They shook hands.

'I can't thank you enough for your help, Hugh. I don't know what I'd do without a friend like you.'

Their eyes met, and Jack flinched under the directness he saw.

'I'm a wretched sinner, Gregson. I wish I could be strong like you.'

'Goodwin, we are all sinners as you very well know. God in his wisdom gave us free will and it's up to us how we exercise it. When I'm weak, then I'm strong in his strength. Remember?'

A sudden burst of angry voices came from downstairs.

'I must go,' Hugh said.

'Of course.' Jack was about to make his way down the path when he heard Hugh's voice.

'Remember me to Lillian.'

'Yes, of course.'

'And Jack?'

'Yes?'

His friend's face was ruddy in the midday sun.

'Look after her, won't you.'

It was not a question. It was a command.

NORTH DEVON, 2010

If it hadn't been for Fran, Ellie mused as the car groaned uphill, she'd probably be half-way to Sydney by now. Instead of which, here they were back in Devon, in a bewildering maze of narrow lanes that twisted and turned between banks topped with hedges so high that you couldn't see what was coming the other way.

She stamped on the brakes. Bang in front of them, in the centre of the lane, a Land Rover shook and shuddered while the farmer leaned out to have a natter with his mate in a van. Her hand hovered over the horn, then dropped again.

'Better not upset the natives, I guess.'

'Here,' said Fran. 'Have a fruit gum.'

Ellie chose blackcurrant and let the deep sweetness spread over her tongue. It was years since she'd had one of these, and the almost forgotten taste soothed her tense nerves.

Last night, exhausted after driving from Canterbury, drained of emotion, she'd barely had the energy to speak. She'd slept like she used to, curled up with two fingers in her mouth, and now here she was, cruising down from the moors on yet another journey. Yet another attempt to find someone who might have been dead for decades. But Fran was convinced that they'd find her. She had a hunch, she said, a feeling in her bones.

'Even if you've given up, I haven't,' she taunted, and that was enough.

One thing was certain. If Amanda really was alive, Ellie was the one who would find her.

She drummed her fingers on the steering wheel, while the two men nattered on. Clearly they had no pressing engagements. Nor did she, come to that. Only a feeble hope of finding parish records, or the gory details of an accident in the archives of a local newspaper. A minister and his family killed in a car crash would probably have been worth a mention.

Deep down she was sure that Amanda had died with them. But the remote possibility that she might have survived still gripped Ellie, and until she knew for certain, she couldn't rest.

A horn honked, startling her. The farmer pulled away and half lifted his hand in apology. The other driver backed into a gateway to let them pass.

'Not far now,' said Fran and clutched the OS map.

They wound through a honeycomb of hills and valleys. Twice more Ellie had to stop to let cars pass, and once for a tractor with a trailer-load of muck that spurted onto the tarmac with every jolt, spraying them with its foul stink.

On a distant hill she could see wind turbines like a troop of Don Quixote's giants, blades whirring with an ominous whine.

Fran was trying to read the map upside down.

'I think we've missed a turning.'

Ellie pulled onto a verge. A horse leaned over the gate, and through the bars she could see grasses, wispy in the breeze, their seed-heads a pink haze. The hedgerows were a tangle of tiny leaves, and where the petals of roses and honeysuckle had fallen, berries were forming.

What she now knew to be cow parsley had gone to seed. The elderflowers had given way to clusters of fruit, still green but gathering a tinge of purple. Beyond the fields she could see hills where a grey tower rose from the tree tops.

'There's a church over there. Maybe that's it.'

She reached for the map. A labyrinth of lanes ran between scattered farms and hamlets, with a church in the centre.

They drove on through a wood, past whitewashed cottages and a farmyard where barns were being converted into chic dwellings. The lane twisted and climbed to a junction. Up ahead, was an ancient fingerpost.

Midford ½ mile.

'So it's *mid*,' she said. 'I guess that's marginally better than *mud*.'

She parked under the shade of what Fran recognised as horse chestnut trees. Dad had told her about conkers, and here they were on the ground, with their prickly sheaths split open over glossy brown nuts. A tiny roofed entrance led into the churchyard.

'It's a lych gate,' said Fran, 'that's where they used to shelter with the coffins till the vicar arrived.'

Her words jolted Ellie back to that hot January day when Dad's body was burned to a handful of ashes. The screeching of cockatoos, the jacarandas in blossom, their purple petals on the parched ground, every fibre in her body screaming in denial.

Now, though, something had subtly changed. It was like when you teased a sea anemone spine out of your foot. You could still touch tenderness where the pain had been, but its sharpness had gone.

She followed Fran into the churchyard. Its silence and permanence made her feel like an intruder, yet strangely at home. Ancient gravestones sank at odd angles into the turf. Several of them leaned against the boundary wall, encrusted with a grey-green growth of lichen. On one she could just make out an inscription.

Josiah Barton departed this life 20th March 1703. His beloved wife, Mary.

Fran led the way to an entrance porch with wooden benches on either side. The stone flagged floor was spotted with confetti. Along the wall was a notice board with lists of church services and other events, tacked on with rusty pins.

Church fete, family fun day, flower rota, PCC meeting.

And a warning to thieves that an alarm system had been installed.

Around the arch, above the rough wooden door, was a garland of flowers like the ones she'd seen in Lyme Regis. Soft, blowsy roses twisted through a rope of green leaves. Above them, tucked into the rafters, nestled the tiny cup of a bird's nest. A soft chirruping came from inside.

'Swallows,' said Fran.

They stood for a moment, listening, then Ellie lifted the heavy iron latch and pushed open the door. Light filtered through the stained glass windows to paint pools of colour on the stone floor. The air was cool and damp, mixed with the fragrance of the wedding flowers.

A strip of carpet trod soft and silent under her sneakers. She made her way to an ancient stone font at the back of the church. She'd read about these but never seen one before.

'Maybe Amanda was christened here,' she said, and reached for a book that lay on a dusty shelf. On the cover were the words

Baptismal Roll, written in red biro. She flicked through the pages but the entries began in 1990, which was way too late. The older records must be in an archive somewhere.

Like a kid on a treasure hunt, she prowled around the church looking for clues. Fran trailed after her. Apart from some cross-stitched kneelers and tattered hymn books, the pews were bare. In one corner was a carpeted space with children's toys and board games, and above it, on the stone walls hung colourful banners. As Ellie glanced at them, she caught sight of a board with a list of names.

Rectors of this parish.

The list ran from the 1300s to the present, and as she skimmed down it, she stopped with a jolt.

'Fran, look! *Reverend John Henderson, 1952-1960.'*

'That's our man. Blimey, I can't believe it.'

Ellie made for the door and sped out into the churchyard while Fran scurried behind. A soft drizzle had started to fall and the grass was wet where they crossed it to reach the graves. One was a freshly dug mound of dirt, strewn with bunches of flowers in cellophane wrappers. She led the way past a row of headstones, the inscriptions clear and sharp, but all were far too recent.

'We need burials from 1960.'

They worked their way down a slope towards the boundary wall. This part of the churchyard was darker and more overgrown, edged by bushes with dark glossy leaves. In one corner was a pile of grass clippings, garden waste and rotting flowers.

'*1990. 1984.* We're getting closer.'

Some of the graves had been carefully tended with fresh jars of flowers or pot-plants. Others were choked with weeds and barely visible. She moved carefully up and down the rows, trying not to step where people were buried. Superstition or respect? She wasn't sure.

'*1965. 63. 61. 60.*'

A shiver ran through her as one inscription shot sharply into focus.

'Fran, this is it.'

Her voice sounded strange. As she scanned the words, all she could hear was the wind soughing in the trees.

In loving memory of John Alfred Henderson, vicar of this parish, and his wife Anthea, whose lives were tragically cut short on 5th December 1960.'

Fran stood beside her.

Beneath are the everlasting arms.

A magpie flew out of the hedge with a loud chacker-chacker.

'So where . . . ?'

As if by telepathy, they both turned to the neighbouring graves. *Ridd. Chugg. Pugsley.* Each unfamiliar surname brought a tremor of hope. Ellie scanned every stone in the section, then walked up and down through the churchyard again.

Fran had sunk onto a bench, elbows on knees, head in hands. She looked up, fearful, expectant, as Ellie drew near.

'She's not here, Fran. I've searched everywhere.'

'So that means . . ?'

Ellie sat down beside her. The clouds had thinned. Weak spots of sunshine trembled and danced through the leaves.

'It must mean she's alive. Or she'd be buried here, too.'

The magpie startled them both with its ugly chatter. Ellie clapped her hands and it flapped away. Her mind raced over the possibilities.

Could Amanda really have survived the accident? And if so, what would have happened to her afterwards? You heard tragic cases like that on the news sometimes, parents killed in house fires or terrorist attacks or plane crashes, their children orphaned.

The family stepped in, didn't they? Wasn't that what the reports said? *The children are being cared for by relatives.* Grandparents, aunts, anyone close enough to offer them a home.

But what if you had no relatives? An adopted child didn't share the genes of the new family. They might make excuses, too many children of their own, money or health problems, other concerns. Those would be the kids who ended up in children's homes, as the responsibility of the state.

Poor Amanda. Adopted, orphaned and taken into care in the first few years of her life.

Fran jumped to her feet.

'Let's get out of here. This place gives me the creeps.'

They walked back to the lych gate and out to the car. The trees rustled as the wind caught their branches. The sun had disappeared again and the air was chilly.

Ellie turned to her aunt.

'Fancy a drink? There must be a pub somewhere.'

Her mind whirled backwards then forwards again.

1960 was half a century ago, but maybe, just maybe there was someone still alive around here who could remember the terrible events of that December day. The day when a little girl lost her parents for the second time.

An hour or so later, Ellie followed a farmer's Ute out of the pub car park. She was riding on a new wave of optimism. Just as she'd thought, the bar had been full of locals, and the man up ahead knew an old lady who'd lived here all her life.

'Just as soon as I finish me pint,' he'd told them, 'I'll point 'ee in the right direction.'

She drove with all her senses alert, ready to stamp on the brakes if he pulled up sharp. A border collie rested its paws on the tailgate, barking back at them.

He turned into a lane that twisted between hedges, and they began to climb steeply. At the top of the hill, the Ute's brake lights glowed and the farmer stuck his head out the window.

'That a-way. Second cottage to the left.'

His tyres spun in the dirt as he roared away in a cloud of exhaust fumes. She turned onto a rough track.

'Blimey,' said Fran. 'This is almost more remote than my place.'

Grass grew along the middle of the track, and wheel ruts sank on either side. Ellie kept the car in low gear and they bumped over potholes until a pair of terraced cottages came into view, fronted by a low stone wall. The roof was corrugated tin like the one they used to have at Narrabeen. Judging by the rust it had been there some time.

She parked on a verge. They both got out and a ginger cat jumped down from the wall. It rubbed at their legs, lifting its tail. From a distant field came the whirr of a combine harvester. As Ellie glanced up at the cottage, a curtain moved, but it might have been the breeze, which was stronger now that they were on higher ground. She opened the gate. A geranium in a china potty stood on an old milk churn beside the door, but she couldn't see a bell or a knocker.

'Here goes.' She thumped with her fist. 'Anyone home?'

The cat miaowed and scratched at the peeling paintwork.

She was about to knock again when Fran gripped her arm.

'Someone's coming. Listen.'

From inside the house came the sound of shuffling. A shadow darkened the square of frosted glass, and the door opened a crack. A minuscule old lady peeped out, her face shrivelled. Wisps of orange hair quivered over her scalp and two bead-like eyes glinted as she spoke.

'Are 'ee the chirp'odist?'

Her accent was so unfamiliar that it took Ellie a moment to realise what she meant.

'Ooo?' the old lady said, when she explained why they'd come.

'Henderson. Reverend Henderson.'

'Ah, him were vicar when me and Bill was wed.'

The papery skin of her face split into a toothless grin. She pushed the door further open and inched towards them, her back bent under a flowered housecoat and cardigan.

'So do you remember the accident?' Ellie asked.

'Oh yes, me lover. What a terrible way to go. Him and his Missus squashed like a pair of beetles.'

Fran bent down to stroke the cat and her shoulders were quivering, but Ellie was in no mood for fooling.

'Do you remember their little girl, Amanda?'

The old lady tutted.

'Them did have a little girl but that weren't her name.'

'Do you know what it was?'

Her forehead creased, the wrinkled face twisted, and her gums worked soundlessly in the effort to recall it. Ellie waited as patiently as she could. Inside the dingy house she could make out a wooden staircase, a stone flagged floor and a table covered with an oilskin cloth.

A gnarled hand gripped her arm.

'Denise. That were it. Denise, poor little mite.'

'Denise? You're sure?'

'Oh yes. It come back to me now. Same name as me niece over to Molland.'

Ellie swung round to Fran in excitement. Denise Henderson – no wonder the name Amanda Latimer had yielded nothing. She turned back to the old lady.

'So was Denise with them when they had the accident? Was she killed, too?'

'Oh no, me lover. Her was at school.'

Fran sprang forward. 'So what happened to her? Where did she go?'

The old lady's hands, shrunken and bony under folds of skin, kneaded together.

'Barnardo's took her in, over Taunton way.' She named a village. 'Hartfield House, I believe the home were called.'

Ellie's eyes met Fran's in a moment of triumph. Just as she'd guessed – the orphaned child had been taken into care. It seemed almost too simple.

At the sound of a car engine, they all turned. A Ford Sierra was bumping its way over the potholes towards the cottages.

'That'll be the chirp'odist now, I wouldn't wonder.'

'We'd better let you get on, then. Thank you so much for your help.'

They were about to leave when the bright little eyes fixed on them one last time.

'So who are ye, then?'

'My aunt here is a . . . distant relative of Denise.'

'And my niece has come all the way from Australia.'

'Australia?' The old lady peered at Ellie with renewed interest. 'I got a cousin in Perth. You wouldn't know she, I suppose?'

'No, I'm afraid not,' said Ellie as kindly as she could. 'Perth is quite a long way from Sydney.'

And that, she thought as they walked back to the car, is a very long way from here.

Dunkery Beacon could glower all it wanted but Ellie almost skipped as she walked away from Fran's caravan. The finish line was so close. At last she had a clear goal, and locating Denise would be child's play.

Fran stood huddled in a jumper to see her off.

'Don't let Dot take over. She's covered this up for years, so why should she call the shots now? Denise is my sister, too.'

'No worries. I'll call you the moment I find her.'

Fran stuck her head through the car window and pecked Ellie on the cheek. A sting of tears took Ellie by surprise. The days that they'd spent together had brought them closer, like old and new growth in the Devon hedges, hawthorn and holly, separate but intertwined.

Rain had filled the potholes in Fran's track. It sent up muddy splashes as she bumped along but her heart was rejoicing. How wild and tangled the banks had grown since she'd first seen them. The grasses had dried and gone to seed. Blackberries glistened on the brambles. She could hear a tractor and smell the sour, pungent odour of muck-spreading. Swallows had gathered along the telegraph wires, ready for the long journey home.

At the end of the track, she joined a lane that dropped into a valley between steep, wooded hills. The oaks and beeches were bronze and gold, the conifers dark against the moor. She paused by a gateway to let a car pass. Through the bars of the gate, across the meadow, a pair of deer stood, their shadows slanting in the evening sun.

She switched off the engine. The window was open, and as stealthily as a hunter she framed them in the lens of her mobile. Their heads were up, looking her way, the stag with his antlers lifted, nostrils sniffing the air. She clicked.

Without a sound, simultaneously, they turned and bounded into the wood.

The grasses and trees were as still as if the deer had never been there. But the image on her phone proved it.

Their ease and alertness. Their curiosity. Their caution. Their togetherness. In this domesticated landscape they conjured up a sense both of freedom and belonging. It resonated with something Ellie recognised but couldn't identify.

She sat, trying to make sense of it, while shadows crept across the valley and stole the colour from the copse where the deer had disappeared.

Night was falling as Ellie reached the outskirts of the village that the old lady had mentioned. She stopped to ask the way from a man walking a dog.

'Hartfield House? Just down there on the right.'

It was a large building, set back from the road, three storeys high and six windows wide, surrounded by lawns. A flight of steps led up to a pillared portico. Lights shone brightly from inside. Several top range cars were parked in the drive. A stylish brass tube lit up the signboard at the entrance.

Whatever Hartfield House had been in the past, it was now a hotel.

The next day, back at Dot's, Ellie scoured every website she could find. Perched on the bed with her laptop, she trawled through records of births, marriages and deaths, directories of addresses and telephone numbers, professional registers, social networking sites, but to no avail.

Denise Henderson had vanished from the face of the earth. If there really was somebody up there, he was making a fool of her and she didn't like it one bit.

She went downstairs. The sitting room was empty but the door to the patio stood open. Dot sat outside in the late summer sun with a newspaper, her pen poised over the crossword.

She looked up as Ellie approached.

'How are you getting on?'

'A dead end. Denise Henderson seems to have gone up in smoke.'

'Did you say that the children's home was run by Barnardo's? I'll ask Raymond. He might be able to help.'

'Raymond?'

'Oh, he knows all sorts of people and has his fingers in all sorts of pies.'

She folded the newspaper and took off her glasses.

'He did a lot of fund-raising for Barnardo's at one time. They must have records somewhere, and he's bound to have a contact who can ferret them out.'

'But Hartfield House closed in 1972. That's a very long time ago.'

'Raymond is a very old man,' Dot said with a smile. 'Nearly as old as I am.'

A few days later as Ellie walked back from the village, a car pulled ahead of her into Dot's drive. It was the dark blue Rover, bodywork polished, chrome gleaming.

Raymond climbed out, his slick of hair neatly combed, a portfolio under his arm. Ellie shifted Dot's shopping bag to her other hand and waited while he fussed over the locks, as if thieves lurked behind every neatly clipped shrub.

'Good afternoon, young lady. Just the person I've come to see. I have news. Dorothy is at home, I take it?'

Dot came out and Raymond lifted his hand, half in salute, half in greeting.

'I bring good news – and bad.'

He halted all Ellie's attempts to question him and made her wait while Dot ushered them into the sitting room, brought in cups of tea, then passed round plates and served slices of home-made Victoria sponge.

'Well, then,' she said, 'do put us out of our misery.'

Raymond swallowed his cake and dabbed his mouth with a serviette.

'I am happy to say that a source close to the charity in question has supplied the information you requested. Denise Henderson was indeed at Hartfield, albeit for a very short time. Almost certainly no later than 1961.'

Dot clapped her hands.

'I felt sure that if anyone could find out, it would be this man. He does have his uses, you know.'

'Thank you, Dorothy, I take that as a compliment. However, I must advise caution. That was the good news. From there on, I'm afraid, we've drawn a blank.'

Ellie listened with growing tension as he explained that the details of what had happened to Denise were sketchy. His contact's authority was limited, so he couldn't press too far.

'This is all off the record, you understand.'

'Do you think that she was adopted a second time?' Ellie asked.

Raymond reached for another slice of cake.

'My word, Dorothy, this is good. You certainly know the way to a man's heart.'

Ellie clenched her teeth, trying to hold back her irritation. Dot came to her aid.

'Do keep to the point and spare us the agony. What else did you discover?'

'It's only a hunch. I wouldn't want you to get too excited.'

'Out with it, man. Stop teasing us.'

'Ah, she knows me only too well. Seriously, though, what I'm about to tell you is no more than a possibility. I must emphasise that there's absolutely no evidence.'

'Well?'

'The suspicion is, and it's only a suspicion, though the lack of records is a compelling factor, that Denise was one of those children who were sent abroad.'

'Abroad?' Dot and Ellie looked at each other aghast.

'Especially since she had no living relatives.'

'You mean none that she knew of,' Ellie said.

Her irritation was hard to contain, but Raymond laced his fingers and waited for their attention.

'So your best option would be to contact the Child Migrants' Trust. You may well have heard of them. There was a television programme not so long ago about the woman who uncovered the scandal. A film, too, I believe. She caused quite a stir at the time.'

'Yes, I do remember,' said Dot. 'Margaret somebody. She set up the Trust in order to reunite the orphans with their families.'

The awful tragedy, she added, was that it turned out that many of them weren't orphans at all.

'Their parents had given them up unwillingly because of poverty, or the hardships of war, and the poor children had never been told the truth.'

Ellie put down her cup so fast that the tea sloshed over the saucer.

Those orphans. She and Josh had talked about them, and how Australia was often used as a dump for the unwanted. Only the other day she'd mentioned them to Fran.

Raymond was talking, but she interrupted him.

'They were sent to Australia, weren't they?'

'Indeed, some of them were.'

'You're kidding. That means I've come all this way and she's been there all the time.'

He wagged a cautionary finger.

'Australia is a possibility. But some went to Canada, or to one of the British colonies in Africa.'

'Then Denise could be anywhere. If that's the case, I give up.'

She shifted Clio's chin off her foot and started to pace. This whole quest was futile. It was all very well for Dad to say that giving up was a euphemism for failure, but when he'd had problems with his family in England, he'd turned his back on them. She'd tried to pick up the pieces for his sisters' sake, but now she'd had enough. Oh yes, people were brilliant at giving advice, while they sat on their own backsides and left you to get on with it. Just like Josh. What was it he'd said? *There's a whole lot more to gain than to lose. You can wallow in self pity or keep fighting.*

Well, she'd fought, and she'd lost.

'1961,' said Dot thoughtfully. 'That was the year that Jimmy left.'

It took a moment for the connection to click. Ellie narrowed her eyes, not sure if Dot was throwing her a lifeline. Her aunt sat there, sipping her tea in that annoyingly serene old ladyish way.

Ellie flopped back on the sofa, her mind swimming. She didn't want a lifeline, not really. After all the setbacks, she'd be just as happy to drown. But again the old intrigue stirred. That chain of improbable connections was too lucid to be illusion, too intriguing to ignore. She'd already realised that it was because of Denise – her birth, the circumstances surrounding it – that Dad had emigrated. But what he couldn't possibly have known was that Denise was leaving the country, too. By a chilling coincidence, they'd both left England in the very same year. Their paths might have crossed, in a crowded railway station, a busy port of embarkation. They might even have travelled on the same boat.

In her mind's eye, as if enlarged on a screen, Ellie saw the two of them pass on deck, a young man and a child, who barely noticed each other, not realising they shared the same father. No, that was too way-out. But however and whenever they'd travelled, both of them had headed in the same direction. Of that she felt sure.

Two exiles on the way to a Promised Land.

Australia. The place that people run to when they want to hide from the past.

Australia. The place that people are sent to when nobody wants them.

Her voice burst out to two startled faces.

'She's in Australia. I'll bet you anything.'

By bedtime, her neck and eyes ached. Frustration had bubbled up again and built to boiling point. This whole attempt at a search was taking her round and round in a maze with no exit. Hope soared like a rocket only to sink as a damp squib.

The website of the Child Migrants' Trust made it clear that Dot, as the nearest surviving blood relative, was the one who should lodge her details. She'd gone out to a meeting, so this would have to wait until morning. Even Ellie's minor breakthrough of finding that Barnardo's had a Family History Service was short-lived. You could trace a deceased family member for the purpose of genealogical research, but, bizarrely, to trace a living one you needed permission from the former Barnardo's child herself.

Everything was stacked against finding Denise.

Even so, Ellie was sure that her hunch was right. If Denise had gone abroad, it would explain why they'd found no trace of her here. Okay, it would be too much of a coincidence if she'd travelled on the same boat as Dad. But if they had sent her abroad, it would almost certainly have been to Australia, whatever Raymond said. That was where most of the orphans had gone. And anyway, an uncanny sixth sense told Ellie that this was the missing piece that fitted perfectly.

'I feel it in my bones,' as Fran would say.

Dad used to talk like that, too. Sometimes events had a pattern, he said, as if they were meant to be.

'Just think, if I hadn't emigrated, I wouldn't have met Mum. If I hadn't met Mum, you wouldn't exist.'

Ellie grabbed a pen and began to doodle. Circles, a mind map, a chain of cause and effect.

No, if Dad hadn't met Mum he'd have met someone else, had different children. Yet it worked in reverse, too. Dad wouldn't have emigrated if his family life hadn't been so unhappy. His family life wouldn't have been unhappy if Grandad Jack hadn't had an affair. Grandad Jack wouldn't have had an affair if . . .

She tossed the pen aside. Who could trace the complex web of reasons that had led him to that? People's lives were made up chances, choices, coincidences, each one leading to another that no one could foresee. Maybe afterwards, if you looked back, the connection became clear, but by then it was too late to change the route that you'd followed, or the place it had brought you to.

The Road not Taken. There was a poem, wasn't there? Who had written it? She couldn't remember.

She glanced at the time. Fran had asked for an update, but it was too late to phone her now. So she showered and combed her wet hair, changed into a nightshirt and flopped on the bed. A quick flick to her *Facebook* page showed that several people had commented on her photo of the two deer by the wood.

Stunning. Where is it? Looks like an awesome place.

She was about to add a reply when the Skype call-sound made her jump. The name on the screen jolted her to a sphere that she didn't know existed. Her hand was so unsteady it could barely move the mouse.

His face appeared in a frame in the corner.

'Hey there.'

His voice, grainy as if he'd just woken from sleep, dissolved all resistance.

'Hey.'

'Tilt the lid a bit. I can't see you.'

While she tilted it, his picture jumped to full screen. His hair was all over the place and a shadow of stubble covered his chin. She had to resist the urge to run her finger over it as he spoke:

'That's better. Now I can see you.'

A tiny window showed what she must look like to him. The fuchsia silk of her nightshirt, damp hair, an idiotic smile. She snapped her mouth shut. Let him speak.

'I saw you were online. What time is it there?'

'Midnight nearly.'

'I just woke up.'

She laughed. 'I can see that.'

His t-shirt was crumpled and behind him was the corner of a bed, unmade, and a window, filled with light. The dog sat beside him scratching itself, its ugly snout lifted with a look of ecstasy. Something like a sound system, chrome, with wires. Clothes strewn over a chair.

'I was about to go to bed,' she said.

'That photo you put on *Facebook*. Those deer. That was really weird.'

'Weird? Why?

'I had a dream. You know that Robert Frost poem, *Two Look at Two?*

So that's who it was – the poet she'd been trying to remember, the one who wrote *The Road not Taken*. He'd written this one, too, and as the uncanny coincidence snaked through her, she blurted the first words that came to mind.

'I didn't know you were into poetry.'

'Yeah, well, whatever, I was reading it the other day. I've been thinking a lot about different worlds co-existing. In that poem the animals are in their natural habitat. They were there way before the humans moved in. Then those two come to live alongside them, but they respect them, so it's all harmonious and sort of okay.'

'So?'

'It was like that in my dream. We were looking at the deer and they were looking right back.'

'We?' The word hovered between two momentous interpretations. 'Who was?' she managed to ask.

'You and me.'

'You and me?' she repeated stupidly. Her mind whirled.

'Yeah,' he said. 'You Ellie. Me Josh.'

Thank goodness he did that ape thing, because it meant she could laugh instead of saying something she'd regret. *Get a grip,* she told herself. *He ruled you out long ago. Don't act like a lovesick teenager. This bloke's not like the others.*

'Duh, you probably had the dream because you saw the photo. That sort of thing happens all the time.'

'Wrong. The dream came first. I only saw the photo just now, when I woke up.'

That *was* weird. No, no, it wasn't. It was making something out of nothing and she refused to do that. Not now. Not ever. She raised one eyebrow.

'So now you believe in dreams, too.'

'I'm not sure. Maybe they just confirm things we already know.'

'What – that you and I both like deer? Guess what,' she went on before he had a chance to answer. 'We've found her, my grandad's love child. She's called Denise Henderson and I'm prett sure she was sent to Australia. You know, along with those orphans we talked about.'

The screen froze and she thought she'd lost him. Then he leaped back to life.

'Australia? Do you know where exactly?'

'Not yet. She's proving kind of hard to trace.'

'So you'll be coming home soon.'

'I need to stay until we know for sure. It's not for me really, I'm doing it for Dot and Fran, you know, my aunts.'

She felt her voice catch.

'That's cool, Ellie. Really cool.'

'Otherwise I'd come like a flash. I miss . . . all sorts of things.'

Did her words come out jerky or had the call turned to robot-speak? The connection stuck, jumped, then a whole torrent of words rushed out like water from an unblocked dam.

'I miss the beaches, the surf, the warm air and breeze, the smell of nature, the rough masculinity of the bush.'

'You're homesick.'

'Is that what it's called?'

'Do you have a better name for it?'

She could think of one but she wouldn't tell him. Change two letters, the *h* and the *m*.

'It's the smell of the dirt,' she said. 'The jacaranda trees in blossom all over the Northern Beaches. The birds that screech in the morning and again like crazy in the afternoons. Did you notice, Josh, that the birds here are little and sweet and peepy? Ours are all big and loud.'

His face creased as he laughed.

'Not everything's good here, Ellie. Some poor guy over in Perth got eaten by a shark last week.'

'Oh no! That's terrible. Yes, of course there are bad things, too. But I still like it. It's where I belong.'

'Take the rough with the smooth, then?'

'If you say so.'

He did that thing with his eyebrows.

'What do you say?'

'Yes . . . no . . . maybe.' She drew deep into herself. 'I'm not sure yet.'

'That's okay,' he said. 'You take your time. It'll wait.'

Had she heard him right? It'll wait? I'll wait? What did he mean? It was just as well that the connection stuttered and gave up the ghost so they had to end the call, because she might have said more than she was ready to say.

She slept like a child again, a deep, sweet sleep undisturbed by dreams. When she woke, pale sunlight seeped past the curtain over the doona and onto her face. It was more than happiness, it was bliss, like floating on swansdown through a cloudless sky.

When she closed her eyes, the image of Dad crept into her mind. He held her for a moment and kissed the top of her head before turning to leave. He was dear, but she could almost let him go. Tears crept down her face, of pain or of joy, she no longer knew.

She stood, lifted both arms and whirled in a pirouette.

'Ellie.'

Dot tapped at the door and peeped round.

'I'm sorry to disturb you, but Raymond's on the phone.' She hesitated. 'Are you all right?'

'Oh, Aunty Dot.'

Ellie rushed across and threw both arms around her. 'I'm so happy.'

'Goodness child. Whatever's happened?'

'Nothing. Everything.'

She planted a kiss on Dot's cheek. Her skin was soft and cool. 'I'm so glad I came here and got to know you and Fran and everyone.' She stepped back, blew her nose and laughed through the tears.

'But now I think I'm ready to go home.'

A week or so later they sat after supper by the open fire. Its warmth was welcome now that the evenings had turned chillier. Dot rested her head against the wing of her armchair and Ellie curled up on the sofa. Raymond had confirmed that the Hartfield House orphans had been sent to Australia, and Ellie's visit was soon to end.

They talked about many things, Dot's career as a teacher, her concerns about Fran, her excitement now that they really might be able to find their half-sister.

The conversation drifted to Dad and the effect that his parents' unhappiness had had on him. Dot began to talk about one particular day when he'd gone up to London with his father, shortly before he applied for the ten pound passage.

The firelight caught her face and glowed on the glass of Dubonnet that she twisted in her hand.

'You are a modern young woman, Ellie, so I suppose you will think me an awful prude, but my life has been so much more sheltered than yours.'

Ellie watched the firelight flicker, wondering what was coming, while Dot gathered her composure.

'It must have been in 1959, I think, because Jimmy had just finished his national service and was about to go back to university. He had some paperwork to sort out, so he went up to London with our father, who had to go to a meeting there. Anyway, they went their separate ways, then met for lunch at Lyons Corner House. Afterwards they had to go to a post office, and while they were waiting in the queue, my father sneezed. He reached into his pocket for a handkerchief, and something fell on the floor.'

Her chest lifted and dropped again.

'It was a condom.'

She clenched both eyes as if to shut out the image. 'Of course Father snatched it up and put it back in his pocket. But not before Jimmy had seen it. You can imagine his disgust.'

'So this was after Denise was born?'

'Yes, several years.'

'Sorry, Dot, if this sounds a bit crude, but had it been used?'

'Yes, it had.'

Dot drained her Dubonnet all in one go, and shuddered.

'So you see, that was probably the last straw for Jimmy. One mistake he could forgive, or try to, but the evidence that our father was still . . . carrying on . . . was too much for him.'

'Was it still with Maureen?'

'That we don't know. Perhaps we never shall.'

Did it make any difference, Ellie wondered? Did cheating with the same person lessen the pain or increase it?

'I don't know about you, but I could do with another drink.'

Dot reached for the bottle of Dubonnet. Ellie held out her glass as the liquid filled it, lit by the gleam from the fire.

'Thanks for telling me that, Dot. It really helps me to understand why Dad felt he'd had enough.'

'I do hope so. Of course, I should have been more open about all this before, but you see . . . it was hard.'

Ellie put down her glass, leaned across and placed her hand on Dot's.

'Dear Aunty Dot, you've been so strong, taking this all on yourself.'

As she fought tears, Dot's free hand gripped Ellie's, so she stroked the skin that stretched as fine as silk over the bones until Dot slid her hand away and reached for a handkerchief.

'Well now, this will never do.'

She blew her nose vigorously and Ellie slipped back to her seat. When her aunt was calmer, she decided to ask one more question. It was partly curiosity, but also because she wondered if maybe, just maybe, it might help.

'Who was that blonde woman, Dot? The one that Raymond said someone saw in town with Dad when he was still at school?'

Dot smiled and shook her head.

'That was me.'

'I wondered if it was.'

'Yes, it was a complete misunderstanding.'

She explained that the busybody who saw them thought she was his girlfriend.

'It was against the school rules to be seen with a girl, believe it or not. Loose behaviour, they called it. A silly overreaction. Mother was furious with them for casting aspersions.'

Ellie remembered how Raymond and Dot had looked at each other with secret understanding.

'He was in love with you, wasn't he?' she said gently.

'Raymond? He was a school friend of Jimmy's and, yes, he had a crush on me for a while, that's all.'

'Were you in love with him?'

'I liked him. He was a nice boy, if sometimes a little pompous. But no, I wasn't in love with him.'

'There was someone else?'

Dot laughed.

'Well, my dear, this is turning out to be a night of revelations.'

'So there was someone? I was sure there must be.'

'Yes, once, a long time ago. It was while I was up at Oxford.'

She drew her shoulders straight, and it took her a while to speak.

'He was my tutor, but he was married, you see, so it simply wasn't possible. I'd seen what my mother went through, her anguish, the way it crushed and destroyed her. How could I do that to another woman? So I just had to accept it and get on with my life.'

'And you never met anyone else?'

'No, my dear.'

Dot cradled the glass and their eyes touched.

'You see, when you've found someone you really love, no one else will ever do.'

CANTERBURY, 1963

It was transparent. It was slippery. It was almost like a membrane, but as Lillian drew it from Jack's inside pocket a stickiness lingered that clung to her hand.

For a moment, as she wondered what it was, she thought of the children's game where, blindfold, you identified objects by touch. In the sickening finale you poked your finger into what they told you was Nelson's Eye, but was really the flesh of an orange.

But this wasn't flesh or fruit. Nor was it paper, like the receipts she'd found as she emptied his pockets to take the suit for cleaning. It was more like cellophane. Jack had a sweet tooth and she often came across melted toffees, still in their wrappers. No, this was silkier with hints of an iridescent crust, and as she held it to the light, she could see its strange shape.

It was almost like the finger-guard Bobby had worn when he crushed his thumb in the car door. She flinched at that long-ago memory. Almost two years had passed since his death, but the pain of losing him, as well as Jimmy, still stabbed her with a mixture of rage and helplessness.

She looked again at the object in her hand. Yes, it was shaped like a finger-guard, but hugely inflated, like a man's penis.

It was a condom.

As recognition stung, venom spread through her veins. She stared where it hung from her fingers, unsure if condom was the right word. French letters, Johnnies, rubbers – how had these alien terms crept into her vocabulary? She had never seen one before, but they were used for one thing and one thing only, of that she was sure.

With a yelp of disgust, she let it drop like a deflated parachute onto the bedspread. Her fingers were tacky and she could smell the telltale odour of sperm. The outside was almost dry, but the inside still damp with a cloudy discharge. This was no relic from seven or eight years ago, when that girl had accused him of fathering her child. This was recent. It was all that had come between Jack's engorged flesh and some woman's vagina.

A rush of blood boiled up through Lillian and she sank onto the bed. So he was at it again. She had agreed to put behind her the shock and humiliation of his illegitimate child, but despite all his promises, he hadn't changed.

Who was it this time? The Latimer girl had been sent packing, the child given up for adoption. She was sure of that. Because Jack was so devious, Lillian had insisted on evidence. Hugh Gregson had written to her, tactful and full of sympathy, to guarantee that he had made the necessary arrangements. Jack, he assured her, had sworn to end all further contact.

So had he gone back on his word and kept in touch with her? Or had he started again with someone else? Lillian's mind raced over the confines of his working world. The college had expanded over the years, and a number of women now worked there. Could it be some new slip of a typist who'd caught his eye?

With a roar of indignation, she seized the condom and ran from the house. His office was a short sprint across the quad from where they now lived. Not caring who saw her or the evidence she carried, she sped towards the arched doorway. Tears streamed down her face. If anyone spoke to her she would shout out the truth, not caring who heard.

'We've lost both our sons, and even that hasn't changed him!'

No, he was as lustful and deceitful at fifty-seven as he had always been. It was hardly surprising that Jimmy, her darling boy, could stand it no longer.

'My father disgusts me,' he'd said when he left for Australia. 'Don't expect me ever to come back, because I won't.'

Lillian had understood why he wanted to go, but it had broken her heart.

Then Bobby, always wayward and disturbed, the poor little mite, had fallen to his death only a month or two later. People said that the accident had nothing to do with his parents' problems, that Bobby had got into drugs, that it was a mishap and a dreadful tragedy. They couldn't see, like a mother, how each painful experience in his life had drawn him towards that tragic path.

Fuelled with fury, Lillian charged up the narrow stone staircase and flung open the door to the office. Three startled faces gaped at her, but none was his.

'Where is he?' she shrieked. She held the offending object aloft, her hair wild, her face tear-stained, but she no longer cared what anyone thought.

'My dear Mrs Goodwin, whatever is the matter?'

A middle-aged lady scrambled to her feet. She was vaguely familiar but Lillian didn't know her name.

'Come with me.'

She ushered Lillian into an office and seated her in a comfortable armchair.

'Canon Goodwin isn't here this afternoon, but perhaps I can help. Just one moment while I bring you some tea.'

She returned with a cup and saucer, closed the door again and introduced herself as Miss Bartlett, the college counsellor.

'A new role, and not yet recognised as a profession, though it's high time it was. Now, my dear, drink your tea first, then when you're ready, tell me what's bothering you. You can be sure that not a soul will hear a word of what you say without your permission.'

Lillian gulped, sniffed and accepted a handkerchief. All her resistance had melted under such unexpected kindness. Miss Bartlett had an efficient but tactful demeanour. Never in a million years could Lillian suspect her of being the receptacle of the disgusting relic that she now took from her hand, placed in a foolscap envelope and locked in the drawer of her desk.

She was more like the understanding mother that Lillian had never had. Faced with such sympathy, for some minutes the poor distressed Mrs Goodwin could do nothing but weep.

Among the theories that Miss Bartlett offered, was the idea that a man, when frustrated, might seek relief alone and in private. Quite what purpose the condom served was less clear. To avoid a mess or tell-tale traces, was the best she could come up with. Lillian was too exhausted to argue against this simple explanation. Deep down, perhaps, she wanted to believe it.

Over the following days it was Miss Bartlett's intervention, as she ran back and forth between Lillian and Jack, that salvaged the wreckage of their marriage, pieced together some repairs, and set them limping towards a more tranquil haven.

The week they spent at Lee Abbey was also Miss Bartlett's idea. At first Lillian resisted. She had no wish to be trapped among a band of Holy Joes, as she called them. In her experience, Christians were either snobs or hypocrites. Some went to church to keep up appearances, others to hide their true nature. They parroted the confession and sang praises, then went out to serve their own interests for the rest of the week.

Jesus Christ of Nazareth she couldn't fault, but his followers were a disgrace.

'And they call themselves Christians!' was one of her favourite taunts.

Years in the cathedral city of Canterbury had shown her the intrigues of the old boy network that still operated among many of the clergy. How Jack could stand it, she couldn't imagine. Whatever his faults, she would never accuse him of being a snob.

As for the well-heeled ladies who called themselves Friends of the Cathedral, arranged coffee mornings and gossiped, they were an alien species to Lillian.

'Dear Mrs Goodwin,' they would say in their hoity-toity voices. 'Do come and cut sandwiches with us for the Dean's garden party.'

'I'm much too busy with four children,' Lillian retorted. 'Why don't you use sliced bread?'

Jack said nothing. He was used to her criticisms. She had others, too. She didn't doubt God's existence, but disliked the way he meted out justice. The good suffered and the wicked prospered. Life was unfair and inherently cruel. The strong preyed on the weak. If ever she made it to eternal bliss, which she sometimes doubted, she would take the Almighty to task over a number of issues. Not least that Jack Goodwin's sins had been rewarded by promotion to Honorary Canon. While she, Lillian the Long-Suffering, was known as a difficult woman. Difficult, indeed, who wouldn't be with all she'd had to endure?

Miss Bartlett, though, was kind, like dear Mrs Denham before her.

'Lillian, my dear,' she said one sunny afternoon while visiting her at home, 'a holiday is what you need.'

'I know, Elizabeth, but not in a beastly monastery.'

They were on first name terms now, a fad that had come into fashion, and of which Lillian disapproved. But in Miss Bartlett's – Elizabeth's – case it was different. She had been so gentle, so understanding, so active on Lillian's behalf, that in the process she had become a true friend.

'Lee Abbey is not a monastery, Lillian, as I keep trying to tell you. It was built as a private manor house, and over the years has been a hotel and even a school. After the war it was bought by a group of Christians. It is now a community run by those who live and work there, to be used in God's service as a place of refreshment and contemplation. It is absolutely what you need.'

'Refreshment, yes. Contemplation I've had my fill of.'

In the end she agreed to go. She had always loved Devon, but never been to the north coast where Lee Abbey was located. It was also true that she and Jack had spent no time alone together since Dorothy's birth, nearly thirty years ago. Now that he was willing to repair the damage he had caused, it was only fair to give him a chance. And with their parental responsibilities almost over, Lillian had no excuse.

The boys, of course, were no longer with them. Dorothy was a more than capable head of modern languages at a girls' boarding school in Hampshire. Only Frances, almost sixteen, was a worr

As the visit to Lee Abbey would be in term time, they arranged for Fran, as she now called herself, to stay with a friend whose parents promised to keep an eye on them both.

Fran was no longer the sweet little girl who once clung to her mother's hand. She had grown sullen and rebellious. Her fringe hung over her eyes. She pouted her lips, painted a ghoulish white. She wore black sloppy-Joe jumpers and tight jeans, and called herself a Beatnik. Loud music thumped from her bedroom, and when asked to turn it down, she did the opposite. Jack, as usual, shirked parental responsibility, and when Lillian tried to reason with her, Fran slammed the door in her face.

The sun was low in the sky as they drove the last few miles towards the North Devon coast. The road snaked up through a thickly wooded gorge, so steep that Jack had to change into first gear. They came out onto cliffs where the moor was purple with heather. Way below, the expanse of the Bristol Channel gleamed like molten gold.

Lights had come on in the windows of the cottages that clustered in the little town of Lynton. A single-track lane led out to the Valley of the Rocks, its dramatic crags dark against the evening sky. The bracken had dried to a rusty red. Lillian saw hills covered with trees, their leaves aglow with autumn colours.

Lee Abbey came into view, its roofs broken by dormer windows. When they stepped out of the car she breathed in the clean, sea air. A breeze rustled in the branches, a sheep bleated, and from the distance came the wash of waves below. High above, an unfamiliar bird called with a mewing sound as it returned to its nest.

Then all was quiet again, and for the first time in a very long time, she felt at peace.

The Abbey was not at all what she had expected. Everyone was friendly and surprisingly normal. As Lillian and Jack checked in, several guests passed them, wearing thick jumpers and solid-looking boots, or shoes that were a bit down at heel. Waxed coats hung above wellington boots in the lobby.

The young woman at reception told them that the weather here was wild and unpredictable, so the only way to keep warm was to wrap up in layers of sensible clothes. A young man came to show them to their attic bedroom. He bent to point out some landmarks from the tiny window.

'Down there is the cove, and a short distance the other way is Jenny's Leap. She was jilted by her unfaithful lover, so the story goes, and jumped to her death.'

'Poor girl,' said Lillian. 'She should have pushed him over instead.'

The young man laughed.

'You'll see it tomorrow if you'd like to join us for a walk. Oh don't worry, there's a railing there now, so you can't fall off.'

'A walk, how lovely,' said Jack. 'We'd both like that, I think, wouldn't we, Lil?'

She bit back a smile and nodded. There was nothing she'd enjoy more, but what really pleased her was that Jack had called her Lil. She couldn't remember when he'd last done that. But she wasn't ready to cosy up to him yet.

At dinner they sat at a big table with members of the community and other guests. Everyone spoke to everyone else, as they passed round bread or asked for the salt and pepper.

'I'm Bill,' someone would say, 'what's your name? Oh, pleased to meet you, Lillian. Where are you from? Canterbury, how marvellous. We're from Cheshire.'

And so the conversation began to flow.

Two community members, one from Ghana and one from Birmingham, served food from huge urns and handed round plates. There was a beef stew, with vegetables from the kitchen gardens, then blackberry crumble with custard to follow. Chatter and laughter rippled round the room. Tea and coffee appeared, and then there was a quiz, or board games in the lounge for those who wanted to take part. Or you could sit in an armchair and read, warm your toes by the log fire. Some wandered out for a look at the stars, or went up to the chapel for evening prayers.

Jack and Lillian were tired from the journey so they went to their room after the quiz. The low-ceilinged attic was cosy, with a metal radiator and twin beds. Lillian chose the one by the window. They changed into their pyjamas and said goodnight. Jack was on his best behaviour, courteous and attentive.

'Would you like a glass of water? Are you sure you're warm enough? Shall I turn off the light, or do you want to read?'

She lay there for some time, listening to his breathing and the sound of the wind in the branches of the trees. From the distance came the boom of waves down in the cove.

The morning dawned bright, with ragged clouds that scudded across a pale autumn sky and sent leaves swirling onto the lawn below. It was such a treat to go into breakfast and have everything prepared for you: porridge or cereals, eggs, bacon and toast, as much as you could eat. Some of their new friends had been to an early morning service, others for a walk on the cliffs.

You could join in with activities or make your own, and nobody seemed to mind which you chose.

Over the next few days Lillian grew to love the wild, rugged coastline, the woods and hills that surrounded Lee Abbey. High in the sky buzzards circled, making the mewing sound that she had heard on the evening they arrived. Squirrels scampered in the dry leaves, scurried up trunks and along branches. Hips and haws glowed red in the hedgerows, and as she and Jack walked, they picked late blackberries, sharp but juicy.

She also loved the atmosphere of the house with its comfortable, unpretentious friendliness. You could have the companionship of others whenever you wanted it, or solitude when you didn't. Nothing was forced, but you felt welcome in people's conversations, and they listened to you with real interest.

Guests and community members came from all over the country and from further afield. One lady was on leave from Tanzania where she taught in an orphanage, another was a shopkeeper from Worcester. Two young men from Switzerland were hiking all round the British coast. A couple from Canada were here to find out about their ancestors, who'd come from this area.

Much to Lillian's surprise, though, she also loved the chapel. It was on the second, or perhaps the third day that they ventured in there. Ever since Jack had worked in an administrative capacity, their church-going had dwindled. Lillian suspected that his faith, like hers, had been affected by the storms that had buffeted them over the years.

They sat side by side on one of the wooden benches among a handful of people, all absorbed in silent contemplation. The walls were rough stone, the only ornament a simple cross. The tiny space was steeped in silence, and a sensation of peace began to settle over her. Then a lone voice sounded in prayer, asking God to take away all their worries and restlessness. Feeling a bit of a fool, Lillian sat as suggested with her palms open on her lap in symbolic release. As the minutes passed, a subtle change took place in her. It was as if her problems rose slowly from the depths of a muddy pool to the surface until all was still and clear.

From somewhere behind her a woman's voice lifted in song, so pure and poignant that tears welled in Lillian's eyes. She could sense that Jack, too, was struggling, and as she fumbled for her handkerchief, her fingers brushed his. They hesitated, then his hand clasped hers. It was like the time when they first met and their future hung on a thread.

More minutes passed, until into the silence a new voice spoke, reading from the prophet Isaiah. It was the passage about the suffering servant, despised and rejected, who took up our infirmities and bore our sorrows. Lillian had heard these words many times before, and always admired their haunting beauty and the poetry of their language.

But here, in the stillness of this simple chapel, for the first time, she understood.

All we like sheep have gone astray; we have turned every one to his own way; and the Lord hath laid on Him the iniquity of us all.

NEW SOUTH WALES, OCTOBER 2010

It was spring when Ellie arrived back in Sydney. The trees by the lagoon trembled over the water, green and feathery with new growth. In the yard the hibiscus had started to open its scarlet trumpets. Cockatoos shrieked and parakeets chattered. The sky was a clear pale blue with wisps of cloud, and when the breeze blew in from the bush it carried the warm, spicy smells that she'd missed so much on the other side of the world.

The season was different, but nothing much else had changed. The porch door still squeaked, the veranda needed a coat of paint. Her old room was as she'd left it, books stacked on the shelves or piled in the corner, the charcoal drawing of Dad hanging crooked on the wall.

He was there and he wasn't there, but she didn't feel his absence like before. He was there in the weatherboard structure he'd put together with his own hands. The dinghy upturned on the bank by the lagoon. His fishing rods that she'd asked Mum to keep.

If anything had changed, it was Ellie herself, or something inside her. It might have been the jet lag, which acted like a sedative, carrying her into long hours of sleep. That and the happiness of coming home to the place and the people she loved.

Everyone made a fuss of her. Mum cleaned off the barbi

and filled the fridge with Ellie's favourite snacks, mango yoghurt, humus and Hunter Valley olives. Karen and Tim came over with baby Will. He'd started to eat solid food, purées that he spread over his face, burbling happily. He'd lost his baby chubbiness and looked more like a little boy. Cindy called to see her, and the rest of the gang asked Ellie to join them whenever they met.

She didn't contact Josh. At first she was too tired from the journey. Better to wait, adapt to the time zone and think more clearly. A week passed. No, she'd leave it till she had something definite to tell him about Denise. It was proving tricky to locate her because she'd divorced, and moved around a lot.

Another week and Ellie was almost sure that she'd found her, but again she stalled. It would be wiser to focus on completing the quest, prioritise professional development, not a pointless fantasy.

Whenever he came to mind, she wobbled and wavered. It would be so easy to pick up the phone and at a touch of a button he'd be there. But nerves always got the better of her.

Had she read too much into what he'd said that last time on Skype? He was probably just being friendly, trying to reassure her. His beliefs and opinions hadn't changed. Hadn't he always made it clear that she was no more than a friend? The last thing she wanted to do was set herself up like a skittle to be knocked flying, now that she was more stable.

It wasn't long before Mum started to nag about work. The excitement of coming home had worn off and things slipped back to the way they'd been before.

She couldn't afford to rent a place of her own until she found a job, but Mum began to get on her nerves. Money was short, and she'd even had to stop using the Subaru because it needed a new gear box and two of the tyres were worn. But she didn't want to apply for any old post. After her experiences abroad, she wanted to do something meaningful, not sink into a monotonous routine, and this caused conflict.

Whenever Ellie went out with her friends, she caught herself watching the clock, wondering how soon she could leave without offending anyone. They were all into their own lives and relationships, and soon the old doubts and dissatisfactions started to disturb her peace.

She had dates with one or two blokes Karen put her way, but it was no good. They were nice enough, but did nothing for her.

'I don't know what you're looking for,' everyone said. 'You're so hard to please.'

Then a rumour reached her that Josh was dating someone. Friends who knew him, but didn't know how well she knew him, said they'd seen him several times with a girl.

'A Christian girl?'

They didn't know, but Ellie was sure all the same. It would have to be, wouldn't it? No one else would meet his requirements. Well, good luck to the pair of them. She hoped they'd enjoy holding hands.

An ex-colleague from the museum had converted to Islam because of her Moroccan boyfriend. A rugby team-mate of Tim's, whose family were Protestant, had become a Catholic in time for his marriage. Someone Cindy knew had a Jewish fiancé and she was receiving instruction from a Rabbi. Danielle and Carl were into Buddhism. Nic was exploring her power animas with earth-centred healing. Pick and mix spirituality was PC.

No, Ellie, it wouldn't work. It would be a sham, and even if you kidded yourself, he'd know. It was the real McCoy or nothing for him.

One sultry afternoon she was lounging on a hammock in the yard when the ring tone sounded on her mobile. It lay just out of reach on the ground beside a novel she'd been reading, and it was too much effort to roll over and get it.

Good, it had stopped.

She closed her eyes, but curiosity pricked and she swung down her hand to reach for it.

1 missed call. Josh.

Her heart jumped, then hammered like crazy. The ring tone started again, but her fingers fumbled and she nearly dropped the phone.

'Hi, Josh.'

'Ellie – great to hear your voice. How you going?'

'Good,' she lied. 'And you?'

'I'm good, too. How does it feel to be home?'

Of course he knew. He knew she'd been back nearly a month without contacting him. She started to babble and make excuses. *Been so busy, catching up with everyone, looking for a job, trying to locate Denise.*

'No worries, you needed time.'

He waited, but she couldn't bring herself to speak. Then he said,

'Look, I've got some news.'

He was going to tell her that he'd got engaged. Her stomach rolled. Or invite her to the wedding. She heard him say something about Katoomba, and she was grasping for a very good reason why she couldn't possibly go there, when Mum yelled from the kitchen.

Ellie interrupted him.

'Josh, I'm sorry but I've got to go.'

In her hurry to end the call she didn't catch what he said.

Speak to you soon? Honeymoon? I'm over the moon?

She located Denise. It really wasn't that hard to do. After marrying again in 1990 her surname was now Cooper. Her second husband, Stan, had been a mining engineer and they'd lived all over Australia before moving to New South Wales in 2005. They now ran a hotel in the Blue Mountains, near the Three Sisters at Echo Falls, which meant, of course, Katoomba.

The uncomfortable coincidence of hearing that name twice in a week unsettled Ellie. With half of her brain she tried to plan a way to go there without running into Josh and his fiancée. With the other half she invented all sorts of tactics to stop him finding out that she had. Then there was the problem of transport. Mum was already fed up with her using her car.

At night she sweated and writhed, and for days she couldn't swallow her food. Mum started to notice and nag.

'You're not eating again, Ellie. Don't tell me you've slipped back into that depression you had after Dad died.'

'I'm okay. Leave me alone. I just need to get the last piece of the puzzle in place.'

She decided to contact Dot and Fran and see how they would like her to approach Denise. They didn't use Skype, and the credit was low on her mobile, so she emailed. That way she could lay out all the facts and give them time to discuss and respond, without anyone flying off the handle.

Dot's reply came surprisingly quickly. She'd spoken to Frances and they'd decided to write to Denise themselves.

Although this might be slower, we thought it would be better than springing a visit on her. A letter would be less of a shock and will give Denise time to absorb our request and come to a decision.

Of course they didn't know it, but they'd also saved Ellie from the embarrassment of going to Katoomba, and bumping into the happy couple.

Barely a fortnight passed before Dot rang to say that she'd had a reply from Denise.

'She thanked us for contacting her, but said she had come to the conclusion that, after such a long time, it would be better for us all not to revisit the past.'

Fran was angry, hurt, upset. Dot was disappointed but resigned.

Morbid thoughts crept into Ellie's mind. The whole search had been a waste of time. All the hope and excitement she'd felt towards the end of her stay in England had sunk into a cesspit of doubts. She would never find a fulfilling and worthwhile occupation where she could make a difference to others.

The wound from Dad's death had closed over, but left a hard, dry scab. It would be so easy to claw it open. Her dreams had turned out to be a mirage. Worse, the memories of Josh at Lyme Bay, the deer, the touch of his hand, the sound of his voice, now mocked her like a seasick hallucination.

A few days later as Ellie lazed around after lunch, thinking that she didn't want to go out or see anyone, a realisation hit her.

The obstacles she refused to confront were like the bars of a prison that kept her trapped. If she didn't exert herself, they would close in and swallow her. The only way to break free was to grapple with them.

She took the boat out on the lagoon where no one could interrupt her. Dad's fishing rod and tackle were just for camouflage. Going through the motions soothed her, but what she'd really come for was to think. It was clear enough in what was left of her rational mind that she couldn't go on like this. Unless she got a grip on herself, she'd spend the rest of her life struggling with regrets, or worse, in some loony-bin, doped out on drugs. The choice was as stark as the banks on each side of her.

What held her back? Pride, partly. Fear that he'd say no, even to this. She couldn't ask more of him, not now that she knew he'd found a mate from an acceptable tribe. But even talking to Josh about something as neutral as Denise, simply being with him, would mean she had to tread carefully, and she might not have the deftness to avoid the pitfalls.

Do you realise, something said to her, *that in all this time you have never once reached out to him?* The bait she was trying to fix on the hook slid through her fingers. Plop, it went, and a swift shadow swooped at it under the surface.

He came to you on the beach at Freshwater. He asked you to walk the trail. He texted you and messaged you and phoned you and Skyped you. He came to England – okay he had other reasons, but he made the effort to contact you and meet up with you. Time after time he listened to you and comforted you and gave you good, sound advice without ever once criticising you.

No, that wasn't entirely true, he'd often criticised her. But whatever he said was always spot-on and never unkind or judgmental.

She reached inside her pocket, took out a piece of paper and unfolded it.

Ellie G's within a cooee of perfect.

Tears blurred her vision. She groped for her mobile. The signal was good here, strong and clear.

'Josh,' she said when he answered. 'Can we meet up?'

He was surprised, she could tell, but he agreed right away.

'I'm in the City – do you mean like now, this arvo?'

'Whenever, whatever, just say what suits you.'

He mentioned the name of a bar near the ferry in Manly. Early that evening. They agreed on the time.

'See you there, then.'

'Yes, and thanks, Josh.'

It was a good thing that no one else was on the lake, because she let out a howl. Of pain and of joy.

He wasn't there when she arrived. She went to the bar for a drink and found a table by the door so he'd see her right away. It was the time of day when people started home from work, and she could imagine how quickly this place would fill. The windows looked out over the harbour, where the green and cream ferries made their way back and forth from the city, spewing out passengers and setting off again. How weird to be at a loose end while everyone else shoved and struggled with the daily commute.

She was half way through her Prosecco and still there was no sign of him. But the alcohol gave her false courage, mixed with a swirl of ideas about how to say what she needed to. Whatever happened, she must keep to the point. The secrets she really wanted to tell him were out of bounds. They were deep and precious like buried gems, too valuable to scatter where they'd be trodden into the dirt.

More people drifted in and a buzz of conversation began to lift. Her glass was empty and she nursed it between her palms, wondering whether to go for a refill.

The next thing she knew he was pulling up a chair. He was devastatingly, unexpectedly smart in a suit, albeit a little crumpled, shouldering a laptop bag, his hair combed through with a bit of gel. A white shirt, soft cotton, open at the neck. A narrow tie, knotted just below it. His skin damp with the heat and sweat of the city and a hint of sea air.

Her mouth spread in an insane grin.

'Do you have you a new job?'

She knew he worked freelance, but she'd never seen him like this before.

'No, but I've just landed a contract to finance a project I want to work on.'

'Half your luck.'

'Thanks.'

Mercifully there was no sign of the dog. Or the girlfriend.

He took off his jacket and rolled up his shirt sleeves. She noticed that one of the cuff buttons was loose. His skin was as tanned as that day in Lyme, and she caught the lean strength of his forearms, a stain of ink across one hand. His eyes danced with a bright light, and his grin sent furrows down each side of his cheeks.

He's happy, she thought, and jealousy flared in her. All this was for someone else. *Don't touch. Don't even look.*

'What you drinking?'

She told him Prosecco and he said he'd get her another

because he wanted her to celebrate with him. It would have been nice to think that he meant his contract, but she feared that he didn't.

He went to the bar, which was busy now with streams of passengers rolling off the ferries. While his back was turned, she touched the lining inside his jacket on the seat beside her. It was soft and silky, still warm from where he'd worn it. Several people ahead of him were waiting to be served, so she had plenty of time. She lifted her fingers and breathed in a confusing mix of city, body odours, and ocean.

'Hi Ellie,' said a voice behind her.

She froze. All the heat that had risen inside her vanished. That voice. It was Brad's, she'd recognise it anywhere. There was nothing for it but to turn and face him.

Sun-bleached hair that touched his collar. Bullish. Confident. Magnetic.

'What are you doing here?' His eyes ran over her.

'Having a drink,' she said as calmly as her voice would let her. 'Is there a law against it?'

Her arms started to tremble. Every cell in her body remembered. His weight, the texture of his skin, the smell and taste of every part of him.

He dropped his keys onto the table and sat down beside her. His face looked leaner, strained.

'I haven't seen you around for a while. Where've you been hiding?'

'I went to England.'

He could have asked for how long, or why, or when she'd got back, but instead he touched her knee.

'You're looking knock-out, Ellie, as always.'

His eyes took in her silky top, the curve of her breast, as though matching it to a map engraved in his memory.

She glanced at the bar. Josh was waving one hand and laughing as he chatted with the barman. *Don't turn round now whatever you do*, she willed him. The muscles all through her body had knotted tight.

Brad's hand slid to her thigh. Through the fabric of her cut-offs she could feel the heat of his palm and the pressure of his fingers. No killer spider could have paralysed its prey more effectively.

'I've missed you, Ells.'

His breath brushed her cheek with a whiff of coffee, whisky, red meat. His voice was deep, caressing, the way she remembered it. When she moved his hand away, hers was shaking. She didn't trust herself to speak.

Unfazed, he hooked one finger in a strand of her hair and wound it towards him.

'I've got a bottle of Bombay Sapphire back at the unit.'

His eyebrows lifted, as if to say, *Do you remember the first time? All those other times?*

'No, Brad. We've been there. It didn't work.'

'Just you and me, Ellie. The way you like it.'

His lips touched her ear, and a shot of seasick sensuality swayed her. Memories flooded. How he worked her hard, like his kiteboard over the surf, with lots of fancy turns and stunts.

Her head began to tilt towards him. Outside, a ferry hooted and she pulled up rigid as another memory hit her. The nausea, the self-loathing when she'd seen that video he'd posted.

If my mates can't have a part of the action, they can at least see what we do together.

She swung round to challenge him but saw Josh weaving his way towards them through the crowds, carrying two glasses, his mouth drawn tight.

She spoke rapidly, lowering her voice to a whisper.

'You've got a nerve, Brad, after what you did to me. Do you seriously think I'd fall for your crap again?'

The lines round his mouth tightened.

'And you look knackered. Maybe you should ease up a bit.'

Josh stood in front of them. Brad jerked his chin with a look of contempt.

'Don't tell me you're with him?'

'So what if I am?'

He stood up nonchalantly, slung his jacket over one shoulder.

'So. You know where to find me. Bring your friend, too, if you like.'

His tone was the same as when he'd sneered at her parents. He surveyed the bar, turned and strolled out to the street.

'You okay?'

Josh put down the drinks and sat beside her. His forehead was creased in a frown, but it was hard to read how much he'd seen or heard.

She nodded, gritting her teeth. She'd already told him enough about that relationship and had no intention of saying more.

'Cheers, then,' he said and they clinked glasses.

Of course, she knew that he'd disapprove. Or maybe he wouldn't care one way or the other. Why should he? Especially now that he had someone of his own.

Each time that she swallowed it hurt. Each time Josh looked at her, she thought he was going to tell her about his engagement. Gloat over his pious and virtuous life. But each time he looked away again. The bar had filled and the volume of voices boomed with the beat of her pulse.

After a while his eyes met hers with a hint of hesitance. She braced herself for the words that she dreaded, but his tone had an edge of contempt.

'So, was that the bloke you told me about?'

All the graphic details she'd dished out that day at Freshwater loomed up between them.

'Was it that obvious?'

'It makes sense, I guess.'

'Do you know him?'

Something about his reaction made her think that he did.

'Only from high school, a bit. He was a few years ahead of me.'

She expected him to dish the dirt but he said no more, just sat with his forearms on the table, hands round his glass, head down.

'What are you thinking?'

He glanced up with a grimace.

'You really want to know?'

'Why not? I've told you enough.'

He drew in breath, met her eyes.

'That I'd like to knock his teeth out.'

He didn't laugh. It was the anger of the righteous, she supposed, spiced with a hint of feral frustration. Maybe holding back from his girlfriend was proving harder than he'd thought.

'When you arrive on a strange shore,' Josh had once said to he 'you can try to change what you find, or adapt, or go back whe you came from.' They'd been talking about the British colonising Australia, and how the decisions they'd made had determined what followed.

His words came to mind as Ellie got ready to leave for Katoomba. She couldn't remember what she'd said in return. Probably that it was pointless to speculate, because nobody knew what would have happened if those first settlers had reacted differently.

The one thing she did know, was that it was all about choices. She'd done a lot of thinking since that day they'd met in the bar by the harbour, and she'd finally made hers. Like swallowing her pride and asking Josh to drive her to Katoomba.

She looked at the clock. Half past nine. He was fifteen minutes late. Was she already beginning to discover his annoying habits? Or maybe it was nerves and excitement that made every second seem like an eternity.

What car would he turn up in, she wondered? You could tell a lot about a man from his choice of car. A family saloon? No, too solid and respectable. A sporty little coupe? Too flashy. A beaten up old Ute? Too boring. She really had no idea, which was probably a measure of how little she knew him.

'Is this your friend now?' said Mum from the veranda where she was watering the jasmine.

A motorbike swept into the yard with a throaty growl. Powerful, black probably under the cloud of dust. Hidden by the helmet, the rider could have been anyone, but the legs under those jeans and the shoulders stretching that sweatshirt were enough to make her knees knock together, even if he was just a good mate.

'Mum,' Ellie said as he took off his helmet and came towards them, 'This is Josh.'

And don't you dare say anything, her eyes warned. Mum had been well drilled – he's got a girlfriend, I'm not interested in him in that way. We're just working on my memoir together.

'Hi, Josh, so you're off to Katoomba. It's a lovely day for it.' A few polite words and she slipped into the house and left them.

'Are we going on that?' Ellie asked him.

'We can go in my mate's car, if you like.'

'Won't I have to wear a helmet?'

'I've brought one for you just in case.' He grinned. 'And leathers, too, if you fancy them.'

'Don't tease me, Bellini. You might get more than you've bargained for.'

Motorbikes are marvellous inventions. For a start she sat astride with her thighs behind his. That in itself was enough to send her soaring from the seat, so she had to hold tight round his waist, and it was perfectly legitimate to lean her head in the lee of his shoulders. And because he had to concentrate on the road, not shoot them both into a ditch, he couldn't see the look of idiotic ecstasy on her face.

All of his warm and intriguing body odours floated into her nostrils. The darling little quiff of hair that pointed into the nape of his neck was just visible below the helmet, so near that she could have rubbed the tip of her nose in it. When he flexed his shoulders – the poor bloke's muscles must have ached from having to control all those vibrations – a peep inside his sweatshirt gave her a breathtaking view of the hills and valleys of his back.

They were only doing some research together. Really, that and the ride were all she had asked him, and he had agreed. There was no law in his religion against it. They were getting to know each other, doing useful things the way that sensible people would.

Like visiting Denise.

'She's in Katoomba,' he'd told her that evening in the bar by the harbour.

'I knew that already. But how did you find out?'

'It's not exactly rocket science to use the internet. You told me near enough everything about her.'

She'd been a bit miffed, actually. He had no right. But at the same time she was pleased that he'd wanted to bother.

'Anyhow, some friends of mine live there. It's a small place. It just happened they knew her.'

When Ellie told him Denise didn't want any contact with her half-sisters, he said he'd see what he could do. If she didn't object.

'God's in the business of reconciliation,' he said, as if to rub in where they both stood.

It turned out that his friends already knew some of Denise's story because she had told them. She'd been a couple of times to their church and asked for prayer about it.

'She what? Why would she do that?'

'People find that it helps. I asked for prayer not so long ago when I was having it tough.'

Tough? What did Josh have to deal with that was tough? Could it be putting up with her? Had he leaped in as do-gooder and then regretted it? He'd probably told his friends every detail of her saga with Brad. Were there pious churchgoers all over New South Wales who knew every tacky thing she'd ever done?

'So, if you're okay about it, my mates might be prepared to act as go-betweens,' he'd said. 'Talk with Denise, and put your point of view. See if she'll come round to meeting you.'

'No. Thank you but no. This is one challenge that I have to deal with myself.'

She had something to prove to the world, and to herself. However much Denise objected to meeting her half-sisters, Ellie couldn't leave Dad's story unfinished. She was sure that in the end all three would benefit from getting to know each other, whatever Denise said. So she'd decided that the best way was to go to Katoomba in person and confront her face to face. This would take courage, and risk rejection, but the element of surprise might make all the difference. The problem was, she had no car, and Mum needed hers for work.

So eventually she'd asked Josh if he'd give her a ride. This would be a final test of her resolve, learning to be with him as a friend, and accepting that it would always have to be this way. But the visit to Denise herself she would make without him.

'Okay,' he'd said. 'If that's what you've decided.'

Several times in the days that followed, Ellie had nearly changed her mind. Then she'd reasoned that if he didn't want to come, or if his girlfriend didn't like the idea, it was up to him to say so.

As far as she was concerned, simply being with him would test all her powers of self-control, but whatever the outcome she was determined to go through with it.

As the road climbed higher towards Katoomba, the mist grew thicker and the temperature plummeted. The forest was lost in a ghostly white haze as if the evil Bunyip had spirited it away. Josh had left the leathers at Mum's so there was nothing for it but to huddle closer and brace herself against the cold. Even misery had its advantages.

After stopping for lunch they felt a bit warmer. Once they reached the town, Josh dropped Ellie at the end of the street where Denise lived. They agreed that she'd call him as soon as she was through. He didn't say what he'd do in the meantime and she didn't ask.

He raised one hand to give her five.

'Go for it,' he said.

The motorbike rumbled away. Silence crept back and with it a snake of panic. The houses stretched in a long loose line, unremarkable little buildings in the English country style, with lawns, porches and dormer windows. They even had English names – *Dartmoor, Windermere, Woody Bay* – and looked strangely at home in the swirling mist, as if people's memories had conjured up the places they still yearned for, years after they'd left them behind.

A fine drizzle began to fall as she made her way up the street. Her jacket and jeans were damp from the ride, her flesh chilled through. Only her hands, deep inside her pockets, held something of the warmth that they'd drawn from clinging to Josh. She counted the numbers of the houses. Forty-four, forty-two, forty. This must be it. Not a hotel, but a Bed and Breakfast, a modest little bungalow. The driveway was empty except for a bicycle propped against a tree. Maybe no one was at home. Hopes and fears fought inside her. If there was no answer, she'd call Josh and forget all about Denise.

She pressed the bell. It sounded two notes, *ding-dong*. Right way she heard someone coming and before she could gather her thoughts, the door opened. A middle-aged woman, plump, fair, in dungarees and a thick cardigan, peered out at her.

'Denise?' The name jumped from Ellie's mouth as if someone else had spoken it.

'Yes?' Grey-blue eyes scanned Ellie's face.

'I'm Ellie Goodwin. My father, Jimmy, was born in England. His father . . . your father . . . was my grandad.'

She watched the woman's face, the slow trickle of understanding, a flush of colour, hesitation. Would she send her away? Slam the door in her face?

But Denise gave her the sort of look you'd give a police officer who'd called with bad news. She sighed, stood back and opened the door wider.

'You'd better come in. My grandchildren were here this morning and the house is in a bit of a mess, but if it's all the same to you . . .'

Ellie followed her inside. On the wallpaper in the hallway, flowers wove through grey-green stripes. The house was bright and clean but belonged to another time and place, with its heavy furniture and thick pile carpets, the woodwork dark brown. Denise led the way into a lounge. She turned and they stood, searching each other's features. Something familiar in the curve of her cheek, the shape of her nose, took Ellie by surprise. It was Dad. Together they stepped forward and hugged, a little uncertainly, but with a rush of emotion as if the complexity of shared genes ran between them. Then strangeness flooded back and they both let go.

Denise signalled to an armchair and they sat opposite each other, uncertain where to begin. A clock on the mantelpiece whirred, clicked and croaked three hoarse chimes. Denise drew in breath and faced Ellie with a pained expression.

'Why did your aunts write? Why did they want to meet me? Why now?'

Her voice was full of hurt and confusion. She was the illegitimate child who saw herself as an outcast, had never expected contact from the legitimate family. Years had passed, a lifetime almost, then suddenly, without warning, a letter had come.

'I think there were a lot of reasons,' Ellie said.

She remembered how Dad used to claim that everything had its time and its season. Events had a way of choosing their own moment. When the fruit was ripe, the seed would fall. But Denise wanted more straightforward explanations.

So Ellie mentioned old age, Dot's desire to right the wrongs of the past, Fran's hurt and anger. She touched on her own father's death, and the grief that had driven her to make contacts that she'd never felt the need to make before.

'When I went to England to see my aunts, it stirred up their memories, and when they told me what had happened, I wanted answers, too.'

She explained about the puzzle Dad had set her, and the trail that had taken her from Canterbury to Devon, on to the children's home, and back to Australia. When she'd finished, Denise spoke, and her pain was obvious.

'What hurts most is all the *whys*. Why was I sent here without any explanation? Why did they want to get rid of me? Why didn't anyone tell me the truth?'

It was hard to know what to say, but Ellie tried to comfort her.

'Social policies that were considered acceptable then, often strike us as shameful now,' she said. 'Change takes time. We look back with horror at what happened in the past, and hope we're doing better. But maybe future generations will see our actions differently, too.'

Still Denise's questions kept coming, one after another, each one unanswerable.

'Why was I adopted, only to be orphaned? Why was I born in the first place if nobody wanted me? Why does God allow such things? Why do the innocent suffer while the guilty go free?'

Questions like these had bothered her all her life, she said, as they sat warming their hands by the gas fire. She found Ellie a jumper because she was shivering with cold. Or exhaustion. Or maybe relief that at last she'd succeeded where defeat had seemed inevitable.

'Stan, my second husband, had to go to Sydney,' Denise said. 'He'll be back at the weekend. Just wait till I tell him. He'll never believe it. We've been married twenty years now, and all that time he's been convinced that I must have relatives back home.'

She stopped and her face crumpled.

'I still think of it as home, even though I can't remember it.' Her expression had the helpless, far-away look of a child. 'But when that letter came . . .'

Ellie thought she meant the one from Dot.

'No, no, I mean the letter from my mother.'

'Your mother?' For a moment, stupidly, Ellie couldn't think who her mother was. Did she mean Grandma Lillian?

'Maureen – my mother – I don't know what to call her. Orphans don't have mothers, it's a word you avoid. But when that social worker said she'd help us find our families, it gave me new hope. We wept, literally wept tears of joy, all of us, hundreds of middle-aged men and women. We'd lived all our lives wondering who we were, where we'd come from and why we'd been sent here. No one had ever told us, you see. We thought we'd done something wrong, that it was some kind of punishment.'

She went across to a bureau, took out a sheaf of newspaper cuttings and spread them on the table.

Ellie saw grainy black and white photos of children disembarking from boats, staring at the camera with startled faces. More recent shots of men and women well into middle age, hugging one another and weeping with happiness. And the headline:

British orphans receive official apology.

'We thought it would mean the end of our suffering. Perhaps for some it was. They were happily reunited with relatives they barely remembered.'

Many of them had been lied to, Denise said, and weren't orphans at all. For others the truth had come too late. Their parents were no longer alive. Her own case was more complicated than most.

'The researchers had to work from the children's home back to my adopted parents, and then through the church, before they uncovered my true parentage.'

Ellie let her speak. No way could she interrupt. Not only because she could see how important it was for Denise to let these emotions run free, but because her own throat was choked with emotion, too.

Denise straightened her back and made an effort to control the trembling that shook her shoulders.

'Do you know, Ellie, I never had much faith.'

After all she'd been through, she said, she was disgusted with the church, the way even they had abandoned children in their care, the harsh treatment they'd given the orphans over here.

'But when I found out that my birth father was a minister, I felt proud. It gave me a sense of – I don't know – value – that I'd never had before. Canon Jack Goodwin, that sounds quite something, doesn't it? He was an intelligent and well-respected man.'

She didn't feel bitter about him. People made mistakes, she knew that, and she wasn't the sort to bear a grudge.

'But when they told me that he'd been dead for years, I realised that meeting my mother was my only hope. So when they found her, I was over the moon.'

'You've seen her?' Ellie asked, astonished, but she shook her head.

The struggle to speak was too much for Denise. Ellie reached to comfort her but she waved her away, just like the stalwart old lady they'd visited in Herne Bay.

After a moment, she lifted her chin.

'I wrote her a long letter and poured out my feelings, told her that I didn't blame her for giving me up. I understood how difficult it must have been, and the only thing that I wanted was to meet her. I was prepared to leave everything at a moment's notice – my job, my family – and travel to England. I couldn't expect her to come here, not at her age.'

She swallowed, fought another wave of emotion, gritted her teeth.

'Perhaps I shouldn't have built my hopes up so high. She wrote me a very nice letter, but said she really couldn't face meeting me. The circumstances of my birth had been very difficult for her, but she'd been forced to accept them and get on with her life. She wished me the very best for mine, but now, after such a long time, she couldn't cope with opening old wounds.'

Denise jumped up, swept together the newspaper cuttings and replaced them in the drawer.

'So there you are, you see. Life has to go on. We can't rewrite the past.'

'That's true,' Ellie said, 'but maybe we can try to repair some of the damage.'

She had come here to build bridges between Denise and her sisters, and that still had to be done. But now she could see that it wasn't the only, or even the most important, goal to achieve. Somehow, mother and child would have to be reconciled, too.

A sigh escaped her. Her quest had burst out of its boundaries. All this would take time to resolve.

The light outside the window was fading. How long had she been here? An hour already? She wondered where Josh was, and if he was fed up waiting.

As she faced her new aunt, who was wracked with a grief she had no hope of mending, Ellie caught a glimpse of herself after Dad died. If there was another bond that ran as strong and deep as that of parent and child, she hadn't yet found it. But she'd also seen Maureen Latimer's steely determination, and knew that the task of persuading that old lady to change her mind would be near impossible.

Denise's voice broke into her thoughts.

'Do you know what, Ellie? The one little thing that I found hardest of all? On my birth certificate I was called Amanda. *Much loved,* is what it means. But my adoptive parents changed it, which may seem a small thing to you, but it hit me really hard. They robbed me of the one gift that my birth parents had given me.'

She stopped, every muscle clenched.

Ellie went across, crouched on the floor at her feet and took her hand.

'So would you like me to call you Amanda?'

Denise hesitated, managed a smile.

'Yes, Ellie, I think I would.'

'So you're my Aunty Amanda,' Ellie said, as Denise's tears started to flow.

Evening was falling. Amanda switched on a lamp and invited Ellie to stay.

'You could have my grandchildren's room. I don't let it out to paying guests, but you're family . . .'

The word overwhelmed her and she had to stop.

Ellie thanked her, and explained that a friend was waiting to take her home.

'But I'll come again, I promise. And I'm sure Mum would love to meet you. Maybe you and your husband could visit us next time you're in Sydney.'

'That would be nice.'

For some moments they sat in silence, then as Ellie got to her feet, Amanda spoke again.

'Your aunts wrote me such a nice letter. I didn't feel up to meeting them at the time, but maybe now . . . now that I've met you . . . would they reconsider, do you think?'

'I'm sure they would. I'll get in touch right away and let you know.'

Amanda stood in the doorway and waved her goodbye.

'Thank you so much for coming, Ellie.'

As the curtain lifted and dropped, so the light on the wall brightened and dimmed. Jack watched it swell and sway as if hypnotised, his eyelids heavy with the haze of morphine. The drug had dulled the pain in his chest, but his mind was ragged with turmoil as he fought to hold onto one last shred of hope.

His confession. He must make his confession before it was too late. It could be only a matter of days.

The countdown had begun a year and a half ago with discomfort under his rib cage, a dull point, always in the same place. When he'd begun to cough up blood Lillian had forced him to see a doctor, who referred him at once to the oncologist. From the very first diagnosis he had been painfully frank.

'You have a tumour the size of a tennis ball on your left lung. Smoker, are you?'

Jack glanced at Lillian who sat beside him, her face ashen, her lips drawn tight. She'd often nagged him to stop.

'I'm afraid so. I started as a lad, and of course in those days nobody knew how harmful it was.'

'And you never thought of giving up?'

'I tried a couple of times, but always slipped back into old habits sooner or later.'

The story of my life, he thought wryly.

'Well, it's too late, now,' the consultant said as he held up the x-rays and pointed to a ghostly shadow. 'I'd give you six months. But it could be more – or less.'

Lillian gasped. 'Can't you operate?'

'We'd have to remove the whole lung, Mrs Goodwin, and by now it's spread too far anyway. Once metastasis sets in . . .'

'But isn't there something else you can do – some sort of treatment – medicine?'

The consultant laced his fingers and turned to Jack.

'You could have chemotherapy if you want to put yourself through that. But it's highly unpleasant and won't do any good. The tumour's too far advanced.'

'What a bedside manner!' said Lillian angrily, once they were outside in the corridor. They stood shell-shocked, staring at each other. An awful coldness ran through Jack's body.

'Well, that's it, then,' he said.

At first it didn't seem real. He kept thinking he'd wake from a bad dream, but the pain grew more intense until he could no longer ignore what it meant. The awful end was inevitable and he couldn't dodge it as he'd dodged so many other unpleasant events. Death would have the last word, whether he liked it or not.

It had come too soon. There were so many things he'd wanted to do, so much to put right. The realisation that he would finally have to face his maker numbed him with fear. *Give me a little longer*, he pleaded, *so I can be ready*. Of course he knew only too well that he didn't deserve special treatment. After all that had happened, he could expect nothing but his just desserts. But the ghastly finality, coming at this precise moment, was particularly cruel.

He was sixty-five years old and due to retire that summer. After decades of struggles, he'd hoped that he and Lillian could make a fresh start, perhaps even relax and enjoy one another's company. The plan was to move to a clergy retirement flat in Devon. Lillian had been happier recently, and excited about this new stage in their lives. Jack, too, had looked forward to leaving behind the pressures and demands of his job. For the first time in their married life they would have the luxury of doing things together – walks on the cliffs, gardening, holidays in their little caravan – and secretly Jack hoped to make amends for the hurt he had caused her.

Now, though, with the diagnosis of lung cancer, those dreams were smashed. From this moment on, each day would take him a step closer to the grave.

'You must come to me,' Dot said when she heard the news. She was a headmistress now with a spacious house in the grounds of the school.

At first they resisted. Perhaps secretly, without daring to utter it, they hoped that a miracle would happen. But as the weeks went by and the pain increased, they gave in and agreed to her plan. Early in May their few belongings were sold and they moved to Hampshire.

Away from work Jack began to feel better. Life went on almost as if he'd had a reprieve. Six months passed, the dreadful deadline, and he was still alive.

'It'll take more than a tumour to finish off an old rogue like you,' Lillian joked.

On good days he could potter in Dot's garden, and at weekends she drove them down to the coast or into the New Forest. Jack would sit in a deck chair, the autumn sun warm on his face, while Lillian and Dot went for a walk. Even with a dreadful illness like cancer he could still enjoy life, and Lillian tended him with more affection than she'd shown for a long time.

Then, in January, the pain intensified. This time the oncologist confirmed that the disease had spread and was tightening its clutches. Jack's strength was sapped, his resistance was failing. He tried to remain cheerful for his family's sake, but he knew it could only be a matter of weeks before he was able to struggle no more.

One morning in early March he felt too poorly to get out of bed. Dot called for the doctor, who sat asking questions, probed with his finger, checked with his stethoscope, his expression grim. After a while he signalled to Lillian and she followed him from the room, but Jack could hear every word.

'My advice is to get him into a hospice. He needs professional nursing care. It could be very unpleasant for you here. If he haemorrhages, the blood could spurt all over the walls.'

There was a shocked silence. Jack waited, holding his wisp of breath, expecting Lillian to explode. But he heard only their footsteps going downstairs and the front door closing. Later, when she brought him a cup of tea, her eyes were red and swollen. That, more than anything, decided him. He would have preferred to stay with those he loved, but it wasn't fair to expect them to suffer on his account.

'These confounded doctors are the limit,' he heard Lillian complain when Dot came home. Their voices continued, lifting and falling like a current that lulled him to sleep.

'We would rather keep you here,' Dot said when he woke, 'but we think it's better for you to be given proper palliative care in the hospice.'

She told him they'd written to Jimmy, but that Fran was abroad and they had no idea where to find her. Jack nodded but said nothing, aware that his failings as a father had driven them away.

Only Dot, his first born, his favourite, remained. While they waited for a bed to be free at the hospice, she made time to be with him. Every morning before work she helped him eat his breakfast, kissed him on the forehead and plumped his pillow. In the evening she tried to tempt him to eat a bowl of soup or a boiled egg or his favourite rice pudding. When Lillian was too tired to sit with him any longer, Dot would take a turn, even if it meant that she got little sleep. They'd rigged up a couple of armchairs face to face with an eiderdown in his bedroom, and swore they were comfortable.

It brought tears to his eyes every time he opened them to see his wife or daughter waiting patiently beside him. His emotions were soft and fluid like those of a child and he could no longer control the desire to weep.

No, he thought, as he lay in the hospice bed, I couldn't have expected them to go on like that. Here was everything he needed – round the clock care, drugs to dull the pain, nurses as kind and gentle as ministering angels.

A soft knock at the door roused him. He must have drifted off to sleep. He opened his eyes and saw the sweet little African nurse of whom he was particularly fond. *Gift,* she was called. When he'd still had some strength he used to tease her that she was God's gift to him in his last days. *Theophilus*, he mused, as the Greek name surfaced from some distant cell of his memory…. No, no, that meant lover of God, not gift, he remembered, as the opening words of Luke's dedication to the book of Acts swirled and faded.

'You have a visitor, Jack,' Gift said with a smile.

'A visitor?'

It was too early for Lillian or Dot. They were due this afternoon at four o'clock. He could see someone standing behind Gift in the doorway, a shadow, indistinct.

'So I'll leave you alone.'

She gave a little wave of her hand as she went out, and the other figure came towards him.

'Hello, Jack.'

He knew the voice but in this strange setting it took a moment to place. She had grown stouter and her hair, once golden, was turning grey.

'Maureen.'

He tried to lift himself but he could not. His heart was beating wildly. *You shouldn't be here, he wanted to say.*

She sat beside him on the bed and reached for his hand as if she'd read his thoughts.

'I don't care. If they see me, they see me, but it's not yet midday and I know that they're not due until this afternoon.'

Her skin was soft and warm, but the brownish blotches were new. He clasped her fingers with his.

'They are coming to take me home. To die.'

'I know,' she said briskly, 'that's why I'm here.'

'You know?'

'Dorothy phoned me.'

He let go.

'Dorothy?'

She stood up and took off her coat, complaining that the hospice was overheated, but Jack had started to shiver. He was vaguely aware of a pale jumper and a beige skirt, and that the vein in her legs were knotted and swollen. She smoothed the hem over her knees as she sat and held her back straight.

'Dorothy telephoned me last night and told me. So here I am.'

He stared at the spots of light on the ceiling while he tried to make sense of this news. It left him in a void of vulnerability, as if his destiny lay in the hands of others. He moistened his mouth and managed to whisper:

'How did she find you?'

'My name and number are in the telephone directory, Jack. I don't suppose it's beyond the wit of your daughter to look them up.'

He tried to absorb what she had said, but his mind was paralysed with shock and confusion.

'So,' he asked at last, his voice hoarse, 'how are you?'

She tossed her head with a huff of exasperation.

'How do you think?' Her mouth clamped shut as she struggled for control.

'Still working?' he managed to say.

'Of course I'm working, Jack. What a thing to ask. How do you think a woman lives if she doesn't work?'

He closed his eyes. A sharp stab of pain made him wince. Her voice reached him again.

'I'm sorry. It's just that – I can't – I can't –' She clutched his hand and her voice rose. 'I can't bear the thought of never seeing you again.'

He tried to respond, but his hand was too weak. *What we shared was important to me, too,* he wanted to say, but the words swirled in his mind, dissolved and disappeared. If only it would go, the conviction of how his pleasure had caused others' pain, he might be able to rest. He wanted so much to find peace, but the knowledge that he had failed again and again, came like a weight to push him below the surface.

'So how are you?' she asked at last, brightly, like a stranger.

'Terrified,' he managed to whisper.

He struggled, he tried to take hold of the lifeline that hovered above him. He drew just enough breath to speak words that might save her, too.

'You must not . . . come . . . again.'

She jumped as if from a bolt of electricity.

How many times had they made the same resolution, but always failed to keep it? Only now, as death hovered at the threshold, his resolution was stronger.

'The chaplain is coming.'

'The chaplain!' she said, with a toss of her head.

'To hear my confession.'

She made no reply. He knew that she understood as well as he did what repentance meant – not only to say sorry, but to turn away from sin.

He summoned his strength one last time.

'You must . . . not . . . come . . . again.'

She sat, stoical, her jaw clamped. He wanted to give her the comfort of hope, as he too longed for it.

'And you too must . . .'

Maureen turned her head away and stared at the window.

'Repent? I can't.'

'So that we'll . . . meet . . . '

In heaven, he wanted to say, gasping for breath, but she understood him perfectly.

'Then I shall go to hell. I can't repent.'

She looked full at him and her face was wild with a bright anguish.

'How can you ask me to repent? There's nothing else that gives my life meaning.'

She stood up, reached for her coat and walked out of the room, her head held high.

NEW SOUTH WALES, 2010

Darkness had fallen by the time they left Katoomba. Soft, deep, with a velvety warmth, the sky studded with stars. Ellie rested her head in the lee of his back and the current of air that ran past them was fragrant with eucalyptus and the hot, spicy dust of the road. She closed her eyes, held tight onto Josh and pretended he was hers.

For a little longer, as they curved down from the mountains to the coast, she rode on a thermal of happiness. The night enveloped them in secret union. The two of them, alone.

When they stopped for something to eat, it was hard to release her grip. They took off their helmets, and Josh turned with a smile.

'You're a battler, Ellie. You kept hold of your vision and saw it through.'

They did the usual hand stuff, but this time they hugged as well. For one delicious moment, with a sliver of new moon in the night sky over his shoulder, Josh held her and she held him, all of him, close to her. She breathed in the hot metal of the bike mixed with a hint of sweat, and was heart-thumpingly aware of how it aroused her.

'Let's eat,' Josh said. 'I'm starving.'

'Me, too.' She gave him a look. 'Ravenous.'

On the last leg of the journey she pressed even closer, soft underbelly against muscle and bone, and clung to him like hope itself. Now that she'd found Denise, it would be hard to invent an excuse for seeing him again. But she didn't want to let him go. For an hour or so more she could still make believe.

Down and down wound the road, the air warmer and more humid despite the lateness of the hour. Way below, the lights of Sydney glittered.

The lagoon shivered inky black when he dropped her at Mum's.

'You want to come in?'

'Thanks, but I'd better head back.'

Nothing would soften this bloke. He was as hard and resilient as granite. She bit back her disappointment and attempted a smile.

'Thanks, Josh. For everything.'

'Let me know what happens.'

He swung the bike round and the red tail light disappeared down the road.

The water was dark and still, the house and the yard were silent. Mum must have gone to bed long ago, which was just as well, because all Ellie's happiness had plummeted into a murky pit of despair.

The next few weeks were agony. She tried to push Josh from her mind and focus on her memoir. In emails to her aunts she trod carefully, step by step, in an attempt to keep the peace. The last thing she wanted was for Dot and Fran to fall out now that they were so close to meeting their half-sister.

Fran's reply came first. She was thrilled that Ellie had seen Denise/Amanda and wanted to 'whizz out to Oz and get to know her' just as soon as she could sell something to pay for the ticket.

Dot's reply was more measured, and contained practical suggestions. She would very much like to come to Australia, and planned on paying the fare for Fran, too.

Since I am a reluctant flyer, I can legitimately say that it would be a great relief to me if she would agree.

On the subject of trying to bring Amanda (*yes, they must call her this*) and her mother together, she had a proposal.

If you have no objection, I will attempt to contact Maureen myself. Your direct approach to Amanda has paid dividends, and perhaps a similar advance to her mother may be equally effective.

Shortly after this Fran sent a long, rambling email in which she ranted against Dot's 'insensitivity in trying to keep a grip on the purse strings and make me feel like a pauper'. The plan to contact Maureen also enraged her.

You saw what she was like, Ellie, the bloody woman gave away her baby and – if what you say is true – she even had the guile to say no when Denise or Amanda or whatever she wants to call herself asked to meet up with her. What sort of a mother is that? Look what she did to our mother (mine and Dot's) too. She's caused enough grief, and the best thing is to forget her. Are we supposed to cart her out to Australia with us, like some sort of long lost relation? That's disrespectful to our mother, and I for one won't hold with it. Dot may think she's got all the answers, but she's as bloody blinkered as always. (Excuse my French!!)

At any other time the email saga would have driven Ellie insane, but now it at least had the advantage of keeping her busy. Since the trip to Katoomba she'd heard only once from Josh. When she'd dropped a hint about meeting up, he'd said he w going away for a couple of weeks to Melbourne and Perth.

'Have fun.'

'It's only for work.'

She wondered if his girlfriend was going with him. The thought of her riding pillion made Ellie insanely jealous, which was crazy anyway, because of course they'd go by plane.

'I enjoyed our trip to Katoomba,' she said.

'Let me know when your aunts come over and maybe we can go again.'

So that was it, she thought as she put down the phone. Her relationship with Josh existed purely and simply around the problems of her dysfunctional family. For him she would never be more than a worthy cause.

In the days that followed, she applied for a couple of jobs. One was as presenter/researcher for an upcoming series on a TV channel, the other as project manager for the preservation and display of a bequest from a wealthy donor to a local museum.

The first was wildly beyond her experience and skill base, and would mean competing with hundreds of better qualified candidates. She was better suited to the second, but it was by its very nature a temporary post.

As a desperate measure she also put in an application for a Masters in Investigative Journalism. Maybe her success in the search for Amanda was pointing her in that direction.

'At least you're trying,' Mum said with a nod of approval. She looked up from where she was vacuuming the hallway. 'And it's about time you cleaned your room. Some of us have to go out to work.'

Ellie dragged the vacuum into her bedroom. She had nothing better to do. With a sigh she began to move the pile of books and papers that had collapsed in an untidy heap in one corner. She dusted them off morosely and stacked them on a shelf.

Right at the bottom of the pile, where it had lain since she first found it, was Dad's book. The dated style of the cover reminded her of the puzzle he'd set her, and how it had led her way back into his past. As she gazed at the title on the lemon lozenge, a strange sensation crept up her arms and into her chest.

She'd felt like this once before, on a dig in the old penal settlements near The Rocks, when her trowel had hit something hard. A nugget the shape of a pebble. Even before she'd scraped away the dirt she'd known that it was special. And yes, she'd been right. Once cleaned and examined, it had turned out to be pure amber, from the other side of the globe, a bead from a necklace that might have belonged to an officer's wife.

As a historian she had learned to take even the apparently insignificant seriously. Evidence was important, but instinct had a part to play, too.

With this in mind, she went to where Mum was drying her hands in the bathroom and held up the book.

'Did you ever see this? I found it ages ago in Dad's things.'

'Oh, that old thing. He was always reading it, at least over the last couple of years. You know what your dad was like once he got his head into a book.'

'Did he tell you what it was about?'

'No, just that his father gave it to him. He said he didn't bother to read it at the time, but now he thought it made a lot of sense.' She hung the towel on the rail and looked at her watch. 'I must go and get changed or I'll be late for work.'

Back in her room Ellie sat on the bed, book in hand. She heard Mum open and shut her closet, take clothes from a hanger. In a few minutes she would leave and Ellie would have the house to herself. She looked again at the title. *Surprised by Joy.* The grey letters stood out clearly from the lemon lozenge, which in turn contrasted with the grey dust jacket. Above the title, in a fluid white script typical of the era, was the name of the author. If she'd noticed it before, she'd thought nothing of it. Her attention had been on looking for clues.

She stared at it, her memory stirring. It struck her as vaguely familiar, but she wasn't sure why. C.S. Lewis. Then it came to her. He was the one who wrote all those *Narnia* stories. She'd read one as a little girl – *The Lion, the Witch and the Wardrobe,* about those four English children who entered a fantasy world. But this book wasn't for children. She'd seen enough when she first found it to know it was about the author's conversion to Christianity.

An icy hand of curiosity gripped her. *Enter here at your peril,* something whispered. No explorer stepping onto a newly discovered continent could have felt more fearful of danger.

'Bye,' called Mum and the front door closed.

Yes, but only a coward would turn away from such a challenge. Even those four well-bred English children had found the guts to pass through the wardrobe into the unknown world on the other side.

She opened the book and flicked through the first few pages. They rambled on with accounts of long-ago schooldays and home life, as dry as dust. The later chapters looked drearier still, tilting like Quixote at scholarly concerns of philosophy and reason.

Then her eye fell on a passage which bore the faint trace of a pencil line in the margin:

*You must picture me alone in that room in Magdalen, night after night, feeling, whenever my mind lifted even for a second from my work, the steady, unrelenting approach of Him whom I so earnestly desired not to meet. That which I greatly feared had at last come upon me. In the Trinity Term of 1929 I gave in, and admitted that God was God, and knelt and prayed: perhaps, that night, the most dejected and reluctant convert in all England. I did not then see what is now the most shining and obvious thing; the Divine humility which will accept a convert even on such terms. The Prodigal Son at least walked home on his own feet. But who can duly adore that Love which will open the high gates to a prodigal who is brought in kicking, struggling, resentful, and darting his eyes in every direction for a chance of escape? The words **compelle intrare**, compel them to come in, have been so abused by wicked men that we shudder at them; but, properly understood, they plumb the depth of the Divine mercy. The hardness of God is kinder than the softness of men, and His compulsion is our liberation.*

She looked again at the pencil line alongside the paragraph. Had Dad put it there, and if so, had he meant it for himself, or for her?

Or maybe Grandad Jack had marked it, intending his son to take note. She could never know for sure.

A shaft of sunlight slanted across the floor from the window. Dust motes hovered and swirled, and for a moment she felt dizzy enough to faint. Could Dad have had some sort of turnaround, and intended this whole search as a cryptic message to her? The possibility was almost too scary to contemplate.

But the undeniable fact was that the author's experience resonated with her. That reluctance, that resentment, the sense of being dragged kicking and screaming to a place where she didn't want to be, by someone whose hardness was really kindness.

She snapped the book shut. It was better not to read it. She refused to be manipulated against her will. But mightn't there be an advantage in reading it? If you knew your opponent you would be better armed. If she understood what held Josh captive, then she'd be in a stronger position to play her own game, and win.

Besides, she'd read the *Narnia* tales as a child and they'd done her no harm. They were an allegory of sorts, but you could enjoy them without seeing them that way. Like Tolkien's *The Lord of the Rings*. That, too, you could read as a dramatic struggle between good and evil, without any religious interpretation. Even if plenty of critics had knocked it for that since.

They were friends, weren't they, Tolkien and Lewis, fellow academics at Oxford? And both, if she remembered rightly, were believers. Despite her resistance, Ellie was intrigued. What was it that drew intelligent men to something as irrational as faith?

She brushed the dust from the cover and took the book out to the veranda. The screen door swung shut behind her. All was silent, apart from the breeze in the branches of the trees that fringed the lagoon.

She flopped onto the swing seat, turned to the first page and started to read. Cleaning her bedroom could wait.

Another airport, another meeting, but this time Dot and Fran were the travellers, and Ellie the one waiting to greet them. She watched as startled passengers appeared from behind the screen and wheeled their trolleys down the ramp. Mum stood beside her, brushing away a tear and pretending to be bright and stoic. The reality of meeting Dad's closest kin was playing with her emotions. Karen was there, too, with little Will. He'd started his first uncertain steps, hanging onto her hand and swaying like a skittle about to fall.

Inside the airport building it was cool, but outside the temperature was thirty-one degrees. In a week's time it would be Christmas, and Santa in shorts cavorted across the entrance with his reindeer. Piped music played a mixture of carols and pop songs. Ellie hummed along, trying not to mouth the words. Yes, you really are all I want for Christmas, she thought.

'Here they are.'

She recognised Dot first, in a dove grey tracksuit, looking quite sprightly after the long-haul flight. Fran trailed behind, trying to control a wayward trolley loaded with bags. She'd cut her hair into something like a bob and coloured it chestnut rather than the old vermilion. When she lifted her hand to wave, her nails were dark purple, though her clothes looked unusually subdued. A white blouse, jeans and sneakers.

Ellie rushed towards them, excited and relieved that they'd actually arrived. In January it would be the first anniversary of Dad's death, so they were planning a family party to remember his life. Christmas would be easier, too, with Dot and Fran to help take their minds off the empty space. Karen and Tim would join them this year, and even though Will wouldn't have much idea what it was all about, they'd have the joy of seeing him open his presents.

Joy. Ellie pushed that word to the back of her mind and hugged her aunts.

'Great to see you again.'

She meant it. If nothing else had been achieved from her trip to England, getting to know these two would have been enough.

She'd planned a busy schedule for them. The first week or so, while they recovered from the flight, she'd show them some of the local hot-spots. Up the coast to Baronjoey Lighthouse, Ku-Ring-Gai Chase National Park, the Hawkesbury River. Down into the City, the Opera House, the Harbour Bridge, the Rocks.

After Christmas they would all go to Katoomba for a get-together with Amanda. Rather than descending en masse at her B&B, they had booked a bungalow to rent for the week. Karen and Tim would take Mum, Dot and Fran in their people carrier.

Ellie had invited Josh to come, as a sort of finale to the project he'd helped her with, and he'd agreed. So the plan was for the two of them to travel together. That was definitely her idea of joy, pure and unbounded.

They hadn't yet decided whether to go by car or on his motorbike. She'd managed to repair the Subaru now that a small inheritance from Dad had come through, so with luggage it would be better to take that. But if she drove, then Josh could bring Gump, and she wasn't sure if she could share the same space as that dog for so long. Maybe she'd have to assassinate it en route. Or lose it in the bush.

The most thrilling and terrifying part of all, was that for the very first time she and Josh would spend the night under the same roof. Though not, she hastened to remind herself, in the same room. That privilege would belong to Gump. No doubt she'd have the humiliation of hearing him whimper and slobber over his master while she lay to the other side of a paper-thin wall. The very thought made her want to throttle the beast.

Oh, Ellie Goodwin, what have you sunk to, that you're jealous of a dog?

She wondered if his girlfriend used to have the same

problem. *Used to*, you notice. It had come to light that she no longer featured. Whether they'd fallen out, or she had ended it, or he had, Ellie didn't know. But at least she and Josh could now be mates without the other girl's image hovering over them. And although his rules about relationships still held as rigidly as ever, she had some new ammunition.

'I've read *Surprised by Joy*,' she told him.

Faced with a rock like him to scale, what woman wouldn't use every weapon at her disposal?

'And were you?'

'Was I what?'

It took her a moment to get what he meant.

Then he laughed. The bastard. He always had an answer for everything.

On the way up Josh said, 'I'm thinking of going to Italy.'

Great, that knocks it right on the head. She was driving so she couldn't see his face, and it was probably a good thing he couldn't see hers.

They'd just passed Glenbrook where the road narrowed as it started to climb to the mountains. The blue haze of gum trees rose in front of them and the scent of eucalyptus wafted through the open window, mixed with fumes from passing cars. The air con wasn't working and Ellie's legs stuck to the seat. It was summer now and hot enough to melt gold.

'What about Gump?' she said, but what she meant was, What about me?

Gump lay sprawled on the back seat with his tongue hanging out, dribbling over her upholstery. Josh sat beside her in t-shirt and shorts, one intriguingly bare leg bent over the other knee, his thonged foot tapping on the dashboard. Jack Johnson's *You and Your Heart* was playing on the radio.

He turned to her with a maddening smile, one eyebrow raised.

'Hmm. I guess he could come, too. Dogs can get passports now, can't they?'

'One day I'll murder that beast.'

'Seriously, though, I'm doing this new project. One of the threads is my own family history. I got the idea from a mate of mine. She went to England and – '

'Don't wind me up, Bellini. I'm a dangerous woman behind the wheel.'

He chuckled. She waited for him to say more, but he started humming to himself.

After a while she could bear it no longer.

'So what are the other threads?'

He explained that it was all about origins, what brought people to Australia, and where they came from.

'What I thought was, it would be cool to do a series of short documentaries, each one focusing on the family history of a different person. It's what I got the backing for, and it's all sorted now. I want to cover a whole range of the population, Aboriginal, British, European, and all the other waves of immigrants that have here come since.'

'Short? How short?'

'I'm not sure yet. Maybe ten, fifteen minutes or so for each one? The idea is to put all of them together on a website, a sort of multi-media resource that people can dip in and out of. Maybe include information about social and cultural issues, with links to relevant agencies, that sort of thing.'

Damn you. That's a fabulous idea. I wish I'd thought of it first.

She glanced at him with pretended detachment.

'Ten, fifteen minutes? And how many months of background research do you think it'll take for each measly ten minutes of film?'

'That's the whole point.' He had a sneaky sort of grin which infuriated her.

'What is?'

'That's why I'm looking for a partner.'

'A partner?'

Her cheeks flamed with indignation. Would she always have to share her best mate with someone else?

'Yeah, a partner. It's too big a project to hack alone.'

She darted him another glance. His eyes danced with an infuriating light.

'Watch out,' he said, and made as if to grab the wheel. 'You'll roll the car.'

'Don't back-seat drive, Bellini, or you can walk the rest of the way. You and that mutt of yours both.'

The car groaned uphill and for a few more minutes neither of them spoke. Josh beat a rhythm with his fingers on his knee while Ellie felt her irritation and curiosity tangle.

'So what sort of partner? A business partner?'

'More of a creative one to help with research, build a storyboard, have a vision for the finished product.'

'Right. I see.'

Or thought she did. She narrowed her eyes.

'So what are the qualifications?'

He counted them on his fingers.

'One, previous investigatory experience. Two, a degree in history, with a special interest in social and cultural issues. Three, intelligence, naturally. Four, a sense of humour. Five, open-minded, prepared to negotiate and discuss.'

'And this partner, would she – or he – have an equal say in things?'

He flashed her the most lovely smile.

'I can't imagine it any other way.'

'Hmm.'

'So what do you think?' He raised one eyebrow.

She didn't just smile. She beamed.

'Mr Bellini, you just might have got yourself a deal.'

'Ms Goodwin, I certainly hope so.'

The bungalow they'd rented was a weatherboard shack with lino on the floors and eau de nil paint from decades ago. The rest of the family had already arrived and were getting changed to go out for an early dinner.

'Will's bedtime,' said Karen, as she bustled off with a dirty nappy. 'Bet you can't wait for yours,' she mouthed with a wink.

Three of the four bedrooms were taken – Dot and Fran in one, Karen and Tim with Will in a travel cot in the second, Mum in the third. Ellie carried her bags in there and left the fourth for Josh.

'Hi Mum. Sorry it took us forever.'

Mum glanced up, a blouse in one hand, a hanger in the other.

'What are you doing in here? We left you two the double.'

'Mother.' Ellie gave her a warning frown.

'What?'

Ellie ignored the mock-dumb expression, unzipped her case, took out some clothes for dinner and grabbed her wash bag.

'You're a grown woman, Ellie, and he's not exactly unattractive.'

'Yes, I know that. I'm not blind.'

'Darling, don't think that just because you're in the same house as us, you can't sleep together. It's not as if it's the first time. You lived with Brad. We got used to the idea that you had a sex life long ago.'

'Josh and I are just good friends, Mother. And colleagues. We share similar interests, but sex isn't one of them. So please get used to that idea, and don't spend the whole weekend dropping hints.'

She strode into the bathroom and turned on the shower.

Much to her relief, the others went on ahead. She couldn't stand any more of their innuendoes. A quick check of her reflection in the mirror – suede jacket, denim skirt and boots for the laid-back hillbilly scene – then she strolled into the room next door.

Josh was lounging on the bed, mobile in hand, Gump sprawled over his lap. If dogs could laugh, she'd swear that's what it did. Josh looked up as she came in.

'You look nice.'

'Thanks. I got cleaned up.'

'Ah, so that's what it is.'

She lobbed a cushion at him. He dodged it, pushed Gump aside and reached for his shoes. Sniffed one before he put it on. The dog had picked up the vibe that he wasn't included in the outing and began to whimper. His pig-like eyes glowered at her, so while his master's back was turned, Ellie pulled the ugliest face she could muster.

They left him shut up in the kitchen with a rubber bone, but his whining followed them all the way down the path.

Despite Mum's snores, and the fact that Ellie lay scantily clad in her single bed while Josh sprawled next door in t-shirt and boxers, she slept remarkably well. The vision of his belly with its fine arrow of hair as he lifted his arms to stretch, yawn and say goodnight, sweetened her dreams. Never mind that the Holy Book was open on his lap.

When she went into the kitchen for breakfast, he and Tim were deep in discussion about the floods in Queensland, climate change and the so-called Niña phenomenon, while coffee boiled over on the stove.

They all had a quiet morning and an early lunch, after which the two blokes lounged on the sofa and continued their conversation, while the rest of them got ready to go out.

Karen plonked Will on Tim's lap, handed him a packet of cookies, and gave instructions for food and nappies. She and Mum had decided to go into town for shopping while Ellie took Dot and Fran to meet Amanda. It was likely to be an emotional time for all three sisters. Karen drew Ellie aside, lowered her voice, rolled her eyes and jerked her chin towards Josh.

'Thought you said he was a weirdo? He seems like a really nice bloke.'

'Don't you start, too. Mum's bad enough.'

Once they had gone, Ellie went to fetch her laptop, where all her notes about the family history were stored. Dot and Fran waited for her outside, ready to walk the short distance to Amanda's house. When she went back through the lounge, Josh still sat chatting to Tim and pinching Will's nose to make him laugh. Gump didn't seem a bit bothered, even when his beloved master lifted the baby onto his lap.

Maybe it was something chemical that dogs picked up around women, which made them act differently.

'See you later,' Ellie said, and Tim turned with a grin.

'Ciao, bellisima. *Non fare nulla che io non farei.*'

Josh handed Will back to his father.

'You speak Italian?'

'A bit. I spent a year teaching English in Rome before I met Karen. Those were the days, fabulous country, gorgeous women – though not a patch on the Goodwin girls, of course. Pity about the politics. That Berlusconi's got them by the balls.'

Sex and politics. Fascinating. But it was time for Ellie to leave. Her last view was of the two of them, deep in conversation, while baby Will dropped lumps of biscuit onto the floor for Gump.

The visit to Amanda began well. Fran was on her best behaviour, friendly and interested, and much to Ellie's surprise Dot seemed a little nervous. Amanda told them her life story, and even Fran, who'd been so upset by the thought of facing the gory details of her father's affair, was full of sympathy for her new sister.

'If anyone was innocent, you were,' she said.

It was when Amanda brought out the letter from Maureen that the mood changed. She handed it to Dot, who read it with little murmurs and smiles then passed it to Fran.

Half way through, Fran gasped. She held up the page in horror, scarlet blotches breaking out on her face.

'So they went on seeing each other right up to his death?'

Amanda nodded, her obvious pride mixed with embarrassment and concern.

'It must be a great comfort to you, Amanda,' said Dot, 'to know that they really did love each other.'

'A comfort?' Fran smacked the letter on the table. 'I bet it wasn't a comfort to our mother!' She leaped up and stormed from the room.

Dot began to pull herself to her feet.

'I'm awfully sorry about this, Amanda, but I suppose I'd better go after her.'

'It's okay,' Ellie said. 'I'll go. You two stay here.'

Out in the street she could see no sign of Fran, so she headed up to the Visitor Centre on the off-chance that she might be there.

Crowds of tourists milled around the viewpoint for The Three Sisters, but she couldn't see Fran. The three massive rocks reared up from the forest as if to mock her. *So much for your quest and the grandiose idea of setting people free.* No, it was hopeless. Her aunts were as entangled in their problems as ever.

With a sigh she turned and scanned the forecourt, where an Aborigine squatted to play a didgeridoo. Its mournful wail echoed through the vast landscape like a dirge for all her dreams. She'd wasted months trying to sort out other people's lives, when it was her own that was tying her in knots. Morosely she looked around her. Where else could Fran could be? Several trails led off into the bush, but it was pointless to look for her there. Virgin forest stretched way into the distance, shimmering in a blue-green haze as it faded towards the horizon.

The only other place where Fran might have gone was back to the bungalow. She sped down the street towards it and saw that the front door was open. Maybe Fran had just rushed inside and left it swinging, she thought, as she hurried across the yard. The sound of the guys' voices reached her and she stopped for a moment, wondering if they were talking to Fran. But no, from what she could hear they were still deep in discussion. And men complained about women talking!

She was about to go and confront them with a sarcastic comment, when Tim's voice reached her.

'I see what you mean, mate, but to say sex is out of order when it's staring you in the face, who but a wowser would miss a chance like that?'

She waited, holding her breath.

Josh mumbled a reply that she couldn't quite catch. Tim laughed.

'You must be made of sterner stuff than me, bro.'

'I used to think I was as solid as steel. But even steel melts when the heat's red hot.'

Neither of them heard her step inside. She could see the backs of their heads over the top of the sofa, Tim's hair thinning on top, Josh's dark and untidy.

'Hi, guys.'

They swung round like a couple of school kids caught having a smoke. On the rug, at their feet, baby Will lay sprawled on his back amongst the biscuit crumbs, fast asleep, his little mouth open. Gump's snout was on a jar of baby food, chasing it round to try and get in for a lick.

She looked straight at Josh.

'It's joy,' she said, paraphrasing Lewis. 'Sex is just a substitute If you have joy, who needs sex?'

They both stared at her, Tim with his mouth open, Josh with

a quiver of something moving across his.

'Joy?' said Tim.

'I'd say it's more like agony,' Josh muttered. 'But joy helps.'

'Is Fran here?'

They gawked at each other as if the name rang bells in some distant cavity of their brains.

'I think she came in.'

'Maybe she's in her room.'

'Well you two had better have this mess cleared up before Karen comes back.'

She nodded towards the carpet. Tim gaped as if an elephant had come in unobserved and left a trail of droppings.

'Bloody hell.'

In a swift movement he snatched up Will, who woke with a yell of protest.

Ellie went to the kitchen, found a dustpan and brush, and handed them to Josh. No need to say anything. He took them from her with an awkward grimace, dodging her eyes, and she knew then that she had him.

First, though, she must check on Fran.

The bedroom was in darkness, the curtains drawn. Her aunt lay face down on the doona, shoulders heaving.

'I'll be right with you, Fran.'

She went back to the kitchen where Josh was tipping crumbs into the bin. He didn't look up, just put the dustpan and brush away in the cupboard and reached for Gump's lead.

'Come on, Gump,' he said and turned to the door. 'Time for walk.'

She stepped in front of him to bar the way. A flicker of consciousness passed between them as their eyes met in a delicious reversal of balance.

'Can you wait a minute, Josh? I just want to have a word with Fran. Then you and I need to talk.'

HAMPSHIRE , 1986

'I think I'll go to bed now. Thank you, darling, for a lovely day.'

Lillian stood by the desk where Dot sat with her pen poised over a pile of papers. Her hair was almost grey now, drawn back neatly into a bun. She took off her glasses and rubbed her eyes.

'I'm glad you enjoyed it. We couldn't let your eightieth pass without a celebration.'

'You're very thoughtful, dear, thank you.'

Yes, Dot had always been the most reliable of their children. She'd achieved everything that Lillian herself had once hoped for – a university education, a successful career – but was she truly happy? Why she'd never married was a mystery. And she worked so hard, too hard most of the time. Like her father, thought Lillian with a sigh.

'You're sure you don't want me to help you with the washing up?'

'Mrs Hammond will do all that tomorrow, Mother, as you very well know. Now stop fussing and have a good rest.'

Lillian clutched her birthday cards in one hand and made her way upstairs, gripping the banister with the other. She took each step with a calm, slow tread. On the landing she paused for breath and gazed through the window. The late summer sun darted shards of reddish light from behind the trees that marked the school boundary. She could hear the babble of girls' voices, shouts from the hockey pitch, the bustle as they went off to their boarding houses.

It was all so different from the world that Lillian had grown up in. At first she hadn't liked it. A private school could be as stifling as a parish, equally populated with bigots and snobs. But after Jack's death, Dot had persuaded her to stay on and make it her home. The head teacher's house was spacious enough for a family and simply aching to be filled.

Lillian could have chosen to live alone. The retirement flat was still an option for a clergy widow. But Jack's death had left her empty and bereft, so she accepted her daughter's offer. It was not the ideal arrangement, she told herself as she climbed the remaining stairs, but when had life ever been ideal?

As always, she tried to be grateful, but how ironic to have a taste of luxury now that she was old and widowed. For the first time in her life she wore good quality clothes, ate varied and plentiful food. She had her own sitting room and a bedroom with an en suite bathroom. During all the years that she and Jack had struggled on a stipend, such comforts had been out of reach. But now that she lacked for nothing, she no longer had him.

Her room was as she had left it, the bed neatly made, the window ajar to let in fresh air. It was too early to draw the curtains, and anyway, she liked to see the tops of the trees and the distant hill as the sky grew dark behind it.

She sat in her armchair, placed the birthday cards on her lap and let her mind drift back over the day. Violet and George had come all the way from Streatham. Elizabeth Bartlett had driven up from Bournemouth, where she had been living since she retired. One or two ladies from the WI, and some of Dot's staff who had been kind to Lillian, had called by, too.

'How are you?' Elizabeth had whispered, squeezing Lillian's hand. She of all people understood, not only her struggles when Jack was alive, but since his death, too. When you lost someone you loved it wasn't easy to fill the gap they left, even when your relationship had been as stormy as theirs.

'I manage,' Lillian said.

'We must go for another of our little excursions.'

From time to time they had a day out together and visited one of the National Trust houses and gardens.

'Yes, I'd like that.'

These treats were the occasional highlights of Lillian's life. They broke the monotony of hour after hour of her own company. As a child and as a married woman she had always been part of a large family, but now she spent most of her time alone. Once she had cooked for six, but now all her meals were provided by Mrs Hammond. So there was precious little for her to do. Dot had a demanding job. Even in the school holidays she had paperwork to catch up with, as well as meetings, interviews or other managerial commitments.

Lillian filled her time with small chores in the morning, then a rest and a walk in the afternoon. In the evenings she worked on her embroidery or watched the mindless diet of programmes on television. Much as she had once loved to read, she now found it difficult to concentrate. Her thoughts wandered, drifted back to the past and replayed the silliest incidents.

Like the time that Bobby had tossed his dinky car tyre in the air, caught it in his mouth and swallowed it. She'd had to make him eat chocolate porridge for a week, until the doctor was sure it had passed through his system.

Her lip wobbled as she swayed between smiles and tears.

Once in a while she went to a coffee morning at a day centre for old fogeys like herself, and sometimes one of the house mistresses drove her into town for shopping, or to the hairdresser's or the doctor's.

Whatever she was doing, Lillian's memories soon drifted to Jack. After his death, when they'd cleared out his belongings and life had to go on without him, she'd suffered what they called a nervous breakdown. The once-quiet Lillian had become hyperactive. She talked nonsense all the time, stopped strangers in the street and told them her life story.

The doctor had prescribed tranquillisers but she'd sunk into a depression. Time passed in a blur, darkness threatened to choke her. Until one day she found herself in some sort of asylum, cooped up with other pathetic remnants of humanity, drooling and dribbling and pacing around talking gibberish.

After two weeks she could stand it no longer.

'If I stay in this loony bin I really will go bonkers,' she told the doctor.

'You've had a psychotic episode, Mrs Goodwin,' he said.

'Well, wouldn't you, if you'd lost someone? I think it's called grief.'

They let her out after that, and little by little life returned to normal. The experience had given her a nasty shock, yet because of it she found the will to survive. Strangely, though, she had lost her sense of self. For decades she had filled a role – vicar's wife mother of four children, betrayed woman – until she no longer knew who the person called Lillian was.

At the same time she became even more self-conscious. She found it difficult to go out alone or meet new people. Dot was a busy, capable woman and didn't understand. But without Jack, Lillian's shyness had returned and her confidence had shrivelled.

'Isn't it strange,' she said to Elizabeth one day. 'You'd think I'd be glad to see the back of him after all he put me through, wouldn't you?'

'You loved him. It's as simple as that.'

She was right. For a single woman, that Elizabeth Bartlett understood an awful lot about love.

'Yes, and I love him now as much as I ever did – more if anything. Life is meaningless without him.'

'Ah, you see, when a person is dead he can't hurt you anymore.'

That was true, too. Only the living can cause real pain. Like Fran, for example, who was such a worry, careering through life in a whirl of chaos. Whenever Lillian saw her, which was rare these days, Fran had a new man, a new hairstyle, a new fad or religion or lifestyle commitment. She babbled on about the state of the planet, or government conspiracies, or food additives, or the famine in Africa, while that poor child, Janis, was dragged from tee-pee to squat to caravan to commune.

No wonder the child was so remote, so sullen and unpredictable. Now that she was into her teens, she wore ragged trousers stuck with safety pins. Her hair was a different colour each time, pink or green or purple, and glued into ghoulish spikes.

'It's the fashion,' Fran said. 'Weren't you ever young?'

'Well yes, but we tried to make ourselves attractive,' Lillian said, though she remembered how Mother had disapproved when she'd coiled her plaits into earphones.

As far as Fran was concerned everything was her mother's fault. It was best to avoid the topic of her vicarage childhood, and woe betide Lillian if she didn't steer clear of the even more unusual childhood that Fran was giving her own daughter.

Perhaps it was just as well that Fran hadn't come to the party. At least this year she had sent a card. Lillian took it from the pile on her lap and peered at the picture more closely. It was really very good, a moorland scene that she had painted herself. Inside, Janis had scrawled her name in huge spidery letters, drawn kisses and written: *'Granny – 80 – wow! – that's really ancient.'*

Lillian smiled to herself. The older you were, the more out of touch you became. She couldn't imagine what her own mother would have thought about the way the world had changed.

'Shoot me if I ever get like her,' she sometimes joked to Dot.

She took another envelope from the pile, the one that she'd been saving till last. This was the best of all her birthday treats, and her hand trembled a little as she opened it. It had a strange Australian stamp of some antipodean creature, an armadillo or an anteater or whatever they were called.

Lillian slid out the card. Inside it, was a photo. Dusk was deepening, so she switched on the lamp, reached for her glasses and peered more closely.

Dear Jimmy, if he'd passed her in the street she wouldn't have recognised him, though he looked a little like his uncle at the same age. The boy she had once called the delight of her life was now a middle-aged man. His hair was steely grey, his face lined, and he had the unmistakable bulge of a paunch. The photo had been taken outside somewhere, in a garden lush with exotic plants. She could see palm trees and a bush with bright red trumpety flowers and one of those things that they called a barbecue.

Jimmy was sitting in some sort of deck chair. His wife stood behind him with one hand on his shoulder. They were both in shorts and those things called t-shirts that everyone wore nowadays, with slogans and pictures on the front. *Fosters*, Jimmy's said, whatever that meant. His wife, whom of course Lillian had never met, looked disturbingly young. She was fair-haired, and so was the elder girl, Karen, who stood beside her.

'Karen is six now,' Jimmy had written, and as Lillian peered closer she could see something of the roundness and solidity of the Goodwins in the child's face.

'And Ellie is four.'

The four-year old sat curled on Jimmy's lap with two fingers in her mouth. Just like I used to, smiled Lillian, until Mother put cod-liver oil on them. And indeed, the untidy hair, the huge eyes that looked up at the camera, gave Lillian the strangest of feelings. It was like looking at herself. Shy, with a touch of wildness, the same bony arms and knees sticking out of her clothes.

'Poor little thing, don't let her be like me.'

She drew one finger over the photo as if to soothe the nerves that were almost visible beneath the surface of the child's skin. That sensitivity, that alertness, that awful capacity to feel deeply that she, Lillian, had struggled with all her life, was there, too, in her granddaughter. The child sat cocooned in Jimmy's arms, and Lillian remembered her own father, and how she had loved to sit on his lap to be cuddled by him. It was obvious that Ellie felt the same.

At least this little one was growing up in an era of peace and prosperity. There was no war to rob her of the father she so clearly adored. Jimmy was not a young man – he must be, what, forty-seven, forty-eight nearly? – but nowadays most people expected to live a long and healthy life. Of course a father must die one day, but happiness in a child's formative years was so important.

Oh, if only she lived close enough to help that little girl. A grandmother might give wise advice that a child would listen to in a way that she would not to her own mother. But, no, it was unlikely that Lillian would ever meet Ellie, or that she could have any input into her life. Of course she could write a letter, but a four-year old wouldn't understand. And even if it were kept for when Ellie grew up, would she take any notice of the words of an old woman she had never met?

No, all Lillian could do was hope, and pray. It wasn't that she believed her prayers were always answered. But somehow, the process of telling God about her concerns, brought comfort.

So she raised the photo in the palms of her hands, bowed her head and closed her eyes. She felt a bit like a fairy godmother as she asked for Ellie to be granted all the gifts that she had longed for herself.

Firstly, a happy childhood with loving parents.

Secondly, a good education.

Thirdly, to be able to use her skills and abilities in a worthwhile career. Plus the confidence to overcome that beastly, crippling shyness. And, yes, might she be spared her grandmother's fiery temper, or at very least learn to control it.

Good friends, too, and happiness. Happiness and fulfilment with the right person, someone who will love her deeply and be worthy of her love. The vision grew clearer behind her closed eyes. She drew in a long, deep breath.

Yes, she whispered, might Ellie find someone to spend her life with, to love as much as she, Lillian, had loved Jack. But, please God, without all the problems and the pain.

NSW, 2010

The room was dark, the window closed, the air stuffy. Fran lay with her face buried in the pillow, her shoulders quivering as she struggled to hold back a sob.

Ellie sat beside her and waited. Her aunt opened one eye, let out a whimper and turned away again. This could take ages. Ellie stood up and pushed open the window until a current of air flowed in, warm but refreshing. Out in the yard she heard Josh call to Gump. How long would he wait? He might get fed up and go. She almost wished he would.

She sat back on the bed and drew in deep breaths to calm her impatience. Fran's breathing grew steadier, too, and she reached for a tissue.

'How you doing, Fran?'

She blew her nose and sniffed.

'Sorry I'm such an idiot but it was seeing that letter that did it. Until then, I felt okay. Oh, I know Amanda's a nice enough person, and none of it was her fault. But hearing about my father and that wretched woman churned up all the pain of my childhood. The rows, the unhappiness, the conflict.'

Her face crumpled, her mouth twisted, her eyes blazed bright with a wild appeal.

'You see – it suddenly hit me – that the rift between my parents had split me apart, too.'

She said it was like having some terrible deformity that hadn't let her grow.

'Every bloody stupid thing I've ever done, all the crazy choices I've made, all stem from that misery. My life has been one big disaster from start to finish.' She gulped, wiped an arm across her nose. 'Well, it's too late to change now.'

'It's never too late, Fran.'

That was easy to say to someone else.

'Oh, I'm strong, don't worry, I'll get over it. It's just that I'm still knackered from the journey, and now this has drained what little energy I had.'

'Yeah, I know the feeling.'

'You won't say anything to Dot, will you, Ellie?'

'Okay, but I think you two should talk. Dot's been affected as well, although in different ways. And she does care for you, Fran.'

'Does she?'

'Of course she does.'

The tears started to flow again. Fran slid down in the bed and pulled the sheet over her face.

'Shall I leave you to sleep now?'

'If you don't mind. Thanks, Ellie. You're a star.' She peeped out and gave her a watery smile. 'Now go and find that hunk of yours.' She sniffed. 'And I hope he bloody well deserves you.'

Ellie closed the door softly, went back through the kitchen and out to the yard.

Gump was scratching up the dirt while Josh buried a turd with a spade.

"Right,' she said. 'Let's go.'

Dogs weren't allowed in the National Park, but Josh knew a trail in the bush outside the forbidden bits. He offered to drive and she sat beside him in silence. Other people's emotions had left her exhausted. But the way he zipped through the traffic pulled her nerves even tighter.

'You crash this car and I'll charge it to expenses.'

He grinned and she glowered. Let him suffer a bit, too.

The road climbed and dipped, twisted and turned through the mountains, kilometre after kilometre of virgin forest that stretched in every direction. At last he swerved onto a patch of dirt and parked. A signboard showed several trails that led into the bush.

They started down one of them with Gump on the lead. The path began to climb until the view opened ahead of them, ridge after ridge of blue-green haze.

Back at the house she'd felt bold and brave, but here all her courage shrivelled. What was she but a tiny speck in this vast expanse of vegetation? The grandeur of the place overwhelmed her. Surrounded by it, you couldn't help sense something bigger and more powerful, whatever you called him or her or it.

She sat on a bench in the clearing and fiddled with a stick. Josh sat beside her, but not too close, like the first time they met, only now the distance between them was spanned by uncomfortable truths. Sweat broke out all over her skin. Even in the shade the evening sun burnt with a relentless heat, and a whole forest of buzzing insects went crazy.

'So,' he said, 'what did you want to talk about?'

She peeled the bark from a twig, exposing its pale tender

flesh, and it annoyed her to think that she, too, was vulnerable. She chucked it on the ground and swung round to face him.

'Look, Josh, if you and I are going to work together, we need to be straight with each other.'

'Absolutely.'

'So the first thing is money. How do we deal with that? I'd say we need to make some sort of contract.'

'Okay. Do you want to discuss the details now?'

The speed of his response made her feel a bit mean. Whatever faults Josh might have, exploiting her wasn't one of them.

'No, let's leave it till we get back to Sydney. What's important is that we agree in principle.'

'Sure, and we might need to get legal advice on the terms of the partnership. Are you okay with that?'

'I'd say it's essential. One lawyer for you and one for me in case we disagree.'

'Fair enough.'

He must have read her irony, because a web of tiny lines shot from the corners of his eyes, and his mouth quivered with suppressed laughter. Tentative, hesitant almost, as if he feared rejection. Underneath it, though, the bones were strongly sculpted.

Sensitivity and strength, what an irresistible combination. Damn it.

Gump chafed at his lead, so Josh unclipped it and the dog flopped at their feet with a contented whimper.

'And the second thing?'

'The second thing,' she said, looking straight at him, 'is how am I going to keep my hands off you?'

He bent for a stick and threw for Gump, but she caught the flash of his smile.

'And more to the point, how are you going to keep yours off me?'

The smile flickered and faded.

'I thought it was just me, Josh. That's why I've been fighting it. But it's not, is it?'

He sat with hands clasped, head down.

'Is it?'

His leg began to jig.

'For crying out loud, Josh, we've got to be honest with each other.'

'Okay.' He let out a long, slow breath.

'So?'

'There's something I need to tell you first.' He met her eyes, but his smile twisted as if in pain.

Oh, no more revelations, please. I've had enough for a lifetime. She sat very still and waited for him to speak. Gump gnawed at his stick with nauseating appetite.

'Okay.' He drew in breath. 'Do you remember that time we walked the trail and you asked me about sex? And I said that I'd only marry a Christian girl, who wouldn't believe in pre-marital sex anyway? Then you asked if I'd ever been with a non-Christian, and I said a couple of times, or something like that.'

Ellie nodded. *Dated* was what she'd meant, but now wasn't the time to split hairs.

'The truth is, Ellie, I put it around quite a lot. It was years ago, before I became a believer, but that's not the point. I wasn't being honest with you. You see, at fifteen, sixteen, I couldn't get enough of it.'

Had the cicadas gone silent? It was as if the world had stopped spinning and now held its breath, waiting for her response.

She should have been pleased. What Josh had just said put a new perspective on everything. But if he *had* been with other girls, then wasn't it even more of an insult that he'd rejected her? She assumed a tone of nonchalance.

'Well, at least it proves you're human.'

'Yeah, too right I am. I didn't give a shit for any of them. Half the time I didn't even know their names.'

Despite the note of scorn, his voice struggled. He wiped one arm across his brow. The heat was intense. Sweat poured down her back, too. The forest buzzed and shimmered, alive with shrieks of birds and crackles. He took the stick from Gump's jowls and chucked it to the other side of the clearing, and the dog went scampering after it, its backside bouncing.

'So, anyhow, one day this girl told me she was having my kid.'

Ellie gaped. His words hit her with a stab of shock, a pang of envy. He was changing shape before her eyes.

'It was around the time that Mum and Dad split up, and I'd crashed the car, and my life was kind of in a mess. I tried to deal with all that by letting rip, but when this happened, it made me stop and think. So that was when I saw what I was really like …'

His voice cracked. He swallowed, took a deep breath, tried again.

'Totally out of order. Selfish and …' He shook his head, unable to finish.

'Shallow? Insecure?'

'Yeah. That's about it.'

His eyes touched hers. Gump sat at their feet, panting, while drops of saliva dribbled from his chin.

'So I decided there and then that I had to change. But I couldn't do it alone. Sometimes you have to hit rock bottom before you'll admit you need help.'

She nodded, remembering the day she'd taken the boat out on the lagoon, the day she'd decided to throw pride overboard and contact Josh. Looking for Denise was only an excuse, but that didn't matter now. They'd arrived at this place just the same. Dad's puzzle had led them here, as if the search was not only for the girl in the photo, but for both of them, too.

No, that was impossible. Dad had never known Josh. At the time of his death she was still getting over Brad. So whatever his quest might mean it couldn't be connected with Josh. Besides, this revelation blotted out all her petty concerns about puzzles. Josh's confession had knocked away her preconceptions and left her reeling.

Somewhere out there was another human being, someone who had claims on him, who probably meant more to him than she, Ellie, ever could. It was all she could do not to stamp her foot in impotent rage.

'So you're a dad.' She expected smiles, photos, eulogies about how wonderful the little he or she brat was. But he shook his head.

'Nah, she got rid of it.'

Ellie was horribly aware of a sense of relief, but it was like being dragged from the water and watching someone else drown. Josh was struggling, she could see. The tendons of his neck strained with the effort to keep control as he spoke.

'I'd have kept it, Ellie, if they'd let me. Looked after it, I mean. At least I was crazy enough to think I could. It kind of choked me to know it was mine. But blokes don't have rights in these situations. We were only kids. Her oldies took over – I couldn't stop them – and no way could I ask her to go through all that just for me.'

'Do you still keep in touch with her?'

The possibility seized Ellie with an iron grip. Was this girl another Maureen Latimer? Get rid of the child but hold onto the man? Was she the one that Josh had been dating?

'It was a one-night stand. We barely knew each other.' A muscle moved as he worked his jaw. 'Someone told me a while back that she'd married. I hope she's happy. I hope I didn't fuck her life up too much. But, no, she didn't mean a thing to me.'

The way his jaw worked as he fought with emotion said it all. 'Never underestimate what complicated creatures men are,' Mum used to say. She'd grown up with brothers. But Ellie hadn't understood what she meant until now. She reached for his hand. It was easy to be magnanimous once all the obstacles were swept away.

'I'm so sorry, Josh – for all of you.'

His hand grasped hers. 'It's just that, from then on, I swore I'd never mess around with anyone until I was sure . . . you know what I mean?'

She didn't, but she could almost imagine. He told her it was like trudging up a long, slow hill, where a lot of the stuff he used to be scornful about started to make sense. People found it hard to understand, but once you'd made a commitment, you chose to do things God's way, even when it was tough. He'd come to believe that sex was special, it combined every part of you, physical, emotional, spiritual, and it was best in a relationship of commitment.

'Like it's an incredibly powerful force, but it can also be the most fragile point of human weakness. Sex makes two people one it creates new life, but it can destroy lives, as well.'

Their hands were linked, but neither of them moved. He

mind whirled, a stranger in a foreign country where all was a dizzy blur. The click of insects rose to a deafening crescendo and the forest sprang into focus. Impenetrable, permanent, intricate in detail.

It wasn't that you lost the urge for sex, Josh said, but it didn't have the same power over you as before. You were part of something much bigger and stronger.

'It's like a candle seems bright in a dark room, but take it out in the sun and it's nothing. At least that's how it was for me.' His fingers tightened on hers and he swung round to meet her eyes.

'Until I met you.'

Her heart leaped to her throat.

'You're gorgeous, Ellie, you don't seem to realise. Do you think it's easy for a bloke to hold himself back from you?'

Was this Josh speaking? Or an insane dream? She wanted to yelp with joy but was scared that if she opened her mouth she'd bawl.

'It really hit me at Lyme, and I thought you'd understood, especially after we talked on Skype. But when I heard you were back in Sydney and hadn't been in touch, I decided you weren't interested, so I tried to forget you.'

That was why he'd gone out with that girl from church, but it didn't work. No, they'd never been engaged, no way.

'When you called and asked to meet up, my hopes revived. Then Brad turned up and I saw how you were together.'

She could have come clean and reassured him that Brad meant nothing to her now. But she hadn't forgotten how this guy had once scorned her, and a dose of jealousy wouldn't do him any harm.

'Look, Josh, don't forget you made it clear a hundred times

that I'm way off-limits. So what did you think? That I'd shrug all that aside?'

'Yeah, I know, I probably came across a bit hard.'

'Hard? That's putting it mildly. You can't reject someone outright, then expect them to be okay the moment you change your mind.'

The trees around them crackled with heat. She watched him struggle, about to break, but Gump began to growl, and a moment later a group of hikers appeared from the bush. Gump ran across, barking, and Josh went and snatched him by the collar.

That was it. If there was one thing Ellie couldn't stand, it was having someone's attention taken away from her. It swept her back twenty years or more to those infuriating times when Mum had barged in with some stupid comment that killed the special moment she'd been sharing with Dad.

Unbelievable – now Josh was actually chatting to the hikers, laughing and joking, while Gump wagged his tail. That did it.

She leaped to her feet and stormed out of the clearing along another path into the forest. If Josh had fallen on his knees and begged forgiveness, sworn she was the only woman he'd ever felt this way about, maybe she'd have melted. But he seemed to think he could treat her like some sort of worm, then click his fingers and she'd come crawling.

He was another Brad, the sort of bloke who thought that just by fancying you he was doing you a favour. Well, he could stuff that right up his backside.

Her toe caught on a rock, she tripped, and her throat tightened with fury. At least Brad knew how to give her pleasure, deep, sensual pleasure that had never been on offer with Josh. What sort of relationship would it be anyway? Just because he sown his two-bags-full of wild oats, then had a turnaround, would he expect her to stick to his outdated rules, too?

Spiky plants, trees and shrubs closed around her as the path narrowed. A bug whizzed at her ear with an angry buzz and she swatted it away. The bush was hot and hateful. Hurt and self-pity welled up inside her. He'd called her gorgeous, they'd clung to each other's hands, but in an instant the spell had been broken.

In that first moment of shock, when Josh had admitted what he felt for her, she'd taken a step onto a bridge that swayed above a dizzy canyon. Josh was the one she wanted, and he stood on the other side. She knew enough about her side, its struggles and wretchedness and emptiness. But did she dare to cross into unknown territory, to the customs of an unfamiliar tribe, to a future out of her control? No, not unless he took two steps for each one of hers.

Up through the branches the evening sky was as hot as metal. The ground burned through the soles of her sneakers and gave off a sharp, rusty smell. Deep in the forest, the air was torrid. Silvery stems of gum trees surrounded her, their slender leaves quivered. Palms and giant ferns jostled for light. Insects clicked and ticked, birds chortled and shrieked. A lyrebird whistled. Something rustled in the undergrowth and slipped into the darkness. Sweat broke out all over her.

Here, alone in the bush, the way was no longer clear. The path twisted and turned, branches lashed and stung. She was about to give up and go back the way she'd come, when the foliage thinned, a patch of light appeared and she found herself in a clearing that opened to a vast panorama.

Only a few steps in front of her was the edge of a precipice. t plunged into unimaginable depths, while way into the distance a sea of vegetation spread, hazy purple in the evening light. On a far-off ridge she caught sight of the three rocks that rose side by side, ablaze with colour, their phallic profiles engorged against the sunset sky.

Three sisters, trapped by a curse, unable to free themselves.

She stared, as if seeing them for the first time.

Three women, in love with men from the wrong tribe, held captive by a spell.

The drop at her feet made her dizzy. She stepped back from the edge.

Could this be what Dad had been trying to tell her? That Brad was wrong for her? Oh, she knew that now, but she hadn't then. Maybe Mum was right. Dad had realised she was unhappy, that even after she'd left Brad, she still pined for him like a junkie for a dirty needle.

'Dad never did like him,' Mum had said. 'He was disappointed, Ellie, that you could fall for someone so shallow. But he didn't know how to tell you. He was afraid of upsetting you.'

'Good,' Ellie had said at the time. 'That's because Dad loved me too much to hurt me.'

Yes, of course he loved her, she'd always known that. But what she saw now was that he'd found another way to get through to her. He'd set her a puzzle instead.

'You can nag all you want but the only way Ellie will learn is by experience,' he used to say to Mum.

Yes, Dad had known she wouldn't be able to resist a trail of cryptic clues. Of course he'd wanted her to find Denise, and he'd hoped that his sisters would come out of it happier and stronger But his real purpose was for her. He'd led her to all those unhappy relationships so that she'd see how damaging hers could be, too.

She gazed across at the rocks. They blazed as crimson as blood in the setting sun, yet stood solid and unchanging in their monumental immobility.

Three sisters, trapped in the curse of the past, unable to free themselves. Three women, held captive by a spell.

But no one had put a spell on Ellie Goodwin. Nothing bound her but her own fears and prejudices. She had bound herself, and her only enemies were stubbornness and pride.

The sun slipped behind a ridge, the shadows lengthened, and Ellie shivered. The future was hers to decide. Would she let bigotry, misunderstandings and preconceptions keep hold of her? Sex wasn't really the problem with Josh, not deep down where it hurt. Any couple could sort that sooner or later.

Did she really care what other people would think of her if she went out with Josh? Was she so hooked on this materialistic and self-indulgent world that the rest of them floated around in?

What if his ideas didn't chime with fashionable fads? Another thirty years or so and a new generation would write off this current culture as empty and meaningless. Josh had values that weren't even in Brad's vocabulary. His integrity, his concern for others, his insight were a big part of what attracted her. Besides, she didn't want another man who treated sex as a performance sport, whose motive was gratification and who displayed her like a trophy. And one thing she did know, which experience had taught her, was how much easier it was to dive into a relationship than to climb out of it. There could be advantages in dipping your toes in the water first.

No, what had really bugged her about Josh was that he hadn't fallen headlong into a hopeless passion from the very first moment he'd seen her. That Ellie Goodwin's brilliance and beauty and wit hadn't knocked him off his feet and sent his values scattering from here to Wollongong.

Yes, she'd resented him for resisting the very hypocrisies that had put her off religion in the past – self-indulgence, people who said one thing and did another, whose human weakness was stronger than their faith. She'd mocked his beliefs, but she'd never once tried to understand them, or why they motivated him to behave the way that he did.

What if he'd given in to her right from the start? She would have gained her pleasure, but he'd have lost her respect, grudging though it was. It pained her to admit it, but deep down she admired his conviction. And the fact that he could keep to it, despite her taunts and provocations, proved it was genuine.

But now that he'd admitted his struggle and come clean about his feelings, she'd tossed them aside as if they meant nothing.

With a groan of frustration she paced around the clearing. Maybe she had overreacted. But it bugged her to go back with her tail between her legs and admit it. Anyhow, by now he'd probably have got fed up waiting and gone off in the car. She could hardly blame him if he had.

The sun had sunk and the sky was fading fast. The small stony patch where she stood was deep in shadow. Night would fall quickly here, far away from human habitation.

She scanned the web of narrow paths that led back into the bush, but wasn't sure which one she'd come on. They all looked the same, barely paths at all, overhung with thick foliage. Panic shot through her. A wrong turning, a simple mistake, and you could wander around here for hours. No one would have a clue where you were. Especially at night.

The vastness of this place overwhelmed her. How had people lived here, navigated their way around, centuries before the benefits of technology? It was too early for stars, but she didn't know the area well enough to work out directions from where the sun had set. Soon night would tighten its hold and she'd be lost in the darkness, with snakes and spiders and wild beasts for company. Croaks and hoots sounded all around, twigs snapped and crackled.

Blank terror seized her and she snatched up her mobile praying that there'd be a signal. From behind her, out of the silence, another twig snapped.

'So that's where you are.'

She swung round. All she could see was a shadowy figure moving towards her through the trees. Then a late glimmer of light caught the head of dark hair and gleamed over the bones of his face. Her heart leaped and she ran to him, arms outstretched, till her feet hit something solid and she stumbled.

'That bloody dog!'

Gump stood there, whimpering at her, wiggling his rump in an attempt at a wag. It was the best you could expect from a creature without a tail.

On the way back to the car, they sorted out a few ground rules. Whatever they disagreed on, it was better to listen to each other's point of view than get into a barney. Go for concord not discord. They were coming at the relationship from different starting points, so the best solution would be to compromise. Get to know each other, see how it went, review progress and move on from here. Take it one step at a time.

As they walked, she tried to explain how she saw things.

'Josh, I know that I've pulled your leg a bit, and sometimes it's hard for me to see life the way you do. But I really do respect you for having the courage to stand out against the crowd. The thing is, it's a lot for me to take on board.'

'That's why relationships are tough when you have different beliefs.'

'I guess.'

He told her what his were, and this time she listened. It was a lot easier with her hand in his. How having faith wasn't the way most people imagined. You weren't poured into a mould, you were free to choose. It didn't make you perfect. Everyone still struggled. The world criticised you, rightly, when you failed to live up to your beliefs, but often it ridiculed you when you did.

'And that's a sort of hypocrisy, too.'

When they reached the clearing where the car was parked, they stopped by a board with a map of the area, peering at it in the dark to locate where they'd been. Ellie pointed to the path that she thought had led her to the edge of the precipice, and he caught hold of her hand as if seeing it for the first time.

'Hey, those are beautiful fingers.'

She laughed. 'Thanks, I always did think they were my strongest feature.'

She was about to turn, but he drew her back.

'Ellie, there's something else I need to come clean about.'

'Oh, fire away. I can take anything now I know how much you like my hands.'

'Something you said once before, back when we walked the Manly trail, really made me think.'

'What did I say?'

'That I should take people as they are, not expect them to be like me – remember?'

'Yeah, the way you dismissed me outright made me feel like some sort of bug that you'd trodden on and kicked aside.'

'It's not that I don't think it's important for people who are in a relationship to share the same values. It is important. But the more I thought about it, the more I realised something.'

'So?'

'That if you accept me as I am, then I should do the same with you.'

'Huh! What's wrong with me now?'

'No, the point is, I was wrong to judge.'

'Yes, you were.'

'And the worst thing is, that I hurt you. So I'm really sorry about that, because . . . '

He broke off and his hands gripped hers.

'Because if there's one person in the world I don't want to hurt, it's you.'

She couldn't speak. His words touched her somewhere that she'd forgotten existed, deep inside her vulnerable self, a soft, tender place that she'd learned to harden like a callus over sore skin. She bit her lip, tasted blood. Strange, how harshness was easier to bear than kindness.

Gump whined, tired of waiting. *Too bad*, she eyed him silently, *your days are numbered*. She stepped closer to Josh and slid her hand round the back of his neck.

'Come here, you.'

That first kiss was bliss. Pure joy. If this was step one, she couldn't imagine what the rest would be like. Not just a country but a continent, a whole new world waiting to be discovered.

So in the car, all the way back to the house, she sang an old Eddie Cochran song, a favourite of Dad's from the sixties.

Three steps to heaven.

Later that night, when the others had gone to bed, she and Josh sat outside with a bottle of wine and talked. Stars spread across the dark expanse of the sky. The temperature had plummeted, so Josh went back into the house and brought out a blanket. They huddled under it to keep warm, blissfully close with his arm around her shoulder, the smell of his armpit sweeter than perfume.

Gump sat at a watchful distance, pretending to snore.

'Tell you what, Ellie,' Josh said cheerfully as he swigged and passed her the bottle, 'being with you is going to be tough. One snog and I'm hooked.'

'Good. Now you know how I feel.' She swallowed some wine. 'And you'd better be careful. The next time you slip up, I might not let you off so easily.'

'You're a cruel woman.'

He pulled her closer and nuzzled her ear.

'Mmm, let me see, you smell of Vegemite.'

They'd had some on toast, they were so ravenous.

'Delicious. Especially with a slosh of Hunter Valley Shiraz.'

She ran her tongue over his lips for him to taste, and for a long moment they kissed. She broke off, and teased him with a smile.

'That's all you're getting. Didn't you want to take it one step at a time?'

As the weeks passed, being with Josh was sweet agony. She felt like a child forced to wait for Christmas while the shops were full of glitz but it was still only August. You knew that when it came you'd gorge yourself. When it came? If it came. They couldn't decide how they'd decide that. Or who would. Or on what grounds.

They didn't see each other every day. Their roles in the film project were complementary, but involved them in travel, often to different places. Ellie worked on most of the research from home, and as soon as she could afford it, from the unit she rented with Cindy.

Josh lived a couple of streets away in a den like a burrowing animal, full of junk. Files slid from the top of a cupboard when you opened the door. You reached for a sheaf of papers and out fell a dirty sock. A pair of shorts hung from the hook of a fishing rod propped in one corner. An empty pizza box lay squashed under the sofa. She didn't risk lifting the lid, just passed it to him with a grimace, nose screwed tight. Wires and cables snaked in tangles from one gadget to another. Gump's basket had a threadbare blanket with stains she preferred not to investigate.

'Don't think I'm going to clean this lot for you,' she warned Josh.

Gump treated her with a grudging tolerance, and sometimes let her scratch his back.

Ellie burrowed, too, for information, stories of people's lives, helped them to uncover facts about their families that they'd always wanted to know. She wrote interview scripts and Josh filmed her talking to fascinating men, women and children who'd come – or whose ancestors had come – from all over the world to settle in Australia. He edited the results, working his particular blend of creative and communicative magic, and she learned about the technicalities, giving them the perspective of a fresh pair of eyes.

He was fun to work with, always buzzing with ideas, original, outrageous, exasperating. She could have throttled him a million times, and often had to take a walk round the block to cool down.

Out of all the bits and pieces, they crafted something with both depth and beauty. Gem after gem appeared on the website, which began to take shape and be noticed. One of the national dailies ran a feature and a TV channel was interested in being involved. They decided to include items on self-help groups, organisations that could put people in touch with their roots and support them in dealing with issues that arose. When funds were low they ate bread and Vegemite. If they hit the rocks, they'd wash dishes.

Amanda had agreed to be interviewed, and Ellie's aunts, too. After Christmas, the three sisters had travelled back to England together, where Amanda had met with her mother, Maureen, only months before she died.

Her aunts still had issues – like Fran's irritability, Dot's guardedness – and occasional letters arrived from one of them berating the other, as they tugged back and forth with their different versions of what had really happened and why.

Amanda was now back home in Australia. Because of the distance between here and England, the sisters didn't know if they'd ever meet again.

'Yes, it is home now, after all,' Amanda told Ellie. 'Maybe I just had to go away, to realise where I belong.'

Ellie and Josh were together more and more. They grew to know each other as co-workers, as friends and business partners. Their interests, opinions and habits sometimes coincided and sometimes collided. That he liked nerdy science fiction film appalled her. He couldn't believe what he called the 'slop' that she read.

They laughed a lot, and argued even more. Often he drove her insane. He could imitate voices and accents, make animal noises, a train running through a tunnel, balance a pencil on his nose. From time to time she lost her temper; he ignored her and she got over it; they kissed and made up. Planning the trip to Italy kept them both focused. It was torment. It was bliss.

She'd met some of his friends and he'd met some of hers. His were surprisingly human. Most of them were in tentative relationships, though they preferred to hang out in groups. There was safety in numbers, they said. She'd even been to his church, where everyone was kind, and no one seemed to disapprove of her. She began to relax around them. They were good fun.

Ellie's friends liked Josh, too, but thought she was crazy to do without sex.

'We're getting there,' she said. 'Slowly but surely. One way or another.'

Josh already knew her family, and one day she met his mother and sisters. The sisters teased him and told Ellie he was impossibly spoiled, the much-wanted male child that every Italian family adolised.

'What Joshua wants, Joshua gets.'

'We'll see about that,' she said.

A lot of people were taking bets on it.

'Those two won't last the year out.'

'Nah, they'll end up getting hitched.'

'But they're way too different.'

'Come off it, they're made for each other.'

The odds changed from day to day.

One afternoon when Josh was away in Brisbane, Ellie felt the urge to go back to the weatherboard house where she'd lived as a child. She chose a time when Mum wasn't there, left the Subaru in the driveway and went for a walk by the lagoon, along the path that she'd followed so many times before.

She sat on the opposite bank, looking across to the little bungalow, the home that Dad had built with his own hands. They'd scattered his ashes on the water, so there wasn't a grave to visit, and this was the place of all places where he felt closest. Where her memories of him came and went like the tides, but were always there, beneath the surface.

Her feet in the water, his hand in hers in case she fell. The soft silt between her toes. Riding on his back while he swam in the strong current. Sitting side by side on the bank, eyes on the fishing line, waiting for it to pull. Feathery trees that leaned over the water, their reflections rippled and mirrored over the secret world below. A dead cat they once dragged out of the sludge. Fallen leaves that drifted, ruffled by the breeze. The silvery light at dusk and dawn.

'Dad, there's one thing I want to say to you,' she whispered into the stillness. 'Not that you taught me how to love, you already know that. Or even that I'm ready to let you go. One simple thing that can never be, but that I wish for, just the same.'

She brushed aside a tear, took a deep breath and looked up to the sky.

'I wish you could have met him.'

Printed in Great Britain
by Amazon

Janet Norfolk is a professional musician and an artist living in Kent who was the founder and conductor of the Detling Singers and now leads the Auguri Singers a group of solo singers who give concerts for charity. These poems were mainly written to amuse her family and friends and are now published for the entertainment of a wider audience.

Carolyn Stevenson is a professional artist living in the North Yorkshire dales.

To

EDWARD

from

BUTTERFLIES

to

ELEPHANTS

by

JANET NORFOLK

Illustrated by

Carolyn Stevenson

from BUTTERFLIES to ELEPHANTS

ISBN 0-9529502-0-0

Published December, 1996
by E.L.S. Norfolk
Gibraltar House, Gibraltar Lane,
Maidstone Kent. ME14 2NG

Cover & production design by: Harry Amson
142 The Street, Adisham,
Canterbury, Kent. CT3 3JZ

Printed by: Whitstable Litho Printers Limited
Milstrood Road, Whitstable,
Kent. CT5 3PP

CONTENTS

1   from BUTTERFLIES to ELEPHANTS

I - BUTTERFLIES

5   A Trip to the Tip!
6   A Day at the Sales
10   A Free Day

II - THRO' THE SEASONS

14   A Far Cry
16   It's a grey day to-day
18   The Forecast
20   The Merry Month of March
22   Looking for Spring
24   Summer Bank Holiday
26   Summer
27   June Memories
28   When Skylarks Sing
30   Another Bank Holiday
32   The Joys of the Garden!
34   Farewell to Summer
36   Regrets
37   A Winter Walk

III - A BIRD'S EYE VIEW

40   Sea Sounds

41   The Hills

42   Far and Away

44   The Moon

45   Might Have Been

46   Easter in the Lakes

47   The Great Wood - Derwent Water

48   Music

50   "Fryton"

52   "Pope's Hall Cottage" ("Moon Acre")

53   Concert At "Stoneacre"

54   Observations on the D.C.A. trip
                up the Thames from Henley

IV - ELEPHANTS

58   Swans

60   Friendship

62   Dogs

64   Trouble With Spiders

V - CHRISTMAS 1991 to 1995

66   1991
67   1992
68   1993
69   1994
70   1995

VI - 'WINKLY WOO' and the CONCERTS

74   The Colourful Concert
76   "Thank you" to the Auguri Singers
78   From the Auguri Singers to their hosts in France
79   Introduction to The Blackthorn Trust Spring Concert
80   "Happy Christmas" to the "Monday Group"
82   "Happy Christmas" to The Detling Singers - 1991
83   "Happy Christmas" to The Detling Singers - 1992
84   "Happy Christmas" to The Detling Singers - 1993
86   "With thanks" to the Detling Singers - May 15th, 1994

LIST OF ILLUSTRATIONS

Part I

4   A Trip to the Tip!
9   A Day at the Sales
13   A Free Day

Part II

15   A Far Cry
17   It's a grey day to-day
19   The Forecast
23   Looking for Spring
25   Summer Bank Holiday
29   When Skylarks Sing
33   The Joys of the Garden!
35   Farewell to Summer

Part III

43   Far and Away
51   "Fryton"

Part IV

59   Swans
61   Friendship

Part V

65   Christmas

from BUTTERFLIES to ELEPHANTS

My mind is like a butterfly
That flits from here to there
It wants to settle on a flower
But flitters everywhere.

I can't decide just where to go
The yellow flower or blue?
I'll climb up on the elephant
To get a better view.

And so dear readers, glasses on
And take a better look
From elephants to butterflies,
You'll find them in this book.

Part I

BUTTERFLIES

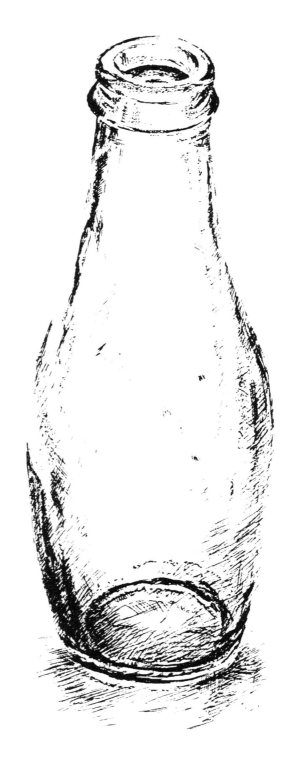

4

A Trip to the Tip!

Turn the key and click the clutch,
And turn the metal crank;
We're taking brittle bottles
To the broken bottle bank!

Bump along the rubble road,
And bounce about the bends -
Then smoother surface silver white -
The long road ends.

The seagulls screech,
The scrawny scrape of lorries coming in,
The clank of metal - breaking bits
When emptying the bin.

The twisted metal, rotting food -
Old sofas - beds - and glass,
These things have had their uses
But their time has come to pass.

So turn the key and click the clutch,
We're going on a trip,
With broken bits of bottles
To the local rubbish tip!

A Day at the Sales

Shall we go to the sales?
What a dreadful idea -
The town will be packed -
And this time of the year
It's freezing outside -
And the shops will be hot,
And whatever you're getting
You've probably got!
No! - I really can't think
Of anything worse
Than returning half dead
With a half empty purse!

Alright - very well -
I will go on my own,
You have more success
If you venture alone.
So, in some excitement
(To some, perhaps, folly!)
I put on flat shoes,
Took a spiky umbrolly -
Which has nothing whatever
To do with the weather -
But might just be useful
in crowds - or whatever.

So I set off at lunchtime
And got in the car;
The excitement was growing -
It's not very far.
Then the traffic stopped flowing -
I sat in a queue -
And I couldn't *believe*
It was quarter past two.
It was certainly hot
And the shops were packed out,
With everyone grabbing
And rushing about.

I tried on a blouse
But the buttons had gone,
And then bought a skirt
(Which was rather too long).
And then to the Top Shop -
It's not very far -
Where I'd spotted a yellow
And mauve spotted bra.
And so time went on,
Then with energy flagging
I aimed for the car
With the poly-bags sagging.
And with legs twice as short
And with arms twice as long.

It flashed thro' my mind
As I struggled along -
There's a meal to be got
And I just hadn't thought
To put food on the list
Of the things I had bought!
And so thro' the traffic
At last I arrive -
And I know that I'm looking
More dead than alive!
But I kick off my shoes
And I put on the kettle -
Already I'm feeling
In much better fettle!
I put out of sight
Where no-one will see
That mauve-spotted bra
In that mad shopping spree!
I'm really quite tired
And collapse in a heap -
Then I think of those bargains
Going terribly cheap!
And I smile to myself
As I think what you'll say!
But it's all been such fun -
Yes! - a brilliant day.

8

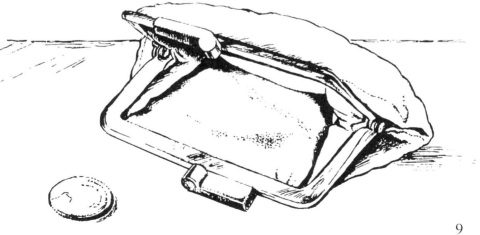

9

A Free Day

I've got a free day
So I'm going to have fun,
I'm going to do nothing
And sit in the sun.
I'll sit by the river
And just take my book,
And I won't do a thing
But I'll read - and I'll look
At the people who pass
And the ducks as they swim 'neath the bridge -
And I won't do a thing!

So I settle myself
And there's nothing to do,
And the sun is all golden,
The sky is all blue.
Then I hear in the distance
The telephone ring -
No! I won't go and answer,
I *won't* do a thing!
But as it rings on
A small voice questions "why?"
I'd better just answer,
I say, with a sigh.

10

"Oh hello there -
Shall we say about five?
Yes, I think that's alright,
A good time to arrive.
Yes of course - we're delighted,
No trouble at all;
Yes - I'll see you then -
And thanks for your call".

So it's back to the river,
Sit down with a flop
And look at my watch -
How much time have I got?
There's nothing for tea,
Absolutely no cake,
But it won't take me long
To have a quick bake.

"Oh - hello there" - I hear,
And I just have a peep -
Do you think I should answer
Or just stay asleep?
She's waving her hand
And she's coming this way;
"Can I join you?
It's oh! such a wonderful day"!

"Yes, of course - yes - please do"!
And my heart seems to sink
As I go to the house
To prepare us a drink.

And there on the carpet
I see a large puddle -
And the house now it seems
In a terrible muddle.
The dogs need a walk
And the cats are not fed -
And I'm feeling right now
I could flop into bed!
So forget all this resting
And nothing to do -
When the sun is all shining
And the sky is so blue -
You might as well *plan*
And find something to do!

Part II

THRO' THE SEASONS

A Far Cry

Damp and dreary drizzle
On a foul and foggy day;
A far cry from the pink and white
And blossoming of May.

The ice and spikes of winter
With the crisp and crunchy snow;
A far cry from the swallows
Skimming swiftly to and fro.

The river with its murky mud
Full tilt towards the weir;
A far cry from the willow trees
Who dream of waters clear.

When once a child thro' younger eyes -
A clear blue sky - and snow;
A far cry now, with ageing limbs,
Those winters long ago.

So on with boots - a scarf - my stick -
My glasses and my hat;
A far cry from the younger me
When hills, it seemed, were flat!

It's a grey day to-day

It's a grey day to-day
It's February
The rain from heavy leaden skies
Falls to eclipse the hills that rise
To seek the sun - too soon.

It's a grey day to-day
And cold
The day, it seems, has not begun
But stays asleep without the sun
Altho' it's almost noon.

It's a grey day to-day
And damp
The murky mist swirls round the trees,
The pavement pools begin to freeze
Beneath the rising moon.

It's a grey day to-day
But then
I saw a snowdrop white, begin
To show her face *before* the Spring
To say she heralds everything,
And comes to welcome Spring.

The Forecast

So Spring is here - they say!
So do not worry ,
Not drifting snow
But just a little flurry!
The forecast for the week
Was lots of sun!
But not today - to come!

What happened to that forecast
"Sun today"?
As far as I know
Not a single ray!
So! - no! we cannot say
That Spring has come - today!

The hailstones lashing at the window pane,
A howling gale -
And then the freezing rain.
So will the Summer come again?
Spring has not come - today!

I've just been out
And walked about
And there - beneath a tree
I found a primrose hiding there,
And purple violets everywhere -
I simply had to stand and stare
'Cos Spring has come - at last!

18

The Merry Month of March

The Spring is sprung and it's hey-nonny-no,
But it's freezing outside and there's lots of snow,
And we're all trying to think as the winds do blow
That it's Spring - in the merry month of March.

It was a lover and his lass -
In the Springtime - the have a little fling time -
That Mick took Madge in his brand new car -
But the lock froze up, so they didn't get far!
All in the merry month of March.

It's thick winter coats, if you're out and about,
There's a Robin on the tree with his feathers fluffed out,
And I think above the wind, I can hear him sing,
'Cos it's March - and we *know* that it's Spring.

Mum's got the curtains down and cleaning in the attic
'Cos it's Springtime now, and everyone is at it -
Dad's in the garden, sorting out the shed,
He's got his bobble hat on, and his fingers have gone dead -
All in the merry month of March.

Fred next door's got a problem with his drain -
'Cos all last week it did nothing but rain,
He's trying to sell his house - said "I'll wait 'til the Spring
Now is the time, as the sun will shine,
The flowers will be out, and the people all about -
Yes! The merry month of March is the time!"

So we've all got it wrong - but the calendar is right -
So we'll just turn the page - keep the Spring in sight!
And we'll sing "tingaling", and a "hey-nonny-no",
And pretend it's the merry month of March.

Looking for Spring

I was hopefully looking for Spring
As I tramped thro' the mist and the mud
By the eddies of swirling water
And the river in fullest flood.
Where is the sun this morning?
And where indeed is the sky?
All wrapped in a grey of silence
Not even a bird flies by.

The trees damply dripping around me
The squidging of mud round my feet,
Perhaps it will never awaken
This world that has fallen asleep.

I fastened my coat even tighter
And just kept on walking, until
In the mirk and the mist of the morning
I reached the tree, high on the hill.

I looked to the valley below me,
I looked to the sky that was blue,
To the shooting of green that was just to be seen -
As the watery sun filtered thro'.

I stood and I looked in the distance
And then as if all that I feared
Had been wrapped in the mist of the winter,
It suddenly all disappeared.

And there from the tree just beside me
I heard the first blackbird sing,
And I saw all the catkins a-hanging
And I knew that I'd found her - the Spring!

Summer Bank Holiday

May Bank holiday - what shall we do?
The sun is shining, the sky is blue.
So, "Come on children - collect your things
And see what this wonderful day can bring".
So with mountains of food and the drinks and the rugs,
The wind-shield, the spray to keep off the bugs,
And the day full of promise, we got in the car
And on to the road - we hadn't gone far
When we noticed ahead a rear light or two
And then, to my horror, I saw the long queue -
And just for a moment I had a slight doubt,
"Is Bank holiday Monday the day to go out?"

It must be an hour that we've been sitting here,
And all we can see is the rusty red rear
Of some clapped-out old van with terrible fumes,
And lots of loud music without any tunes!
Then, "I want a drink" and "I need the loo",
About which of course there was nothing to do.
"You'll just have to wait - now think of the fun
We're going to have soon in the sea in the sun".
Thank goodness! We're moving! They all give a cheer
As I switch on the engine and lurch into gear.
How far are we now from the beach and the sea?
The day is half gone and it's quarter to three!
So we stop for the picnic and spread out the rugs,
The food and the drinks and the plates and the mugs.

The winds a bit chill and it's starting to rain,
We mustn't be long - let's get going again!
Yes, we're all feeling better, so back in the car,
We know now for certain it's not very far.
The car climbs the hill, and before we descend
We suddenly see as we go round the bend
The reason we came! The sand and the sea,
And they're all so excited (except perhaps me!)

In no time at all sand castles are made
And they all splash around with a bucket and spade.
And so as I sit, and I think, and reflect,
Things don't always work out just the way you expect -
But - we went to the sea, and the children will say -
"Remember the fun that Bank Holiday?!"

Summer

Beyond the green
Where distance sees,
A mist of bluebells
'neath the trees;
And there the cuckoo calls -
And lilac blossoms gently sway,
So now I know - it's May

The buttercups in meadows fair,
The scent of blossom fills the air,
And here the blackbird sings,
The fragrant roses now in bloom,
Tell me - it's June.

The air is soft with summer breeze,
And petals drop from
Full-bloom roses there.
And drifting - drifting butterfly -
It means to me - July.

June Memories

The sound of water over stones
Where little streams and rivers pass,
And softly lowing cattle pass
In buttercups, and long green grass.

Shadows and shades of green on lawns
From shafts of sunlight thro' the trees -
And scent of bluebells in the wood
that lingers on the breeze.
And in the heavy honeyed flowers
The drowsy hum of bees.

And hear the sound of sea in shells
Along the pebbled shore -
Sounds of a distant ocean
And Summertime's allure.

Like butterflies, go on your way,
Live for another summer's day,
And see the dark red velvet rose
And blue delphiniums sway.

For summer passes all too soon
And darkness comes where no flowers bloom.
Remember then, and see again
The warmth and light of June.

When Skylarks Sing

Stillness! - and the early dawn
Mist on fields of young green corn,
The moon reluctant, goes her way
Before the sun announces Day.

Midday! - the sky intensely blue
Reflects to perfection fields of flax,
And in the viewing now, perhaps
A glimpse of Heaven too.

And then she sings! - I've never heard
A song from such a tiny bird
That rises from the ground.
As feelings stirred beyond the mind
Transcending light from darkness, find
Such beauty in that sound.
Soaring towards an endless sky
That little bird that flies so high,
The Halls of Heaven must rejoice
To hear the sound of such a voice -
When skylarks sing.

Another Bank Holiday

We've got another holiday
So do let's have some fun,
We'll pack some lunch
And take some booze
And go out for a run.
We won't waste time,
Or take too long -
We'll hurry to the car.
We'll go to Rye - perhaps the sea -
Somewhere that's not too far.

The sun is shining, not a cloud
To clutter up the sky -
So hurry up and let's get off,
We're feeling on a high!
So children get your trainers on,
And all your swimming togs;
And as we're going to be all day
We'll *have* to take the dogs.
So that means leads and doggy dish,
And don't forget a towel,
We'd better take a brolly -
Just in case the day turns foul!

And have you got a jersey?
And I *almost* then forgot
To go and get the suncream
Just in case it's *really* hot.
And what about binoculars?
The camera - in that bag -
"It hasn't got a film in"?
Oh! that really is a fag.

Now, have we got the salad?
What! - not got any bread?
We'll have to go to Marks & Sparks,
Buy sandwiches instead.
The whole idea is wearing off;
Not sure I want to go -
The sun's gone in - the wind's got up -
I saw a flake of snow!
So may I ask in dulcet tones
Who has the final say
On where to go, and what to do
This Spring Bank Holiday!

The Joys of the Garden!

Sing a song of summertime,
Fill up the gin and tonic,
The swing-seat's in the garden
So go and sit upon it.

Oh! Sing a song of summertime,
The hosepipe ban is on,
So you do it all at midnight,
Or you carry cans along.

The weeds are coming on apace
But not much else is growing,
'Cos the pigeons in the springtime
Had the seeds that I was sowing.

And not a shoot has yet appeared
In boxes on the sill,
Perhaps they're in the shadow -
And the wind is very chill.

Sing a song of summertime
And roses' prickly thorns,
Of digging in the garden
And mowing of the lawns,
Of sorting out the potting shed,
Of weeding in the sun,
And wheeling all the rubbish
When the barrow weighs a ton.

32

Yes - we'll sing a little ditty
Now it's tidy and quite neat,
So if my back will make it
I'll just try that garden seat.

Sing a song of summertime,
Fill up the gin and tonic,
The swing-seat's in the garden,
So I *will* now sit upon it!

Relax - enjoy the sunshine
And admire the lovely view,
But only for a minute -
There's a thousand things to do!

Farewell to Summer

The scarlet poppies nod their heads
Amongst the waving corn,
And Summer wanders thro' the fields
Towards an Autumn dawn.
The harvest moon in all her gold
Hangs in the midnight sky,
And softly from the scragged oak
I see the barn owl fly.

The dew is heavy on the grass
And spiders' webs a-glisten,
The morning air is cooler
And as I quietly listen
I hear the far-off whispers
And the cornfields gently sigh;
Farewell - the poppies bow their heads
And Summer says "goodbye".

Regrets

It is as if the Summer's never been,
As if I've never smelt the flowers or seen
The golden sunrise and the crimson set -
The rising moon, or heard the Nightingale
This should have been the summer,
But its past -
I was too busy and it didn't last.

* * *

A Winter Walk

Deep is the snow -
And white on white,
The freezing landscape fades
Beyond vision - into grey and smoky mists
And somewhere meets the sky.

Rattling twigs
A-tangle on the trees -
Pointing their frosty fingers in the wind
Upwards - to where the silent
Silver moon sails by.

Crisply the crackling ice
Crunches beneath our boots,
Heads bent towards the wind
Dreaming of fires - of soup
And hot mince pies!

Part III

A BIRD'S EYE VIEW

Sea Sounds

Soft sea sounds-
On the shingle shore!
Up on the wind
The sea birds soar -
Blue is the sky
And the murmuring sound
As the distant waves
On the shingle pound.
Soft sea sounds
On the shingle shore.

The Hills

The sound of lapping lakes upon the shore,
Above the mist the silver sea-birds soar,
Look up towards the purple mountain range,
One hundred years from now they will not change.

This world of strife, and man's destructive ways
Hath no demands upon the mighty hills
Which lie a-lazing - sleeping in the sun,
As they will be, for all the years to come.

Shadows of clouds and mists of driving rain
Blot out the view - and then the sun again.
See how the colours change with every light,
And yet they change not in their strength and might.

Oh that we might remain as calm as they,
So constantly the same each passing day;
And in this changing life look up again
And know those hills of strength and peace remain.

Far and Away

Far and away from the towns and the people,
Far and away from the noise and the sounds,
Far and away are the sights of the summer,
Green are the meadows and hills all around.
Here you will find in the golden of summer,
Here you will find in the silence of snow,
Far and away from the sights of the cities,
Peace from the hills and the valleys below.

Far and away there's a stream by the meadow,
Trickling clear as the fish swimming there,
Buttercups lifting their heads to the sunshine,
Far from the cities of smoke and despair.
Far and away there's a tree on the hillside
Blossoming fair, as the bluebells in May;
There you can join with the bird-song at even
All that is peaceful, when far and away.

Far and away on the blue of the ocean,
Setting the sails with the wind running free,
Sailing on silver towards the horizon,
Far and away where the sky meets the sea.
Here you will find, as the seabirds are flying
Free as the air on this beautiful day,
Peace, with a breeze that is blowing you on
To an island of solitude far and away.

43

The Moon

The moon like a lantern
Hangs from the sky
And the clouds make way
As she passes by
And over the hills
She is riding high -
The shadows form
As she casts her light
From behind the trees -
And she's out of sight.
She continues now
On her midnight flight
As she travels onward
Thro' the night.
And her smiling face
Is a silver white
As she greets the dawn
And her crimson light.

Might Have Been

Into my dreams my thoughts intrude
I wake in an Italian mood -
Lake Maggiore's where I'll stay
I'm going to Italy - *today*!
No preparation, just my case.
I feel the warm sun on my face
And feel that lovely lakeland space.
Blue distant hills that setting make
As sun sets on the glassy lake.
I love this place that I have seen
Altho' in fact I've never been!

On Monday I shall pack and go
To Switzerland - to see the snow
The mountains and the clear blue sky.
The trees like white embroidered lace
and feel the snow flakes on my face
And look at valleys far below
Where silver-ribboned rivers flow.
I love that place that I have seen
Altho' in fact I've never been!

I know as we get in the car
We won't be going very far
And all the places I have seen
Are simply just a "might have been"!

Easter in the Lakes

The silver look of light upon the lake,
The greenish fuzz of buds about to break.
Surrounded by the blue of distant hills,
The peaceful sheep on green and grassy slopes
Lie with their lambs amongst the daffodils.

* * *

The Great Wood - Derwent Water

The lofty larches lift their leafy arms towards the sky,
And sighing gently, wave backwards and forwards with the breeze.
And buzzing bees a-bumbling on the bluebells far beneath
Join in the songs of summer softly sung.
White butterflies flip past on silent wing,
All gifts of gladness in the summer sun.
Damp mossy cushions cover stones
And lichen-covered branches hang over trickling streams,
Meandering their way towards the lake.

The cuckoo and the lark they sing and sing,
I feel as if it is forever Spring.
Open the closed windows of despair
And know the light and sunshine waiting there.

Music

Listen to the lapping of the lake,
The dripping and the dropping of the rain;
Music in silence - music in the breeze,
And music in the singing of the trees.

There's laughter too, in music of the brook;
Rippling, poppling under mossy banks
Guggling and gurgling as it rushes by;
Music for the dancing dragonfly.

Music in fountains, splashing in the pool,
In gushing torrents, streams and waterfalls;
So listen to the music to be found
In all of Nature's orchestra of sound.

"Fryton"

Soft is the air, and soft the sounds of doves
Cooing in the tall pine trees.
No breeze stirs
And no other sounds disturb the stillness of the summer
afternoon.

Shapes of fields like a patchwork quilt
Draped from the hills as far as the eye can see -
Green - and gold with the ripening corn,
Separated by weathered stone walls.

The house of stone lies long and low
With roses round - and lawns.
Inside such welcome warmth -
Fitting like an old slipper
Waiting by the hearth.

Here faded memories recall
Other visits long ago
Of "Ivy Home" where lilacs grow
Grandparents wait to welcome us
And give us tea.
And Auntie Jessie did her special dance
For us to see.

These things are long past dead
But woven here a past and present thread
And "Fryton" holds the key

50

51

"Pope's Hall Cottage" ("Moon Acre")

From distant woods the cuckoo calls
And tells us it is spring,
And in the sunlit garden
You can hear the blackbirds sing.

No sound of cars or people
As the world goes rushing by,
But all is quiet and tranquil
As you hear the breezes sigh.

All mauve and green the wisteria hangs
And lilac trees a-sway,
The owl is in the yew tree,
It's "Moon Acre" - in May.

Concert At "Stoneacre"

Old English songs and silvery harp,
Turn back in time the book and page
To voices from another age
At "Stoneacre".

Long cobbled path with borders green,
Long-fingered shadows on the lawn
As other days have seen;
And all is still - but birds do sing
And join the chorus there within
At "Stoneacre".

As evening sun glints on the diamond pane,
The sounds and shadows of the past remain,
The fragrant flowers - these tranquil days belong
Where time it seems doth linger long
At "Stoneacre".

Observations on the D.C.A. trip up the Thames from Henley

My dear, we went on the river,
We're members of D.C.A.
With ties and boaters and Henley hats
On a perfect Summer's day.
On the river the views were enchanting -
(The people not quite so much),
"My dear - have you seen Davinia?"
" - She's there - with Lord 'Such-an-Such'".
They're there at the next-door table,
Sipping their D.C.A. wine -
It's one-fifteen, so now it would seem
It's time for us all to dine.

The man on the next-door table
Had several bottles of wine -
It's all thrown in with the tickets,
So when we came to dine
We asked politely to join him -
But he said, "No you can't! - It's all mine!"
It's all most *frightfully* classy,
You can see by all the signs -
The Gucci shoes and handbags
And everyone reading "The Times"!

"We've just travelled up from Ashford -
My dear! - what a *ghastly* place!
That mess with the Channel Tunnel -
It's really a perfect disgrace!"
"I don't know what's happened to England,
Things are not what they used to be -
These people arrange to make all this change -
Don't know what they're doing you see".
"Now what do you think of James Goldsmith?
Referendum might just be the thing -
John Major has made such a mess-up,
And Lord Howe is so *awfully* left-wing!"

"You know Belinda Hampton?
She's made a most suitable match -
She's married again for the second time,
To a Lord, whose a wonderful catch.
She wears such extraordinary garments,
And has fish tanks in her *loo*!
So that when you flush the system
The goldfish go up and down too!!"

"My dear - do you have our problem?
Things are just not quite the same -
Everything's changed in our Service -
Ever since the new Vicar came!
I like to be quiet with my thoughts -
But everything's got out of hand -
They're *kissing* and things in the Service,
So I've just *had* to make a stand!"

It's now two hours since lunchtime -
And nearly a quarter to three,
So it's everyone down to the diner
To tuck into cream cakes and tea..
Who are these extraordinary people?
Are they really someone or not?
And does it really matter
If your drawer's from the bottom or top?

Oh well! - It's all been different -
A most entertaining day,
But I don't think I'll go touring
With the members of D.C.A.

Part IV

ELEPHANTS

Swans

Soft white feathers
Like a cloud in summer sky,
Long stretched necks
As the swans fly by.

Grey the misty morning,
River shadows loom;
Distant snowy feathers -
The swans are coming soon.

Gliding past the rushes
Soft and light as air;
Fluffed with snowy feathers
The silent swans are there.

Soft white feathers
Return another day;
Long stretched necks
As the swans fly away.

Friendship

This poem is based on a true story of a lone swan and Canada goose who formed an extraordinary friendship on the Medway:

Bereft she is - honking and looking to the sky
Watching her friends, and wishing she could fly.
She looks - and longs to feel the air
Passing her wings to join them there.
Shaped in a V, away they fly
Canada Geese in a crimson sky
Flying towards a setting sun
But here on the lake - she's the only one.

Resigned now to his lonely state
The swan who last year lost his mate -
Missing his partner still so dear
He inwardly sheds a silent tear.
Then way beyond the river bend
The white swan hears her plaintive cries
And stretching out his neck he flies
To find his lonely friend.
So swimming near, and so forlorn
Quite different in their feathered form,
With burdens that they had to bear
They had a bond they both could share.

The lonely goose with damaged wing,
The swan with broken wedding ring,
Can now be seen upon the mere
Swimming in waters cool and clear -
This bond of friendship closely tied
They're always swimming side by side.

Dogs

Why do we have them?
I really don't know,
For who wants to go
For a walk in the snow?

I come down in the morning
And undo the latch,
Then what do I see
But a nasty damp patch.

And who has been sick
Just inside the front door?
So, still in my nightie,
I'm scrubbing the floor!

They pooh on the pavement
And pee on the trees,
The next thing you know
They've got terrible fleas.

They're waiting and waiting,
And two pairs of eyes
Are staring unblinking
At all those meat pies
You've only just cooked -
And they don't seem to know
That you've only just fed them
Two minutes ago!

But the welcome they give you
All affection and licks,
And they know - and you know-
You love them to bits.

* * *

Trouble With Spiders

They really are enormous,
They're hairy and they're brown,
They've got their "welly boots" on
And they're plodding up and down.

I'm just about to have a bath
And there it is again.
It's climbing up the side.
It must have come up from the drain!

If I do the washing up,
Its waiting by the plug
And now I want a coffee break
It's sitting in the mug!

I know they're really harmless
But I simply cannot *bear*
Those wary hairy spiders
With those eyes on stalks that stare.

Part V

CHRISTMAS 1991 to 1995

Christmas 1991

Take time!
Watch with the stars that gaze with crystal sight -
On wonders known to us on Christmas night.

Take time!
Listen to whispering trees,
Of wonders told to us in gentle breeze.

Take time!
Sing with the Angels bright,
The songs of glory sung on Christmas night.

Take time!
Stand in the silent snow,
Wait with the silver moon - And know!

Christmas 1992

Snow drifts like people
Where to go? - to stay?
"No room at the Inn" they say.

Poor people driven from their homes
Without a place -
The freezing wind
Forever in their face.
"No room at the Inn" they say.

Here in the Christmas glow
The fires burn bright -
All is a-pleasure
In the Festive light.
Will there be snow for us on Christmas Day?
Is it really true?
"No room in the Inn" they say?

Christmas 1993

Fanlike they softly fall,
The flurried flakes of snow;
And thro' the frosted fronds of trees
The freezing winds do blow.

For some, the warmth and firelight burns
And everything aglow;
For others - coldly turned away
Like Christmas long ago.

Betwixt, between our different worlds
We ponder yet again
Of tinsel hangings, warmth and fun
And those in Winter's pain.

And yet in darkness came the Light
And in that stable bare
The Angels sang - the stars came out
And joy was everywhere.

The world keeps turning - such extremes
Of light and dark appear,
And we must ever hopeful be
With every turning year.

So welcome now this Christmastide
And open wide the door -
As full of hope we enter in
To Nineteen Ninety-four.

Christmas 1994

As with gladness men of old
Did their guiding star behold.
Is the star still shining there
Brightly o'er the stable bare?
As they climb the steepening hill
Does it guide the Wise Men still?
Do they still look up and see
Which direction it's to be?
Finding out how wars can cease -
Searching for eternal peace -
For Bosnia wrapped in dismal shroud
The star has gone behind the cloud:
For Ireland now the star is bright
And shines again with silver light.

Do men look up for guidance anymore?
To try and find the star that once they saw -
Now looking down, and bumbling around,
Busying about - where once they found
A clearer view, a more harmonious sound.

So as another year goes by,
Look up and search the darkened sky;
And there perhaps, we will behold -
Just as the Three Wise Men were told -
The star still shining in the sky
To guide us as we search, and try
To find the peace that's waiting there
For all of us to have and share.

Christmas 1995

Fast away the old year passes
Moving as the shifting sand,
Man and all his worldly visions
Hanging by a spider's strand.

Men are trying to solve the problems,
Talks and meetings - something new!
Things look better now in Ireland,
Hopefully in Bosnia too.

France it seems has many problems,
Strikes and marches take their toll;
Israel hovers in the balance,
How will China reach its goal?

Half the world is moving forward,
Half the world is looking back;
Half the world is bright with sunshine,
Half the world is dark and black.

So it was on that first Christmas,
Turmoil then was just the same;
In the darkness of the stable
Came in love - that little flame.

Shedding light into the darkness,
Giving warmth that frosty night;
Giving hope to all the people
In their poverty and plight.

So look up, and hear the Angels -
"Glory to the New-born King";
Echo back the great rejoicing
Sending back the song they sing.

Part VI

"WINKLY WOO" and the CONCERTS

The Colourful Concert
For Rebecca

I once had a cat called Winkly Woo,
He had large wings and away he flew
Over the fence, and over the shed
And all he would eat was granary bread -
His whiskers were red and his tail was yellow,
He was known by his friends as a handsome fellow -
He had a friend called Sambo Sid,
A particular, portly, purple pig,
And he'd fly to his house on the top of the tree,
Where he'd drink his excellent nettle tea,
And sing his crimson and orange song
Which he'd surreptitiously brought along.
Said the pig, "I've a yellow and pinkish pipe
Which you've never heard me play.
I think we should give a concert
One beautiful summer's day".

So the portly pig and Winkly Woo
Found friends from far and near,
And announced the wonderful music
That they were about to hear.
The song was extremely orange,
And the pipe was extremely pink,
And their friends who had come to listen
Didn't quite know what to think.
They sang and they played for hours
Without a single care,
Completely forgetting the audience
Who were sleeping and snoring there.

"The crimson song was a pleasure"
Said purple pig with a wink -
Said Winkly Woo, as away he flew,
"And the pipe was a perfect pink!"

"Thank you" to the Auguri Singers
after the concerts in France - August 20th, 1994

This note is just to thank you
For your company in France,
The quartets and the solos
Which gave us all a chance
To make some lovely music
And all have lots of fun,
Whilst drinking wine, and eating cheese,
And sitting in the sun.
And J.McConnell's playing
Is really very good -
Adjusting notes if needed!
Doing everything she should!
And Dave with all the plans he made
And bookings in advance,
And rendezvous in massive crowds
Beneath some tower in France!
It all worked like a miracle -
We always seemed to find
That green car in the car park
(Altho' we're miles behind!)
We can't forget the drivers
In the heat and all that sun,
The supporters and the helpers
And all that they have done;
The lunch in Brian's lovely house,
The salads and the wine,
The wander thro' the village -
We had a *lovely* time.

76

Your voices in those churches
In memory lingers long,
Each one so very different -
Each one a lovely song.
The hypermarket visits -
And the picnic place we found,
And opening all those paper bags
With chickens all around..
The visit to the Chateaux
Amongst the milling throng -
No hope of meeting - yet we saw
Dave ambling along!
It's rather a mistake I found -
For O.A.P's when merry -
To war-dance on the tarmac
Whilst waiting for the ferry!

And so, dear friends, I really want
To thank you very much;
I'll look thro' songs and make some plans
And then I'll be in touch.
Then, hopefully we soon will meet
With yet another chance
To sing again, and have some fun,
Just like we did - in France!

From the Auguri Singers to their hosts in France - August 19th, 1994

The Auguri Singers thank you
For the fun we had in France -
Fantastic hospitality -
And giving us the chance
To travel thro' the countryside,
The Dordogne and The Loire -
To sing in lovely churches -
Bovila and St.Croix.
The food and wine you gave us -
Relaxing in the sun,
And meeting all the people -
It really was such fun.
We hope the money that we raised
Will add a little more
For the Medieval Churches
You so beautifully restore.

So many thanks from all of us
For all your kindness shown;
We really had a lovely time -
And glad your funds have grown

Introduction to The Blackthorn Trust Spring Concert
April 15th, 1994

So Spring is here! We celebrate in joyful song -
Welcome her presence, knowing she is near,
And Winter's melancholy mood has gone.
Watching her now in gown of silken green
Passing barefoot, with flowers in her hair,
She walks beyond the farthest fields now seen,
Bringing us joy and new life everywhere.
The blossom on the trees and softest breeze to her belong,
And like the birds who whistle overhead
We join with them in welcome and in song.

"Happy Christmas" to the "Monday Group" of The Blackthorn Trust - 1992

Sing a song of Christmas -
Carols soft and loud -
Four and twenty Monday Group
Waiting in a crowd.
When the door was opened
They all began to sing -
The patients in the waiting room
Decided to join in!

The merriment soon started
And spreading all around
They soon forgot why they had come -
It was a joyful sound!
The building rang with merry tunes,
The doctors joined the choir,
Then John joined in with several friends
To harp, upon the Lyre!

The gardeners came with rake and hoe
(And mud! it must be said!)
The bakers all put down their dough,
"Oh never mind the bread!"
They all came in to join the fun -
Sopranos - baritones -
The altos and the tenors
Joining in the dulcet tones.

So "Merry Christmas" everyone -
Keep singing - young and old,
The wonders of the Monday Group
Are wondrous to behold!

"Happy Christmas" to
The Detling Singers - 1991

Another year of singing gone,
Another year to come -
With songs from nations far and wide,
We should have lots of fun.

So sing in sorrow, sing in joy,
And sing to make you laugh,
Just keep on singing every day
If only in the bath.

We'll have a break, then meet again
As it has always been -
In wondrous voice! - a perfect sound!
All-sparkling and keen!

I wish to you a happy time,
A Christmas of good cheer,
And most importantly of all -
A musical New Year!

"Happy Christmas" to
The Detling Singers - 1992

Across the meadows white with frost
The Christmas bells ring out -
With sounds of cheer - quite loud and clear,
The singers are about -
To sing a song of peacefulness,
And watching, as we sing
The light around the Manger
For the birth of Christ the King.
And so with joyful heart we'll see
The star along the way -
And with a song, we'll go along
To Nineteen Ninety-Three.

"Happy Christmas" to
The Detling Singers - 1993

"Rejoice and be Merry"
I hear the choir sing;
And the "Ding Dongs" and bells
As they happily ring.
"Vast numbers of Angels
Appeared in the sky" -
I hear the choir sing
(With a bit of a sigh - !?)

Twas a wonderful sound -
And the notes were so high
That the ladies took off
With their halos awry!
"Christmas is coming"
The gentlemen sing -
The notes getting louder - !
And now everything
With enormous crescendo -
With Jingles and Drum
Leaves no-one in doubt
That Christmas has *come*!

In spite of the cold
When your fingers are numb,
"Rejoice and be Merry"
And have lots of fun.
So good wishes dear friends,
"Leave your worries and strife"
And get carried away
With the "Rhythm of Life"!

"With thanks" to the Detling Singers - May 15th, 1994
(After the party on my retirement as their conductor
and the presentation of a picture, 'Memory Book', and a cake)

How beautiful the painting is
Now on the wall to see -
The song you all stood up to sing -
All memories for me.
The time it must have taken
And the trouble that you took -
With all the lovely things you said,
And memories in that book.
And Cathy's cake with pictures round,
Too beautiful to eat;
The card Jack made, and you all signed -
The evening was complete.
We've had many years of music,
So many years of fun,
And many lovely concerts
With all the songs we've sung.
We've had our anxious moments
When rehearsals - "only two
Before the Christmas Concert -
And four altos off with flu!"
"We've got to get the notes right -
And will it be in tune?"
We've only got a fortnight -
The concert's very soon!

But on the night you all turn up
In white, in red or green,
The Detling Singers now present
A sight that must be seen.
Ian's got the speakers in -
And Gavin's got the blocks -
With all the helpers humping -
"Yes - we need that extra box".
And David's got the drums in place
And now the piano's in -
The choir's got themselves arranged
So now we can begin.

The audience has packed the hall,
They've come from near and far,
The sound is perfect harmony -
How wonderful you are!
Forgotten are the notes I wrote,
Impossible to see!
The missing parts the Tenors need
And - "Is that middle C?!"
John fills in notes with expert ease -
"We'll try it all again -
We'll note-bash with the ladies first,
And then we'll have the men!"

You've come thro' rain and hail and wind
And every kind of weather -
With tours and trips and barbecues -
Done lots of things together.
And so, dear friends, keeping singing -
And thank you very much;
I know I'll miss the Mondays,
So please - do keep in touch.
But keep on looking forward
To all that is to come.
Good wishes for the future,
And all have lots of fun.
So with voices in good order
May you all be bright and merry
When you start in mid-September
With conductor - Ian Perry.